Blue Sky

The Gypsy Flag

*Born Free
Like a river that flows,
Like the birds of the air
and the wind that blows;
We are born free to follow a star
Jesus*

Romany Rye
Gypsy Gentleman

From New York to Texas,
2,000 Miles All the Way

By Nelson Jack Boswell

A Tachnue Romney-Chell

Published by New Generation Publishing in 2014

Copyright © Nelson Jack Boswell 2014

First Edition

The author asserts the moral right under the Copyright, Designs and Patents Act 1988 to be identified as the author of this work.

All Rights reserved. No part of this publication may be reproduced, stored in a retrieval system or transmitted, in any form or by any means without the prior consent of the author, nor be otherwise circulated in any form of binding or cover other than that which it is published and without a similar condition being imposed on the subsequent purchaser.

www.newgeneration-publishing.com

New Generation **Publishing**

Cover photo:
Scotch Isaac Boswell, my Grandfather, and his Sister-in-law Flory Boswell, of The Isle of Man. Photographed around 1910.

Thanks to my wife Delly, who helped with all the spelling; my love for always.

Many thanks to Samantha and her husband Paul On The Dot Typing Ltd for the typing up of this book and their patience with my constant alterations. Samantha was always happy, always ready to help.

Thanks to Neil & staff at Copyshop Hinckley for their help and the cover designs.

Last but not least my good friend John F McDonald, Author of many books including films of his books, thank you John for advice, suggestions and pointing me in the right direction to the publishers and always having time for me. John F McDonald (A true gentleman).

All the gypsy characters in the book are real my ancestors, some names changed except for Queen Victoria which is 100% fiction, the fight scenes are real most of the incidents were real, especially the son Jack with the Lords niece, how they fell in love and eloped to Hereford. Actually my Grandmother Blanch, her true life family and great Uncle; little stories are built into the book even the Duckering (Fortune telling).

Cushdy-Boc
(Good Luck)

Jack

This book is copyright © of Nelson Jack Boswell

Contents

CHAPTER ONE - 'THE SHOW IS OVER' 6
CHAPTER TWO - 'A ROYAL PERFORMANCE' 26
CHAPTER THREE - 'HORSE DEALING' 34
CHAPTER FOUR – 'THE TRAIN JOURNEY' 46
CHAPTER FIVE – THE YORKSHIRE DALES................................. 68
CHAPTER SIX– ON TO ABERLINE... 93
CHAPTER SEVEN - MEMPHIS TENNESSEE 104
CHAPTER EIGHT- A VERY ROYAL VISITOR CALLS............... 118
CHAPTER NINE – ABERLINE... 137
CHAPTER TEN– A ROUGH DAYS HUNTING 157
CHAPTER ELEVEN - IN THE NICK 173
CHAPTER TWELVE - RETURN TO ABERLINE 181
CHAPTER THIRTEEN - THE TRIAL... 199
CHAPTER FOURTEEN – THE QUEEN AND THE GYPSY EARRING 208
CHAPTER FIFTEEN – LADY AND THE GYPSY 229
CHAPTER SIXTEEN– STAGECOACH 258
CHAPTER SEVENTEEN – GUN FIGHT AT FORT MONTROSE 279

CHAPTER ONE - 'THE SHOW IS OVER'

<u>New York City 1868 – 3 Years After The US Civil War</u>

Sitting on the edge of the bed, Adam pulled on his elastic sided boots. He turned and looked back at Anita. 'Five minutes and I'll be gone' she answered. Stretching out her arms and laying back on the bed.

Adam walked down the steep steps between the shafts of the gypsy living wagon, then reaching into a box on the front board he stuffed some paper into his pocket, walking past the men's bog, a smelly hole in the ground with a sheet around some frame work. As he walked down the field, he breathed in deeply. It was an early April morning. Halfway down the field, he went through a gap in the hedge leading into a small side field.

Having finished what he had come to do, he looked at his pocket watch. 'Five to seven' he said aloud. As he walked further down the field, breathing in deeply the fresh early morning air, he came to a fallen rotten tree. There lay a cock pheasant, it was still warm. Taking out his pen knife, he cut the cat gut that was hanging out of its mouth, then going into a tiny snuff box, and taking out another small fish hook, he threaded the cat gut though it. Then picking up the two biggest raisins from the few that were sprinkled on the ground, he threaded the fish hook into them, then placing it back on the tree trunk. He threaded the clear cat gut down through the mossy bark of the tree. Then standing hard on the long heavy steel stake that the cat gut was tied to, sending it right down in the ground, finally, pulling the grass over it to hide it.

Sitting on the tree trunk, he thought about his Great Grandfather Byron, who had showed and told him so many things of the old Romany ways of life. He had taught and learned him so much. Catapults, guns, running dogs, and gooDellynig-fish and so on, he had brought out so many sharp, shrewd ways that was in young Adam's blood, which would have taken many years to learn. He would never forget him, also Adam's younger brother Layton and his older brothers Jack and Steven, who was a loner, they had all spent a lot of time with their Great Grandfather Byron.

As he sat on the trunk of the fallen tree, he looked down at his boots, wet with the early morning dew off the grass. It made him realize what he was, and what he came from, a Romany Gypsy background. Things in life you so often take for granted how important they are and you suddenly realize this when your way of life is likely to change. Adam wondered what would be next for him, now the travelling Wild West Circus he had spent so many years with was finished travelling. He doubted if he could live in or around a big crowded city permanently like New York. He didn't really want to try.

'Moving around the country in an horse drawn living wagon by yourself, with no other wagons, and on your own, in a new vast country like America could be lonely, and dangerous' thought Adam. He had lived in a horse drawn wagon all his life. He had been born in one on Perth-Inches Scotland. Adam's Father was Nelson, and his Mother Delly. Both were gypsies, which made him a thoroughbred Romany, (a tachnue rumney-chell) a real gypsy. He had come over to the new world, with his parents brothers, and grandparents five months ago.

He had been with The Wild West Circus for nearly eight years, travelling over most of Europe. They all had come over hoping for a better life in America, the new world. Being gypsy men, his father Nelson and Grandfather Isaac dealt in a few horses now and then, also guns, fishing rods. They usually kept three or four horses for trade. Adam and his younger brother Layton had grown up around horses all their lives, and learning from the older men how to doctor a horse up, present it at its best. Any spavins on its legs being dead crumpled up sores, would be burned off with a mild acid, filed down, then coloured in a plain horse, being a tan or brown - After being trimmed, it would then be gyped up, bleached or tinted in the right places, being mane, tail and socks. Then lightly brushed in with a mixture of halibut and olive oil till it shone like satin.

After more work and know how, finally looking, a beautiful palomino and would fetch nearly three times the price of what they had bought it for. They are shrewd men, always ready and keen for a deal. More at home in the countryside than a city, but can adapt getting a living in either place. The women, his mother Delly, Grandmother Nellie, would (ducker), tell fortunes, palm reading from the living wagons. Nearly eight years ago, they joined up with the Wild West Circus at Perth, Scotland. The woman before that would go from door to door selling lace dawb or lucky charms. The crystal ball would always be in the bag or basket. Selling was a living and a get in, the (duckering); fortune telling was the main earner.

He suddenly sensed something moving. Turning his head very slowly, he could see (a leveret), a young hare, jumping up and down, about 40 yards away. Slowly going into his back pocket, and coming out with a catapult, placing a small lead ball in the leather tab, then pulling the tab right back level with his ear, slowly taking aim, knowing he would only get one shot. The young hare seemed to do a half forward summersault and then laid still. The lead ball had hit the back of its head with such force it nearly come out through the front.

Three quarter ways back up the big field, he stopped to give his arms a rest from carrying the hare and pheasant, he lit a thin panatela cigar, then drawing in deeply, and blowing the smoke out. 'There was nothing like the first smoke of the day' thought Adam. As he got closer to the big tent, with its red, white and blue panels, he noticed people standing in small groups pretending to be talking or doing something. Really they were watching the row with Anita and her husband Carl. He was dragging her by her blood stained blouse, bawling and shouting, she was crying and shouting back at him. Her lips and nose were split and puffed up where he had been smacking her in the face.

Adam stopped, dropping the pheasant and the hare. Then taking a deep puff on the cigar, he started to walk faster. 'She must have fallen back to sleep, and Carl had caught her in my bed' thought Adam. 'You're just a dirty little two timing whore' shouted Carl. He was the circus strongman and it was a fact that he had the strength of three men. He stood seven foot three, and over 32 stone.

Seeing Adam, he started to beat his chest. Adam glanced at Anita, lying on the grass he felt very guilty and sorry for her, he wished he had not gone with her. But she had just kept coming around and he knew he had not been the first. Carl was from Germany. He had fought with two men in a tavern in Dusseldorf where he lived. Both men were seriously hurt, were taken to hospital, they had both been out barely three weeks, when each one died. It was rumoured that it had been taking such a beating from Carl that killed them. When the Wild West circus came, Carl was very pleased, he and his two nephews joined up with it to be out of Dusseldorf.

Carl was in a rage, and it was no good trying to fast talk him out of it. Adam suddenly realized he did not notice too much the size of such a man, being with him every day for years you just accepted it. But this morning Adam did notice the size, and as he glanced around, he could see nearly half of the secremengers – (show people) were out and looking on. 'I just can't leave, walk away from a challenge. I have to save face. I have to think of my name' thought Adam.

'When I get my hands on that gypsy bastard, I'll break his bones. I'll kill him' shouted Carl. 'Hey, low life, I am your gypsy boy and fighting is my game' shouted Adam, accepting the challenge as he tore off his shirt; the buttons at the front seemed to fly like little bullets. Carl came at a trot; his fists held very high, Adam could see he had not had a lot of experience, 'but who the hell would want to fight such a man anyway, only a fool like me' he thought.

Adam deliberately had his guard low, and Carl thought it was his chance he threw a right. Adam eased back his head; the fist sailed by, missing his face by some three to four inches. He quickly bought his left over the top of Carl's outstretched right arm, stubbing and twisting the red end of the cigar into Carl's right ear. He let out a low deep little scream as the hot cigar disintegrated into his ear.

Carl started to brush his ear fast backwards and forwards several times with his right hand. There was the smell of burning flesh. 'Go for it Adam' shouted a woman. 'Don't get in too close, he's big' shouted someone else. 'Take him apart, break him up Uncle Carl' shouted another. As they sparred up, Adam looked like a teenage boy; Carl stood some 15 or 16 inches taller, and was double his weight.

Adam was jabbing hard with his right, bringing Carl slowly around on to his left, being his best and hardest punch. Carl's lips were split. The big man made two swings, a right and then a left. Adam stepped forward underneath throwing his right punch. His fist seemed to go in three inches below Carl's belt. He had punched so hard Adams left foot had come off the ground as he gave it everything he had. He just did not want to hit Carl's stomach. He wanted to go straight through it to the other side, as his grandfather had taught him, and called this punch 'follow through'. His punch had sunk hard into a grizzly hard fat. Carl moved back flat footed, slightly bent, grunting, and blowing out. Adam opened and closed his hand several times. He felt like he had hit a padded oak door. Carl was trying to smile, but that low belly punch he had just taken; it was hurting really bad. Adam could see this, he had dropped several men over the years with that punch, but Carl, he was not being dropped. He was not a normal man.

Adam's mother Delly was shouting at her husband Nelson, 'why don't you go over there and do something?' 'That borie mush (big man), he could maw (kill) our Adam. He is a giant. I can't very well go over and two him with a weapon, 'when it's a fair fight can I?' because that's what it would take to floor him, when half the circus is out watching the fight can I' answered Nelson. Ignoring her husband, she ran up the wagon steps, then going through several cupboards, she found what she was looking for, a bar of iron as thick as your thumb, about 15 inches long. 'Don't worry about it, Adam will break his arm, then drop him with a left jaw breaker, just give him five minutes' said Nelson. 'You sit there talking like a dumb (gorger), a none gypsy. He is fighting a giant. He could get (mawd) killed. I don't think even Layton could stop him.'

She wrapped the bar of iron in a thin towel, and started to walk over towards the fight. Carl was now moving a little slower. Adam seemed to still have that bounce as he circled Carl but he was now breathing heavier. Maybe it was those 4 or five cigars he smoked every day. Carl's right hand dropped for just a couple of seconds, it was more than enough. Adam seemed to jump a little to get it there. As his left fist hit Carl's right eyebrow, it split. It had been aimed at his jaw. He went in again with a right that caught Carl square in the mouth. Getting his guard back up and pulling himself back together the big man smiled, spitting out blood. 'When I do get you, you're dead meat'. Adam had dropped quite a few men in gypsy bare knuckle fights but this man was something else.

To quote an expression, Adam was sick as a pig. He was giving it his best, and he could see he was no good to this man. The strength and endurance that he had was unbelievable. 'I'm just going to have to keep chopping at him, and try to wear him down. 'My arms are starting to get tired. If i can just stay away from him, and let him keep hitting fresh air. A few more low belly punches, then chin him, and he should go down' thought Adam.

The blood was now slowly trickling down the side of Carl's face from the one inch cut in the end of his eyebrow. Adam realized he was having to jump to hit him, and because of this, his punches were losing power. Carl rushed forward lashing out quickly with a left, and a right. The left caught Adam above his right ear. Adam seemed to walk fast sideways, then went down. He could see little sparks blinking in and out. Carl then tried stamping on him, Adam looked like a boy under Carl's feet as he rolled again and again as fast as he could to get away, then quickly scrambling to his feet, shaking his head several times dancing away. It only took Carl 3-4 strides and he was there. His massive arms wrapped around Adam, he had him squeezing again and again. He was laughing, eyes staring wild, as Adam was gasping.

The little sparks that Adam had been seeing was back again, this time mixed with a grey. His arms were pinned down to his sides as Carl continued to squeeze. Adam was bringing up his knee several times as hard as he could, hoping to knee him between the legs, he was so tall all he was hitting was Carl's thighs. The sparks had now stopped blinking in and out and everything was now going grey, and starting to slowly spin around. 'My god, he's going to kill me' thought Adam. His left hand had finally found what he was hoping for, Carl's privates. He started to squeeze, pull and yank as hard as he could. Shouting in pain Carl had to release him.

Adam was free again. Shaking his head several times, he staggered a little, trying to get himself together again. He looked sold out. Carl's long left hand was stretched out in front of him getting ready to throw his right. Adam grabbed his wrist. Stepping underneath, he twisted it around as best he could. He then jumped to bring his left hand down in a chop with maximum force. But Carl's arm was as thick as a man's leg, and Adam did not hear the elbow joint snap as he had done a few times in the past.

The squeezing that Adam had received had zapped quite a lot of his strength and his head was throbbing. Carl's face looked in a mess, he had taken a lot, but he also looked like he could go on a lot more, Adam knew. He was no good to Carl he was too big and too strong. I will go for his head with a drop kick, both feet, but his heads to high.

Suddenly Delly, the little woman was there, jumping up and down between them, and shouting for all to hear 'you call this a fight. You look like a couple of girl's ugging and pulling each other. Why don't you stand back and fight like men' she shouted. She was standing between them, and the size of Carl blanked her off completely from the onlookers in the distance. As she was jumping up and down, she quickly hit Carl as hard as she could twice high on the forehead. There was no blood, no cuts from the iron bar it was padded with a towel. Everyone was laughing at her jumping up and down waving the towel and shouting.

Carl was staggering, his eyes slightly glazed. It looked like everything had suddenly caught up with him. Delly quickly slipped the iron bar down the inside of her skirt, holding it with her hand, as her other hand waved the empty towel, as she stepped away, then shouting 'fight on boys, fight on'. Carl threw a half hearted punch that caught Adam a glancing blow on his shoulder, but there was not a lot of power behind it. Eyes glazed legs a little wobbly. Suddenly he wasn't sure what had happened. The (Divas) is Lestys Deiel him dewey (the day, is yours hit him twice)

Adam stepped to one side then with a very hard low belly punch that made Carl gasp. Adam then stepped back. His knuckles hit Carl square on the chin and his elbow following through, it was a double hit. Carl went down and stayed down.

Adam had washed and cleaned up as he sat on a stool at the front of his father's wagon. His head throbbing as his father held a cold wet pad on the lump that had come up on the side of his head.

Albert the owner of the Wild West Circus came walking over. 'Morning Nelson, Delly' he said, as he sat down on the stool. Delly went back to the large iron frying pan that hung on a hooked kettle iron over the stick fire, the bacon sizzling as she turned it over. 'Will you have a bacon sandwich Albert?' 'Thank you, it smells good' he said. The kettle iron started to bend over too much into the fire. 'The cavey saster, (kettle iron), is going to fall into the yog (fire)' said Delly Nelson, grabbing a thick rag to hold the hot iron and press it further into the ground. 'You put up a long hard fight Adam. That big gorilla could have killed you' said Albert as he got up off the stool to look closely at the lump on the side of Adam's head. 'It's like a small egg; you should see a doctor with that'. 'It'll go down in a couple of days' answered Adam. 'You must have been mad bothering with her'. 'It's hard to keep saying no. She just kept coming to my wagon' answered Adam. Then looking away and feeling a little embarrassed at what he had said in front of his Mother. 'I know what you mean, one of these days your good looks is going to get you into big trouble' said Albert.

'I've just had the big trouble' answered Adam. Albert looked at Delly, 'That was quite an act with the towel. What was in it, a hammer?' Delly and her husband exchanged a quick starry glance. Nelson picked up the coffee pot as if he hadn't seen Delly's knowing stare. It couldn't have been more than two seconds. It was just as well to have been a 2 minute conversation, it is said gypsy Romany people can speak to each other with their eye contact. Nelson poured the coffee, then handed them around. Nelson had noticed that Albert had also picked up the quick knowing stare. He doesn't miss much, thought Nelson, looking at Albert's tanned face and arms, dark eyes, the Romany Gypsy blood in him could be seen.

'Thank you' said Albert, then biting into the bacon sandwich and washing it down with a mouthful of coffee, clearing his mouth and looking at her with a smile. 'You know there's not many women would have had the nerve to do what you did, and you made it look very natural.' Delly just smiled and nodded, then putting more bacon in the pan. 'And where is all this conversation going?' asked Nelson. Albert was trying to bring the conversation round in a joking friendly way, he knew this family really well. They had been together, and travelled together for nearly eight years.

He pointed the half-eaten sandwich to the short two-sided blade roman sword that was stuck in the ground by the shafts of Nelson's living wagon. 'That's where the conversation is going' said Albert. He had had enough hinting. 'I have seen you use that sword when we were ganged up on in Dublin'. 'Listen Nelson, I just can't afford any serious trouble. This is New York, not Dublin. There is a wagon near the gate with three (Musgarers) police officers in it every day'.

'Now you listen to me Albert, I am 58, not 28, and I am five foot 10, not seven and a half foot with the strength of three men. If he comes round me, they'll be no fair play; I'll open him up like a fish on a slab, and make no mistake about that.' Just at that, Carl went past, his arm around the shoulder of one of his nephews as he glanced over.

Nelson pointed at the short sword, then pointed at Carl, as much as to say that is for you. Carl looked away and walked more quickly. He'd seen Nelson use it and wanted no trouble with him. 'That is the trouble with these gypo's, you fight one, and you've got them all to fight.' Said Carl to his nephew. 'I know what you mean Uncle Carl, we'll sort him out one dark night.

'You know right now I can't afford any complaints, any enquiries of violence. All this Wild West show is supposed to be an act, not for real. The circus is finished, closed down in a few days and the new thing I am starting at Coney Island, and I don't get a license through till next week. I can't afford a stink to follow me there' said Albert.

'You have my word, I will do nothing, I will start nothing, unless he starts it first' said Nelson. 'That's good, I can see Carl wants no more trouble. I am worried about Layton and Carl's nephews. We all want this new thing they'll be no other tick off workers, fortune tellers there'll be only your family. You will have sole rights. Do you want to ruin that?' said Albert.

Nelson looked at him and realized what he was saying made a lot of sense. Any serious problems or trouble and they would be out and stuck in this new country, not sure where to go. 'You have my word' said Nelson. 'No trouble will start unless he starts it first.' Adam then stood up. He turned and looked straight at his mother. 'Thanks mother, I was just about finished. I couldn't have beat him'. 'Most men wouldn't have even tried son'. They just stood there for a few seconds and stared at each other. Neither of them spoke. Adam could see signs of love in his mother's eyes. 'There's been enough (tugness) trouble son, stay away from the (luverndey) whore.'

He just nodded, to his father and Albert, then turned and walked away. 'Come and see me later on, I have to show you something and talk business' shouted Albert. Adam turned and waved. He needed to get to his wagon, to lay down. His head felt like there was someone on the inside with a little hammer trying to get out. Maybe the two askit powders, instead of one, his mother had given him would start to work soon, his arms and ribs hurt when he breathed in deep. 'I feel like lying down for a week' he said to himself.

Sylvia put the coffee cup down and looked at her husband. 'Do you really think we are doing the right thing Albert with this amusement park thing?' 'If I was worried about it, would I want to put 70 thousand dollars into it?' 'That's what I worry about' she answered. 'I am not questioning your business ability, I never have. It's such a big step and it's such a lot of money, three quarters of every penny we have. We were buying that hotel just outside of New York with 90 bedrooms. It would keep us very comfortable for the rest of our days, for just 40,000 dollars, and you're putting 72 thousand into something brand new.' 'Of course I am. I just can't see myself in a monkey suit. Yes sir, no sir, it's not me, he answered.

There was then a knock at the door. Sylvia looked down at Adam standing at the bottom of the steps. 5 feet 10 tanned with black curly hair. 'No wonder he always has woman trouble' she thought. 'Come in Adam, that's some lump on your head'. 'Oh it looks worse than it is. I took two asket powders. The ache and the pain went in about half an hour, but it comes back. 'Would you like a coffee?' 'No thanks, I will have a glass of milk though.' 'Clear the table' said Albert as he took a rolled up plan out of the robe, spreading it out on the table and placing cups on each end.

'This is a 35 acre site, it will be an amusement park; I've got it on a 99 year lease with the New York council. There'll be many stalls and amusement games, a boxing booth show, and other side shows. Swing boats for children.' 'I have seen them when we were round the London parks' said Adam. 'I know you have just listen, and you will learn what has taken me months to get together. I have had pictures, photos and drawings sent to me from Berlin, been in touch with them on and off since we have been here. A 60 feet long cake-wack that shunts back and forth, and one called a Noah's Ark that spins around with seats on, these rides hold up to 40 people. A big wheel, 45 feet high, made of light steel frame. This fun or amusement park will be the first in America, and being its biggest city New York, it will be a success.'

Adam looked at Albert as if he was mad. 'These rides weighing many tons and with people on them, what on earth will make them go.' Albert smiled 'do you remember when we played Berlin in Germany?' 'Yes I do, three years ago' answered Adam. 'Didn't we have a day out and went on a big wheel that went round with seats on it?' Adam nodded. 'That big wheel was sent around by steam pressure, railway engine steam, working off coal or logs. Two big steam engines could work four rides. Very clever people the Germans. They now have two rides at that park. Standing next to that big wheel, and a few side shows. The first, real big fun amusement park in Germany, probably the world. I have ordered a big wheel, and a cake walk, and a Noah's Ark ride, and I have had a brilliant idea of my own, and I know it will be a success. I have asked them to make three more rides only half the size, and I am going to call them juvenile rides. They will be for children. I have ordered three Stevenson's steam engines from England. They are the power fullest in the world. Most of this is finished, and will be here soon. The park will open this summer. What do you think about that? Have you got any ideas?'

Adam put down his empty glass and just looked at Albert. 'I think it will be 10 times busier than this Wild West Show because there is so much more for the people to do to go on the rides again and again, you've got a good head for business.' Albert smiled 'we would be closed Wednesdays and Sundays, and there will be a café with 25 tables. I have made a lot of money in Europe over the past nine years, and I am now back home for good, and I am going to do just as good. I had a rough idea when i came back; the Wild West Circus would be no good here. The cities are too far apart, hundreds and hundreds of miles apart. More time travelling than show time and most of the towns are too small compared to Europe.'

Adam held out the empty glass to Sylvia. 'I am finished with a tent, the buildings will all be made of wood and they will be painted red, white and blue' said Albert. 'Do you think New York is big enough?' asked Sylvia. 'What is your opinion Adam?' 'Right now it is really half the size of some of the European cities, Berlin, Birmingham, only a quarter of London. But New York is growing fast, and so will Washington. This is the country of the future, answered Adam.' 'If that is the case I will grow with it, I'll put on coaches to bring people here, and even train trips as well. Sylvia and Adam looked at each other then at Albert, what a brain, said Adam. The kids will love it, the small rides, going on them again and again, and the Wild West Show will still be there, and so will the other shows as well. It will be a full park of entertainment with lawns and paddling pools as well' said Albert. The first in America 'Whatever will this cost?' asked Adam. '72,000 dollars, probably more' answered Albert. He was pleased with Adam's opinion, giving him confidence; he felt his fortune was safe.

Adam looked at Sylvia don't worry, don't worry at all. It's a brand new idea, and the right mans running it.' As Sylvia cleared the table, Adam glanced at the big solitaire diamond ring on her finger. One stone, 10 carat. He had seen it many times over the years, it was so big, so full of life, fire colour. He was with them at Hatton Gardens in London when Albert bought it for her anniversary. Twelve hundred and fifty pounds he had given for it. Adam's father when he heard was shocked at the price he had said back in Scotland; you could buy a 350 acre farm with barns and a cottage on it for twelve hundred and fifty pounds.

Albert looked at Adam. 'The Western Circus, stage coach scene, gun fights, you and your brother Layton run it, work it, all of it right through. My hands will be full with this park. You's can work it on fifties instead of a wage and ten% of the take. Adam looked up, it's a good offer, full half, and I thank you, I really do but I've been around this Wild West show life nearly eight years. I'm in the new world now, a new country and I want to see what's out there. You don't know, I could make my fortune, become somebody, as you yourself now we're a wandering race of people, and I'm only 26.'

Albert quickly glanced at Sylvia. He needed Adam. He was one of the main attractions of the Wild West Show. Adam had seen the glance between them. 'What about my mother and grandmother with the tick offs, (fortune telling stands?) Will they still be the only two on your park?' 'Two is enough, just the one family. They will have sole rights. I am very satisfied with them, they help pull people in. No one else fortune telling' answered Albert. 'And if you leave, as you think you're going to, your brother Layton will run the stage coach scenes and the gun fights. He will be in charge of the Wild West Show on a third. If you stay, you can run it together on 50/50'. 'Oh I know I had something to tell you Adam, that dealer Johnny Goldfield we was talking about, he is very interested in your surrey and pair of greys. I set him up good for you and I have heard from my younger brother Gilbert he's got some new idea he's been involved with and he's coming over here to the states with it within a year.

Then walking down the wagon steps Adam wonders what Gilbert was up to? Must have something big up his sleeve, Adam had known both of the brothers from being a teenager when his family had first joined up with the Wild West Circus at Perth. They were both very sharp business men, Romany gypsies but it was rumored they had Jewish blood as well. No bother getting up early in the morning to put one over on them, you would need to get up the night before thought Adam. He made his way over to his father's living wagon. Noticing he had hung the (duckering) signs up, fortune telling signs. One sign was showing the palm of an outstretched hand with various lines and words by the lines. The other one, a picture of a head with various areas and writings by the head. There was a third bigger sign with pictures of many nobles, celebrities and some royals that had their palms, their fortunes told when coming to see the Wild West Show in Europe, showing Adams mother and grandmother Nelly duckering (fortune telling) the nobles and royals. This was obviously the main flash for the clairvoyant customers, young rawneys gelling over akay (young lady's coming over this way)said Nelson

'It should be a (Custy-dives)good day. Plenty of (ryes and rawneys) gentleman and ladies' said Nelson. 'Some of the young ladies was giggling with each other about having their fortune told, comparing the palms of their hands to one another. Then looking at the picture in the frame of the outstretched palm and the writings and signs on it.

'Good day, young lady, I can see in your face you are searching, said manx Nelly, Adam's grandmother. The young lady glanced at the painted sign it read Clairvoyant star gazer past, present and future, advice on romance, family and financial matters.' And then on a smaller sign it read 'Manx Nelly, The Royal Gypsy, clairvoyant to Royalty, also Presidents and Prime Ministers'. 'That's quite a statement,' said the young lady. Nelly looked at her and smiled, 'I am known as the Royal Gypsy Clairvoyant, all these photos with crowned royalty and heads of countries, who have all seeked guidance or advice from me, again and again.' Some call me Mother some the Stargazer.

'I can tell you a lot my dear,' said Nelly holding out her hand, the young lady placed her hand in Nelly's as she walked up the wagon steps. They each sat down on a small box type seat, Nelly sat facing her; a small table top with a drawer underneath between them. Martha slowly looked around the living wagon it was highly polished mahogany with a glass cupboard in each end corner over the bed, The glass fronts were so beveled they were nearly half moon shaped. They had a small star cut in the centre of each one, there was a pair of china plates, mushroom color background with two gold pheasants sparring up. In the other cupboard were two square dinner dishes, just touching each other, it was a highland scene, a castle away in the background. Two long horned highland cattle stood in a pond drinking their reflection in the water making a second scene. There was a thick gold plaited rope that went around the edge of each square platter.

'You have lovely china, it's beautiful, 'Thank you, that one is Royal Crown Derby and the other is Royal Worcester', said Nelly pointing to each cupboard. My name is Nelly, most of my clients call me 'Mother'. My name is Martha. 'I will call you 'Mother' because I feel at ease with you.' 'I do find it, she paused, glancing at the Welsh plaited rug that covered the bed, then the Hostess Stove, with square oven door the long stainless steel polished hinges so bright. It's all so clean and tidy, 'it's so cozy and dainty said Martha, placing her right hand on the table. 'How much is it?' she asked, ' two dollars for one hand, three dollars for both hands,' 'Martha snapped her purse shut, then placing the three silver dollars on the embroidered table cloth. 'Open both your hands my dear', said Nelly picking up the coins. She made a cross on each of Martha's open palms and then dropped the coins into a drawer under the table.

'I see a tall young blonde haired man,' said Nelly hesitating. 'Yes, yes tell me what is he thinking about me?' Nelly noticed her third finger of the left hand had a slight ridge around it where a ~ring had been she had seen her and her friend get out of the horse drawn trap with a tall blonde haired young man. Martha smiled and looked away, she knows and probably seen me come through the entrance into the circus field. We seem to be trying each other out, thought Nelly.

'How long have you been having the affair?' Martha looked surprised, then answered, 'four months.' 'This young man, he is not the first is he?' 'No he's not,' said Martha looking down at her shoes a little embarrassed. Nelly glanced down at Martha's button sided suede boots, very good quality, her clothes, skirt and jacket is tailor made for her, thought Nelly. 'Don't be embarrassed Martha, I am here to advise you,' said Nelly staring into Martha's open palms, her eyes then slowly looking into Martha's face. 'I see you are expecting.' 'How on earth can you know, I have only known three weeks myself?, said Martha. 'I read a lot in your face as well as your hands, answered Nelly as she looked at Martha's fingers and nails, she does do very little work, if any, thought Nelly, noticing again a slight ridge on her third finger of her left hand.' Are you separated or still with your husband, and you have a child, don't you?' 'I am with him and have a little girl of ten.' 'This young man I see he is a lot younger than you?' 'Yes he is, 22 and I am forty. 'I can see your husband is older than you, isn't he?' 'Yes mother he is 51, eleven years older than me.' 'And I can see he has a profitable business doesn't he?' 'Yes mother, a Livery (Horse) stables. 'And this young man, I can see he is the father of the child you are expecting isn't he my dear?' 'Yes, mother, he is and some evenings, works in the Livery stables for my husband, he is lovely and he makes me feel young again. 'You don't go with your husband a lot do you Martha?' 'Maybe every seven or eight weeks, replied Martha, a little embarrassed.

'There have been others haven't there, but this one is special to you, isn't he my dear?' 'Yes there have been four before John' 'I can see that John is the one for you, the one that you want?' 'Oh yes as I have said,' he makes me feel so young. 'Your husband Martha, I can see he is suspicious, he jealous?' 'Yes I think so, he saw me laughing and working, helping John.' 'And of course, you don't usually help the staff do you Martha?' 'No I don't, he was suspicious and he hit me.'

'I see big problems for you, but it's now starting to get cloudy, I would need to use the crystal to go deeper. 'Oh please do Mother I need to know what my chances are for the future,' said Martha glancing at the crystal. Nelly pulled it into the centre of the table then removed the small black velvet cloth that covered it, the light from the lamp above seemed to bring the crystal to life.

'The crystal Martha is 5 dollars. For the very deep reading, it has to be paper money, it must be folded and placed under the crystal'. Martha folded the 5 dollar bill and then placed it under the crystal, she then leaned back looking slowly at Manx Nelly whose eyes were now closed. The top of her black dress was hand crochet with tight little rose buds; her black grey streaked hair was pulled back tight into a bun. Her complexion was slightly tanned, around her neck was a chain with large square gold beads, every third one was a square red coral bead, earrings were small Canadian half dollars with a maple leaf down each side. Nelly's eyes opened and her hand slowly wavered over the crystal ball. Martha noticed her wedding ring was thick barrel shaped with a half carat diamond set in a star being gypsy set.

She was an impressive figure and spoke well, thought Martha. 'What is your accent mother? I can't place it. 'I was born and raised on a little island off England called the Isle of Mann until I was sixteen, I then spent many years in Scotland, Edinburgh and Perth. 'You must not interrupt anymore Martha, I am deep in the movement of the planets, the past is now going into the present don't interrupt any more I may see a little of the future in this reading'. The future is so misty, your lover wants you to leave with him, but not to leave empty handed, he knows the wealth your husband has and he wants more than you, what your husband has worked for all of his life, and he is encouraging you to take it all for him and you, I see a little more now. He is wanting your husband gone, done away with isn't he?' Martha hesitated before she answered 'Well yes mother I have been good to him, a good wife, kept his home clean and entertained his friends, after being with John my husband seems so old, and so un-interested in me, he's more interested in his business. I have been with him 22 years, since I was nineteen'. That might be so my dear,' said Nelly looking away, to hide her disgust and thinking you are not clean, "My Dear" you have been with men behind your husband's back, a good hard working husband, looking after you, you are a well-dressed and well-spoken whore, thought Nelly.

'You must try to tell me more Mother' ' I am trying but there is a lot of mist around the planets, replied Nelly. 'The future is also looking misty for you Martha as it can go either way, this young man he is wanting and planning a dark deed, which you would be more involved in than him.' Nelly stopped for a few seconds and looked at Martha, rubbed her eyes slightly and stared deep into the crystal again. 'Yes Martha the deed would be very black, this is New York and it carries a death sentence in New York.' 'How do you know this, how?' 'It is my gift and my talent, I see a dark cloud for you and your lover, you could lose everything including your daughter.' 'Tell me more mother, what about my daughter?' Manx Nelly suddenly sat back rubbing her eyes,

'Enough, enough Martha, the mist is now covering the planets, it's gone, you must come and see me for another reading next week, It might be a good idea to bring your lover with you, if I could do his reading separate from you, I could then give you a lot better reading'. Nelly placed the black cloth over the crystal then pushed it away leaning back. Next week the Wild West Circus will be at Coney Island permanently.' Martha went to speak, Manx Nelly held her hand up, 'I am tired Martha'.

'The show starts at two o clock, two o clock the show starts. Tickets are now being sold at the box office' shouted the man with the mouth funnel as he walked about the field. 'Howdy there Adam'. Adam turned as he felt the tap on the shoulder. 'Hello Mister Parva what brings you here again?' It was John Parver, a true Westerner, he had been to see the Wild West Show before and had built up a short friendship with Adam. He was very interested in things and places of Europe, and Adam was interested in how things really were out west.

'I really enjoy talking to you about Europe, and the little lady of course well she wanted to have her palm read again' said John. 'We're going back home tonight. We've had a nice break. Two weeks in Washington, and two weeks here in New York. I thought I'd come and give you some support when you ask for volunteers, I've bought my own gun as well.' Adam glanced down at the big 45 under his coat. 'So you're wanting to get in on the act with that cannon' said Adam, introducing him to his father. 'And where would that be?' asked Nelson, as they sat round the fire. 'You could say it's one of the last towns in Texas.' 'So what's it like out there?' asked Nelson. 'Well it's vast, it can be lonely, valleys, canyons. When you get to what you thought was an end in the distance, it's not. There is more, again and again. It's so big, so vast, open and wild. It's a man's country, what Scotland probably was, but on a lot bigger scale before England took it that is.'

'My mother was Scottish, my father Irish. There are still parts, untouched, only Indians. Thousands of square miles, a lot of it isn't even mapped up yet.' 'What about the people?' asked Adam. 'All immigrants, their parents or grandparents. Nobody is special, or well bred. The real American is the Indian. We all go down the same road. Some make it big, some don't. But nobody goes hungry, there's plenty there for everybody, and plenty of chances. Of course there is a lot trying to get rich quick, and some get dead quick' laughed John Parver.

'Does anybody own these vast areas? What of the farms, ranches?' asked Nelson. 'Well the Indians owned it all at first. It's their country. They didn't need even a quarter of it, but still they fought because they knew they would eventually loose most of it. When my father and his brothers built our place, it was out of the wilderness. They fought the Indians back and that would be only about 30 years ago. They had rifles. The Indians, they lost a lot of braves. There is thousands of square miles out there. It just keeps going down on to Mexico, and the Indians, well they just move back a bit more every five years or so, making room for the settlers for the ranches and farmers. There are ranches big and small. The odd mixed farm arable, growing stuff. Very big areas of free range for cattle.'

'You have a ranch?' asked Nelson. 'Yes I suppose it is a ranch. It was a small valley with mountains at the back and some lower hills to the front. It's called The Fish' said John proudly. But he could see Nelson and Adam were not impressed by the name. 'A valley' said Adam, 'and you made it a ranch. It must be big.' 'Yes it is. 65 miles long and eight miles wide' answered John. 'That's about the size of a big county in England. How many acres would that be?' asked Nelson.

'Some say it's the biggest in Texas, But I don't rightly know if it is, I don't know how many acres. My father and his two brothers came over from the free states of Southern Ireland Dundork first town over the border in the South, I was born on The Fish. In them days they mostly lived off the land at first, trout, salmon, Jack Rabbit, dear, it was all there. There was other families farming, small ranches nearby. I suppose there was more game, a lot more than what was needed, and everybody seemed to get by on it, then everybody got their own stock, and land, they just settled there and took it off the Indians, said Nelson. Yes I reckon so. Other settlers stayed away from the valley, too many Indians. Dad, his brothers and two cousins fought them off for a few years. They started The Fish, there were two bulls and 10 cows, and just let them roam free range. There is now about three and a half thousand head or thereabouts. We have a cattle drive every four years.'

'They must have been tough determined men to survive. Was there any doctors?' asked Nelson. 'A few, not many. Some homesteaders died in their 50s.' 'It sounds so new' said Adam. 'It is, and things are improving. We have a doctor in Glen Parva. This last fifteen years and the one we now have his wifes a nurse. Nice people, they came out two years ago from Bristol, England.

'As I said to you before John. I'd like to see it, try my luck' said Adam. 'We'd like to see you out there; I'll help you if i can. Nothing's stopping you. Trains, stage coaches, head for Fort-Worth, then Aberline, then Fort Monrose, next you're at Glen Parva. You'll have to stop off in Aberline, be careful it's a wild, open town.

'And how far would that be?' asked Nelson. 'I don't rightly know exactly, around two thousand miles' said John. 'Two thousand miles that must be from one side of this country to the other' said Nelson. 'Nowhere near it, they say it's nearly four thousand miles this America from the bottom up to Canada. It's not all been mapped out yet. It's a continent. There are hundreds and hundreds of miles with just the odd little place; they call them settlements, no law, no order, your knife, your gun. Self-protection and it pays to carry one.'

'How long have you been here in America?' 'About six months, the towns are too far apart and too small for the circus to travel' said Adam. 'If you do decide to come down Adam, when you leave Fort Worth, that's about the end of civilization so to speak, it gets a bit wild and you should always carry a gun, especially in open country. Not just men, but also animals, and as I said before, there's plenty of chances for a young man, especially if you have a knowledge and have skills. It is needed. How you shoot, you could become a sheriff or maybe a highwayman' said John with a laugh. He put the coffee mug down on the ground as they sat round the fire. Taking out a pencil and a piece of paper, he wrote John Parver, The Fish Ranch, down from Aberline, passed through Fort Monrose, Glen Parva. 'Thank you' said Adam as he folded it and put it in his pocket. He looked at John, 'that's your name Parver, and that is the name of the town. It must have been named after your family'. 'That's right, it was' said John. 'The Parva's are Irish. That was my father, and the Glen's they are Scottish, my mother.'

A pair of horses pulling a cab pulled through the encampment entrance. A young man got out with a big box of chocolates. As he walked over, a few ladies heads turned. It was Layton, Adam's younger brother by fifteen months. He was dark like a Greek or Turk. With sharp features, and long black curly hair which touched his shoulders. He stood 6 feet 4, about 16 stone. 'Morning father, morning Adam'. He had stayed the night in New York. Taking a mug of coffee, he handed the box of chocolates to his mother. As she went to kiss him on the cheek, he pulled back, embarrassed in front of the men.

Adam introduced him to John Parva. Nelson broke the story gently to his younger son before anyone else did, making as less as possible of it. Whenever there was any trouble with drunks or fights around the big tent, they usually called for him. Layton could handle himself and loved a fight, like most young gypsy men, they had to fight to survive, and they liked it. He put the half empty coffee mug down as he looked closer at the lump on the side of Adam's head. Then stared at the fire, then back at his brothers head. 'Did he say any insults to you father?' 'No, no, it's all over, it's all finished son. Adam knocked him out. It's finished' said Nelson. Not mentioning how hard the fight had been for Adam, and Layton's mother's involvement with it.

Layton glanced at the lump as big as a small egg on the side of Adam's head and his ear swollen deep red. He stood up 'I'm not bothered about his size, or how strong he is lifting his silly weights. He's no good to me. I'll destroy him; I am the best man on this field.'

'It's all finished son, just leave it. Albert wants no more trouble or complaints because of the amusement park going ahead' said Nelson, trying to calm him down.

Nelson and Adam were having difficulty keeping up with Layton's long strides. There was a little froth at the corner of his mouth and his eyes was staring straight ahead and looking a little wild. John Parva followed seven or eight yards behind. He loved to see a good fight and he could feel there was going to be one.

Carl the strong man could see Layton coming with Nelson and Adam trying to calm him down. 'You've caused some trouble this day' he said to his wife. Anita could see as big as Carl was, he wanted no trouble with Layton. Layton stood about 4-6 feet back from Carl. 'If ever you again go near any of my family'. 'All this is not my fault; it was your brother who started the trouble.

'You're interrupting when I'm speaking low life'. 'The one in the fault was your wife. She's a whore.' 'You Romany lot think you're so well bred' said Carl. He had had enough; he was ready to fight again if he had to.

'That's enough Ley, come away, it's over and finished' said Nelson, getting hold of Layton's arm. 'I don't mean to be disrespectful father, but go away.' Nelson stepped back and went and stood over by Adam. Carl stood up, his hand hanging low on a golf club. 'Have I got to fight the three of you' he said, staring down at Layton. 'I don't need any help, you're a bucket of shit' said Layton, taking a few steps back. 'I am the best man on this field; bring your golf club if you want. I'll make you eat it.'

He jumped two and a half feet off the ground as he was in mid air, both feet kicked separately. Then slowly swaying from one side to the other, Carl looked at him now unsure of himself. Nelson stepped forward his left hand holding his coat open. His right hand then pulling the small short roman sword half out of its sheath staring up at Carl. 'You're about a foot taller, and double his weight, use that golf club and I'll take one of your arms off.' Carl could see there was no hesitation, no bluff. He'd seen Nelson use that sword before. He threw the golf club under his wagon and stepped forward beating his expanded chest and standing up to his full height grinding his teeth. 'My god, he's the biggest man I've seen, he's a giant' said John Parva.

'Enough talk, let's see what you've got' said Layton. All of a sudden the three New York police officers were there on the scene. Long navy blue coats with shiny brass buttons and light grey helmets. Each held a 15 inch long baton. 'Break it up now' said the Irish Sergeant. The three officers stood in front of Carl. Albert Miller stood in front of Layton. 'He had obviously brought them to stop the fight' thought Nelson. The officer in charge was pointing with his baton to Carl and then Layton. 'It's up to both of you, walk away now. Let that be the end of it and they'll be no charges made. Keep it going or any cheek, we'll throw each one of you in that black Mariah' said the Sergeant pointing his baton to the big heavily built wagon by the entrance. 'You listen to the Police Officers son.'

Nelson was speaking loudly to Layton, a bit of a show so as the Sergeant could hear, the Sergeant could see they both took his warning about jail. As they walked away, Albert between them, Carl bent a little holding his stomach. Layton had that confidence as he walked. 'I've got the Sergeant squared. It has cost me 10 dollars, so as no complaints go back to town. Don't let me down., said Albert' 'I won't' said Layton. Carl just grunted. 'This argument, fight, has to finish now. If not you will both have to leave my show, no amusement park. You're throwing away a very good living for a lot of years. I can't have this on the boil ready to start at any time. I am putting a fortune into this park. It stops right now, because one of you could possibly be dead, and the other doing 20 years. Is that what you want?' said Albert, looking from one to the other.

'You have my word' said Carl, shaking hands with Albert. Then Layton done the same. Albert got hold of Layton and Carl's right hands and put them together. Layton and Carl shook hands; each looked the other way not interested. It was only for business and Albert. 'You keep away from me and I'll do the same' said Carl, as they walked different ways. 'Hey' shouted Lay, the big man's head turned, 'what is it?' shouted Carl. Chummer mandes bull – ('kiss my arse')shouted Layton. 'Bloody gypo's, you can never understand them' said Carl walking away.

Albert looked the other way. He was ready to laugh. 'What do you think son?' asked Nelson. 'I think it's over with dad, finished thank god. They have both given their word, he's still holding his chest, and he could have a broken rib.

'Mandy's shoora (my head) feels like there's someone in there trying to get out with a hammer'. If it had been a fight to a finish, one of them might have ended up dead. 'All over a hot arsed woman' answered Adam.

'Are you alright Uncle Carl?' asked one of his nephews. 'No I am not, my head and my belly feels like I have been kicked by a horse'. You should have given it good to that Nelson. He's supposed to be a Gypsy bare knuckle fighter and he comes out with a sword, said the other. 'Let some time go by till it's all settled down, he's got it coming, it's not finished by a long shot, he'll get his one day', answered Carl, glancing back.

CHAPTER TWO - 'A ROYAL PERFORMANCE'

Adam went to the cabinet and brought out a leather pistol box. Placing it on the table, he flipped back the lid. There was a smell of used gun powder and oil. The small square window in the side of the wagon situated above the table where he sat let in little light. He lifted the glass globe on the crystal angel lamp that was bolted to the wall, then lit it. Taking the pistol out, he quickly stripped it down. He went back to the oil lamp, and turned it down slightly as it was starting to smoke and black the inner glass globe.

Holding the revolver examining the chambers which held 6 bullets. Satisfied, he slowly put it back together. Adam glanced at the engraved silver plate on the inside of the lid, Adam Boswell, wiping his hands on a wet flannel and then a towel. He lit a cigar, as he leaned back, blowing out the smoke and just staring straight ahead. His mind went back, back two years ago. They had just landed back in England from the tour of Europe and they were in one of the great parks in London

Never had he thought he would see so much of the world and learn so much of places and people. It was eight o clock in the morning as he walked through the park. Birds singing and the odd rabbit running. He could have been out in the countryside. 'These great London parks are beautiful, some, four miles around them, and yet in the heart of the biggest city in the world' he thought. Adam's favourite area he loved had been Perth, Scotland and Blackpool. 'But this London, there is a magic about it' he thought.

He lit his first panatela of the day. Albert had said to him and his family 'it might not work out when I get back in America. It is a vast country. Cities they are hundreds of miles apart. This new world America,' 'My brother Layton and myself, we want to see it. Our people are Romany's. 'So we are wanting to roam,' said Adam, with a smile.

He walked away further down the park leaving Albert. He had been told tomorrow night's show was very special. Queen Victoria's husband, Prince Albert was to visit the show. The Wild West Circus would be in London for 4 weeks, then moving on to Bristol, Cardiff, Birmingham, and so on, three-four weeks in each place throughout Britain's big cities. The Prince was known to be a pistol marksman himself and he had really come to see Adam's act.

Yesterday Albert had the full staff out. He explained what a day it would be. Newspapers, writers, some from other countries, even pictures being taken, every act would give their best for the royals. Everything would gleam and sparkle, the full Place was so busy all day it was just like when they had performed for the titled families in Berlin. The stage coaches, wild Indians, their attack, the cavalry rescue. Then there was Carl the strong man and his two nephews. After the interval, there was then Layton's wild horses, trick riding, somersaulting off one on to the other. The Royal's had constantly applauded they seemed very pleased enjoying the show. Horse riding and then a shoot out with three Indians when this was finished there was a 10 minute interval.

Albert walked forward into the centre of the arena holding a large funnel putting it to his mouth. 'Your Royal highness Prince Albert, Lords, Ladies and Gentleman, I give you Adam Boswell, the main event. A pistol crack shot, who has entertained royals and presidents of Europe. A pistol marksman that has yet not been equaled, wherever he has been' 'That's quite a statement' said the Prince to his companion, Lord Rogers.

The band started to play very faint, the roll on the drums gradually getting louder. As Adam reached the centre of the ring and the drums died away, there was a loud applause. He was dressed in white buckskin. Gun holster and low crowned Stetson and boots in black. He slowly walked forward, stopped and stood in front of the royal box.

'My god' whispered Albert, 'What is he going to say? Please, please Adam be careful' said Albert under his breath. As he removed his hat, he bowed and smiled to the Prince, and then to the Princes Companion Lord Rogers. 'Your Royal Highness Prince Albert a loyal subject I am and here to entertain you's. I am honored to entertain you.' The Prince smiled and nodded.

His black curly hair hung over his ears. He had quite a tan where they had been on the continent, which seemed to show off his white teeth. 'Oh what a handsome chap' whispered Lord Rogers, the Prince gave a quick glance to Lord Rogers. Adam noticed a higher row behind the royals, there sat four heavies. Each had a bulge in his jacket. Putting his hat back he bowed, then turned and went to the centre of the ring. As the section of the sheeted tent roof was sliding back, a section of the side sheeting was also sliding back by another four men that was pulling ropes, to reveal a high wall of what looked to be thick wood planking. It was 150 feet to the shelf that was on the planking. The four targets was metal, being thick hollow square cubes painted in silver, that started at six inches square, then four, then two, and the last one only one inch square.

Albert asked for the two volunteers that was good shots. A Police Officer of about 30 proudly walked forward. 'One more, we need just one more' shouted Albert. The Prince turned to the back row of Bodyguards. 'Geoffrey, you knew this was coming tonight, come along, you're the best. Show them what you can do.' 'Yes sir' he said standing up. 'Yes, we have the other one' shouted Albert. As Geoffrey held up his hand striding into the sawdust ~ring there was applause from the audience for the two challengers.

Each man refused Albert's offer of a pistol, each explaining he had brought his own. Bill the Police Officer went first. He was using a 22 caliber target revolver. He took the first two targets off the shelf, one straight after the other. Slowly and carefully taking aim. After five seconds he took the third one off the shelf. The audience gave him a good applause, again slowly taking aim he fired at the last target. The bullet passed so close to the small one inch cube, it rocked it, but it did not fly off the shelf.

Adam smiled and held out his hand towards the target, motioning him to try again. Taking aim, he fired twice, one straight after the other. The cube jumped in the air. Albert lifted the funnel to his mouth and shouted to the audience 'that small cube is only one inch square, and the distance is 150 feet, 50 yards. They are using pistols, not rifles.' The audience gave a good applause.

Bill went to walk off. Albert took hold of his arm not to leave, telling him there was a lot more to come. Geoffrey the body guard stepped forward, keen to show what he could do. As well as being known as a royal body guard, he was a British pistol champion. As he was taking off his jacket, the targets was being put back up again, pulling out the six shot 38 caliber revolver from its shoulder holster he nodded to Adam. He seemed very confident as he stood on the line, pistol in hand. He went down the line. The first three went down, one straight after the other within 10 seconds. He then stopped, slowly taking aim.

'Get on with it man' said the Prince under his breath. The last shot came another 3 seconds later, taking the last cube off the shelf. Geoffrey smiled, pleased with himself as he reloaded and received a good applause from the audience.

Taking off his hat, Adam stepped forward, after checking his revolver then holstering it, he stood on the line, 'hit it Adam' he whispered to himself. The gun was suddenly in his hand. Shooting from the hip. Four shots rang out, one straight after the other. His gun then took two spins forward and one back, landing it back into its holster. The four cubes was gone. Everyone stood up clapping. 'The gun back in its holster in eight seconds' said the Princes companion Lord Rogers. 'Are you sure?' Asked the Prince. 'I am sure sir' came the answer, 'it was eight seconds.'

'And Geoffrey?' asked the Prince. 'Yes sir that was 17 seconds.' Albert stood in the centre of the ring pointing up with his cane. All eyes went up to a large box at the top of the planked wall. There was four big oil lamps, one on each corner that had been lit. There was a roll on the drums as Albert stood in the centre of the sawdust ring. Lifting the funnel to his mouth, he started to shout. 'This time it will be falling targets.' Bill the Police Officer was now standing on the line, 50 yards from the plank wall, gun in hand. The man up in the box waved that he was ready.

Albert shouted again 'two pint glasses, whenever you are ready, just shout drop' said Albert to the young Police Officer. Bill had his 22 pistol out, his arm very loose, the pistol moving from side to side at various heights up and down. 'Drop' he shouted. Two glasses fell for the practiced fall for all to see. 'Maybe it's the height, why they seem to fall so fast' thought Bill. They had seen the practice drop and this time it was for real.

'Drop' he shouted again and he hit both. The second glass shattering only nine feet from the ground. Geoffrey the body guard surprised them all. Both glasses shattered half way down. The royal box gave him a good clap including most of the audience. 'He must have regular practice with moving targets' thought Adam reloading his gun.

As he stood on the line Adams fingers seemed to play a tune on the side of his holster, 'drop' he shouted. The holstered gun was suddenly in his hand. Both glasses shattered and then his gun was holstered, he went back to where the other two stood. There was little applause, Adam was used to this, as it was expected of him. There was now two men in the box above, and Adam walked back to the line, turning to the audience, he held three fingers up, standing slightly crouched, his finger tips moving as if playing a tune on the side of his holster again. 'Drop' he shouted. The first two shots rang out, the glasses shattering nearly side by side. The last shot hit the third glass three quarter ways down. The full audience was up on their feet applauding as he holstered the gun he smiled. He had them back again as always, but there would be more to come, thought Adam much more, he could tell these were not the usual Top Gun Club Members. Adam knew this Royal Bodyguard was not the usual A Class marksman. This Geoffrey would be Double A, which would be the best in either England, Wales, or Scotland, and Bill the Police Officer would be a London Champion, a single A.

On the next drop of three glasses, Bill hit two out of the three, and Geoffrey, he hit all three, but the last one barely five feet off the ground when it was hit. Bill looked at Geoffrey, who was the second best pistol shot in England. He would now have to give it his very best to beat this American cowboy, who seemed to make it all look so very easy.

The Prince leaned over to speak to Lord Rogers. 'By damn this American cowboy can shoot. There's no effort. He seems to do it with such ease. I would like to see him in a shoot out with Johnny Burt from Birmingham.' The targets seem to get more unusual and difficult. There was now a big seesaw brought in and placed down the far end in front of the planked wall. On one end of the plank was a square flat basket. The other a square padded end standing, some four feet off the ground. Albert stepped forward with a whiskey glass, holding it up for all to see, then placing it on the basket end. He then pointed to a heavy built man who was standing on a trestle some six feet above the padded end.

'Up' shouted Albert. The heavily built man jumped. The weight and force of him sent the plank down hard, and the small whiskey glass went straight up 60-70 feet in the air. Bill and Geoffrey nodded as if to say thank you for the trial show. Both of them hit A small whiskey glass, and so did Adam. Albert stepped forward, this time placing two whiskey glasses on the plank, one went straight up. The other went in a different direction, some 6 feet off to the right.

Bills first bullet found its target, the small glass shattering into pieces. He had to drop to one knee to get the angle of the second glass, and having to fire twice, so as to hit it. Only six or seven feet off the ground, the glass shattered. The audience clapped and cheered him. It was a good show of marksmanship, especially going down on one knee to hit the target.

Geoffrey hit both glasses, and hit them well. One half way down, and the second one some 10 foot off the ground, but the second glass took him two shots to hit it. 'Good show Geoffrey, damn good show. He's giving the cowboy a run for his money' said Lord Rogers. The royal box and all the rest of the audience gave him a good applause. Albert's expression seemed to look like a question mark as the corner of his mouth pulled up to one side. This was not the usual shoot out with some local shooting club. Both these men could shoot, especially the bodyguard. He gave Adam a nod. Had Adam finally met his match. Albert had heard of this Geoffrey Royal bodyguard, he was Triple A Class, being the highest. There would probably be only six or seven in the country. Number 2 Kevin, from Bloxwich, he was a triple A, and of course the best in the country, triple A was Johnny Burt of Birmingham. Geoffrey was equaling Adam, hitting everything that was put in front of him. But some of the shots were taking two to hit the target and Adam was doing it all the time with one. 'So he is not in this Cowboys class', thought the Prince.

As Adam turned, he noticed his father and Layton standing over by the large exit curtains. They both smiled showing confidence in him. Albert was now pointing to the target. 50 yards away on the target shelf was three white thin candles each one no thicker than your finger. Adam ignored Albert and walked back over to the box which the targets were kept in. He brought out three whiskey glasses. ' And just what are you trying to prove with three? It's probably impossible in mid air at that distance' said Albert.

Ignoring Albert, Adam put the three small glasses on the plank. Smiling he waved over Geoffrey. Geoffrey nodded. He was accepting Adams challenge. 'There's three, so whenever you're ready' said Adam. Geoffrey finished reloading. 'What about the candles?' he asked. 'They'll come later' answered Adam.

Albert explained to the audience if a target is hit with a second shot, it is only one point in a competition. If it is hit with the first shot, it is three points. Gun in hand, Geoffrey stepped on to the line. 'Up' he shouted, the three glasses seemed to stop in mid air for a fraction of a second as they had reached their maximum heights, they were at different heights as they started to fall. 'They're so far apart' thought Geoffrey. The centre one was at twelve o clock, the left one nine o clock, and the third one at four o clock. They were all dropping at the same time, and falling different ways. He took the highest centre one first.

His next shot hit the second glass on the left, three quarter ways down. Swinging his gun fast to the right, too late, the glass hit the sawdust ground in one piece. There was a loud sigh of disappointment from the audience. Bill the Police Officer looked at Albert and shook his head from side to side in answer as saying no. He knew Geoffrey to be the third best pistol shot in all Britain, even he had only just managed to hit two glasses. Was such a target possible, 'I don't think so, at this distance, he thought.

Bill was champion pistol shot of all London Counties Police Force. He did not want to make a fool of himself. Adam walked over and shook his hand. 'Stay for the candles' he said. Geoffrey glanced at the royal box and looked away disappointed. 'I was too slow' he said to Adam. 'One more' said Adam out loud. Placing another three glasses on the plank. Albert nodded. 'Why not' answered Geoffrey, reloading his gun. His first two shots sounded nearly as one. The first glass shattering, the second missed, the third shot hit the third glass shattering it. But the second glass lay on the sawdust in one piece.

'Too fast' said Adam as he stepped onto the line. This time his gun was in his hand, not holstered. He stood like a prize fighter. One foot behind the other. Some 15" apart. The gun in his left hand, wavering from side to side like a clock pendulum. 'Let us watch and learn' said Bill sarcastically to Geoffrey. He had taken a lot of swagger and boasting from Geoffrey the body guard at the gun club in London on several occasions. This cowboy was showing Geoffrey up at every shoot thought Bill.

'Up' shouted Adam. He took the lowest glass first, then the second one, across from the first, the third bullet found its target and the last glass shattered, the pieces fell to the ground, the small heavy bottom part of the last glass went diagonally spinning up through the air. Adam fired again and the thick small bottom of the third glass exploded into pieces. There was no applause. Not a sound. Everyone just stared. So did Albert, Nelson and Layton.

They had never seen this before. People was talking and pointing. You would probably need a double barrel shotgun to do that. 'Is that really possible with a pistol?' said the Prince. 'Well we've just seen it with our own eyes' answered Lord Rogers. You're right, said the Prince just staring he then stood up and started to clap, suddenly the full arena 1,500 people followed him, they were on their feet. Everyone was clapping and cheering. Bill and Geoffrey both walked over and shook hands with Adam refusing to take part in the candle shooting. Both had obviously seen enough.

Prince Albert sat down turning and speaking to Lord Rogers Who then waved Adam over to the Royal Box, Adam walked over removing his hat giving a bow. Prince Albert reached in his waist coat pocket and handed Adam a card. 'Thank you your highness, thank you for a lovely evening', said Prince Albert.

Suddenly there was three loud knocks on the wagon door. 'You're on Adam in 15 minutes.' Reaching to the ash tray he picked up his cigar and relit it. His hand went to the lump on his head. It was throbbing. His fingers going over it very gently. He cursed Carl. Then pouring some water into a glass, he emptied two asket powders into it. Swirled it around, then took it back in one swallow. As he flipped the lid shut, he looked at the revolver. Taking the holster out of the belt, he turned the two small catches on either side of the edge of the holster, opening it up. Inside the bottom of it was a leather covered small metal plate. It was seated in a groove on either side. Underneath of the plate was two small powerful little springs as he pressed it up and down several times with his thumb, he was satisfied that it was still oiled enough.

Folding the face of the holster back over, then turning the two small catches, he strapped it on and tied the holster cord round his thigh. Then pressing the revolver slowly down into the holster, as it stopped there was a little click. Adam stood slightly crouched, his fingers just touching the top of the face of the holster. As he pressed just once, the gun seemed to jump into his hand.

Satisfied, he gave the gun two forward twirls, then one back, landing it in its holster. Then pulling the safety cord over the hammer. He unstrapped the gun belt and hung it over the chair then started to get dressed into the white buckskin suit for his act. Adam thought about what Jim Parva had told him. Rich farmlands, ranches, busy silver mines, working. 'I could become part of it, maybe make my mark. A new town with new people, from different countries, a new life' thought Adam. 'I've not come thousands of miles to the new world to stay in this tent the rest of my life. There'll be chances for me, I may buy a small holding and maybe breed horses. If I get the right breaks maybe I can clean up with the Wheel of Fortune and the Silver Lady and own a big casino one day. Who knows! I've got a nice few thousand dollars behind me. To try my luck'

He cupped his left hand to the side of the top of the glass globe, of the oil lamp and blowed down it, then turned the wick right down. 'It's about time I worked for myself and was my own man' thought Adam as he closed the wagon door. There was a young man tanned up and dressed like an Indian walking straight towards his wagon. 'You're on in a few minutes.' 'I was just on my way Billy Joe' answered Adam.

CHAPTER THREE - 'HORSE DEALING'

Next Morning

'Whoa easy there whoa' said Layton as he pulled on the reigns, pulling the rig into the roadside. 'Excuse me fella, is this area called Patterson?' 'It sure is sir' answered the nigro man. 'We're trying to get to Station Road, a fella called Johnny Goldfields, general dealer.' 'Yes sir, you've passed it. Turn around and take the second road on the right. Go straight. Straight down to the bottom, it'll be a good half a mile, then it's right in front of you.'

'You're not from round here sir are you? Where are you from?' 'Scotland' answered Layton. 'That's fine, thank you sir' said the nigro touching his cap. It wasn't often white men spoke to nigro's so friendly. They went down a long driveway, and at the bottom there were three big buildings. Each one being twice the size of a farm barn. Layton pulled the pair of grays up in front of the office. Jumping down Adam tied the leather strap of the bridles to the hitching Rail.

'Johnny Goldfield, general dealer, we buy and sell anything' said Adam, reading the sign out loud. 'Good morning to both of you. Which one of you is Adam?' he asked. 'That's me, and this is my brother Layton. Are you Johnny Goldfield?' 'I am' he said. 'How did you know us?' asked Adam. 'How could I not know you? Albert said you may be selling that waterman's'

Adam looked over to the left, there was a yard half full of wagons, trailers, traps. It must have been half an acre, and there was one low flat roof that covered it all. He looked over to the right to a field with some loose boxes in it.

Layton looked at Adam, then the field of horses again. There must have been 20. Thoroughbreds, paints, palominos, ablutions, and a rare pair of white Arabs. 'That's the best stock of well-bred gryes horses I've seen in years' said Layton. He loved horses. Doctoring them up, getting them right, selling, even training them. Johnny had taken them on a tour of his stock. As they came out of the last building, Adam looked back. 'You've got some stock, however do you keep count on what you've got?' 'I can't, I just keep buying and selling, wood glass, furniture, horses, guns, anything.' 'Could one man own all of this? Just how much of this stock is really his, he seems very self-important' thought Adam.

'Come on up to the house' he said. 'You seem proud of what you've got and what you've done' said Adam. 'I am, I landed in New York 22 years ago. A Jew boy of 18 with only 15 pounds in my pocket, about

70 dollars, and I started dealing in anything, a few guns at first, then some horses to the army. It was the army that put me on my feet. They were taking all I could get them for the war. No knackers, good middle stock. The horses you see over there are for private sale. That field is usually full. I then went into property. An odd shop here and there, then houses, a few fields on the edge of town.'

'Does he ever stop bragging' thought Adam. I'd tell him I do not want his success life story but I don't want to rub him the wrong way. 'I've seen your show and it's good' said John. As they walked in the house, Adam and Layton glanced from one to the other. The place looked very, very wealthy. 'Aren't you frightened of being robbed?' asked Adam as he glanced around waving his arm at what he could see. There was a silver bowl you could sit a child in. Paintings, Royal Worcester and Crown Derby, large pieces and Dresden Figures Bukhara Persian rugs. 'It's like Aladdin's cave' said Layton. 'Probably three quarters of this stuff in here will be (chordy), stolen. I bet he's a fence for nearly anything' thought Layton.

'No I am not scared of being robbed. Only a stranger to New York or a fool would try to rob me. The Chief of Police and the Mayor are personal friends. Every gang in New York sells me things. Layton smiled, I know you were a fence, he thought. I have five of a working staff who all live here in that row of houses as you came in. All well-armed, all well paid and all loyal.'

'Please sit down gents' he said, as a pretty half cast girl came in, pushing a trolley. There was a platter of beef sandwiches with mustard on the side. Two pots, one coffee, one tea. A smart woman of about 45, a little overweight came in and sat on the chair facing, with practically a ring on every finger. 'She should sell them all and buy one good solitaire' thought Adam. 'This is Adam and Layton Boswell, and this is Vivian my wife.' 'Good morning gentlemen.' 'Good morning ma'am'

She then clapped her hands. 'Jessie, Jessie, where is the cake?' 'I forgot it, I'll get it right now Ma'am' she answered rushing out. 'Let's get down to business about this Waterman's'

Adam's and Layton's eyes met, just for two seconds then looked away. Adam smiled, 'he's keen, this could be my day' he thought. Layton smiled back at Adam, looked down and then looked up. 'I know brother. Caution, use caution. He could be a dangerous little man' thought Layton.

Jessie came in again with another platter and on it was a large Dundee cake, the top of it smothered in almond nuts. Vivian handed out three small plates, then picked up a mother of pearl handled knife, and started to slice the cake up. 'Just help yourselves to what you want.' 'This cake is the best I've tasted since I left Scotland' said Layton, as he buttered a second slice. 'I'll agree with that' said Adam.

'So where in town do you get them?' 'You don't. I love to cook' answered Vivian. Adam finished his coffee, Layton his tea. 'So let's see this rig' said John getting up. They all walked out. Adam offered Johnny a cigar. 'Not bad, not bad at all' he said, as he drew on the pale thin cigar. 'And why are you selling such a lovely waterman's coach?' asked Vivian. 'You and Johnny have a good look around it. Take your time. We're going to have a look at your horses' said Adam. Layton soon left Adam behind, his long legs taking big strides. He just wanted to see the horses. That was his business, he loved them.

Adam leaned on the top rail, standing next to Layton and looking at the stock. 'That pair of Arabs are beauties, what I wouldn't give for them' said Layton. 'How could you turn them out. Povv them in a field (put them in a field), no loose boxes, left out all night, probably get them (chord) Stolen' said Adam.

As Layton climbed over the five barred gate, Adam followed. 'Probably all these horses will be for sale'. 'So what are you thinking?' asked Adam. Layton picked up a bucket of oats and walked towards the two white Arabs that was over in the corner on their own. After patting them for a few minutes, Layton held out his hand several times full of oats. The horses had accepted him and did not trot away. Adam held the bucket of water. The first one had a good drink. Knowing that a horse will not drink straight away out of a bucket or bowl that another horse had been drinking out of.

Adam taking out his handkerchief he soaked it in the water and opening the second horse's mouth, he washed it inside several times. Then opening its mouth to look at its back teeth. 'This one's four to five years old.' 'This one's six' answered Layton. Their legs are clean, no spaverns'

'Anything that's not up to the mark Layton' asked Adam. 'We were both taught horse trade by the same old grand dad, you know as well as I do they're good stock, but their manes aren't quite up to being full Arab. They have slight dark streaks in places. A mild powdered bleach, then olibat oil, would bring those manes pure white and shining'. 'I'd like one of these, if you could pull it in the deal at the right price.' 'How would you value them' asked Layton.

As we both know what makes them so high in price is that they're rare. They've got to be worth at least a thousand dollars each. I've never seen any pure Arabs since we've been in America. I suppose there will be some.' 'Anyway Adam, I'd like one. I've never had a white Arab.' 'Okay Layton, let's see, let's see how it goes.'

'So what do you think Adam your waterman's? It's really a copy isn't it? If ever he found out, he'd have you done over, and if you're going away.'

'I suppose you're right Lay, he looks a proper little hound doesn't he, a fence, he'd scream his head off.' 'No I don't think he would. He'd be too laged (embarrassed), to let anyone know two gypsy boys had had him over. I must use caution, as granddad Isaac says, we have to leave ourselves an out. He is nobody's fool or he wouldn't have what he's got. Let's give him plenty of rope.'

'Be a little on his side Layton when the dealing starts.' 'I've got you brother, we've been there before, I won't overdo it' said Layton.

'So Mister Boswell, why are you selling such a lovely rig, are you needing the money?' asked Vivian. 'What a cheeky piss-taking bitch' thought Adam. He never showed his anger, he looked her straight in the eyes and smiled, then turned to Johnny. 'I believe Albert told you he's starting a big amusement show park in New York. I've been in the circus game too long and I'm thinking of going out west, going to try and make something of myself, make my mark. I might start a ranch, go into some sort of business.'

'Johnny just ignored Adam's remarks. He was looking all round the coach and that was all he was interested in. 'I'm not looking for faults to run it down, there is none. The colours' said Johnny. 'The colours I chose' said Adam.

The coach was light grey over dark slate grey with a gold leaf double line through the belly between the greys. Even the spokes of the wheels, each spoke was shadowed by the other shade of grey with a double gold thin leaf line round the hub. The shafts was all dark grey. All the metalwork was highly polished white metal. On the door handles was the initials WM with a Leicestershire crest. At the bottom of the front board was the badge, Hanson Cab Coach Builders, Hinckley, Leicestershire, England, then in brackets the Waterman's.

'It's a nice one, isn't it?' Johnny just nodded in agreement. It was the best he had seen. 'I suppose you know there's only six over here, four in New York, two in Washington, they can sell all they can make to Europe' said Adam. 'So where do you want to be with it?' said Johnny holding his hand out, palm up, the show of a dealing man.

'Five thousand, that's including the pair of greys, the harness, the lot.' 'you're mad, I can buy two good shops with a house above for less than that.' Adam looked at him. 'The pair of greys that pull it are worth 12 hundred dollars for the pair all day. The harness patent leather platted in two greys, especially made for the rig. Then there's all the white metal buckles and clasps. Is there anyone in New York can make such a set of harness and metals? I don't think there is yet.'

Johnny never answered. 'that's got to be worth 500 dollars anyway.' 'So' said Adam, 'that's 17 hundred dollars isn't it, leaves only 33 hundred for the Waterman's, how can it be dear? It's obvious you know the name, but not the coach. It's double floored, there's a metal floor underneath of that wood floor and the roofs the same. That's real hide over all the wood paneling interior. All hand worked. They make lots of handsome cabs, but the Waterman's type or model as they call it, they only make 15 a year. Seven coats of paint and two varnish sanded in between coats. You know it's mostly titled people and big land owners that have these. You have to buy them out of the back door on the quiet. They don't like common people having them.'

'Just a bunch of puffed up snobs' said John. 'Oh you're right there' said Layton. 'So how do they get the name Waterman when they're called the handsome cab?' asked Johnny.

'We was there with the Wild West circus only a little country market town Hinckley, but it's halfway between Leicester and Coventry, two big cities, only eight miles each way from Hinckley. So it's a good place to have the circus for six weeks. Layton, me and Albert went to the Handsome Cab Works.' Layton looked at him smiling as if to say 'I don't remember that Adam.'

'You see they make 70 cabs a year, that's a lot of cabs, but only 15 Waterman's, they're not built to a dead price. They're made with the very best of materials, and the three men that make them are the best that's there.'

'You're very good with the story' thought Layton. 'I don't remember any of that'.

'The old man that started the business was Harry Waterman and his two sons. They made that model in his name, in his remembrance. We went there with Albert when he ordered his. He was waiting five months to get it, and if he hadn't been in England, he'd have waited 12 months. Now I haven't got the name of a crook, and I don't intend to be classed as one, I respect you and I tell you the truth. This Waterman's has been repaired. It has been slightly re-built, not fully re-built only slightly. It went over, only the back wheel was broke and the door, and the paintwork was badly scratched up and he gave it a complete repaint job. The coach worker repaired it and completely re-built it and improved it in various places in his own time. It was repaired out of the works; he spent a full year on it. I gave him a lot of money and a pair of very good shot guns for it. I tell you this to show you respect.'

'It's a good tale' thought Layton, 'and I think he's going to swallow it'. Johnny looked at Adam 'You do show me respect, maybe you know I would not be taken for a fool. There's a saying in Scotland your eyes is your judge, your pocket is your guide, and your money is the last thing that you part with, said Adam. You're a dealing man Johnny and that's how you get your living, you would not have what you've got if you was a fool would you?' 'Thank you' said Johnny smiling. Layton turned his head to have a quick little smile; we've heard our father say that a few times, he thought. 'You know the mayors got one of these, and there's only three others in New York, I've seen Albert, this one, it's better, it's so well finished, so much detail, answered Johnny.' Johnny suddenly stopped, I must not keep mentioning how good it is or I'll never be able to bid him and get the price down, but it's such a good buy, thought Johnny.

'Yes, the young craftsman worked nearly a year on it, weekends, I must have seen 10 at different times in places over there, they're the best, so well finished, said Adam.

'But if you don't fancy it Johnny I can put it in the big monthly auction next month. I believe they sell anything and everything.' 'They certainly do, the New York monthly sale, is something not to be missed answered Johnny, 'I'm there every time.'

'Trouble is I'd have to wait another 2 weeks, by the time the auctioneers paid me, it would be three weeks, and I'm wanting to move on' said Adam. 'It looked and sounded good, he'd covered it well' thought Layton.

The last thing Adam wanted was to put it in a sale. 'A Waterman's would probably have to have receipts from the Handsome Cab people, paperwork would probably be expected for such an expensive and rare piece of merchandise' thought Layton. It was simple and it was convincing. Really it was many pieces, the name plates, hinges, brackets, even the paint and leather that the young man had taken out of the works in the evenings. The only thing he did buy was the wheels and some sheets of thin wood. It was a very beautiful copy, but the young man could not use it. They would want to know where a worker at the works could have built such a thing and so expensive bits and pieces. How could he own it?

'Can I see you a minute Johnny?' said his wife, speaking loudly and standing some 40 to 50 feet away, not wanting to interfere when men was dealing. 'What is it?' he answered a little annoyed. She looked in an aggravated mood thought Adam 'If he changes his mind and takes it to the New York monthly sale they'll be a dozen bidders after it'.

'I don't need you to tell me that, go in woman and do your house work, men's dealing'. 'You listen to me, next Sunday all the best people will be at the big park in New York. I want to be getting out of that Waterman's dressed in my best. You can well afford it Johnny, now stop farting around like some old man and get it bought before he changes his mind and wants to take it the New York sale.'

'Alright' he answered with a put on smile. Layton looked at Adam; I've got a lot of money laid out. I see you like them Arabs, will you deal?' asked Johnny. Sharp people these Jews, he's got plenty just wanting to deal something in, I fancy one of those Arabs, thought Layton.

'I'll deal to a walking stick if I can have a good deal, draw enough to swap' joked Adam. 'The stock you've got here and this place, you're probably a millionaire.'

Adam could see Johnny liked the praise. He knew Adam was moodying him along, but he loved it. 'How much are the Arabs?' 'Two thousand dollars' answered Johnny. 'I'll take one Arab and four thousand dollars'

'I don't see five thousand dollars in the Waterman's, anyway the Arabs are a pair, I can't split them up, I want two thousand dollars for the pair, and I think they're not dear. They're the only match pair of pure Arabs I know of in this part of the country. But I have been told there is a pair in Kentucky.'

'I have to pull back some money on this trade' thought Johnny. He had been asking 15 hundred dollars for the pair of Arabs, 'that 500 dollars I've spliced on top will give me some slack to deal' he thought. Layton could see it would be a hard deal; they were both two very shrewd men, thought Layton.

Johnny held out his hand palm upwards as if waiting for a bid, but he was giving the bid. 'I will give you two thousand dollars cash and the pair of Arabs, you're making four thousand dollars of the coach and that's a very good price.'

'It's not a bad price at all, but you'll go more, you'll go a good bit more because I can see that you want it, and if you don't get it, you're gonna have problems with the little lady, thought Layton.

Johnny walked away supposing to look round it, giving Adam time to think of his bid. He needed to get it together in his head. 'There was too big of a gap between' thought Johnny. 'This gypsy was like dealing with another Jew' he thought.

'Thanks for the bid Johnny, one bids worth ten lookers on. But I'll have to wait and see what it will make in the sale. I can only sell it once, and I need to get as much as I can. The Arabs are very good stock. I'll agree to that, but I don't see two thousand dollars in them, especially with their manes being streaked.'

Johnny nodded. 'And my pair of horses, those grays that go with the Waterman's, they go very well.'

'They're alright, they're a nice pair and I can't fault them, but they don't do the Waterman's justice. I would have to sell them. 'What is wanted for that Waterman's is a pair of grey abolitions and I know where there are a pair 300 miles away, the other side of Albany, said Johnny

Layton gave Adam a quick glance as much as to say 'you've got him. He's got the horses picked out already for it. He wants it bad. He'll go more. Get to him brother; I'll pull it together for you.'

Layton looked at Johnny 'you know when you see that rig going round New York and everyone's admiring it, and you could have had it, you'll realize Johnny, ready money is nice, but it isn't everything.' These people, they're very convincing ' thought Johnny looking over at his wife who was smiling at him. He smiled back; he realized if he didn't get this deal together, he would probably be sleeping on the couch for a month.

'Come on Johnny' she thought. 'You've had deals for more than this?' It was now Layton's turn to move into the deal gypsy style, but Johnny did not realize it and what was coming. 'Adam had asked him a bit high' thought Layton; he had give him enough rope to hang himself. But it was a bit too much to drop. Johnny might smell a rat. Layton looked at Johnny slowly, 'the deal is starting to go a little cold' he said, giving his brother Adam a quick glance as much as to say 'he's no fool, you need to get it together.' 'Give me your hand Adam, and you Johnny.' He held each ones right hand. 'Sell the full rig with a good heart Adam, you'll only sell it once, and you Johnny, it'll be yours for a lot of years. You might not see another one for sale in this area for who knows how long. Don't begrudge the extra money Johnny, you can afford it, buy it lucky.' There's too big of a gap, you're a bit greedy Adam and you Johnny, you value your money too high' said Layton, holding both of their right hands. 'You're asking five thousand dollars Adam, and you Johnny, you've bid two thousand, and the Arabs. They are worth two thousand you say' said Layton giving Johnny a quick stare. Johnny looked away.

'Adam wants five thousand dollars, he wants three thousand dollars to swap, you've bid him 2000, say yes to 25 hundred Adam, let's see a deal.' Adam made out to hesitate. 'It's too much of a drop' he said.

'No way with the Arabs that's four and a half thousand dollars' said Johnny pulling away. 'I'm trying hard here for both of you to make a deal' said Layton. '25 hundred dollars Johnny, you're not paying it all out, 25 hundred dollars Adam' said Layton, squeezing Adam's hand. Adam made out to pull his face in a sour sort of an expression and slightly pulling away. His top lip curling up a little. 'It's too much to drop it's 500 dollars' Layton said Adam.

Johnny felt him trying to pull his hand away, as if no deal. 'Were born actors' thought Layton looking at his brother. 'Bid again Johnny, bid again' shouted Vivian. Johnny looked over at her, she was so excited. 'She looks lovely, so beautiful when she is excited' he thought.

Johnny's eyes met Layton's; he never said anything he just nodded his head twice as if to say 'yes I'll deal'. 'Come on Adam, come on, he's trying to deal with you, if it was me I would deal' said Layton.

Adam made out to hesitate, then said 'Okay it's a deal I'll stand on at that,' and shook Johnny's hand. 'That's it said Layton, that's the deal then. Johnny you've got to give him 25 hundred dollars and the Arabs.' Johnny nodded. 'Adam you've accepted the deal 25 hundred dollars and the Arabs for your full rig.' 'It's a deal then, said Adam

Vivian ran over and threw her arms around Johnny's neck 'thank you Johnny, thank you.' They went back up to the house. The deal was finished and Johnny was as pleased as his wife. They sat down and coffee was brought in. Johnny went to a safe and pulled out a leather bag. He tipped it up on the carpet. There must have been about 30 thousand dollars or more in it. Layton and Adam looked at the heap of money, then at each other. It was obviously done for a flash, but it was a good flash, 'a nice sight' said Adam.

Adam then counted the two wads of money; it was in 20 dollar bills and 10 dollar bills. He peeled off 20 dollars and stuffed the 2 rolls in his front two cash pockets of his trousers and buttoned them down. 'There would have been no deal only for Layton getting us together', 'and it was a four and a half thousand dollar deal' said Adam, placing the 20 dollars in front of Layton's coffee cup.

Johnny nodded then folded a 20 dollar bill and put it on top of Adam's, He hesitated for a minute, then looked at Adam, 'Does your people have a word for a third man in a deal?, Who helps bring a deal together' asked Johnny.

'A guinea hunter' answered Adam. Johnny nodded; he had never heard the word before. 'It must be British' he thought.

Layton folded the money and put it in his cash pocket. 'Thank you gents, I just love horse dealing, there's so much fun with it. Now the dealings all over Missus Goldfield, we want something off you before we leave.' 'What might that be?' she asked. 'One of those Dundee cakes to take home with us' they all laughed.

Layton and Adam, had done this for each other, in many places so many times over the years, they had lost count. 'I'll need a receipt a bill of sale. I can read and write, but I'm a very poor speller' said Adam. Johnny looked at Layton, who just shrugged his shoulders. Maybe it would be better if Missus Goldfield wrote it out and Adam signed it for you.' 'Make it a good one Vivian; I might want to deal it on again sometime in the future.' Layton and Adam helped themselves to another thick slice of Dundee cake and a second cup of coffee. 'That's it' said Vivian, placing the sheet of paper and pen in front of Adam. He quickly read it through and signed it. He smiled, and then read it out the second time for Layton. It was made out for an extra 15 hundred dollars more.

'I won't need any previous paperwork from England, it wouldn't count anyway, and no one would want to check it out so far away. The name plates and the rig speaks for itself' said Johnny, giving Adam and Layton a knowing smile. 'You Romany boys must have a little Jewish blood in your veins.' 'Maybe you're right, who knows, probably some of our wandering ancestors spent some years in Jerusalem before they went down to the Mediterranean' answered Adam with a smile.

The pair of greys pulling the waterman's came through the entrance. Johnny Goldfield and his wife sat up front. Adam and Layton sat in the back. The white Arabs were tied at the rear. 'Over there Johnny on the right hand side' said Adam. They pulled up near the gypsy wagons, Johnny held his wife's hand has she stepped down from the coach. Isaac shook hands with Johnny. Vivian glanced at the signs that were hanging on the sides of the living wagon. 'Have you started yet, are you open? She asked. Isaac glanced over to his wife.

Johnny looked at his wife and gave her a quick smile, then slowly shook his head as if to say 'I am surprised you believe in it'. Adam's grandmother stepped forward and held out her hand, 'I am Manx Nelly, The Stargazer, many call me The Royal Gypsy, 'Come my dear let me tell you some answers to what you are seeking.'

Isaac walked round the back of the coach, as Albert made conversation with Johnny. Looks like you've had some trade Adam.' said Isaac his grandfather very quietly. (Mandies Bickened the Dewy Grys and the tista. Drew Dewy Arab Grys and dousta-luver, answered Adam) I've sold my two horses and coach and drew back plenty of money, answered Adam. Layton was talking to Johnny. 'These gypsy wagons are very romantic' said Vivian as she slowly looked around and then sat down.

You bought the full rig then Johnny? Asked Albert. Yes, I had to Vivian had fallen in love with it. If I hadn't have brought it I'd have been cooking for myself and sleeping on the couch for a month. Albert and Layton started to laugh. Albert slowly walked around to look at the white Arabs, Johnny and Layton following.

'Are they for sale? 'He asked holding out his hand, palm up. The sign of a dealing man. 'One is,' a quick deal, no fooling around, I'll take eleven hundred dollars, Albert, and I'd want fourteen hundred off anybody else, answered Adam. 'I can see no fault with them but you value them too high, I'll give you eight hundred dollars, Adam'. 'That's a lot of money for one horse.'

'How can eleven hundred dollars be a high price, when there's not a horse in the full circus, that's anywhere near the quality and breeding of one of those Arabs?' 'Imagine the ballerina on its back going around the sawdust ring. 'I don't know', answered Albert as he shook his head, then looking at the Arabs. He wanted it, he knew it would be a hard deal, and he won't have it all his own way. Layton went to follow Albert. But his grandfather Isaac touched him on the shoulder. 'What is it grandfather? Asked Layton. Isaac looked at him straight in the eyes and shook his head once slowly, then looked down as if to say, leave Albert be' he's far too wide to be (moodied) kidded into a deal. 'I'll give you fifty dollars back out of the eleven hundred, that's a thousand and fifty Albert it's the best horse on this field.' 'I'll go up another fifty; eight fifty answered Albert, holding out his right hand, and not a penny more that's it - Adam.

I'll just leave it with my brother Layton to put in the New York monthly sale.

'You can't value a thorough bred and a rare breed to the last fifty dollars because once it's sold it's gone,' you've lost it said Isaac. Albert turned to look at Isaac, words of wisdom from an old man that's had horses all his life' answered Albert. Then feeling in his pocket and coming out with a silver dollar coin, 'You've always liked a gamble Adam, are you game?' eight fifty or a thousand and fifty. 'You can't count your bidding Albert, it's got to be nine hundred or eleven hundred. Spin it up and I'll call. 'You're on, answered Albert, as he placed the coin on his thumb. Then flipped it high, the coin shone brightly as the sun caught it spinning. 'Heads' said Adam. The coin hit the hard mud pathway then bounced once. Its tails, said Albert pulling out a thick wad of 10 and 20 dollar bills from his front cash trouser pocket and started to count. 'You can't win them all', said Adam with a slight smile. As he stuffed the roll of dollar bills in his pocket.

CHAPTER FOUR – 'THE TRAIN JOURNEY'

<u>4 Days Later</u>

The young man jumped down from the back seat of the surrey, then tied the horses bridle strap to the itching rail. Layton looked slowly around 'some size of a train station this for a new country. Billy-Jo, don't leave the surrey, this is New York. If you do it'll go, horses as well.' 'I'll stay here Layton. I won't leave it.' Adam felt in his pocket; he then peeled off 2-10 dollar bills and pushed them in Billy-Jo's shirt top pocket. 'Get yourself something with that.' 'Thanks Master Adam' I'll miss you said the teenager. I'll miss you too.

   Adam carried one case, Layton carried the other. He stopped, looked back again and waved to Billy-Jo. There were two ticket kiosks. 'Yes fella, can I help you?' 'I'd like a one way ticket to Glen Parva, near Aberline, and I've been told that I take the Washington train.' 'Never mind what you've been told. Come on, I've not got all day.'

   Layton reached over and grabbed the man by the shirt front, then pulled him half way over the counter. 'Listen fat boy, I'm not in the mood for you today.' 'You let go of me now, right now, or I'll call a police officer.' Layton pulled him over a bit more and looked closer into his face, 'And by the time the police officer gets here, you'll be lying in your own blood. He asked you a civil question, and he's waiting for a civil answer. You hear me fat boy?' 'Alright, alright, let go of me then.'

   Layton let him go with a push. Getting up off the floor the ticket clerk came back with a large thin book. 'Now you say it's near Aberline. The rail track finishes at Aberline, but there's a lot more country right down to Mexico, and this Glen Parva that you're talking about, I've never even heard of it.' He now had a map out of Texas. 'There's a small Mex town called San Angelo, is it near there?' 'I've found it, it's about', he stopped then looking at the distance and judged it in inches, measuring it with his thumb 'it's about 200 miles from Aberline, first time I've heard of it, just a dot on the map.'

   The ticket clerk glanced at Adam's clothes, shoes, and the heavy gold ring he wore. 'These places Mister, they're rough little towns, in the middle of nowhere. Some you wouldn't even call a town. No place for a gentleman like yourself just big settlements some of them. It's only a dot on the map. Aberline, that's a very rough wild place. That's a hell of a town mister. Who knows what this Glen Parva's like; I'd take a gun with me, if I was you. A gent like you must be nuts going down there. You come into a big inheritance or something.'

'He's minding his own business, like you should be doing' said Layton. 'Okay, okay fella, no offence meant.' Layton looked at Adam, 'these Irish New Yorkers, they're ignorant people, very ill mannered', he said aloud. The clerk glanced at Layton, and then looked away. 'Right I've got the book, tables of travel. You'll need sleeper carriages of course with it being so far.' Adam nodded. He wasn't used to train travel. 'Okay fella as you said, you do take the Washington train, the New York Flyer, into Washington, change at Charleston, West Virginia. Then catch the Kentucky Rocket, the fastest train in the world by the way. You go right through Virginia, Lexington, and then onto Nashville, Memphis, Tennessee, and then on through Little Rock, that's in Arkansas. Then it's Texicana, then Fort Worth, Texas, that's the last big civilized town, then Aberline, end of the line. Aberline is the end of the line fella, give or take a hundred miles, it's around 2,000 miles.'

'That's only three changes in 2,000 miles?' 'That's right fella, its America, there's not that many big towns around to change for. It's a new country, do you want a ticket or not? If so that's 150 dollars one way. It's the New York Flyer from Charleston on to the Kentucky Rocket, then change again at Little Rock, it's then second class all the way through to Fort Worth. All meals you pay for on the train, the diner carriage that is. And the last part of the journey to Fort Worth, no sleepers to Aberline, there's no diner; you take your own food on board. Then onto this Glen Parva, that's by Wells Fargo Stage Coach. Are you sure it's still there? That it exists?'

'I'm sure it's there' said Adam. He counted out the 150 dollars, and the clerk gave him two tickets. 'You know fella, some of these places, they only last for 15-20 years, then they're gone, ghost towns never to be seen again. You'll need both of them tickets, they're separate. One goes first half, and the other one goes to the second half.'

As they walked away, the clerk shook his head slowly from side to side. 'Glad to be rid of them Greeks or Turks, he speaks good English though' said the Irish ticket clerk.

'Thank you', said Layton, as the waiters put the two coffees on the table. 'You know you're breaking the old people's hearts with this thing don't you?' 'I don't mean to Layton. It's what is in us. I love the old people as much as you do; it's now time for me to move on. I'm 26, they're settled down now, and they'll have a good regular living in that big amusement park. Somewhere to belong to, to call home.'

He knew that Adam was right. He felt the same way himself sometimes. 'It's not hundreds of miles like Scotland down to London, it's two thousand miles' said Layton. 'We may never see you again.'

They'd been such a close family. Parents, grandparents, even great grandparents, they had always travelled together.

'Will you miss New York?' 'Yes, all the different races of people. It will be a big city in future, full of character. A lot of the old world making a new world, quite a place to live. I think it will be the London of America. I like it, but everyone's on the grab. You'll have the number one spot now I've left.' Layton never answered. 'It's time for me to be my own man. You can't tell me you've never felt that way'. He's right thought Layton. 'Yes, I know what you mean', he answered. 'The Purey Fokey (old people) they've done it, Scotland, England, and then Europe. They're now ready to settle down because they're Pory (old).' said Adam

'I can see you need it Adam, so do it.' 'You know my brother, you're the one I'll miss the most. We've done so much together haven't we, and we're still young men' said Adam, then putting his hand under the table. 'Take this Luva (money) Pange (five) hundred bar dollars there. If I have to come back, I'll have something to start with if Mandy's low for Luva, (if I am short) for (money).' Layton nodded 'Let me pay you for the Arab.' 'No it's a present. I insist you have it as a present.' Layton just nodded; he knew it was no good arguing Adam had given it him as a going away present.

'So how did you come out of the deal anyway?' asked Layton? 'I sold the other Arab Gray (horse) as you know to Albert, for 900 dollars. After taking out what the full rig owed me, I came out of the deal 950 dollars in front, after having the fun of it for nearly 2 years, I'm very satisfied. I've got a kitty of 7,800 dollars to take with me. It's all in my money belt, and I've got a lot of knowledge and know-how from a wise father and grandfather. I am just a bit trashed, frightened, of carrying all Mandy's lover money with me. (Ashar) you know John Parva told me it's a new place for new people, I'll swing it by its tail, if it's no good after six or seven months, I'll move on, there's a lot of country out there.'

'Your game Adam', said Layton. 'We're both game. Its men like us this new country needs.' 'I'll write you now and then, you understand my writing' said Adam.' 'If I drink anymore coffee, I'll piss all day' said Layton, putting his second empty cup down. 'You look tired Layton.' 'Yes their gypsy weddings go right through the night till the next morning.' 'It was good, I enjoyed myself. The roum people are different from us, more old fashioned character, and yet they have more gorger ways than us.' 'Do you think you will marry this roum, Lilly?' 'Truthfully Adam yes, I just don't want to lose her.' 'So how long have they been In America?' asked Adam. 'She was only about five when

The Book Everyone is talking about

Romany Rye
Gypsy Gentleman

From New York to Texas
2,000 miles all the way

By Nelson Jack Boswell
Cushdy-Boc (Good Luck)
Published by New Generation ISBN No:
9781785070907 on Amazon / Kindle
Available in all good book shops

Romany Rye
Gypsy Gentleman

A British Gypsy family "The Boswell's" arrive in New York in 1868.

Adam, a gypsy wheeler dealer; the hero of the book leaves on a 2,000 mile journey to a boom town in Texas.

On a Train stagecoach with many stops and places, he encounters a couple of con artists, moody jewellery, a pretty gypsy girl in West Virginia and a Marshall. In Memphis; pit dog fights, a Creole girl, the Mississippi boat, a killing and in Aberline; gambling, a knife fight, gun play and a mafia beauty.

His thoughts regularly going back to full chapters of a gypsy family life in old England; of Hare coursing, fishing, hedgehog hunting, real gypsy fortune telling, travelling and occasionally the real gypsy language. Six long winters camped at a Lord's Manor; two cultures each learning from the other, a family feud settled in Hereford, romance and much more - two stories coming together as one, 20 years apart, coming together in America.

Adventure, romance, animal interest, fights, travel and culture, but his main problem.... Women!

By New Generation Publishing
ISBN No. 9781785070907

they came over from Europe, so they've been here about sixteen years. Never done no travelling, they're all in houses, different areas, different ways from us, and they ducker from the kerr's houses (fortune tell).'

'When you get out there Adam, see if you can get something started then when Liley and I get married we will get married.' 'Well if I do' answered Adam, putting out his hand. 'However big it is, it will be partners all the way, just give me a year to get started', answered Adam.

A man was walking round with a big shouting funnel in his hand 'The 12.30 Washington train now on Platform 4 leaves in 15 minutes, that's the New York flyer' he shouted, then repeated it several times. Layton helped Adam in with his bags. 'These carriages are nicely finished' he said, looking at the oak paneling and the padded seats as he sat down, even ash trays in the wall. 'God I wished I was coming with you.' 'So do I, but both of us can't leave the Purey-Fokey (old people) at the same time, you know that Layton.' 'Get them well settled in to this amusement park thing, for the women duckering (palm reading), and help your father and grandfather, get good contacts for (Bickening the Grys) (selling horses), maybe a year who knows, you could join me.'

'All aboard, all aboard. Doors now closing. New York flyers leaving for Washington. Doors closing' shouted the railway guard. Gypsy families don't shake hands; they hug each other, with a quick kiss on the cheek. Adam put his arms around his younger brother. 'Don't worry about it Layton, there's always a hill to get over, your time will come. I'll miss you Lay.' 'Me too' said Layton as he got off the train.

Adam leaned out of the window and waved as the train gathered speed. Layton was still standing there, hands in his pockets smiling. He then turned and walked away. Adam closed the window, then leaned back in the thick mockette padded seat just staring into space. There was no thoughts in his head, none. His mind was a blank. He was usually very proud to be what he was, a gypsy, a wanderer. He now wished he was something else. He felt guilty about leaving his younger brother, and he knew there was no one or nothing he could blame only himself.

It was the second day as Adam looked out of the window. Virginia looked something like Perth and Fyfe Scotland. Rich green farmland, there was farms as far as the eye could see. Mixed some livestock, some arable crops. 'Breakfast is now being served' said the train attendant, as he walked through the railway carriage. Adam hadn't seen much of Washington. The train, seemed to go around the small city, it had been night time. Sleeping had been easy with the rocking of the train. And the faint clickety-click of the track it never stopped, it never seemed to be quiet. The diner car was nice thought Adam, clean good cutlery and table cloths.

The nigro waiter, a heavy man of about 60 with a slight limp came up to Adam's table. 'What would you like sir?' '3 bacon well done, 2 sausages, tomatoes, 2 eggs and toast please.' 'How do you like your eggs sir? Hard, sunny side up, or just over easy?' Adam never answered for a minute. He was having difficulty with some of the American expressions and sayings. 'Sunny side ups, a little sloppy aren't they?' said the attendant with a smile. 'I think just over easy.' 'You've got it sir.' 'And a pot of coffee.' 'You have a good appetite? You get on at Washington?' asked the man at the next table. 'No, New York. Yes I like a good breakfast. I don't bother with a day meal. Where are you from?' asked Adam. 'We're from Washington originally, we're now living in Charleston, West Virginia. Why don't you join us instead of sitting on your own?' 'Thank you' said Adam, moving to their table. 'Most of these Americans seem forward, and friendly' he thought.

Breakfast came. 'Can I have some butter?' 'Butter for my toast' asked Adam. 'Yes sir you want butter.' 'I am Pierre Carrington, this is my wife Constance. Our family is originally from Paris, France.' Adam mentioned a few main boulevards and suburbs when he had stayed around Paris. 'I was there for five weeks' he said, not mentioning the circus. He tucked in to the breakfast. As he sat back enjoying his second coffee, he looked down the railway carriage. This must be about a 80ft long. Everything is so big over in this country he thought. He just stared out of the window, his thoughts going back.

He remembered the last time he was on a train. It was going down to Slough, near London from Sterling Scotland with his grandfather Isaac, to keep him company. Adam was only 8 at the time. His grandfather's sister she was called Missy. He never knew her. She was married to a London Smith, Elijah Smith, but they had spent years over in Ireland, and then came back over, and travelled all around the London counties, because that's where Elijah's people was. It was a big funeral, as most Gypsy funerals are. Grandfather Isaac seemed to like the area, and they stayed there for five days after the funeral with relations, gypsy cousins, that was on the big field where in horse wagons and tents they were, Lees, Balls, Smiths and Boswells. There was also some travelling families on the field in tents, and wagons not dark, not gypsies. That spoke with a London accent they called themselves travelers.

Adam's great grandfather, old Byron was of a great age, and too old really to make decisions. His son Isaac being Adam's grandfather made the decisions, and the rest of the family usually went along with it. His grandfather, Isaac was impressed with the London area, and the company that stayed there, when they got back up to Scotland, he told all of the family this, and everybody seemed pleased to go and see a different part of the country. They coupled up the wagons, great grandfather Byron and wife Louisa, granddad Isaac, wife Manx Nellie and Adams mother and father, Nelson and Delly and their elder brother Jack, four wagons in all. They travelled down from Sterling passing Glasgow, then the beatak moor, which was very bleak. Granddad always called it border country adjoining England and Scotland. Very cold with just a few cottages here and there, mostly mountains and sheep.
    When they got to the start of the beatak moor, being Lanarkshire the Scottish side, they stayed the night, the next morning, barely daylight, they had breakfast by the stick fire outside. The horses would have a drink then be coupled up to the wagons while the women cleaned things up, they would leave daylight just breaking to cross the Beetick moor, 40 miles of desolate rocky country a very hard winding road.
    The horses went at a fast walk, it was steep in places, and too difficult to trot, though a few times they would trot. Occasionally the men would jump down off the front board of the wagon, where they would sit with their legs hanging over as they held the reins when the going was hard for the horses, they would work leading them holding the bridle to keep them going. Each man taking a turn, including Adam, because he was a big youth for his age. Layton was too young, they would stop twice for half an hour, a snack and a drink, and a break and drink for the horses. We must have walked seven or eight miles most days. I suppose that's why the men are so fit, he thought. Yes, it was some hard going to cover in one day the Beetick Moore. Early morning till nearly night.
    'You seem miles away' said Pierre. Adam turned to look at him. 'Yes I was' answered Adam. 'I'll be back in 5 minutes' he said, standing up. Adam looked at him. There was something about this couple, very friendly. Some Americans were like that. Maybe it's me being a bit reserved like the British people, he thought.   Adam's cunning gypsy mind was ticking over, always taking notice of what was going on around him. Most gypsies have no business, they are the business. Their appearance, the way they act, speak, represent themselves. You could say living off their wits. Sharp people, with no definite trade, but tended to know a little bit about many things, and being well travelled.

They could easily mix with different people, and impress and convince them.

'Is there anything else sir?' asked the attendant, as he cleared the table. 'No thanks that was fine.' 'And you Ma'am?' 'We're finished, that was okay' said Constance. They had tea and toast. 'So where are you from originally? You haven't developed an American accent, yet you don't seem to have any particular accent?' she said. Deliberately bending forward, the low cut dress with the first two buttons undone, it did not leave much to the imagination, thought Adam. Her head turned gazing out of the window, it's the come on if ever I've seen it. She's about 30, nicely put together, but a bit too much paint and powder, he thought. She could do a lot for a man thought Adam. 'Thank you sir' said the waiter placing the bill in front of him. Adam read it, Atlantic Rail Diner, breakfast, one dollar. Adam placed a dollar and a 1/4 on the table. 'That's fine, it's okay.' 'And what did you think of the breakfast sir, no complaints?' 'Very good, I won't want a midday meal. Thank you sir.'

Pierre was back, as he stood at the side of the waiter, Adam's eyes was quickly looking him over. Everything he was wearing had been the best. The suit was tailored, lapels hand sewn. But it was starting to go just a little shiny at the cuffs and knees. The expensive handmade skin shoes was now starting to crack a little with wear and polish. Everything had been the best, but now like its owner, getting past it. The ring on his hand looked to be nearly a two carat single stone diamond in a pale 18 carat gold shank. It was similar to his wife's, but hers was white gold or platinum. As Pierre sat down, Constance never bothered to cover up any. He's got to be 25 years older than her. Is she really his wife? She's not with him for his money. He probably was well off once. But it looks like a lot of it has gone, thought Adam.

'The trains slowing down' said Adam. 'Yes it's a slow trip through West Virginia, it's a slight uphill pull most of the way. Its speed goes down to about 20.' 'I've had horses a lot faster' said Adam. 'Yes you probably have for a mile or two, this train keeps it up hour after hour, day and night, and on the downhill it'll do 35 miles an hour.' Adam nodded. 'How did you sleep last night?' he asked. 'I had a good night sleep, except for the clickety click' answered Adam.

'Are you going far?' asked Pierre. 'Down past Aberline, I don't expect you've heard of it, a little frontier town called Glen Parva', taking out his cigar case. Pierre refused and took out his own cigarette case, offering his wife one, then taking one himself. He lit both. A very forward young woman smoking openly in a public place thought Adam. Both cases lay on the table. 'Do you mind?' Said Pierre, picking it up. 'Help yourself.' 'It's very heavy' said Pierre, noticing the gold initials in the centre. 'It's silver?' 'No' answered Adam, 'it's stainless steel plate. It took my eye one day in an antique shop in Rose Street Edinburgh, and I then had my initials in gold put on it.'

Adam got up and walked to the end of the carriage, then went out onto the outer platform. He stood there smoking, leaning on the handrail and looking out across the open spaces. It's big, and open, it's a lovely country. He could feel the weight in his coat pocket. He hadn't got used to it yet. The last day he had with his people (family). They had insisted on taking him round New York that was growing so quickly.

Billy-Jo drove them, Granddad Isaac and Nelly, and his parents Nelson and Delly. Layton stayed home. It was Adams day with his family. The next day he would be leaving.

'Every time you come into town it's growing. No wonder, it's now the top city of America, the new Capital.' 'Yes it used to be Philadelphia. That's the Americans, can you imagine altering London to not being the capital', said Nelson.

'I bet there's more Irish in New York than there is in Dublin' said Isaac. 'Yes it's that famine they had in Ireland 10 or 12years ago, and they'll be as many Italians here as there is in Rome.'

'That's New York, it will have all nationalities except the true American, it will be full of character' said Nelly. 'Or as the old professor would say at Sir Johns, it will be cosmopolitan' said Adam with a smile. Isaac and Nelson shared a quick look, not knowing what the word meant. They made their way up Mulberry Street, which was on the East side, now heading for the city centre.

'This is now Broadway starting 42nd Street. I was duckering (fortune telling) a Runny (A Lady) last week, and she was telling me there are 3 theatres on this one street. Pull up here Billy-Jo.' He stopped right in front of an ice cream parlour. 'Stay with the rig, and I'll bring you a big one out.'

Nelson took the reins while Billy-Jo tucked into his large ice cream covered in strawberry sauce and nuts. Adam pointed out a ladies shop, and they pulled in to the kerb. He wanted to buy his mother and granny Nelly a present, but they would not hear of it. 'No, no Adam, it's you that's leaving, so it's you that has to have the going away presents.'

Isaac pointed over to a large open area that seemed to nearly disappear. 'It's nearly finished, they were landscaping areas, and planting trees.' 'It will be a lovely Park' said Delly. 'Yes, they say it's a mile square. But they're going to make it longer. It's called Central Park. It's big, but you could drop it in Hyde Park. They're looking at

London, Paris and Rome, copying.' 'I think it will be the business city of this country' said Nelly. 'It will be a city of people of the world', said Adam, as he turned looking around.

Adam looked slowly at the shut knife, it was the best he had ever seen. The black boon handle with silver leaves, and an acorn on the end, the blade was only five inches. Engraved in script made in Germany, made to last. It had no notch to put your finger nail in, but a very small flat plate near the hilt, you just flicked it, the blade was out, and locked in two seconds, very handy, but very dangerous in a fit of temper. It was a present from his father and mother. His grandmother had bought him a scarf, paisley pattern, Macclesfield silk. His grandfather had a ring for him, and granny Nelly also giving money. They had the full day around the new city.

His mind went back to the morning he was leaving. It was only days ago, but it felt more like a week ago. He could see his mother. 'You may be fully grown, but you're still my boy, and you're not too big for me to give you a big hug.' He had felt the wet from his mother's tears on his cheek. 'It's so very far you're going from us son, it's not from Perth, down to your cousins at Blackpool' wiping her eyes with her long pinny. 'We covered about 2,500 miles when we left England and travelled the continent with the circus.' 'Yes son we did, but we were all together. You'll be on your own. You don't even have a wife to look after you.'

His father smiled, pulling him close to him, and kissed him on the cheek, 'I love you son' he said. It was the way of his people, shaking hands was for friends. 'I know how it is son, you want to see what's out there, now you live in this big country. We've been the same way haven't we?' said Nelson, looking to Isaac his father. Isaac nodded. 'I know you don't look for trouble son, but when you get out there in them places, there's very little law and order.' 'Father I think a lot of this wild cowboy thing is exaggerated. By what John Parva was telling me, it didn't sound a lot wilder than Glasgow, or the rough end of London'. 'The Gaubles, Glasgow, London, White Chapel and the Elephant and Castle, if it's any rougher and wilder than those two places, it would be a human jungle' said his father with a smile

'Do you need any Luva (money)? We can let you have some.' 'Thanks father for asking, I'm okay, I'm not short.' Adam stood in front of his grandmother and grandfather. He could see the old man was upset. He had grown up with them. He had taught him and his brothers so much, and he had always had time for them. How to hunt, trap, game, course with a dog, guddle trout out of a stream, how to sense when a fight was coming. And how to fight when it had to be done.

Adam had learned a lot from him, especially the fighting. It was regularly needed. There was always someone to skit his race to put you down and blame you. Being a gypsy you sometimes had to fight to survive.

As they stood there they slowly looked at each other, Adam could sense what his grandfather Isaac was thinking. He's gone old to how he used to be. His jet black wavy hair was now grey with the odd streak of black, and he now walked slightly bent. What a man my grandfather Isaac had been, he thought. Only 5 feet 9, but had to have a 21 inch shirt collar. Built like a Staffordshire bull terrier. It was said very rare he had to hit a man twice to put him down. They usually went down with the first one. He would take no lip from two men, never mind one, and he would shout his challenge as he went forward, 'Isaac Boswell no surrender, no surrender', he would repeat. Meaning he would not give best, it would be a fight to the finish. One of them down and out, and the other still standing.

Adam looked at his old knuckles. Some of them had moved back a little where he had hit so hard when he was younger. Layton seemed to take after Grandfather Isaac for his aggression. Granny Nelly was so short. He had to bend for her to kiss him. She was a Boswell, being one of the oldest gypsy names, from the Isle of Man family; her father Tommy had a farm there. She was well brought up. Her father Tom had brought trotting horses over to Mussleborough, Edinburgh, where the British Cup was trotted for. They were a well to do family, the only Romany gypsies on the Isle of Man. She was like a young lady only 16 at Mussleborough, when she met his grandfather Isaac; they fell madly in love, him being only 16 as well. They ran away to Gretna Green, put their ages up and got married. She was always showing the boys, and telling them the right way. 'Keep your appearance up. Hold your head high. Anyone can be a low life, a dosser' she would say, kissing Adam. Whereas granddad Isaac, he was a Scottish gypsy, and also a Boswell, rough tough, a man's man. Usually well dressed, never a tie, always a Dicklow, silk hanky around his neck he would not wear a shirt the second day. His shoes always polished.

Adam looked at his left hand; the two ounce heavy pale gold ring, the top was a square block, in the centre a small square and compass on it in white gold. On the left shoulder of the ring was a triple 'T' sign of the Royal Arch. On the opposite shoulder of the ring was a small diagonal ' T' with a ball on either side of the stick, this was a tubal cane, a sign of the second degree. His grandfather Isaac had pulled it off his finger, and put it in Adam's hand. 'Take this with you; it might open a few doors for you.' 'But I am not a freemason grandfather, and you are.' 'I don't need it much now. I am old, I want you to have it. I have the fellowship in a lodge, and enjoy it. Wear it, and if anybody asks you, are you a free mason, just say no, I am not, my grandfather is, and has been through the vales, that means the Royal Arch, and it might help you, if you are speaking to a freemason, he will respect your honesty.'

Adam had refused to take it off the old man, but he was brought up, when an older member of the family insists, you agree, that is the way, and grandfather insisted. 'I was going to leave it to you one day, and my heavy chain and watch to Layton, and my diamond tie pin to Jack, and my cuff links to Steven.' 'Take it young Adam; we may never see each other again.' 'Don't say that grandfather. I will see you again.' The old man looked away. He seemed to know, thought Adam. Granny Nelly looked at Adam.

'Be careful, you can accept the ring as a present off your grandfather, you don't have to wear it, the deeper you go into that, the darker it gets.' She took a small roll of notes out of her pinny pocket, and put it in Adam's hand. He looked at it. 'I won't take it off you' he said. 'I've got money. You will, or I won't read your letters, I insist. We're not short.' 'You can't have too much' said his Grandfather Isaac, smiling at him.

High-Youne and his wife Yeton walked forward. 'So you are leaving, it is true, gypsy Adam.' 'That's right High Youne. I leave today, 2000 miles down into Texas.' 'We will miss you.' 'Yes we have all been good friends for many years' said Adam, jumping down out of the trap. Nearly eight years ago when the Boswell family had joined up with the Wild West circus at Perth, the two families had quickly become friends and it had lasted.

High-Youne was a Tibetan Monk of the highest order of self-defense and attack. He would walk on hot coals and lay on a bed of nails. Over the years, he had taught the gypsy brothers such a lot. High-Youne held a purple sash, the highest order. He was a disgraced monk who took a 16 year old girl for his wife. He was 41, and he had been put out of the monastery. There was quite a few misfits that made up the Wild West circus. 'I wish you much luck gypsy Adam.' 'Thank you' said Adam, as they both bowed then shook hands. 'I have made this for you.' It was a purple sash with one silver line that ran through it, whereas High-Youne's had three silver lines. 'Thank you, I will never forget you' answered Adam, as he hung the long scarf around his neck. High-Youne smiled, taking the sash from around his neck, then tying it around Adams waist. 'As I have taught you, never forget

Adam, just look around you, everything is a weapon.' High-Youne and his wife gave a quick little bow, turned, then walked away.

As the trap was going past the living wagons. 'Good luck Adam', shouted some of the circus people. 'We will miss you, shouted others. Albert and Sylvia walked over. Young Billy Joe pulled on the reins of the pair of horses that were pulling the large trap. Adam jumped down. Albert ignored Adams outstretched right hand, putting his arms around Adam, he hugged him. 'If ever you decide to come back, you're more than welcome, don't even bother to ask.' 'How are you fixed for money?' 'I am okay, I've been a good saver.' Sylvia stepped forward, and kissed him on the cheek. 'Good Luck, Adam. Me and Albert will never forget you.' 'I know the amusement park will be a big success' said Adam, as he climbed back into the trap.

He had never counted the money they had given him until he was on the train, it was 500 dollars. Also the roll of notes his father Nelson had given him, there were also 500 - 1000 dollars in all. Adam took a match out of his waistcoat pocket and struck it on the metal handrail of the railway carriage. His cigar had gone out, inhaling it deeply then blowing out again. 'Yes grandfather' he said out loud, 'I wonder if we will ever see each other again' as he looked at the ring on his finger. He was glad to be out of the railway carriage. He came from outdoor people, and preferred to be out. They would even eat outside when the weather was warm enough. The carriage door opened. 'Everything alright sir?' asked the assistant. 'Fine, I just needed some air, sat in there hour after hour, day after day, I feel like a chicken in a laying shed.' 'I know what you mean. My name is Charles' said the assistant. 'You look the outdoor type sir. Are you Italian or Greek?' 'My families from somewhere over there, the Mediterranean I believe, I'm pleased to meet you. My name is Adam Boswell.'

Sometimes he would not say what he really was. But that was in England. Being in America, he was now starting to admit his race quite a lot. Many people were racial and did not like gypsy people, with them moving around constantly, they were very easy to blame if there had been wrong where they had been. The gypsy was often used as an escape goat. 'Those two that are sat with you, they're on these trains every week, always making friends' he said, giving Adam a knowing wink. 'Thanks, I thought they were up to something.' 'What's the train slowing down for?' asked Adam. 'It's a station stop there called a settlement, taking on coal, logs, filling up with water, on loading, and picking goods up it'll stop for at least an hour, maybe more. If you want to stretch your legs?.' 'That's a good idea' said Adam.

About 30 people had got off the train. Adam noticed two guards walking up and down, each had a rifle. 'What's the guns for?' 'Oh last year there was a couple of hard cases on horseback, rode amongst us with pistols, robbed four or five passengers, until the two guards chased them off with rifle fire. Now we have armed guards for all stops.' 'A good idea' said Adam, noticing his carriage was the first one back from the diner. Then another two carriages behind his, plus three big packing trucks. He walked over to Charles the attendant. 'That's a lot bigger engine to what I've seen in Europe.' 'These engines are bigger, they've got to be, what they pull day and night. The hundreds of miles they do, they're sent over from Robert Stevenson's in Lancashire, England. This ones the New York Flyer. Got a top speed fully loaded of 28 miles per hour. That's pulling all this as well. You like to know a lot about things.' That's right Charles, that's how I was brought up to ask, listen and learn.'

'What's that massive big metal cover over the chimney or funnel?' 'That's a hot coal catcher, it stops any sparks coming out which would catch wheat or dry fields on fire.' 'Is that so?' said Adam, 'I suppose that big guard at the front is for pushing aside anything in the way.' 'That's right, it's called a cow catcher, mostly lazy cattle that don't want to move, sometimes a small fallen tree.'

Adam nodded. A big 12 ft wagon with high sides, had a four-in-hand horse team pulling it, and was struggling, loaded up to the top with coal and logs. 'They'll do another two loads' said Charles. Adam looked around as he slowly walked with Charles. On the other side of the track was a water tower. He stopped to look at the settlement. There were two big barns, 5 houses, a general store, and a saloon. He couldn't help but notice everything was made of wood. There wasn't a brick building in sight. On the side of the barn was wrote 'Cambridge, West Virginia.'

Adam nodded; noticing there was another two wagons loaded with sacks of tobacco leaves being taken to the train, the two wagons would then make another trip and there would probably be other goods to sell.

Also another wagon loaded with skins for the train. 'You know sir' started Charles, 'My names Adam, I'm not sir.' 'You see Adam, these pockets of people alongside of the railway track, every 80 or 100 miles or so, it's a link with civilization. They get goods and they sell their goods.' 'But what if there is no rail track?'. 'It would probably stay a settlement, maybe never become a town', answered Charles. 'Four years ago, there were only two houses here. Just one barn for the railroad workers that was it. Now there's two barns, 5 houses, a general store, a saloon, and a smithy. It's started, it's now a big village, it will become a town within the next 6 or 7 years' said Charles. Adam nodded in agreement. 'It's a brand new country, and it's growing quick' said Adam.

One wagon that had been emptied was now leaving. The train loaded with crates was coming from the end of the train. On one of the crates sat a man with two cases. A young woman sat up front holding a child. 'New blood' said Charles. 'Yes I heard them speaking at New York Station, they're Dutch. She's a dressmaker' said Adam, wondering to himself, and what could I, a gypsy offer out here, he thought. What skills can a Romany gypsy offer? A sharp mind, a keen eye, maybe fight for a good cause? A heavily built bald headed man of about 50 was making straight for them. 'Hello there Charles' said the big man with a strong Irish accent. 'I've got what you want, a New York, Washington, and Chicago, papers, and they're only one week old.' 'This here is a new friend of mine called Adam Boswell from New York. This here is Bob the Blacksmith of Cambridge' said Charles. 'Pleased to meet you smithy' said Adam, putting out his right hand. 'I notice you're from Ireland.' 'That's right friend, the free states Dublin.' 'I've worked down O'Connell Street a few times. Lovely city' said Adam.

He could see he was a hardworking man. He had a leather apron on. Big boots, his face was black with smoke dust, and so were his massive arms. 'I see the new couples arrived from Holland' he said. 'She's a dressmaker. I can use him at the smithy shop, if he's strong enough' said Bob. 'I thought you had a man?' said Charles. 'He left for good, 5, 6 weeks ago, shot dead in a saloon card game. He pulled a knife on a cow hand and tried to stab him. Cow hand had a 6-gun shot him. He died the same night, just bled to death. We couldn't do anything for him.' 'I suppose it was self-defense. What did the Sherriff do about it?' asked Adam. 'He couldn't do much, nearest ones in Charleston, a hundred miles away. We all agreed at a meeting it was self-defense. Let him go next day, but we'll report it when we see the sheriff. If ever there's a big problem, we can get on the telegraph' said Bob, pointing to the telegraph wires alongside the rail track. 'Have you got a doctor yet?' asked Charles. 'No we haven't, but we've got a good nurse, helps and does the best she can. Used to be one of the three dance hall happy night girls. Packed it up and started nursing. I think she was a nurse in New York where she came from. She's getting a lot more respect and making a good honest living. I sent a letter off to Dublin saying there's a post here for a Doctor, had a letter back two weeks ago asking how many people are in Cambridge and 10 miles around it. We will hear in the next 6 weeks if we're getting a doctor. I think we will. The widow of the man that worked for me who was shot, she is in big demand, quite a few farmers after her. Women scarce in these here parts.'

The wagon with the crates on pulled up. 'Bob, this here is the new people' said the driver. 'Howdy there, I'm Bob the smithy, my place is over there next to the blacksmith shop. Martha's in. She'll show you your room. Make you some food. Give it a week, all here will lend a hand. Have you a house knocked up in no time.' 'Thank you sir, thank you.' 'I'm no sir, the names Bob. I need a man to help with the smithy, and this here settlement can use a dressmaker.' 'Good luck, I hope it works out for you.' 'It will sir, we work hard, make new life, Copenhagen, long, long way away. New start, new life' said the Dutch man. 'You're right, it's a long way.' 'It's the other side of the world man' said Bob as the wagon pulled away.

'What do you think they've done?' asked Adam, as he turned to Charles. 'Most of these Europeans have had enough of how things were run by the powerful and titled ones. They're wanting a new way of life, a change. Some are running as hard as they can to a new life and from who knows what. It's not my concern or my business.' 'I suppose you're right.' 'This is a new country, made up of all sorts of people.' 'That's a fair way in looking at it' said Adam.

Well dog my cat, 'that's two gypsy wagons over there' said Adam, pointing to a fenced paddock way back behind Bob the smithy's place. 'Bob, do you know who owns those two gypsy wagons?' 'The gypsies that live in them' answered Bob with a laugh. 'Tell me about them.' 'Well there's two families, youngish I'd say in their 30s, dark people, keep themselves pretty much to themselves. Don't seem to bother anyone. The women tell fortunes, and do a good trade. Folks from miles around here go to them, and the two men make knives, deal horses, guns, anything.' 'How long have they been here?' 'Oh about 8 or 9 months. You seem pretty interested' said Bob. 'Thanks, I'll see you later Charles. Are you going there to get your fortune told?' joked Bob. 'When you hear the train whistle, you've got 10 to 12 minutes, then its leaving. There's no being late.' 'Okay, Charles' said Adam, walking away quickly.

Charles looked at Bob. 'Do you think there's anything in this fortune telling thing?' 'A lot of folk around here, especially the ladies say the gypsy women are very good at it. My Martha goes.' As Adam approached the encampment, he slowed down to take it in. They had a nice piece of land, he thought. Must be nearly three acres fenced off. Four horses were grazing down the far end. Over to the left of the wagons was a building, open at one end, a loss box for the horses. 'Hello there, cushty dives, (good day)' said Adam. The men stared at him and smiled. 'Romny cinty' asked the little one. 'Mandy is a British rumny chel, British Gypsy.' Adam could only make out half of their short conversation. He felt a little embarrassed. Their dialect was different. They looked from one to the other.

'I am the same' he said, his hand going over his body. 'Shurra - head, yokkas -eyes, danyas-teeth knock-nose moy-mouth.' 'Enough, enough' said the small one. 'We know you are gypsy, we accept you as gypsy. How long has your family been in England?' 'Three generations, maybe four.' answered Adam. The little one nodded. 'My name is Nickey, and this is my younger brother Peppe. We are Robinson's.' 'Yes, I have heard of the Robinsons. My name is Adam, when we landed we were Bosvills and now we are Boswells.' 'We have heard of the Boswells, Lees, and Smiths. I think your people came from France didn't they?' 'Maybe when we first landed in England, nearly 200 years ago. But we do originate from the Mediterranean.' 'So what are you cinty, roma? asked Adam. 'No, we are caldaresh gypsies. I was not classing you as a gorger, non gypsy, but you have been in England so long, you have lost some of your language. For instance you say danyas for teeth, we say danyo, and your shurra for head, its shurree. How you say dog?' 'Juckle' said Adam. 'We say Juckella.'

Adam was starting to get a little annoyed. 'So maybe you have got some of it wrong as well' he said. 'Where are you from?' 'I have already told you, we are caldaresh, we are from Romania.'

'What would you call a train?' asked Peppy. 'There is no word because it's a modern thing, so I would make up a word.' 'And that would be?' asked Peppy. 'Saster-grey, Iron-horse' answered Adam. The two brothers nodded smiling.

'Did you bring the wagons over with you?' 'No we made them here ourselves.' 'They're very big. I thought a Reading Wagon or a Bill Wrights was a big wagon, 12 feet, they look even bigger.' 'They're 16 feet' answered Peppe. 'Big country, you need big wagons.' 'Does your women ducker?' 'Palmistry, read palms, fortune tell' said Peppe. 'No, no' said Adam with pride. 'Gorgers call it that. The gypsy word for it is ducker.' They both just stood there and stared from one to another, accepting what Adam had said. 'So' asked Adam 'did you emigrate here, come over here for a better way of life as I have, or were you transported her bitcherd-a-par?' 'Yes we were transported over here from Romania for horse dealing, accused of horse stealing. Not even tried. We were transported to a place called Georgia, many hundreds and thousands of miles from here, to work in the cotton fields with black people. But we left. We ran, and we kept running for many weeks till we were well away, and then we made one wagon, and we travelled for many more weeks until we got here, Cambridge village, Virginia. Then we made the second wagon whilst we've been here. That word you used bitcherd-a-par, I have never heard it before.'

Adam smiled 'It is a very old gypsy word, bitcherd-a-par is transported', he said, sitting cross legged by the fire. One of the women brought him a cup of coffee. The woman looked at Adam. 'Your dress and how you speak, you are a Romany Rye, a gypsy gentleman' she said. 'What is your name?' 'Adam' he answered. 'Romany Rye Adam' she said. They all had a little laugh, including Adam. The other woman came over and gave him a plate with several pieces of cooked belly pork on, it was cold and crispy. 'Morra and kil' (bread and butter) she asked. (Owerly) 'Yes please', he said. She then put two pieces of crusty buttered bread on his plate. 'Do you want more?' mass or morra (meat or bread) doster 'I have (plenty)' answered Adam. More Bullermass (pigs meat). 'Will lesty Beshakye' (Will you stay here?') asked Adam. 'I think so, we are accepted, no one bothers us. Everyone here, or their parents are all from Europe.' 'The real American is the Indian' said Adam with a smile. 'We are not looked down on or beaten, like in Europe. We are accepted as equal. We do alright with a few horses, guns and knives, and the women have people that come back again and again for palmistry, duckering' he said, correcting himself. 'Definitely a gypsy gentleman. He speaks lovely, such words, so clear' said the other woman who had gave him the food.

A pretty tanned little girl with black curly hair, about 7 or 8 stood staring at him. 'What is your name?' 'Victoria, after the great Queen' she answered. 'A great lady. I have met her, and her husband Prince Albert.' They all smiled, and looked from one to the other. He wasn't sure if they believed him or not. 'Where are you going?' asked Peppe. 'I have come from New York, and I am going to a town at the end of nowhere called Glen Parva.' 'We have heard of it, down past Aberline.' 'Do you know much about it?' asked Adam. 'It's wild like Aberline. They say its wealthy with silver and cattle.' 'I was told there are 2 gypsy families already there, called Lees' said Peppe. 'They will be English gypsies' said Adam.

'Do you have a gun? I can sell you two good pistols if you need them.' 'It's okay, I have a gun and a rifle. You have a nice piece of land here, private, well back' said Adam looking around. 'Anyone can have half an acre of land free. After that, it's 35 dollars an acre, as long as it's 150 yards back from the village, giving the village room to grow, and no more than 2 acres.' 'I suppose that's to give the village room to expand as the years go by' said Adam. 'Expand?' said Nicky. 'To get bigger' answered Adam. 'After 2 miles you can buy whatever and as much as you want. 10 miles out there near those mountains, you can have 50 acres free, and you can then buy what you want at 15 dollars an acre, good grazing or arable land.' 'Is there many out there?' asked Adam. 'Yes 14 farms. They all run alongside of the river. 4 of them are 500 acre farms, 3 are 3000 acre farms. Every 1000 acres you get a 100 acre free. We have friends here. We are accepted as equals, we're happy' said Nicky.

'I am pleased for you' answered Adam. 'What part of England are you from? Are there many Romany chells (gypsies) in England?' 'Yes there are 3 or 4 families in Scotland. Many in Wales, and some round London and Blackpool, maybe 20 families in all' answered Adam. Nickey nodded, he had heard of Scotland, but not Blackpool, and Wales. Nicky could see by Adams appearance, and how he spoke, that he came from a good family.

'Why go down to Glen-Parva? It's dangerous there. This Cambridge will grow, we will all grow with it, it's good here. Esmeralda come here my sister' shouted Nickey. The wagon door opened. She walked down the steep steps between the shafts. Adam looked at her slowly, then looked away, then back again. She was one of the beautiful lest women he had seen, maybe 20, he thought. Dark gold coloured, short, tight, curly hair, probably ¾ gypsy and her skin was slightly tanned, a long dress of many colours, with a broad belt around her narrow waist, her skirt hung to her ankles. Large gold hoop earrings in her ears. A thin gold chain with a cross on it, hung around her neck. 'I'm sorry, I do not mean to stare' he said. She smiled, came over, and stood by her younger brother, Peppy. She was as tall as him, about 5ft 5inches. 'This is a gypsy visitor off the train. He is called Adam Boswell from England.' She smiled, 'I am Esmeralda.' Her big dark eyes flashed, her teeth we're like pearls. She had taken Adam completely by surprise.

Adam put the plate down and stood up. 'I have heard of the Boswell's, Smiths, and Lees in England' said Esmeralda. Adam held out his hand to her. She placed her hand in his.

'You speak so well, like an English gentleman.' 'Thank you' said Adam. 'She is a very good duckerer (fortune teller), a good getter (earner)' said Nickey. Adam squeezed her hand as he looked into her big dark eyes, then her teeth, then let go of her hand. She could feel his eyes on her as she walked away, and sat down with the other two women. 'There is none like ourselves anywhere near here for hundreds and hundreds of miles, all gorgers' said Nickey. 'I don't want her to end up with a non gypsy.' He gave his sister a look, then looked at

Adam. 'I know what you are telling me, she is beautiful, a good getter (earner)' said Adam, a little louder for her to hear. 'Tell me what gypsies do in England, Scotland?' asked Peppy. 'We horse deal, buy things, clean them up to look good, then sell them, prize fight, the women ducker (tell fortunes).' 'That's the same as us, but we do not prize fight, we usually fight with knives' said Peppy.

'You are suggesting marriage for her, aren't you?' said Adam. 'I can see you come from a good family, and your name, a real gypsy, represent yourself well, If you come and see her a few times, and only if she accepts you, we would say yes to marriage' said Nickey. 'Do I have your permission to speak to her alone?' Nickey glanced at Peppy, then back at Adam. 'Yes, but you stay in the encampment.' Adam smiled at Esmeralda, then holding out his hand, as he slowly walked away. She caught him up, putting her hand in his. They turned, and stood at the back of one of the wagons. 'What should take a few meetings to say, I say now, because I will be gone soon, within the hour. If we will ever see each other again, I do not know. You are what I am, very beautiful, Rumney-Chel you are dusta cushdy-dicking and (very good looking)', he said, looking into her big dark eyes. He still had hold of her hand, lifting it, he then placed it slowly around his neck, kissing her gently on the side of her nose, and then the corner of her mouth. She slowly placed her other arm around his neck, as her mouth opened slightly. The kiss was long and passionate. They separated, then kissed again. His left hand went to her breast. 'Please stop, don't, you must stop now' she said, slightly out of breath. She was what a gypsy young woman should be, clean, decent, waiting for marriage, and then to explode. 'Forgive me' said Adam, as he kissed her again, his left hand slowly playing with her ear.' 'I forgive you. I want you to stay. Don't go' she said.

'I will write you.' 'None of us can read' she answered. 'Some Gorger (not gypsy) will read it to you, and write for you. It is the way of most of our people' he answered. They was just walking back holding hands, then let go. As Peppy, her younger brother looked at his watch, 15 minutes had passed, 'Esmeralda' he said loudly, 'come over here'. His elder brother Nickey gave him a long hard stare to cool it.

'Maybe this is the English Romany way', said Nickey to him. 'They have only talked in private' he said aloud. Peppy nodded in agreement to his elder brother. 'She is far too forward, not showing gypsy shame, probably too much talk with the gorger women that she duckers', said Peppy. Adam looked at Nickey, 'we have talked and we are both in agreement. I will be a 900 miles away, because she is beautiful and the same as what I am, I will write, I do want her, maybe it will happen, we don't know.'

'I am being honest. We would welcome you into our family', said Nickey. Adam turned to go. He felt in his pocket, and came out with a shiny silver dollar. 'Look what I've found for you to go to the general store with Victoria. You could buy sweets, and maybe a dolly. It is yours for a kiss.' She looked at her mother, who smiled and nodded. Adam kneeled down on one knee. She ran to him, kissed him quickly on the cheek, then grabbed the silver dollar, and ran back to her mother.

Adam stood up and turned to look at them. Just then the train whistle went. 'I must go'. 'Wait Adam', said Nickey. 'Yes what is it?' Nickey undid his belt, and pulled the knife and sheath from it. 'Take this.' 'I can't, it's yours.' 'You cannot refuse a gift, you may need it.' 'It's a present from me and Peppy to you. I made two of them, one for Peppy, and one for myself. I will make another one. 'It has been fired 22 times, it will never let you down.' 'Thank you' said Adam, their eyes met. There was a friendly stare, and time stood still for a minute with thoughts of their families and far off lands.

'We are thousands of miles from where we both really belong. Different countries in this new land, this new world, but were the same' said Adam. 'Yes, we are the same. The blood ties feel strong.' Answered Peppy. 'Yes it does' said Adam. 'Goodbye Romany-rye' shouted little Victoria. 'Good bye little Princess.' 'If ever we can help, you just write.' 'Thank you' said Adam. They both smiled. He turned to look at Esmeralda 'If I don't come back and see you before a year has passed, I won't be coming back. I will write you' he said, giving Esmeralda a smile as he said it. She undid the chain and cross around her neck and gave it to little Victoria, whispering in her ear. Victoria ran over, and pushed it in Adam's hand. 'She said for you to write.' He kissed the cross, and dropped it in his shirt pocket. 'God bless you Adam, Romany Rye.' 'This sister see is too forward in front of her family ' said Peppy, looking away annoyed.

Adam started to walk quickly back to the train. 'All aboard, all aboard. Train is leaving in a few minutes' shouted Chris. The train whistle blowed twice. Everyone was now onboard. It waited for another 3 or 4 minutes, then the whistle blowed 3 times. It then started to move forward. The gypsy family were waving, so was Bob, the Black Smith.

'Did you get your fortune told?' asked Charles. Adam just smiled and didn't answer, thinking of Esmeralda. God, she's beautiful. I will write. They're a nice family. I wish she was in Glen Parva, he thought. 'Do they always come out to the train like this to wave us off?' asked

Adam. 'I suppose so. They might not see as many strangers for months. Most of the trains go straight through' said Charles.

Some of the settlement women ran towards the train. Passengers let the windows down, finished newspapers and magazines, they threw them out. A woman and a teenage boy were picking them up, then just standing there. 'My god' said Adam, 'we are witnessing the birth of a big town one day, maybe a city. It's the start of a new vast country of the future, free and equal for all.' 'I have been too many places, but never have I felt like this before' said Adam. 'You know I never looked at it like that' said Charles, looking at Adam, he could see the experience had really touched him. 'God bless this America. May it always be free and open for all' said Adam, raising a hand waving. 'What a nice thing to say. You know how to use words. You could be a Congressman one day' said Charles under his breath, as he walked away.

The rain was now slowly trickling down the windows. Adam looked over in the distance. The caldaresh gypsies had gone back in to their wagons. Bob the Blacksmith stood in the rain in front of his house waving to the train.

Adam looked at the knife, the present he had received. The blade must be 8 inches. Obviously, a hunting knife. The bone handle was brown and black. Let in to the centre of the handle was a silver plate. On one side, it had engraving across it, (cushty-bock) Good Luck, the other side, the plate was plain. The hilt that separated the handle from the blade was stainless steel, it was a thick wide plate. What craftsmanship. These caldaresh, they seem more skilled with metal than our people, thought Adam.

He pushed the knife into its sheath, then hooking the safety cord over the hilt. Nickey had said the knife had been fired 22 times. It was usually 6-7, maybe 10 at the most. The only blades that were fired that many times were rapiers and very expensive dueling swords. Maybe that's why it seemed so light, thought Adam, and the balance so good.

He looked up at the molly croft roof. Another small roof built on top of the main roof. It was a lot narrower, running the full length down the centre, with the small side Molly-Croft windows let in each side, exactly like the horse drawn gypsy living wagons, the small windows opening to let fresh air and light in. How it reminded him of the horse drawn gypsy wagons that he had grew up in.

The train had gathered speed. The carriage started to rock a little from side to side. Within less than 5 minutes it had reached its maximum speed. These engines are so powerful. They needed to be to cover this vast country he thought. He closed his eyes and listened to the rain beating on the windows, thinking how Nicky had offered his sister in marriage to him. She was beautiful, would make a good wife, and be a help if a man needed it, his parents would have encouraged it, and accepted her, if they had been there.

'Excuse me sir, you go to Aberline, yeah' said the little man.

Adam turned, 'Yes that's right and I'm going on a bit further again.' 'I understand sir. Is there more of Texas again.' Adam looked and just smiled. 'Where you from fella?' 'We are from Sweden yah, my younger brother and me. I am a youl, joiner, and my younger brother, he helps, he is fifteen. I have had letter from America, Aberline yah, to say I will get plenty work there.' 'So you should be alright' answered Adam, looking up at the two bags on the rack above the mans head. 'Is that all your tools?' 'Yah, I have tools, big box full in packing wagon at the back.' 'To answer your question fella, there's a lot of Texas, I've been told there's over 400 miles down past Aberline to Mexico.'

'By the way, the first thing they'll ask you is do you have a gun.' 'Yah, I have shotgun.' 'No, a side gun, pistol, and you'll need to learn how to use it. You're in a very rough wild part of the world here.' The little man and his wife looked from one to the other; he then looked at the little girl sat next to his wife, and the younger one on her lap. Adam noticed a slight fear in him. 'What part of the world did you say you came from? Asked Adam. 'I come from Sweden yah.' 'You've come a long way. There's hundred's coming every week from all over the old world to this new world America' said Adam.

'You are English gentleman, yah?' Adam just nodded, then leaning back in the seat, and listening to the rain on the windows, his thoughts going way back.

CHAPTER FIVE – THE YORKSHIRE DALES
About 1853

'Happy Birthday' 'Happy Birthday Adam, you are ten, I wonder how much you'll get' said his younger brother Layton. 'I said, I wonder how much you'll have Adam for your birthday.' 'How can I tell you that until I've got it?' said Adam. The old gypsy way for children with their birthdays was usually money. They always got money pushed in their hand, and very rarely a present until they was grown. It was Christmas they got presents, not birthdays.

'This grass lay by is going to be soft to get them carts off this morning, that's if we can get them off. We might have to forget taking the women out horking. It's still slightly raining, just a little' answered Adam. The stable type door on the gypsy living wagon they lived in suddenly opened. A heavily built old man of about 75 came in and slammed the door. 'Just look at your boots old granddad, they're very muddy.' 'I know, I know', he said, as he pulled his boots off.

They called their great grandfather Byron' old granddad' so as they did not get mixed up with their grandfather Isaac. Old Byron, his wife called Louisa, known as "Blackpool – Louise Smith". They let the two boys sleep under their bed, being a bottom bed, the main bed being a top bunk double bed, and this gave the boys' parents, Nelson and Delly some privacy in their wagon. 'Happy Birthday young Adam', said his great grandfather, pulling him to him, and kissing him on the cheek. Adam threw his arms around his old granddad. It was the Romany way for family showing their love for each other, always a kiss on the cheek. The Romany people were deep in their traditions, culture and ways it had not changed from generation to generation, because they kept themselves, well to themselves. They preferred it that way, being a very small race of people that had came to England in the 1700's.

His great grandmother Louise was sitting on the side of the bed. 'Happy Birthday young Adam' she said, as she pulled him to her, and kissed him on the cheek. 'Give him his present' she said to her husband. Old Byron felt in his waistcoat pocket and came out with a shiny silver six pence piece. 'Thank you, thank you old granddad. and you old grandma. Are you sure it's not too much?' 'Of course it's not too much Adam, it's your birthday'. His brother Layton looked on. He was not jealous, for he knew he would get the same on his birthday.

The (Yog) fire being an iron range, with a small oven adjoining at the side of it, called an Ostis Stove. The fire was just lukewarm; it had stayed lit nearly all night. The old woman picked up the hooked handle, and lifted the round iron top off the fire, then pushing a small balled up piece of brown paper down, and throwing a few pieces of thin wood. Finally, a small log that had been split in two, she struck a match, and then pushed it through the bottom of the front bars to the brown paper. Within three or four minutes the thin wood started cracking as flames rose around it. She then lifted the top again and put a full shovel full of coke on top of the split log.

'I wonder how the hawking will be around here?' she said. 'Don't you worry old girl, you'll have your chance to find out' said her husband Byron. 'Yes, I think I'm looking forward to seeing the villagers around here', said young Adam. He would drive the trap out with his mother Delly, his grandmother Nellie, and great granny Louisa. The women would hawk the villagers, usually houses and various shops, but never (kitchemers) public houses. The women wouldn't go into them. Offering lucky silver charms, Nottingham handmade lace, and sometimes daub, which was a polishing paste for wood, a mixture of various pastes and a nice scented smell to it, sometimes Lavender. This was made by the men in the evenings, in their spare time, and tinned up ready for the women to sell when they went out hawking. A grocers shop was always a good call, or butchers. They would sometimes get half a basket of groceries, while from the butchers, it was meat, and sometimes with a Florin 2 shillings to go with it. There was always a lady, or old maid, who wanted to know of her love life, and of her so-called friends.

"Tell me Gypsy woman" they would say, and the Gypsy woman with the crystal could do just that. Yes, the crystal was always in the bottom of the bag. You could say the cream of the hawking so to speak – no stock, no costs – just the tale! Some were very gifted at it, and could tell a mark, a client, what they wanted to know, or very near to what they wanted to know, and the young married Gypsy women would listen to the older women and learn. Shopping would be taken usually in part exchange for fortune telling. Sometimes even the odd item of clothing from a clothes shop. This would be usually (monged) begged. The crystal was always the special reading. Palm reading was usually silver and the crystal, well, however much you could possibly get for it. A good coursing dog and a good hawking woman would be the backbone of many a Gypsy family. She would keep the table, always full, and she would always have a nice few pounds kept to one side for herself. This was usually kept in a stocking and knotted. When out in a big Town, she would have her own money to buy something, to please herself. Gypsy men would joke and say to their wives, "I bet you've got a nice lump in that stocking!" He usually got a smile and a laugh – but no answer.

The men were well into horse dealing, and would call when in the small Town at the Blacksmith's shop and tavern, to see if there were any horses, or if they knew of any horses in the area for sale, or someone wanting horses. Adam would sometimes drive the women out hawking, with a trap, when there were no horse sales to go to, with his father Nelson, or his grandfather Isaac. Layton loved the horse sales. There was so much to see and learn, and sometimes, a good fight to watch. All gypsy men and boys liked to see good fights, one to one. Jack and Steven were Layton and Adam's eldest brothers from Nelson's first marriage. Steven and Jack's mother had died when he was barely in his teens; she had died of the new dreaded disease, called Cancer. Their father Nelson, then married his first wife, Jane's cousin, Delly, who was Layton and Adam's mother.

Adam held the thick slice of bread in front of the bars of the fire, with a long toasting fork "Another slice old Granny? This one's done" Jack opened the door and old Byron handed him a mug of tea with two rounds of toast. He placed them on the front board, and sat on the top step with them – the wagon was full. "What are you doing today Layton?" asked Jack through the open door. "I'll stay home with old Granddad. What about you?" "I'll go with our father to enquire around a few villages for horses and guns" said Jack. He had picked it up, and learned very young, as Layton was now learning. He knew how to present a (Wafferty Gray) – a bad looking, miserable horse. He could "doctor" one up, and nearly present it as good as the older men. All the men were surprised, and often wondered how good Layton would become one day with the horses. He knew so much for his age.

The bacon was sizzling in the pan. Adam had a long fork getting toast ready for the bacon sandwiches. Jack held out his plate. He had eaten one piece of toast. His old Granddad shook the fork. The two slices of crispy home cured bacon fell on the round of toast. It had been raining off and on all night. "Thank God it's stopped" said old Byron, snapping the lid on his heavily carved gold watch, and dropping it back in his waistcoat pocket. "What time is it? asked Louise. "Half past eight" he answered. "We've left it a bit late, but we will soon be on our way" she said. "You get off out hawking. I'll tidy the (Vardow) living wagon up for you" said the old man.

The bacon was crispy, the toast thick, and well-buttered, and no one was talking. The old woman put her plate on the sideboard, and filled the teapot up. She then went back to her breakfast. Old Adam would dip his sandwich in the bacon fat, and the 3 boys doing the same, until the pan was clean. The boy's father, Nelson, was standing with his father Isaac, by the outside (Yog) fire. The 3 boys went and stood over by their father, "Happy birthday son" said Nelson, giving him a shiny silver 6 pence piece. "Thank you Father" he said. His father pulled him to him, and kissed him on the cheek "Happy birthday young Adam" said his Granddad Isaac. "If you go to your Granny Nellie, she's got something for you" said his Grandfather Isaac. Adam looked over towards his Granny's wagon – the 4 wagons were pulled in a circle, his parents, his grandparents, Isaac and Nellie, and his great grandparents, old Byron and Louisa, eldest brother Jack had his own small wagon, an open lot. The wagons were pulled in a circle with some 6 or 7 feet between each one, the front board, with the steps going down pointing towards the fire in the centre of the encampment. Adam's Granny Nellie came over. A small well dressed woman. She held out her arms to him. Adam walked over to her. He was just 10, and he was nearly as tall as her. She went in her pinny pocket, and came out with a purse, which had a wallet on the opposite side. She held out a silver shilling "Happy birthday young Adam." "Thank you Granny Nellie" he said, kissing her on the cheek. "This is a shilling piece, that's a lot for just an ordinary birthday." "That's alright young Adam. Your grandmother wants you to have it" said his grandfather Isaac. His Granny Nellie was a clever woman. It was said she could go into a village, or a row of houses, where other gypsy women had hawked, that same day even. She would call after them, and still come out with money, sometimes big money, (a bory ducker pen) finding a good mark, a client, for big money fortune telling. This would cause jealousy sometimes amongst other women. His Granny Nellie and Grandfather Isaac always had the very best of whatever was available; wagons, and coloured horses to pull them. They would eat from Royal Crown Derby and silver cutlery, and wore heavy gold jewelry. They had the nickname amongst other Gypsy people and travellers of Flash Isaac and Nellie.

Everyone sat in their wagons eating and drinking. The horses were tethered, tied to the back of the wagons. Nelson and his father, Isaac, had brought the horses from a field down the road, nearly 2 hours since the horses were put out in the field for the night to eat free grass. It was the Romany way, and it was called "Puvven the grays". The horses would be led to a field, usually down some quiet side road, at 11 o'clock at night. They would have their fill of fresh grass and then sleep and the men would then take them out of the field, early, 5 o'clock the next morning. This being free grazing, free run, (holling for chitchey) eating for nothing, especially any foals, they were reared free.

They had travelled down from Scotland, and were now stopping in Yorkshire. Their Grandfather Isaac had said they were stopping somewhere between Borough Bridge and Elmsmere, not far from a big village called Essingbold. It seemed to be very open country. The farms well spread out, with the odd village here and there. Isaac said he thought it was called the Yorkshire Dales, but he wasn't sure. Adam and Layton, standing one on either side lifted the shafts of the trap, as his father backed the horse up, and the boys slipped the harness loops over the shafts of the trap. The three women placed their shopping bags on the floor, and then climbed up into the trap from the back. It had a seat on either side. Old Louisa was the last in. Young Adam closed the centre door at the back, and then sat up front.

"So where are you taking us young Adam?" asked his Grandmother. Jack came walking over fast "Whoa wait" he said "I forgot to give you your birthday present brother Adam". He went into his pocket and brought out a 3 pence piece. "Oh thank you Jack." said Adam looking away. Granny Nellie went into her bag and came out with a small bag full of glass sweets "These fruit suckers are very nice, tasty" she said, handing them round. Adam glanced down at the 3 shopping bags, his mother's, his Granny Nellie's, and his old Granny Louisa's. Granny Nellie's was the smallest of the three. Different bags, sometimes baskets were used in different areas by Gypsy women. The Gypsy women from the Midlands, Blackpool, and Yorkshire would use a shopping bag for their stock to sell charms, droub and paper flowers.

The London Gypsy women, West Country, and Welsh Gypsies would use a basket, usually with pegs in, or flowers. Many times they would sell flowers such as daffodils and tulips, and when there were none of these to be had, sometimes early in the morning, they would be taken from a park or large Government buildings which seemed to have far too many flowers. Yes, his Granny Nellie had the smallest bag, but she didn't need a big bag. She could speak so nice, like a (bitty rawny) little lady. Manx Nellie, as she was known, because she originated from the Isle of Mann. There would be a few rolls of crocheted Nottingham lace, and a small purse with a handful of silver charms in, and the main thing, her crystal. He had a lot of respect for her. He had once said to another Gypsy boy who was asking about his Granny Nellie "She doesn't need a big bag or basket. She could quite easily get a good living working out of her pockets". The horse had kept up a steady trot for some 10 or 12 minutes. About 2 miles away in the distance was a big country village called Essingbold.

Layton and his old Granddad Byron sat around the outside stick fire. There were 3 big rabbits on a spit over the fire which Layton had been turning now and then. He may have been old, but his hearing and senses were still sharp. "I hear horses at a good distance" said old Byron. Layton stood up and looked one way then the other "You're right old Granddad – 2 in the distance." "Sit down Layton we have nothing to fear. We have done nothing wrong. Let me do the talking". 4 or 5 minutes passed, but it seemed like 20. The 2 horses approached from behind old Byron. "Good morning Gypsy." Old Byron got up and stood beside Layton. "Good morning Sir. My name is Byron Boswell, and this is my great grandson, Layton". "I am Lord Sir John William Bates, and this is my grandson, Walter." "I am pleased to meet you my Lord" answered old Byron, removing his cap and bowing. Layton noticing that his Great Grandfather had gone a little humble. He gave Layton a quick glance, and he did the same, with a slight bow. "Do you know your wagons are camped on my land and you are cooking my game?" "I say to you with the highest of respect my Lord, we are only camped on a lay by, not in a field, and we are only cooking rabbits, which as we both know is not game my Lord, and also there are plenty of them." "You speak well Gypsy, and you show respect. Where do you hale from?" "Originally Blackpool, but we have spent a lot of time in Scotland my Lord." "Forget calling me my Lord. You may address me as Sir John" he answered, starting to climb down out of the saddle. Layton stepped forward, and held the horse's bridle. "I have some crusty bread and fresh butter, and the rabbits are cooked, would you like a snack with us Sir John?" "It does smell good. I am a little hungry". Layton ran over to a wagon and brought his father's outside table placing it near the fire. Old Byron had placed a large loaf with a butter dish and a knife on the table. As they ate, old Byron threw the bones in the fire. "A good snack and tasty, where did you get the bread?" "The women folk make it Sir". Layton came over with 2 wet cloths, placing one in front of Sir John, and one in front of his grandson. Old Bryon wiped the grease from his hands, rubbing it into his elbows, then wiping his mouth and hands with the wet cloth. Layton did the same. Walter looked on, with a smile. "Different people have different ways" said Sir John to his Grandson. Byron placed a small stainless steel milk can on the table, and pulled off the lid. He then poured sweet cider into 2 cups, and half-filled 2 more for Layton and Walter. Sir John finished the drink, placed the empty cup on the palm of his hand and flicked it with his fingernail. "Fine bone china" he said, turning it over, Royal Crown Derby, then looking at Byron's thick gold watch chain "You are a proud race."

'The Robinsons sometimes camp here.' said Sir John. 'My great grandmother, was a Robinson called Blanche", said Layton. "So, have you come down from Scotland the last few days?" "Yes Sir, we have made about 6 or 7 weeks of it, stopping here and there. We buy and sell horses, and the womenfolk hawk." "And of course, they will read your palm and tell your fortune, won't they gypsy?" "Yes they do Sir. My name is Byron not Gypsy." "That's a very well-bred animal you have there Sir" said Layton "And what would a young boy of your age know of a horse?" Layton walked over and started to look around it. He then looked at Sir John with a smile. "It is our life Sir. We are brought up in the country and with animals." "I see. Do you go into Town very much?" "Now and then Sir, only when we need to get something." "So what can you tell me of this horse young man?" "It's an Ablution grey over black, or should I say silver. It would look a lot nicer if the mane and tail were (jipped) dyed in places to match up with the silver markings. It's big, probably about 17 hands." He walked over, reached up, and opened its mouth. "Looking at its back teeth, it's about 7 years old." He ran his hands slowly down the front legs, one after the other, "There's a spavin? Just starting on its front left leg"

"My stableman could not tell me all that, not in 5 or 6 minutes like you have done. He would need a good half an hour and I do not know a lot of dyeing horses but I have heard of it." Walter looked at Layton, "I am 12." "How old are you?" "9" answered Layton. "Can you read or write?" "No I can't. I can't see much use for it" "You will later in life young man" said Sir John. "That's a fine lurcher dog, what breed is it?" asked Sir John, looking at old Byron. "It's crossed twice, specially bred for the job. It has speed, cunning and staying power." "It's a lot bigger than a Greyhound, and its coat is unusual – who bred it?" asked Sir John "My Grandson – its mother was Saluki and Greyhound crossed, and then the father was an Irish Stag Hound for the second breeding." "Does it chase well? Can it kill?" "It can hunt, kill and carry back" answered Old Byron. "I'd love to see it course. Coursing is my favourite sport, and I have some powerful hares on my Estate." "Do you have a lot of land Sir?" "23 farms, nearly 7000 acres" said Walter. "Your Grandfather must be a very wealthy man" said Layton. "One of the richest in all Yorkshire" answered Walter. "And where is the rest of the clan?" asked Sir John. "The womenfolk are off to the nearest town to hawk with my other great grandson driving them, and the men are off looking for horses to trade for." "I might have a few horses that you might be interested in. I am getting rid of a few from some of my farms. I will be back tomorrow morning, as I want to see that dog course. Tell the men I will show them some horses, and I will be selling them, and giving them a chance at them. Thank you for the meal" "See you tomorrow then" said Layton to Walter. Walter looked disappointed at his Grandfather "Alright, you can come tomorrow then, I will tell the teacher you can have the day off. But you must not make a habit of it." "Thank you Grandfather. I will see you tomorrow Layton" "Yes, we will have a day's hunting" said Layton "We will hunt, eat, and we will talk tomorrow, and it will be a good day Sir John" said old Byron, touching his cap as Sir John climbed into his saddle "Yes, a day of sport tomorrow" said Sir John. Walter turned in his saddle to wave as they left.

The women had a good days work. Louisa had sold half of her lace, and got in with a baker. She had told the fortune of the baker, and gave his wife a reading with the crystal, who had insisted to have it separate on her own from her husband, and she confided in old Louisa that she was having an affair with one of the workers, a junior baker, some 15 or 16 years younger than herself. Louisa had told her more or less what she wanted to know, and what would please her, and had pushed the crystal reading, knowing it was the best one for her client and of course the dearest reading. The baker's wife gave her a Florin (2 shillings), and wanted to see her again for more advice of the future – and how things would turn out for her. The baker was only interested in his business, as he wanted to open another baking business in the next town, and he had given her a florin (2 shillings) for both hands being read. She had as many cakes and bread she could get in her bag. Delly had done some business as well – she had sold some silver charms and told 2 fortunes.

Manx Nellie got into the butcher's shop. She (duckered) told their fortunes, palm reading of the butcher and his wife and son for 2 half crowns, and had managed to (mong) begin with the readings half a bag of meat, chops, a dozen eggs. Nelson and his father Isaac, and Jack, had managed to buy 2 horses from the blacksmith. So all in all, it had been a very good day for the full family. They were more than pleased. The large frying pan with the hooped ring handle hung over the fire, on the slanting (Kavvie saster) kettle iron, 7 or 8 inches above the fire. It was full of lamb chops and thick slices of home cured bacon and sausages, Nellie was taking out of the iron pot, potatoes which had been cooked with their skins on, while Delly was cutting up two crusty loaves.

All were sitting round the fire eating and enjoying the evening. Old Byron stood up to speak. "We will need to have a day home tomorrow. The (rye) gentlemen of the boorycare, the gentleman of the big house, will be here tomorrow for a course, and we are on his land, we must make him very welcome, and give him a good days sport. The womenfolk will need to cook a good meal. He might not come alone".

They all ate and continued to talk. Then old Byron brought out his button keyed accordion. Old Byron played the accordion and Jack bought out his violin. There were several Scottish and Irish reels played, and the 2 boys, Adam and Layton, went under one of the wagons and pulled out a large square sheet of wood. Nelson started to tap dance on it to the music as the sweet cider was passed round. Layton and Adam sat by the fire cross legged clapping their hands to the music, as their father tap dancing to the accordion and the violin playing.

When Nelson finished he had been tap dancing for some 15 or 16 minutes. He sat down a little out of breath. His wife Delly stepped forward, standing in front of the fire, and started to sing, old Adam accompanying her on his accordion, with Jack playing his violin. When she finished, all gave a little clap, then Manx Nellie stepped forward and started to recite a gypsy rhyme.

9 months of the year were an open and a free way of life for the Gypsy families. It was November, December and January, the 3 months of winter, which were hard. No house, business, or job can hold a real Gypsy. They are a born free race, as free as the birds in the air, and as free as the wind that blows. A real gypsy will often say I am born free.

It was a lovely spring morning, birds whistling, and the grass wet with early morning dew. Nelson had taken Fawn, the lurcher for a short walk, and was just coming back with him. Layton brought a small enamel bowl of water for the dog to have a drink. The boy never gave him any food, as it would slow him down if he was coursing. Layton had a stiff horse brush, and was starting to brush Fawn down. When he had finished, Jack started to run his hands down the dog's legs and thighs and back, massaging him slowly. Old Byron came over and looked at the dog "Don't you let me down this day Fawn" he said. A good hour had passed when 3 horses came into view. "I can see Sir John and his grandson. Don't know the other" said old Byron. "Probably a companion or bodyguard" said Isaac. Old Byron stepped forward. "Good morning Sir John." "And good morning to you Byron and grandson Layton." Old Byron introduced him to the rest of the family, as Sir John shook hands with them. "This is my gillie" he said, the man nodding to them. Then Manx Nellie came forward "Good morning my Lord. I am Manx Nellie, Isaac's wife. This is my mother-in-law Louisa, from Blackpool, and this is my daughter-in-law Delly, from Manchester and Birmingham area". Sir John looked at Nellie, "She speaks well, her dress and style is something above most Gypsies" he thought. Around her neck was a necklace of square gold beads, there was a red coral bead, every third bead. On her left hand was a heavy gold ring with a half carat diamond Gypsy set in a star. Her earrings were small gold Maple leaves with a Canadian half dollar in the centre. Her complexion was not as tanned as the rest of them. Her grandmother had been a gorger, being a non Gypsy in the Isle of Man. Her raven black hair was tied back and hung in ringlets with a few curls at each side of her forehead, and her eyes seemed speckled as if laughing. Sir John removed his hat "I am pleased to meet you Manx Nellie." He was a little taken aback at her style and good looks, "of course, all you other ladies as well." Delly came forward with 3 mugs of tea, "milk and sugar is on the table my Lord" she said. "I believe you have a lot of land my Lord." "Yes I do. Please just call me Sir John. The Lord is the son of God" he said. Isaac smiled; he liked this man, this Yorkshire Lord. "Not a truer word spoken Sir" said Isaac. "Yes, I have 23 farms. Mixed arable and grazing, which are rented out, and my own farm, which we work ourselves, is about the size of 3 farms." "So where will we hunt today?" asked old Byron. "There" he pointed to a high hilly land in the distance, with a large wood on one side. "There's 2000 acres there, barren rocky and wild land. It's a vast open area, hills and woods; it's just left as open range. That is where you will see the most powerful and fastest hares in the country. We also have venison there as well. You say you have spent time in Scotland?" "Yes we have Sir John, at Bridge of Earn, just outside of Sterling, the vast moorlands there, of open land. The white hares there, the biggest and fastest in the land, in all Britain" answered Isaac.

 Sir John smiled putting his empty mug down and stepped nearer the fire, holding his hands out for a warm. "Maybe not the biggest and fastest" he said. Isaac and Nelson looked from one to the other, surprised "Nearly 100 years ago Sir Walter McGregor of Stirlingshire was a very close friend of my Grandfather. My Grandfather would have a week up there now and again, for the salmon fishing, and Sir Walter McGregor would sometimes come down here to stay with us, for a few weeks hunting. He was so impressed with the silver hares here; they caught some 10 or 12 of them, and took them back to the open wild plains of Stirlingshire, where they bred. But they did have trouble with the first few breedings, for the hares to adapt that is to the cold Scottish winter weather on the Stirling tops." "I have seen them Sir. They are nearly white not silver" said Nelson. "Probably the cold Scottish weather has altered their coats a little" said Sir John. "But here on them vast open Yorkshire Moors, on that wild open top up there, that's where the Stirling big white hares hail from. Here are the originals, nearly silver, and as big as a Corgi dog. So fast, they have to put 2 good dogs on one course. The one dog will turn it, for the second dog to kill it." Isaac looked at his father Byron, a slight worried expression. Sir John smiled. "Come, come Isaac, faint heart never won a fair lady. I believe this big Lurcher of yours will give a good account of himself. You say it can hunt, kill, and bring back?" "So it can Sir John, hunt, kill and carry, but we did not have him when we were at Stirling. That was 5 or 6 years ago, and we had to put 2 dogs on 1 white hare, which we don't believe in doing that, but we needed the meat for the pot."

As they climbed in the saddle, Sir John glanced back at Manx Nellie. Isaac reached out, getting hold of the bridle of Sir John's horse, pulling it to one side, and letting the others go on a few yards ahead. "Don't you keep staring and looking at my wife. Lord or no lord, there will be trouble" said Isaac. "No offence meant no offence. Your wife is like an oil painting. Please accept my apologies and take it as a compliment." "I accept that" said Isaac. They dug their heels in and quickly caught the others up.

After 20 minutes of slow trotting they came to a farm road. A wooden plank painted black with the words in white on it 'Wild Moors Farm'. Sir John's man trotted ahead and opened the 5 barred gates. As they approached the house, the farmer came out. "Good Morning Sir John." "Good Morning Norman. We're just here for a day's hunting. We will stay to the paths keeping away from your crops and stock." "Will you have a mug of hot tea before you go?" asked Norman's wife. "Thank you just the same, but we want to get on our way."

They finally came to the end of the last field, which had got quite steep; there was a small paddock, a water trough and 2 stables with feed in. They unsaddled the horses and left them loose. Nelson looked slowly round it. It was a high walled paddock, about 3 acres. "You seem to have this well set out Sir John." "Yes I do, I love hunting this vast open land, and game is very close to my heart up here. I am away from all the pump and ceremony and parties. I was thinking once of building a summer cottage up here, but it's never happened yet." As they went over the stile into the other side of the walled paddock, he pointed up. "Table Top Mountain Gentleman", the land rose steeply, the mountain looked to be about a quarter of a mile away, was poor land, tufts of grass here and there, with large stone gravel areas, and rocky. Then there would be big patches of good fresh grass, with the odd few bushes here and there.

They kept walking to the left along side of the forest; occasionally there was a deer to be seen. Nelson put a slip lead around Fawns' neck. Old Byron stopped, looking into the woods, "I smell water, and I think I can hear water over the rocks." Sir John and his man glanced from one to the other. "What you can smell and hear, it is in the heart of the forest" he said. "There is a spring on the hilltop that goes down both sides." As they continued up, a pheasant suddenly jumped, taking to flight some 30 yards ahead of them. It was flying straight across from left to right in front of them.

Adam's catapult was out, and he placed a lead ball the size of a small finger nail in the leather. It was at arm's length. His hand was alongside of his left ear when he let fly. He aimed a good 8 to 9 inches in front of its head. The lead ball whistled as if fired from a rifle. It hit the bird in the bottom part of the chest. It was about 20 feet of the ground. Feathers came down like snowflakes. The bird dropped to the ground, and lay still. Sir John and his Gilly just looked from one to the other. "That would have been a good shot with a rifle, Adam" said Sir Johns man, then walked ahead of them, and picked the pheasant up. "He uses a catapult well" said Sir John. "Yes sir, we all do" answered Isaac. Their heads were turning one way then another looking for hares, but there was none to be seen.

"Don't worry, you will see them soon gentleman" said Sir Johns man. "But we're getting steeper, and the going is slower." He had stopped halfway, and had a 10 minute rest. Sir John's man had taken some flasks of water out of his bag, giving 2 to the guests to share, one for Sir John, and one for himself. Another half an hour passed, and they finally reached the top. "What a sight" said Jack, "it's like a small prairie, how long? How far is it Sir?" "I don't rightly know. Some say it's nearly 2 miles square. It is gravelly here and there, but there are good areas of grass also, as you can see. It's far too high and cold to feed sheep here, especially in winter. The snow up here gets quite deep. We lost half of them when we tried it – just can't get the feed up to them, and too steep in snow to get them down." "I suppose they might do something with Tabletop Mountain one day." "I'm not really bothered, as I have more than enough land to bother about".

They walked slightly behind Nelson, who was some 4 or 5 strides ahead of them. He stopped and had a drink. Then taking a handkerchief out of his pocket, he soaked it in water, then opening the dog's mouth, he rubbed the wet hanky into its mouth, and then squeezed the drops that were left into its open mouth. Fawn stood still, nose pointing straight ahead then, looking from left to right. Old Byron lightly tapped the back of his hand for attention, and then pointed to what looked like a large stump of grass, some 80 yards ahead. All stood still, staring, Nelson could now see the top half of the two large ears. Luckily, it had its back towards them, and the light breeze was blowing in their face, or it would have picked up their scent. Nelson motioned for all to stay still, as he went forward slowly. He had only covered some 20 yards when the hare's ears went down. "It's a (bory Caningra) a big hare, and look at the size of it" whispered Layton to Adam.

The hare suddenly sat upright. "My God" said old Byron, "it's as big as a full grown Jack Russell!" Nelson could not hold the dog, seeing the hare some 60 yards ahead, it lunged forward. As he did, Nelson slipped the leash, and they all rushed forward. Nelson was running as hard as he could. "Go Fawn go! You're on it boy, go!" he shouted, encouraging his dog "Look at that dog cover the ground! He's got some power and speed!" said Sir John. All of a sudden the hare went to the right, 7 or 8 strides. Fawn took the right bend after it, but by the time Fawn had straightened out, he had lost the distance he had gained. It took him around 20 yards to make the turn that the hare had made in 5.

Then the hare made a short right turn and again gained another 12 or 15 yards, as the big dog was a lot slower at getting out of the turns, and on the straight again. The greyhound coursing breed, the speed was coming out of Fawn. There was no let up, because he had the stamina of the big Irish Staghound, he was taking it in his stride with no problem, and the hare was turning again, as Fawn closed the 60 yard gap to 35, the hare made it up again, another turn, this time to the left. Most greyhounds by now would have been spent out, finished. But the big Irish Staghound breed that was in him for running down deer's. "What a course, what a chase!" shouted Sir John. The hare was ready to turn yet again, and that's when the cunningness of the Egyptian Saluki breed came out. Fawn did not turn as before, he continued straight, and when the hare had finished 2 turns, and straightened out again, Fawn was on him. The hare stopped dead, and Fawn landed straight on top of it, his open jaws going into the ground.

"Up Fawn! Up!" shouted Nelson, running behind the dog, a good 45 yards back. But the hare was up first, covering the ground. It was tiring more quickly than the powerful dog. Fawn, landing on top of it, had knocked the wind out of the hare. The hare was soon up and gone again – it had picked up speed. It would have definitely taken 2 good greyhounds to have brought it down – one would turn the hare, for the other to make the kill, but that was not the Gypsy way of coursing. They believed in one dog for one hare, and that's when you know it was a good dog, a good sport, and it was usually needed for the pot. "But there would be very few dogs that could kill one of these silver hares on its own ground" said Old Byron. The hare was making good time; he now had a lead again some 60 to 70 yards ahead, but he was trying. Fawn had been slower in getting up from the fall. "There Fawn! It's over there!" shouted Nelson, as he ran towards his dog, his hand pointing. Fawn now could see the hare; it was doing bigger and slower turns. The hare thought he had lost the dog. Fawn got straight down to the job – his strides were strong and long, his deep chest was brushing the ground with his massive strides, the stamina of the Staghound was now coming out again.

The distance between them was quickly disappearing; it was really something to see, a course that a lot of men would have travelled 50 miles to see. Fawn was now showing the authority. He went in a straight line occasionally zig zagging, his large body swaying from left to right. Fawn had out smarted him. The hare now did not know which way to turn, he feinted a left turn, then made its real turn to the right. Fawn's large jaws were there – one heavy snap, a low little scream, and the hare's neck was broke. Fawn threw it in the air, and picked it up, then came trotting towards his master with it in his mouth, dragging his kill, as it was too big and heavy to carry.

Sir John and old Byron slowly walked over to the dog. Fawns tongue was hanging out to one side, and he was panting heavily. "That would have taken 2 good dogs to do that. You're a champion Fawn! You're a champion!" said Sir John, patting him. "Good boy Fawn, he was bigger than you thought wasn't he!" said Layton. Walter stood smiling. He was enjoying the days sport. Nelson stood there, he was proud of his dog. He soaked the hanky heavily with water, and rubbed it in the dog's mouth, finally squeezing all the drops into the dog's mouth. There was now nothing in sight, with all the noise that had been going on, and Sir John started walking over to the right, being the opposite side from the woods. Nelson put the slip lead on his dog again, then, taking a few big, fast strides, he caught the others up. "Let us take our time. We all need a rest. Fawn's not ready so soon for another chase. Let's give him a while. I don't want to burn him out".

When coursing on vast open areas with no ditches or hedges, coursing men usually took 3 dogs or 4, so as to give the pair that had just had the kill and the race a good rest, before putting them on another hare. Hearing a noise, they all turned – it was 2 pheasants, a cock and a hen. They had stayed down low, some 25 yards to the right, as the hunting party had passed by. All turned, quickly – squawking and crowing – they took to the air. Suddenly the catapults were firing. The lead balls could be heard whistling through the air. Then, there were feathers floating down like snowflakes. One pheasant had been hit twice. "Good shooting! Damn good shooting! What a fine days sport this is I am having!" said Sir John.

In the next 2 and half hours, with rests in between, they had another 2 hares. "These hares are so big and powerful for one dog. Fawn has killed 3 out of 5. I'd like to stop now if that's alright with you Sir John. I don't want to burn my dog out." "Of course you don't Nelson, he is a fine animal, and we have enjoyed it" answered Sir John "Up Fawn, up" said Nelson. The big dog stood on his back legs, and placed his front paws, one on either side of Nelsons shoulders, his head level with Nelson's face. "He's the finest lurcher I've seen, and I have seen a lot of them. I have a smoky silver coloured greyhound bitch. I call her Smokey. She's fast, can kill, if another dog courses with her – not in Fawn's class by a long shot, but, she's a good dog. She'll be coming into season soon, would you put your dog to her for me?" "I will do that for you Sir John, of course. I would expect the pick of the litter, one pup." "That would be fair" answered Sir John. "You say this greyhound is fast, Sir John. How would you compare her to Form?" "One hundred yards straight, she would be faster than Fawn, then she would just fade out. She would possibly turn quicker than Fawn, being smaller and lighter, then she would be burned out, finished but I would definitely say Fawn has the staying power of three greyhound bitches. Also Fawn has such cunning and skill – I have never seen it's equal. That will probably be the Saluki breed coming out. If your big dog put my bitch right for pups, they would be good coursing dogs, better than the mother. Can any of you use a gun?" "I have a small rifle, a .22" said old Byron "It's old, but it is in good order. Young Adam and Layton are very good shots with it" said Isaac. "That is good" said Sir John "My Grandson here, Walter, is a very good shot as well with a rifle. For his age that is. We must have a day's sport, target shooting, at my Manor House. I have some revolvers as well" "It sounds good Sir John, and we would all enjoy it that's for sure. But you see, we have to think of going out and getting a living, it would need to be a weekend. We need to find a few horses for trade" answered Isaac. "On our home farm, we have working horses, five or six are a bit slow and have grown too old. I usually send them to the knacker's yard, they don't make a lot, that's for sure. Every three or four years we just write off six or 7, and get fresh stock in, younger blood. We could work something out to suit both of us, as they are ready to be got rid of" said Sir John. "Thank you, thank you we all enjoy shooting, especially the boys, young Walter looked on he seemed so happy".

350 maybe 4 hundred yards ahead was the water spring. There was some young trees in a half circle, with bushes here and there around the

small lake, which was some sixty yards across. In the centre was a cluster of boulders, protruding up out of the water. The spring, a fountain of water shooting into the air. They came to the edge of the water, and Jack slowly looked around. Adam pointed to a cluster of bushes the other side. There was a young buck, a deer. Adam went to get his catapult out. Old Byron reached out and placing his hand on Adam's arm 'leave it be son, it's too far for a clean kill, it's only six or eight months old it has had no life yet and we have plenty of game for the pot,' 'Alright old grandfather. 'Would that have been a powerful enough shot with a catapult to kill a young deer at that distance? Asked Walter. A head shot especially near the ear would drop it, at fifty or sixty yards, answered Adam.

It's beautiful up here, so quiet, just the noise of the spring water and the birds, this must have been like this for hundreds and hundreds of years,' said Nelson as he let his dog have a drink for just a few minutes, then let it have a second drink about ten minutes later. They just stood there. 'I can see a stream at each end of the lake, where does it go? asked Adam. It runs down each side of the mountain servicing the farms below Tabletop Mountain, answered Sir John. Is there fish in there?' asked Nelson. Yes, I believe there's trout, we should have brought a rod, said Young Walter who needs a rod, said Adam, his eyes going slowly along the bank. He walked over to where the ground protruded out with a miniature cave so to speak that looked to go back underneath where he stood I'll bet there's (doosters) of (bory matchy) lots of big fish in this lake. Very quietly taking off his jacket he lay belly down, his arms went down into the water and back into the pocket under where he lay, he slowly felt around and back as far as he could, then got up. 'What is he doing asked Walter? 'He's guddling for fish; you stroke and tickle the trout's belly and slowly get your hands under him, then throw him up over your head onto the bank, answered Layton

You're kidding me aren't you? 'I kid you not, said Layton. What if it's a Pike you could lose your fingers'. 'No a Pike would not let you get that close to him, he would be gone. Just then Jack got up and went further along the bank, as he did Nelson gave the lead to young Adam to keep hold of Fawn, and he went the other way down the bank. Suddenly there was a splashing of water has Jack threw a large trout over his head. Walter looked on in amazement. Nelson had gone along to where some of the trees threw shade on the lake, there were several pockets going back underneath the bank where a lazy trout could rest in the cool. Fifteen minutes passed, and Jack had another trout. Sir John's gilly pushed a thick string through each of the fish's gills and out the other side stringing the fish together.

'I have heard of fish guddling but never seen it; i have learnt from your people this day, said Sir John. Isaac stood there smoking his pipe slowly looking over the area. 'You are truly natural hunters, people of the open countryside, said Sir John. 'What a place this is, I have travelled Scotland, Wales and a lot of England, never have I seen or enjoyed a place like this flat top mountain, fresh water full of game, even deer, and not a soul in sight, what a place this would be to pull your wagon. A gypsy's paradise away from the world.' said Old Byron. And how many coursing dogs do you have? Asked Nelson, Just the one I lost 2 with dry pad. You say you have 2 empty stables Sir John, how would you like to breed a really special coursing strain. I have thought about it, but I don't have the time and experience you have.' said Nelson and Isaac nearly at the same time. Very well come up to the house tomorrow and we will talk about it, said Sir John

'I can just see them coming, said Delly. Two of the women carried a second table then opening the legs up and placing it next to the first table. The womenfolk had got a good fire going. 'Do you keep it going all day?' asked Sir John. 'Yes as soon as we're up till we go to bed', 'If the weather is good we sit around it, only going in the living wagons to sleep.' 'We'll share the game up and be on our way, it's after five,' said Sir John, pressing the lid down on his pocket watch and dropping it back in his waistcoat pocket. The women will be insulted if you do not accept our hospitality, they have cooked a meal for you your man and your grandson,' said Old Byron. 'Thank you then, Byron, answered Sir John, it's a pleasure to eat with you.

Layton and young Adam were the first to dismount then as Sir John and his man dismounted. The boys led their horses away and tied each one to a wagon, then giving them a drink. After seeing to the guests horses they saw to their own horses. Delly walked over to Sir John and gave him a towel and soap, there is another bowl of water over there for you and your man, Sir John. Walking over to a bowl of water they washed their hands and face. There was an oval shaped large black boiler hung over each of the two kettle irons, one on either side of the fire, a thick cloth was lapped around the hot handle then two of the women one on either side of the pot lifted it from where it hung off the curled hook, on the end of the kettle iron. They placed it on the table taking the lid off. A thick metal skewer was pushed through the knotted cloth at the top of the big basin was tied up in. As it was lifted out of the iron pot, hot water fell back into the pot, steam rising. It was placed on the table and the cloth was undone. The thick pot basin, was then turned upside down onto a platter, it was a steak and kidney pudding. As it was cut into many pieces small chunks of steak and pieces of kidney fell out of the thick pastry and a thick gravy trickled out filling the sides of the platter.

The second pot was emptied out full of new small potatoes and sliced runner beans onto another two platters, it was all served out thick slices of crusty bread filling a third platter. Two stools were brought and placed by the table.' We would be honored Lord John if you and your man servant and grandson would eat with us,' said old Louisa, Byron's wife.

'It smells delicious said the gilly it certainly does, answered Sir John, picking up the large spoon and filling his plate and then a piece of crusty bread. He suddenly put down his fork and stood up, 'i am so hungry please forgive my manners offering his stool, his man seeing this done the same. 'Please sit down Sir John with the men at the table, we very rarely use chairs,' as she pointed Sir John glanced around him. Some were sat on very low stools there were two thick scotch tartan blankets. Some were sat cross legged on them as there were only three chairs. Old Byron sat on one, being the head of the family and the other two was offered to Sir John and his man. All had a plate full of food and a fork.

Manx Nellie and her daughter-in-law Delly went round handing out mugs of a sweet cider as she placed one in front of Sir John. 'Thank you,' he said, glancing the other way. She smiled to herself as she filled the gillie's mug. I'll expect you along at the hall tomorrow Isaac about ten o'clock, I'll show you the horses. 'Can you bring Layton along?' asked Walter. I'll bring Layton and young Adam, said Isaac. Nearly an hour had passed as they ate heartily and discussed the days hunting. Sir John got up from the table 'Thank you ladies for the meal you laid out for us, truly I enjoyed it, it was delicious. I have not enjoyed myself so much in quite a long time. You are a proud and traditional race of people. I look forward to your company tomorrow. Leaving the encampment he turned in the saddle and waved back to them.

The trap had covered about 4 miles of the road as it turned a sharp bend to the left was two broad stone pillars each with a shield on it. The one on the left had a coat of arms on it with some writing in Latin, and the words Rascliffe Hall. The shield on the opposite pillar were the words 'Fortune favours the brave' this is it said Nelson we are here. He was the only one that could read. Look at the size of that,' how can one family live in it, it's half as big as a village,' said Adam. There'll probably be twenty servants to look after them,' said Jack. Today you will see how the other half lives or should I say the Lords and Ladies of this country live,' said their father. With a flick of the reins on the rump of the horse, it suddenly broke into a steady trot. I'll bet these people have met the Royal Family,' said Byron. Adam and Layton, best behaviour boys today, you show me up in front of these people and you won't sit down for two days,' 'watch, listen and learn because it is rare to mix with such people.' 'We will be good father', said Adam and we will learn said Layton. Old Byron had taken the other trap, driving the women out for a days hawking.

There were long lawns and flower beds on either side of the drive as it went up to the big house. Nelson pulled the trap up in front of the entrance. There were fifteen steps leading up to a paved area, you could have put a cottage on it. One of the two eight foot doors opened a grey haired man of about fifty well dressed in a black suit and tie stood there. 'Tradesman's entrance is around the back of the hall,' he said. He speaks more posher than Sir John and he looks very important. 'Who is he? Asked Layton. He's just a butler, a servant in charge of other servants ,' said Jack, loud enough for the butler to hear. Nelson glanced at his eldest son with a slight smile and a quick stare as if to say you put that very well. 'Be good enough to tell Sir John his new friends are here,' said Nelson. Be off with you now, or I'll call for the dogs to be let loose. 'And what is all this commotion about?' the butler turned around Sir John was stood at the back of him, 'these people, tinkers or gypsy's won't leave and they say they are your friends Sir John.' 'And so they are and until you know the nature of a caller and who they really are, you must show friendliness, 'Do you understand Jeeves?' 'Yes, Sir John, and my apologies gentleman. I'll call for the gilly said Jeeves.

Is this really one house?' 'It is Layton. 'You must have a big family?' Sir John smiled. 'And how many rooms does it have?' Ooh lots and lots, I sometimes forget, answered Sir John. 'Good Morning Nelson and where's Isaac this fine morning?' asked Walter the Gilly. 'He's home cleaning down and grooming two horses. Welcome to Rascliffe Hall, you and your boys, 'never forget Nelson you are my guests here. please feel at ease.' 'Thank you Sir John. The Gilly got into the trap. Your horse and trap will be around the back whenever you need it,' he said. 'Thank you,' answered Nelson.

Jeeves the butler took Jacks cap from him and went to do the same with Adam and Layton, they pulled away and kept hold of their caps. Nelson smiled at them and was pleased to see they had both removed their caps as they entered the house. It had 2 fireplaces, one at each end. 'it's so big we could pull our wagons in here,' ' yes you're probably right it's one hundred and fifty feet long by sixty feet wide, very handy if you have a row with the good lady, Sir John. 'That's a good one, by Jove it is, I must tell my friends that.' Jeeves stared sideways at Nelson he was surprised how he made himself at home, and speaking to Sir John on a level, ignorant and very disrespectful thought Jeeves. Adam could see Jeeves slyly looking at his father. 'Why is this hall so big Sir John?' 'Yes I think my ancestor, my great great grandfather went a bit too far when building this hall this Manor House, let me show you some of it.' 'This where we are now is called the Great Hall, the broad staircase at either end leads up to the open corridor that runs right around the top, there is some fourteen rooms at the top, most of them bedrooms, and most are kept for guests. There is also a small kitchen, a library and a study up there.' 'And this hall is only used for banquets, parties and so on.'

Jack stopped as the others walked on, looking at the shields, pennants, flags and weapons that were pinned on the walls. 'I can see you are interested,' said Sir John as he turned and walked back to Jack. 'The flags and swords, have you used them?' 'No but my ancestors did.' 'You must have met the King to be knighted?' 'Well, yes and no, I have met the king several times I inherited my knighthood from my father. The first knight in my family was my great great grandfather he was knighted by the king then, in the field of battle for bravery for fighting alongside the King. 2000 acres of the land was bestowed on him with the title. Many farms were bought by my ancestors and I have also bought several farms making the estate what it is today, it is the biggest private estate in Yorkshire only second to the Crown Yorkshire Estate'. Sir John continued walking. There are various rooms leading off the Great Hall and of course there are the servant's quarters beneath the stairs.'

They went into a side room there was a long grey haired man stood in front of a black board, at a desk sat young Walter Sir John's grandson. He waved Adam and Layton over pleased to see them. The teacher tapped several times with a ruler on the table. 'Quite please Master Walter, now I'll continue. 'If I go to York fair and I buy four barrels of apples, three of them has fifty apples in and the last one is only half full and has 25 in, what is the total amount of apples? The three full barrels they cost 20 pence each and the half barrels is 10 pence, how much is the total and how many apples are there altogether?' 'Walter was struggling, it's seventy pence altogether, he answered, he whispered his mind wasn't on it, seemed to be more on sport with his new friends.

Nelson glanced at Adam, then at the black board it was as good as ten words to his son. 'I'd like my break now please, I've put two hours in.' 'You'll break when the teacher tells you,' said Sir John. Walter said nothing. Adam stood up. 'Yes young man,' Adam pointed to the black board, 'Come on up then,' said the teacher. Adam picked up a piece of chalk and spoke as he wrote, 'three twenty's makes sixty pennies, and ten pennies for the half barrel being seventy pence in all.' 'That's very good and so quick,' 'where do you go to school young man?' 'I don't sir, the teacher smiled ignoring Adam and looking to Nelson. 'He tells you the truth neither of them as had one days school.' He picked up the piece of chalk passing it quickly several times from one hand to the other. 'Which hand is it in? Layton looked quickly from one to the other. 'That one,' he said.

'That was a lucky pick young man. 'No sir your left hand the centre knuckle is a little white through squeezing the piece of chalk,' 'Does either of you know how, or should I say who the old Kings father was?' Layton shook his head 'We don't know sir, because it's of no help to us,' answered Adam. 'Can either of you read or write? No sir,' said Layton and Adam, nearly at the same time. The teacher walked over to Nelson 'your boys are quite remarkable, they are so quick why haven't they had any schooling?' 'We don't seem to need education; we deal, hunt and by horses.' 'And where are you from, Italy or maybe Turkey? 'No we are Romany Gypsies our ancestors are from the Mediterranean. 'If you's were to stop wandering and establish yourselves permanently in one place, your business would be very successful, just as the Jews have done, it is a waste, you need to let them have schooling, said the teacher. 'I don't know about schooling, we live in the countryside, we're hunters, dealers and horsemen.' 'One day we must talk about your schooling, you could bring them up here with Walter i would not mind, said Sir John.

'So these are your new friends, John?' Nelson and his three sons turned. A well dressed woman of about fifty stood in the doorway, a young lady stood at her side. 'Yes, darling, these are my hunting friends, they are a genuine Romany family, this is Nelson Boswell and his three sons, Jack, Adam and Layton, 'gentlemen, my wife, Lady Florence and our niece, Lady Elizabeth Hilton from Scotland. She smiled holding out her right hand. Nelson placed his hand in hers, 'It's a pleasure to meet you, My Lady.' The two young boys gave a slight bow. Jack held out his hand, 'it's a pleasure my lady.'

'This is my niece, Lady Elizabeth. Jack placed his hand in hers, she stared into his dark eyes and quickly glanced away, then looked back still holding his hand. 'You are beautiful' he whispered as he squeezed her hand, she then slowly pulled it away. 'Come now Elizabeth, we will leave your Uncle John to his hunting friends. As they walked away, Lady Elizabeth turned, opened her mouth slightly then smiled at Jack. Lady Florence was standing in the doorway, Nelson, Yes my lady, being true gypsies your women folk will be experienced in Clairvoyant fortune telling. Yes they are, answered Nelson. We are having a night with refreshments, a few of my friends will be here, would your ladies like to join us? Yes Lady Florence they would be honored. Thank you Nelson it will be in three nights, Thursday, 7:30 and it might be a profitable evening for your ladies. Nelson smiled back. Does your women folk read the tarot cards?' No, we consider them to be evil, of the devil, our women are clairvoyant stargazers of the planets, past, present and future. That does sound very interesting, we will be entertained. Good day Nelson. He pulled his two young sons to one side, 'Watch and listen and, learn how a real gentleman acts and speaks,' he advised. Nearly an hour had past and then they were out in the courtyard

Nelson and Jack were looking and examining seven horses. 'How do you value them, said Sir John, holding out his right hand. Nelson glanced over towards the stables. 'You have shown me some fine horses, well bred, jumpers and hunters, but these workers, Nelson stopped and walked away. 'Speak your mind, don't be embarrassed, I am as good a judge of men as you are of a horse,' said Sir John. 'Well they are spent out, as they are, it would be probably the knackers yard, we would need to put them out to grazer for a month, also plenty of oats, then wash, cut and groom them, to get them back to how they used to be. But after three months hard work they would slip back again to what they are now. 'If you could find another three or four it would help, up to Lanark sale and back is a long way.'

'That's just into Scotland said Sir John. You see Sir John Lanark sale is a big sale very good sale for big working horses, they make top money. 'So you say after three or four months of hard work they would slip back to what they are' Yes they would Sir John. 'When horse dealing I was taught your eyes are your judge, your pocket is your guide and your money the last thing you part with. 'So it is up to who is buying them, to really look over what he his bidding for.? I would sell them sold as seen, no guarantees,' said Nelson.

Sounds fair, said Sir John, and where would you want to be, the price asked Sir John. 'Well we will do all the work, we would need them for six weeks, I would need young Jack with me to help and I would bring you back receipts from the sale. We would need to take them up by train, the deal, half of what they make. I will have to give some of my share to Jack because of him helping. 'How you would do it sounds a lot of time and hard work involved. It is Sir John. Give me a week to get some more new stock in and I'll try to make the amount up to twelve or fourteen horses it will be worth all the trouble and bother then won't it, and the deal will be a three way cut, you, Jack and myself.' said Sir John.

Nelson quickly put out his right hand he knew once he had shaken Sir Johns hand the deal was clinched. Sir John smiled, knowing how Nelson was thinking about the handshake 'that's a deal then Nelson and I will find more horses to make it all worthwhile. Lady Elizabeth and Lady Florence came into the courtyard. Each wore a ladies top hat with a long ribbon tied around it, hanging low at the back they both looked what they was, real ladies. Each carried a riding crop. An old man came out from the stables, walking between two horses holding their bridles, he let go of one then stood by the other. 'Whenever you are ready my lady' he said handing her the reins and looking at Lady Florence. Lady Elizabeth walked over to the other horse and stood there, the old man waited for Lady Florence to put one foot in his cupped hands, he gave a little lift and she seemed to jump into the saddle. Lady Elizabeth slowly turned and looked at Jack.' I think the lady needs a lift into the saddle' said Nelson smiling at his eldest son Jack. 'You're right father.' Mounting from the left into the saddle then lifting her right leg over the saddle horn to ride side saddle, thank you Jack, she said. As they slowly trotted off.

The end of summer is York fair, are your family going? Yes I think so Sir John, the women will do fortune telling there. We will pull on the fair field with the living wagons (caravans) and some horses for trade, we have never been to York fair, Nottingham goose, Musselburgh trotting which is The British championships near Edinburgh and of course, Appleby the biggest horse fair in the country. Yes, so I have heard' I have visited Appleby not Musselburgh' 'does a lot go on there? asked Sir John. The British cup, is a three day event. Of course there's goods sold and brought, horse dealing, bare knuckle fights. 'So what of this York Fair, Sir John? Oh it's a jolly good fair, full of character, probably like your Musselburgh event, but on a smaller scale. It is a two day fair, but the trader's stalls all pull on a day before the fair, the fair is on Friday and Saturday.

I never asked, 'Do you have any family Sir John? Only one brother and sister, we're a small family; my sister married a bit of a cad, a bounder, fortune hunter. She lives down at Weston-Super-Mare on the far side of Bristol. He bought a farm with her dowry, and my brother junior by twelve years, actually the baby of the family left for the Americas about six years ago.

It was suddenly Thursday the three days seemed to have passed so quickly. The women had not gone out horking. There would have been too much to do with a night time meeting as well. Manx Nellie and

Louisa her mother-in-law agreed to go to the manor. Both were well dressed in black, each with gold on, which is how a gypsy woman is usually dressed for fortune telling. Delly wasn't really keen on the duckering.

It was 6:45 when the coach arrived that Sir John had sent for them, as the coach went through the driveway entrance Dordy-Dordy (Deary Deary me) Vater borry-keer (Look at the big house).' said Louisa as she gazed at the Manor House ahead' It looks like a palace. 'Don't worry Louisa' Nelson has told me they are lovely people. Ryes and rawnys (gentleman and ladies) they know what they are, it's the middle class that is arrogant and wanting to be what they are not.

As the coach pulled up in front of the two 8ft doors a footman quickly came down the steps and opened the coach door first flipping the step down. 'Good Evening ladies' the butler Jeeves will escort you to the pink room 'Good evening to you ladies, may you have a nice night. 'I am Jeeves,' 'Thank you Jeeves I am Manx Nellie, she said, her head high with enough style and pomp for a titled lady.

As they walked into the room they just stood there looking around. Manx Nellie had been in a few similar places before at such parties and knowing how the evening would go. We will get dousters of lover varter the rawnys, how they are riggered, said Manx Nellie (we will get lots of money here tonight look at these ladies) how they are dressed. Lady Florence welcomed them in after Sir John had introduced them, there was four tables, 1 with food on, cold meat, salad, the other with bottles of wine and glasses. Lady Florence looked at Jeeves, 'I would like these 2 footmen gone we can see to ourselves. It's a girl's night tonight. 'Very good my lady. Manx Nellie and old Louisa went first to 1 table then the other being introduced to the lady guests, there was six ladies in all at the 2 tables joined together. Louisa stood still slowly looking around the room, it was in pink and cream the long pink satin curtains touched the floor there was five bay windows. The pelmets over the windows went right around the room in one piece. 'You have a beautiful home Lady Florence , said Louisa, then looking down at the thick Grosvenor Wilton carpet, cream with pink heavily embossed pattern. I'm so glad you like it Louisa we call this the pink room. Louisa smiled as she looked around the room, you could put my home, in this room twice she thought.

Sir John walked over to Lady Florence, I will see you later darling, let me know when you are finished and we will come and join you we will be in the billiards and snooker room. As he walked down the corridor a footman stood at the door, thank you said sir john as the servant opened the door for him.

Manx Nellie looked at her mother-in-law. I hope I'm as good as her when I'm 76 she said to herself looking at Louisa. Manx Nellie had just finished with the first reading, they would do 2 each have a break then continue to complete all the readings. This is a lovely night said Louisa, and when it's finished I'm really looking forward to the food and wine with these ladies. Manx Nellie was slowly looking around she could see they were making a good impression, we will see most of these ladies again I would think, Louisa smiled, yes let's hope so she answered.

CHAPTER SIX– ON TO ABERLINE

"Mister Adam sir" said Charles, pressing on his shoulder for the second time. "Yes what is it?" answered Adam looking around. The rain had stopped a good hour had passed. "You told me to wake you; sandwiches, coffee or tea will be coming round in a few minutes, served in the diner." "Thank you" he answered, then getting up, and walking down the corridor through to the next carriage.

Choosing a table, he then turned around and sat down. Facing the way he was travelling. Pierre and his wife came walking down the corridor. "Hello again" he said smiling. "Well what did you think of Cambridge settlement and the people there?" asked Pierre, as he sat down facing Adam, too forward and over friendly thought Adam. "Well they have come thousands of miles to make a new start, a new life in this vast open country. They've got guts I'll say that for them." "A Dillinger" said Adam, pointing to the pearl handle just showing out of Pierre's waistcoat pocket. "Yes they're a little big one" said Pierre, placing it on the table. "The gambler and would be gentleman's best friend" said Adam with a smile.

Picking it up slowly examining it, "it's a nice one" he said, admiring the engraved nickel plated barrels. "44 caliber 2 shot under and over, it'll have a lot of punch for a short distance 40ft then drop." He cocked the hammer right back in a clumsy sort of couldn't careless way. Pierre quickly moved to one side. "For god sake man, at this range, it would go straight through me." "Is that so" said Adam, letting the hammer slowly go back down, then placing it back on the table.

Pierre quickly picked it up and put it back in his waistcoat pocket. "Coffee and sandwiches, beef or cheddar cheese?" Said Charles, as he moved slowly down the corridor pushing a large trolley full of coffee and tea pots with cups underneath, another attendant pushing a second larger trolley full of sandwiches.

Just then Constance came back and joined them. "Hello Adam" she said, squeezing his hand as she sat down. Adam looked at her bulging bust, short blonde hair with blue eyes, she was full of life. I don't think she would pull your hand away, she'd put it there, he thought. Yes I'd like to spend some time with her, a week he whispered to himself, "what was that?" asked Constance. "Oh nothing" said Adam. "You look lovely darling" said Pierre. "What will you have ma'am?" "A pot of coffee please." "Very good" said Charles. "What time will the evening meal be served?" asked Adam. "It's not sir, it's served on the other train that you change onto, at Charleston."

Constance was slowly rubbing her leg up and down Adam's as she sat facing him. He didn't mind, it was making him feel good. She's the sort of girl you take out, but not home to meet mum and dad he thought. "Are you always as forward as this with strange men?" "Very rare, only with one I really fancy." Pierre was suddenly back again. "I've got you a beef sandwich and tea" she said to Pierre, not bothering to look at him as she spoke. "That's fine" he said, glancing away. Adam didn't like him, but he did feel sorry for him

Pierre noticed Adam looking at his ring. "Do you like it?" he asked, pulling it off his third finger. "Yes it's very nice" said Adam. He was judging the weight of it in his hand. "Its 18 carat solid gold, and that's a 1 and 1/2 carat diamond, it's for sale. I'm financially embarrassed" said Pierre looking down. "A big gambling debt, I might even have to sell my wife's engagement ring as well. If I offer it up towards the debt, they will want to beg it off me. It's worth about 900 dollars. I'll take 750 for it as a quick sale. Please don't take my word for it, there's a well-known jewelers shop in Charleston, the next stop. You can have it valued if you wish."

"Alright" said Adam, "I'll give you 600 dollars for it." "Thank you, thank you very much. That will pay a third of my gambling debt, do you think you might be interested in my wife's engagement ring as well? It's the same size." "Yes I would at the same price." "You're making a good investment Mister Boswell." Adam smiled, "when the train pulls, into Charleston." "Yes" said Pierre eager. "We will get off, but we will catch the train back to Washington, and I'll pick a jeweler in Washington, maybe two jewelers" said Adam looking at the ring on his little finger. "It does look nice on your hand, but that's not necessary, it's all time and trouble back to Washington and then back here again." The big jewelers store in Charleston is very reputable and well known said Pierre, "I don't think so" said Adam. "If I'm going to part with 1200 dollars, that's 300 pounds in English money, I could buy a house for that, I would take no one's word for that sort of money. I'd want it vetted by a jeweler that I chose and I would keep it on my finger."

Adam took the ring off and placed it on the table "your tales good, believable, alright for some farmer or shop keeper. It's not got the weight for that big heavy looking shank. Gold is heavy, in fact it's heavier than lead. That ring will probably be brass, dipped three times, and as regards for the stone, a diamond, un-marked absolutely white, very rare. There's usually a little bit off colour, which looks good in yellow gold, and many stones have a tiny speck of some sort in them, but that's absolutely clear white. A very good, cock up, cost you about 40 dollars apiece, well made, a good flash for a greedy man, I am not greedy, but I am always looking for a good deal and the jeweler friend in Charleston, well he would be the convincer for you wouldn't he, he would receive a nice little slice of the cake each time."

"I resent this. I resent this very strongly Mister Boswell." Adam put up his hands as if to say stop. "I come off a very old fashioned sharp race of people, who has lived off their wits for centuries. I worked with my father and grandfather when I was only 7-8 years old. My old grandfather would find a mark, and my father would serve him. A heavy gold double buckle ring eighteen caret with a half caret diamond in the centre, supposed to be hot stolen from who knows where, which could not be sold in a jewelers window. The mark would be interested being greedy, and he would insist on taking it to a jeweler of his choosing that he knew sometimes even in another town. The jeweler would acid test it, and would be satisfied with it. When my grandfather and father would be coming out of the jewelers shop, I would pull my hand out of my grandfather's hand to rush forward, I would fall off the step on to the pavement, hitting my knee, and I would cry and hold it. They would bend down to pick me up, as they did, my father would switch the ring, all it would take him would be 3 seconds, he was that fast. It would even have the asset tests on it. That had been dipped over so as it still showed gold. I was always taught a greedy man is the one you want. He will fall. He is always a customer."

"My father's name is Nelson. He was named after the great Lord Nelson at the battle of Trafalgar, my grandfather said when he was born Nelson would be a clever man, and my father is a clever man. Quiet and not bragging of what he knows. He always had three or four of them made heavily gold plated, usually a spinell. Half carat stone he would have it in his hand, the real one, it had been tested, he could quite easily ring it parm it from one hand to another as he was speaking without anybody even expecting it. My father and grandfather were masters. You're making a mess of it, as I've said. It's alright for a shop keeper or some greedy farmer. We would look for a mark a customer who thought they were shrewd, it became a little dangerous, a lock up job. They were very good, you could wear it for five or six years, before the heavy gold plate started to wear off, but the stone would go first with every day wear it would go a little cloudy, but if a person kept it for best the chances are they would never know. But you came down too quickly, you should have let me bid you, then haggle, finally selling them.

My family has gone back to horse dealers now. We buy good horses and sell palominos and thoroughbreds."

"I can assure you Mister Boswell I am not." Adam held up his hand. "That silly put on french accent you're using Pierre, you're about as french as my arse, you want to drop it. You just picked the wrong man." "Please leave now, you are insulting my intelligence." Pierre nodded and said nothing, putting the ring back on his finger; he glanced at Adam, then out the window. He felt a fool. How quick this young man had seen through his scam. I bet these people could sort you out with a horse thought Pierre. He could see Adam was now getting annoyed

"Is there a problem gentleman?" asked Charles. "There is no problem Charles. Mister Carrington and his floozy are leaving my table right now. If not I'm going to kick his arse right down that corridor, because he's trying to take me for a fool." "You haven't heard the last of this I say. This is an insult, and I'll lodge a complaint when we get to Charleston." "Mr Carrington?" "Yes what is it?" he said turning to Charles.

"Be very careful how you make any complaints to Charleston Train Office, there has been a complaint lodged about you there." Adam sat back. It's a new one working trains, this America is a fast country. I'll bet two women could get money duckering (palm reading) clients, while the men are casually selling something, straight and simple, no complaints, he thought.

"It was nice knowing you and talking with you about the settlement. I always enjoy learning" said Adam, as he shook hands with Charles. "Something?" said Charles. Adam unfolded the piece of linen cloth between two slices of bread was a big sirloin steak. "Looks good" said Adam putting his hand in his pocket. "No" said Charles, as he held Adam's wrist, "I've enjoyed knowing you." "Thank you', I'll see you again somewhere, take care" said Adam.

"Jesus loves you" shouted Charles. "I hope so" shouted Adam, turning smiling, and looking back a little bewildered as he walked down the platform. It was the end of the line for the New York Flyer. "I'll have a coffee and two of these buttered pancakes please." There were only 4 tables in the crowded little café.

A platform worker sat down at Adam's table. "Thanks" said Adam, as the waitress placed the hot mug of coffee and 2 buttered thin pancakes in front of him. "35 cents sir." Adam placed a quarter and two five cent piece on the table. "You going far fella?" "Glen Parva near Aberline." "Never heard of Glen Parva, heard of Aberline, that's the end of the track Aberline." "It's a hell of a place, a frontier town." "Have you got a gun? A colt?" Adam looked up from his coffee. He was sick of everybody telling him to get a gun, these frontier towns would be exaggerated, he thought. "You think I'm going to walk around a town with a big colt revolver strapped on my hip" like Buffalo Bill out of a Wild West magazine. "Where are you from fella?" "Just come from New York, originally from Perth, Scotland." "Never heard of Perth, i've heard of Scotland." "That'll be Scotland England."

Adam just nodded, "how long for the Lexington train?" The man looked at the clock on the wall, "nearly an hour, Kentucky Rocket, 30 miles an hour, a Stevenson Express from England, got the name of the fastest train in the world. With no carriages, it'll do 40 miles an hour." "That's some speed, however would it stay on the track going around corners at 40 miles an hour?" said Adam looking at the clock.

"Train now standing at platform 2 is the Kentucky Rocket. It's leaving Charleston in 15 minutes, heading for Lexington, Nashville, then Memphis Tennessee, leaves in 15 minutes. Boarding now, boarding now" shouted the guard with a funnel held to his mouth. "Thank you for the hand with the cases." "You're welcome fella, and good luck in Aberline" said the guard.

As Adam looked out of the window, Charleston was nearly gone. He noticed the train had leveled off, reaching its maximum speed. "This thing's got some power." It takes the British craftsman. We are showing the world, he thought, looking out at West Virginia, it's a lovely country like Worcester & Hereford you'd need to live twice to see all this country.

"Tickets please" said the conductor coming down the corridor. Adam held up his two tickets. The conductor punched a star hole in one with a pair of pliers. "Don't lose it sir, if you can't show it at Memphis, you'll have to pay for the last part of the journey again." "Can you spare me two minutes" asked Adam motioning with his hand to the seat. "Of course sir, what is it?" he asked sitting down. "These two cases, I could do with a private lock up. I am tired of babysitting them. I don't mind saying thank you" said Adam, pushing a silver dollar in his hand, taking one of the cases. "That will be no problem at all sir. I'll get them locked up for you. Just follow me."

"Coffee or tea sir?" "I'll take a tea strong." The attendant placed it on the lift up table. Adam unfolded the linen cloth on the table. "It does look good" he said quietly to himself as he cut the steak sandwich in two halfs, with his lock knife. "It sure does mister." Adam turned, the seat across from him was now occupied by a woman of about 40, and a freckled faced youth. "Don't you be so cheeky William." "That's alright ma'am, he's okay." Cutting one half in two he gave it to the youth. "No I can't it's your meal" she said. "That's alright ma'am, you take it, and I've still got half left." "Thank you, that's very nice of you." "Mr?" "Boswell, Adam" he answered. "This is William, and I am Susan."

"The Kentucky Rocket will be pulling into Memphis Tennessee for half an hour, it's straight through, no changing, straight through Memphis Tennessee, Lexington and Nashville and stopping at three settlements over 700 miles in two and a half days and nights", said the attendant. Susan's son, Young William was practicing his fast drawer with his toy colt. 'No young fella, you slap the face of the holster as your hand is coming up, cocking the hammer back.' 'You explain it very well mister for a man who doesn't carry a gun.'

Adam turned, a man of about 40 dressed in Levis, pockets trimmed in buck skin, also an expensive three quarter length tan leather coat he was standing in the passageway. In western boots, the lapel off his coat pulled back just showing his colt 44 peacemaker in a shoulder holster. 'Gosh mister, that's a real one, can I have a look at it?' said William. 'You sure can sonny' he said, as he drew it out of the holster and pressed the safety down. Young William was impressed. 'Thanks Mr 'some call me Tex, because I come from Texas, but my name is really Joe.' The colt 44 in Williams' hand seemed to look so big and heavy how he was handling it. 'Don't touch anything William' said Adam. 'I'm going to be a gun fighter, like my Pa was' he said, trying to twirl the big heavy colt around. It fell out of his hand, hit the floor and went off. The sound inside of the carriage was deafening. The bullet went straight through the side of the carriage wall.

Everybody went down for cover, a woman started screaming. 'It's okay folks, it's okay, and just a little horse play' said Tex loudly. Adam had picked up the pistol. Two of the guards came rushing in, each one carrying a rifle. They came straight over to Adam who was still holding the colt. 'What the hell do you think you're doing mister, letting off a gun in a railway carriage?' 'This man gave it to the boy to look at.' Tex had suddenly lost the cowboy act and looked down embarrassed. Adam pushed the safety catch back on, weighing it in his hand giving it two fast backward twirls, then two forward, then pushing it in the man's belt. 'You're fast mister ' said William.

The Kentucky Rocket was now crossing at its maximum speed through West Virginia. It's been lovely country that Kentucky, 'the grass I don't know, it seemed to look a sort of a blue green' said Adam to Tex, as they stood on the outside platform at the end of the carriage. 'My name's Adams Boswell.' 'No hard feelings fella about the gun, I am Joe Steve Junior, a lot of my friends call me Tex because I was born and raised in Texas.' I should have known better. 'So what's the

Junior?' asked Adam. 'My father was a well-known man for horse breeding and hunting and my mother for her cooking. So I had to use Junior for a lot of years, but some started to call me Tex

'Yes Kentucky is sometimes called the blue grass country, and they say the best horses in America are now coming from Kentucky, they got a lot of their breeding stock from Ireland' said Tex. 'Tennessee by the way is moonshine country, many small oldens with whisky stills, is that right?' said Adam. 'You've got it fella' said Tex as they got off the train to stretch their legs.

'Jackson and Brownsville Settlements' shouted an attendant. 'Stopping for water, logs and coal. We will be about an hour. Adam took out a cigar, then offering one to Tex. There was a white board nailed to one of the telegraph poles, pointing straight ahead. It said Memphis 80 miles.

Tex was looking Adam over. You say you come from New York, is that right?' 'No, I said I was travelling from New York.' 'That's what I just said' answered Tex. 'I'm really from Scotland.' 'Is that Scotland England?' 'That's right' said Adam, drawing deeply on the thin cigar. 'How far you going fella?' 'Glen Parva, I suppose you've never heard of it' said Adam. 'Yes I have, it's a new small frontier town, and it's doing well, and getting bigger. That's where I'm going. I work there off and on.' 'And what do you do, if you don't mind me asking?' 'No I don't, these cigars are good, they're mild and a little sweet, I hire out my gun, mostly to the saloons overlooking the gambling tables moving the drunken losers from the bar. I sometimes ride shot gun guard on the stage coaches as well.' 'If trouble starts you're in the middle of it, it must be dangerous' said Adam. 'Not always.' I wear a badge.' Going into his waistcoat pocket, he put the badge in Adam's hand.

'It looks nothing like a law man's star' said Adam, looking at the silver egg shaped badge with small letters 'contract lawman' in gold plate across the centre. He then turned it over, license number 5 'Joe Steve Texas'. 'Nice badge' said Adam giving it back, as I was saying it must be a dangerous job, said Adam.

They know you're good, or you wouldn't be doing the job.' 'And are you good?' asked Adam. 'You trying me out fella?' a slight aggression in Tex's voice. 'No I'm asking you a straight question Tex.' 'Well I can more than handle myself in a fight. I am good with a six gun. Got a little wife called Cheryl, and 2 boys, they sometimes worry me a little. I've put two in Boot Hill in Aberline, and one in Glen Parva and 1 in Washington. I don't work away unless it suits me. There's no hard work to it and the pay is good. I've got my own room in the last chance saloon with all meals. It's mostly nights I work, 20 dollars a day or a night, whatever you want to call it, and all found but it's mostly nights, and 20 dollars a day whenever I ride shot gun guard. 'That's a good job all in, it's got to be 70 - 80 dollars a week, and all found as well, you could save plenty every month and no hard work' said Adam drawing deeply on the cigar.

'I wouldn't want to be a target for a drunk with a gun or a loser with a knife every week' thought Adam. He gave Tex a quick glance. He was slightly red cheeked, long brown hair, broad built about 6 ft 4, big hands. He looks to be a rough handful, got plenty of nerve I would imagine, and seemed straight forward thought Adam.

Does your wife like it living in a saloon? No, I have a place 2 miles out of town, a house and forty acres, I breed horses and I only sleep in town at the weekends.

'So now you know all about me, what about you Mister Boswell?' Adam smiled, I know a good horse when I see one, and deal in the same. I like a gamble, I'll nearly bet on anything, and I'll nearly buy anything and sell it again, if it's at the right money. I'll avoid a fight, but if it comes I won't walk away. I can use a gun, but I'm not a gun fighter, and I'm a friend if you need one.' Adam put out his hand. 'You don't lead a false trail, I can't have too many friends' said Tex, shaking hands. He sensed something about Adam, and felt he could be a good friend.

'You know you've got a slight Glasgow accent' said Adam. 'Is that so, I suppose that's because my Ma and Pa was from there, but I was born here in Texas, near Amarillo, my folks had a ranch there till the common charros wiped us out. My brother, matt and me re-built the ranch, but I'd had enough and I wanted out. It's a lonely life on a ranch 26 miles out on a prairie, getting in to town for supplies, maybe once every three weeks'

'So what's a common Charro?' asked Adam. 'A murdering low life treble mixed breed, Comanche apache mixed, and the other part is Mexican, more cunning and sly than a pack of coyotes and deadlier than a sack of rattlesnakes, that's a common charo, looted and burnt our home to the ground, raped and killed my mother and pa. Me and my brother Matt were away two days branding cattle, when we got back, that's what we found.

'I'm sorry to hear that, it must make you very bitter' said Adam.' 'Bitter? If one of them looks at me the wrong way, he's dead meat.' 'So how do these mixed warriors look?' I like how you speak posh, you're English aren't you, Adam just smiled not answering. 'Well they're different, not all Indian got high cheek bones, not quite red like an Indian, and not really as tanned as a Mex, slim looking, fit like the apache. The Mex side, big white teeth, black hair, like the Mex, they like a knife, and then there's their language, nearly impossible to understand. They mix it all up, bit of both, Indian, then some Mex and little English, all in and out of each other. Some Indians don't even know what they're saying, you fight one, he goes down, don't turn your back and walk away, he'll crawl after you with a knife, a rock, a piece of wood, anything, they would like to cut the throat of every white man, woman and child that's within fifty miles of where they live, that's what they are. But there's plenty of law now and a fort sixty miles passed Glen Parva, a sheriff and two deputies in most towns these days'

'Well is there any Common Charros around Glen Parva?' 'Oh they're in and out, passing through, always come in three, four, fives, never see one on his own. A lot of people class them as Mexicans, most shop keepers and saloons will accept them as Mexican. They're good spenders. The Sheriff knows them for what they are and leaves them be unless there's trouble.'

Adam just nodded and never passed any comment, he could see Tex really hated these people and he understood why. 'So my accents slightly Glasgow you say? I've been told that once or twice. You speak good English; you don't have much of an accent though. Adam never answered; British real gypsies don't seem to have an accent.

The first whistle went, 'The train leaves in 20 minutes' shouted the Conductor, then repeated it. He walked over to a fat man with a bowler hat and a coat that was two sizes too small. 'Sir we are not running a wholesale whiskey train, if you pay for that barrel you'll have to leave it at Memphis. If you want two bottles in a bag that's okay, one bag, no barrels, Revenue Men at Memphis will take the barrel off you.'

'It must be good Tex how the people are buying it.' 'As you know real whiskey comes from Scotland by the time it gets here, it's very dear, but this Moonshine, you could say it's sort of an homemade whiskey, Kentucky Pure Mountain Spring Water, some call it a Tennessee Bourbon. 'Come on' said Tex, jumping down off the train. 'I want a few bottles to take with me, how about you?' 'No thanks I don't drink a lot of spirits, a beer now and then does me.'

There was a long table with three rows of square bottles with two men standing behind it. The bottles had no labels on. Also a pile of small cloth bags. 'Is it still 4 dollars a bag?'. 'It sure is Mr, one bag 2 bottles, 4 dollars, do you want me to get a bag for you?' 'That's a swell idea Adam, you carry it' said Tex giving the man a 10 dollar bill pocketing his change.

Adam and Tex stood watching the man tapping the big wheels with a hammer. 'Got it. It's the second one back.' They followed the attendant. 'Is it bad?' 'Bad enough, loose bearing, you won't make Fort Worth, it'll need a new bearing, good job you're only eighty miles from Memphis.' Tex looked at the attendant. 'How long we going to be in Memphis?' 'it's hard to say, I know they keep small stuff like bearings if the wheels not buckled, they can do it in one day. If it's buckled, it would have to come out from Winchester train yards near Lexington. Times it's all done and balanced, could be three days.' 'Is there another train going down to Fort Worth?' 'No, only two a week and it went two days ago.' 'So when will we now?' 'No more questions gents, this train will be running late. Could be over an hour late.' 'All aboard, all aboard, train leaving' he shouted, giving the engine driver a nod.

Sitting back in the seat, Adam reached in to one of the bags, looks pale in colour, he said unscrewing the top, and doesn't smell too strong. 'Have a taste, see what you think' said Tex. Adam took half a mouthful, swilled it around slowly in his mouth, and then let half of it go down. Three seconds later, he let the other half go down. 'Well?' said Tex. 'You know, genuine good malt over here it's three times that price, and it doesn't taste a lot better. It's a little like a pure malt, mild smooth, not a lot of fire, but this is slightly sweet, and after a while you can taste the fire down in your belly, it slowly gets hot. It would be nice with some orange juice in it. That's how my grandfather drinks his malt whiskey.' 'I'll have to try that, have some more.' 'No thanks ' said Adam, giving him the bottle.

Tex had two mouthfuls, and then put the bottle back in the bag. He leaned back in the deep cushion seats. 'You must have something really special cooking in Glen Parva to come all the way from New York, man it's gotta be over two thousand miles to Aberline, then the stage coach to Glen Parva.' Adam thought for a few seconds, he was just going to answer then the attendant was standing there 'Coffee or tea, ham or beef sandwiches.' 'I'll have a pot of coffee, cream if you've got it and a ham sandwich with mustard.' 'Make that twice, but forget the cream' said Tex. 'We have no cream sir, only milk.' The attendant reached up to the rack above Tex's head and bought down a fold up small table. 'That will be a dollar 25 cents.' Tex placed 2 dollars on the table then put the change in his pocket. 'Cheers' said Adam pouring himself a coffee. Tex smiled 'what's cheers?' 'Bottoms up, all the best' answered Adam. 'Oh well then cheers' said Tex with a smile.

Adam now had more time to answer Tex, it would soon spread round the small town once John Parva and his wife had told them of their meeting with Adam and his family at the New York Wild West Circus, they would be back home tomorrow. Over the last twenty minutes or so he had told Tex a lot of his previous life, and just a little of the Wild West Circus 'you've seen so much, man I'd love to have travelled like that, seen other countries' said Tex.

'So you're curious, why I come so far to a little place like Glen Parva that isn't even really on the map yet.' Tex nodded. 'It's in my blood like I told you Tex what I am. I was reared, brought up to travel a nomad life. I just did not want to live, spend the rest of my life with the circus until I became an old man. John Parva told me of Glen Parva, what it was like, new, how it was growing, lots of chances for a young man, and as he said to me, two weeks and you're there, well maybe, and there's another four days, don't forget the stage coach, nearer to three weeks' said Tex.

John said its wide open, 2 silver mines, cattle ranches, plenty of money, and still a small town, I want to make my mark there, I've done a lot of gambling and I've done a lot with horses, so I'm going to give it a whirl. 'You do that fella, there's plenty of chances for a young man in Texas. If it doesn't turn out, you can always try somewhere else. This country is so big, you would need 3 lifetimes to see it all answered Tex.'

'You know Adam you must be really good with a six gun to challenge the best wherever you went.' 'Good enough' said Adam. 'Oh ho, who's boasting now' said Tex. 'Well Americans aren't too modest are you, and when in Rome, do what the Romans do.' 'Trains travelling more slower' said Adam, looking out the window. 'It's because of the busted wheel' said Tex.

'When we get to Glen Parva, maybe, we can have a competition, say fifty dollars a side' said Tex smiling, thinking a bet like that would dent his ego. 'Let's make it interesting, a hundred dollars.' 'You're on Adam, a shoot off for a hundred dollars. You know out here, we don't go to some shooting club once a week, were bought up with a gun, a 22 rifle for shooting game and then it gets to a thirty/thirty Winchester. At eighteen you're packing a colt 44 and you're starting to get good with it. There's some good guns at Glen Parva, we could get big money in the pot, arrange a shoot off.

'I know what you mean, and I am game' said Adam. At fourteen I didn't need a rifle, I was killing game with a 32 revolver' answered Adam.

'You seem to know about guns for a dude, a competition with big money in the pot might just liven the little town up a bit' said Adam. 'Oh you'll find Glen Parva lively enough' answered Tex with a mischievous smile.

CHAPTER SEVEN - MEMPHIS TENNESSEE

The crippled engine came to a stop as it pulled into Memphis-Tennessee.

'Those who want to leave the train to go into Memphis; it will be here all night. Please feel free to come and go to your sleepers, the guards will stay with the train' shouted the Attendant.

Adam waved him over. 'I am an attorney at law Adam Boswell, and this is my bodyguard.' Tex went along with him pulling back his coat showing his badge and gun. 'And what can I do for you Mister Boswell?' 'I am handling important land documents and I would like to see Memphis, maybe stay the night.' 'Yes I understand Sir.'

'To put these papers in my case, in the locked cage with our bags.' The attendant turned the key twice of the heavy padlock. 'I take it you have two keys?' 'Yes sir, one for you and one for me,'

Adam pushed two silver dollars in his hand. 'I'll take them and give them both back to you.'

'Nice move, now we don't have to worry about getting robbed' said Tex, walking over to a horse and cab. 'Let's walk' said Adam, 'it's a downhill walk and a nice view' as he looked out at the Wolf River in the distance, 'and it's flood free location above the Mississippi.'

'I've never been on one of those' said Adam, pointing to the two Mississippi paddle boats. 'I'll take you on that big one, it's full of entertainment, gambling, bar restaurant and Creole girls, the other ones for hauling goods.'

'So what's a Creole -girl?' 'They're about a quarter coloured and half French, tanned flashing eyes, have slight French accent, just takes your breath away.' 'Sounds good to me, let's go there' answered Adam. 'You know Tex; I've never seen so many black people before.' 'Must be one in five or six, they're free now, can just about go where they please' said Tex.

'That's how it should be, we all bleed red when were cut, were all human. Tell me about the river boats.' 'The bottom stores goods, slaves, and animals. Second deck is all private cabins. Third is restaurant bar lounge and casino. Top outside deck usually piled high with cotton.'

'Sounds okay, a lot of French accents here' said Adam, as they passed people on the street.

'That's right, even the kids speak with the accent, and they class themselves as French American. They use it as much as English.'

'I thought the British owned Memphis and New Orleans?' 'That was a long, long time ago. The French took it back for a while, then lost it, now it's all America.' 'These Memphis people must be mixed up with it all' said Adam. 'That's a good way in putting it. This countries so big everybody wanted a piece of it' answered Tex.

'These outside tables and chairs with the big verandas sun shades over the shops it's a lot like Paris.'

'No kidding, fancy a beer?' 'Why not' said Adam, following him in to the bar. Two Deputies' came in looking all around, then walking over to Tex and Adam. 'I see you're wearing a gun fella, it's not allowed anywhere in town limits. If you give it to him I'll give you a receipt and you can pick it up when you're leaving town', the other had several gun belts thrown over his shoulder.

Tex held his coat open showing the law badge, 'I am not carrying a gun' said Adam holding his coat open wide.

'You speak like you're from England.' 'No Scotland.' 'Well it's all the one I suppose, evening you all.'

'I had difficulty understanding him.' 'Yes he has a strong southern drawl, from down the other side of the Masan Dixon Line.' Adam never replied. He wasn't really sure what Tex was on about.

'Unusual name Memphis.' 'I believe it's named after some ancient Egyptian city on the Nile River' answered Tex, feeling very educated. 'You like to know.' 'That's right, my father used to always say watch, listen and learn.'

There was a group playing quite loud in the far corner, two guitars, a clarinet, a piano, except for the drummer, they was black or half-cast.

'I never have heard music like that before, it's just great' said Adam. 'Some call it New Orleans and country, others jazz; you'll only hear it round Memphis New Orleans Dixie Land' said Tex. 'Bit of a mixture, like everything else round here I suppose.' Adam could have bit his tongue. 'Well now we can't all be English gentleman can we' answered Tex.

No offence meant Tex, none taken.

Adam started clapping in time to the music. 'There seems to be no music sheets, each one does his own thing' he said.

Suddenly there was shouting. 'You've marked the corners off the cards with your nail. It's a big pot and I am not sitting quiet for it.' 'Listen nigger, you're not even supposed to be in here.' 'Games over, I am the winner.' 'Get out'. The half-cast pulled a big hunting knife. There were two cracks from the small 32 caliber. The gambler stood there smoking, revolver in his hand.

The Deputies was by the batwing doors, turned quickly walking back over one with a gun in his hand. 'I'll take that gun right now.' 'He pulled that big hunting knife on me, I had to shoot him.' The Deputy turned the man over. One bullet has missed; the other had hit him just above his left eyebrow. 'Your under arrest, it's the jail for you.' 'He challenged me with that big hunting knife.' 'Listen fella, there's no law in what size knife you carry, but law says no guns.' The Deputy turned both hands over. He had three queens and two ten's. 'You had two aces and these cards are marked at the side.' 'Are you accusing me?' 'You listen, that man had no gun and the winning hand, you've shot him dead.' 'Look closer, he's a nigger, shouldn't even be in here.' 'I am an upright citizen of this town, you jail me and there'll be uproar in this town.'

'I'll go good for his bail or bound. I know him we'll. I am the owner of this Saloon as you both we'll know. That half cast shouldn't have been in here.' 'Okay, name, address, and don't leave town. They'll be a court hearing about this. These blacks have now got rights, don't leave town.' 'What about that money, it's a big pot; there was only the two of us left in?' 'I'll see his family gets it' said the other Deputy stuffing it in his pocket.

'They'll never see it.' Said Tex. 'Probably manslaughter - seven to eight years' said Adam. 'No trial, a quick hearing, and let off with self-defense, could be a big fine.' said Tex.

'Where's the justice?' said Adam.

'There is none for them yet, they've only just stopped being slaves. It's the British and French that's brought most of them by the boat load here as slaves a hundred years ago, they're now called African-Americans.'

Adam felt embarrassed for where he came from. 'Think straight Adam, and keep your voice down, more than half the wealth of this town, state of Tennessee and Alabama has come from slave sales and labour.' 'Let's change the conversation, it's not healthy. This is what started the war.'

'Another drink?' said Adam. 'Yes I'll have a beer with a whiskey chaser.' 'Scotch steel.'

Four men picked the body up carrying it out.

They stood on the sidewalk smoking. 'You want to see a dog fight?' 'I've seen a few, some countries just let them fight to the death, don't really like it, but I'll go along' answered Adam. 'It's a bit early; steam boat doesn't really get going till about 11.'

Tex waved to the cabby across the street. He brought the horse and carriage around in a half circle. 'Where to gents?' 'Fills dog fights' said Tex. 'So how's things in Memphis these days?' asked Tex. 'It could be a lot better, cottons gone high, slaves now get paid cash' answered the Cabby. 'That's grown since I was here two years ago' said Tex, pointing to the sign Village Africa. 'I hope you're not taking us in there.' 'No, that's where most of the slave families these days live in those shacks. Farmers and businesses employ them as they need them, and a lot of them have left to who knows where.'

The carriage turned off the main road going down a dirt road, straight in front was a farmhouse with two buildings. There were quite a few carriages and traps scattered and horses tied, men were walking, exercising their dogs. 'There's usually three fights' said Tex. There were five or six big flat carts with dogs in pens. 'They're for sale' said Tex, as they walked over to the smallest building that had a serving hatch. 'Mines a beer' said Adam. 'I'll have the same with a whiskey ' said Tex. 'Cheers' said Adam. 'Cheers' answered Tex, not sure what he meant.

A big man in a leather jacket and trousers, a pair of studded gloves that was tucked in his gun belt. 'Good evening Gents to you all, I am Fiell-Anderson. For those that do not know me, and my brother Ted. All are welcome; we have a dog fight here twice a week, its five dollars to enter the building. If your dog wins, we want 10% of the purse, and ten dollars for dog entry. If you seal a dog it's 10% commission to use. Anyone trying to welsh or doping a dog will be barred for good, thank you. Have a nice night.'

There were some very mean looking men. Three half breed Indians and two half black young men back woods men and quite a few towns' men. 'Must be a hundred in here' said Tex. 'Glad I left my money belt locked up' said Adam under his breath.

'What's that you said?' asked Tex. 'Nothing, just thinking out loud.'

Adam looked around the barn; it was kept especially for dog fighting. In the centre was a pit about 4ft deep by 20ft across. The ground went steeply up all around right back to the sides of the barn. There was a thin metal rail standing about 4ft off the ground. Bolted to six steel bars sank in the ground, the rail went right around the pit.

'This is one of the best organised dog fights I've been to, and I've been to quite a few countries.'

'Thank you sir, your English yes?' 'That's right; I am Adam Boswell from Perth and New York.' 'I am Fiell-Anderson and this is my brother Ted. My mother was English from Bath.' 'I know it well about fifteen miles from Bristol, a lovely roman city.' 'So I have heard and seen photos of it. I would like you and your friend to come up to the house tomorrow to have dinner with us, meet the family.' 'We were going to' said Adam. 'I insist you will have dinner with us, tell us about Bath, England, make way there, I say' said Fiell, pushing his way through. The row of seats bolted in the ground close to the pit rail went right around. Each one had reserved painted in white on the backs. 'You sit here, you are my guests. Have a nice nights sport.' 'Thank you' said Adam. The brothers both shook hands with Adam and Tex.

'You do have a way of getting known, you ought to take up politics' said Tex. 'Who knows' answered Adam. 'We've got the best place in the building' said Tex.

'The first fight tonight gents, Tennessee Bills - Staffordshire Bull Terrier, The Penkridge Lad, against half Doberman pincer, half German Alsatian, the Berlin Warrior. You have fifteen minutes to get your bets on.'

The Doberman Alsatian was the first in the pit. It looked an ugly big black and tan mean animal. The owner held it muzzled over the far side. 'The rules gents, the first dog to coward down and whimper, or run, loses. It is not a fight to the death.'

There were some cheers and laughs as the Staffy was brought in, it was short, very broad and muzzled. It stood in the opposite corner, sandy coloured with a white chest and feet. Short little legs with a square head as big as a shovel. He looked quite happy wagging his tail as his owner was patting him.

'I am having twenty dollars on the big German' said Tex. 'You could be making a mistake, I've seen these Staffordshire's before, they can fight.' 'On the Staffy' said Adam, holding out a twenty dollar bill to one of the runners for the bookies office in the far corner.

'Got you' said the man, giving Adam a red ticket with twenty dollars stamped on it. Adam turned it over. Memphis A B C Gamblers. Taking off the muzzles, the two dogs were brought up to the scratch line. Each man had a seat on opposite sides of the pit.

'Get the job done Penkridge' shouted one of his fans. The Staffys head turned a little on the mention of his name. 'Rip his haggly big head off' shouted Alan Merger, the owner of the German dog. Tennessee Bill stood up. 'Hey you, a private side bet one hundred dollars.' 'You're on' shouted the owner of the German dog as he climbed out of the pit. All of a sudden the building was silent. The big German dog snarling, slowly circling, ready to pounce. The Staffy would go three or four paces to left then to the right like a boxer waiting for an opening. Both dogs jumped nearly at the same time. They seemed to clash, teeth snapping, they both hit the ground, the German dog on top, snapping again and gnashing his teeth, torn the Staffys ear. It was completely split, which now matched his other ear. His beady little eyes set so far back, seemed to be going from side to side, his head was very bloody. They went to it again and again for the third time the big German dog was on hurt or damaged. He'd put several holes in the Staffys long snout. If it had been a point's fight, he'd have been a mile ahead.

'Take your time Penkridge, you'll get him' shouted his owner. The dog turned, his head for a second in quick acknowledgement to his Master. He could barely hear him above all the shouting. It was the fourth time the German dog came in, this time for the kill. He looked very confident. The Staffy went underneath, his big mouth opened wide then snapped shut around the other dogs front leg. His jaws were locked. There was a snap that only the two dogs heard.

'Look at the strength of that little dog' said Tex. 'He's not so little, he's heavier built than the tall one' said Adam. The Staffy was now shaking the big German dog like a rag doll by the broken front leg. He let go and the other dog hit the wall. The Staffy was on it, his teeth around the other dog's throat.

Fiell and his brother Ted was in the pit. With a thin bar of iron forcing the Staffys mouth open. The two dog owners were now in the pit.

'Be careful with that bar, I don't want his teeth broke' said Tennessee Bill, pocketing his one hundred dollars side bet.

They had the other dog on the lead, then hobbling out on three legs.

'The winner by a full attack, the Penkridge Lad.' Tennessee Bill put the lead on his dog, parading it round the pit being cheered. He bent down patting the Staffy, he was wagging his tail. 'He seemed to enjoy it' said Tex. 'Yes, great dogs, born to fight' answered Adam.

'How long?' asked Tex, '18 minutes' said Adam, pocketing his watch. 'Long fight' said Tex. There was an interval for fifteen-twenty minutes, letting the men get a drink and bets on the next fight. The owners stood in the pit talking with their dogs muzzled. The back woods man had a wolf. The towns man a big ugly half breed Doberman crossed with who knows what. Fiell walked round the circle shouting 'an unusual fight gentleman'. The second bought Monten Man Irish Doffys Wolf Shamrock, a none fighter against John Seers, the town gents Mississippi Warrior (Doberman Rottweiler).

'This is not a fight to the death. The first dog to whimper back off, turning tale to run loses the fight. Out of the pit please gents.'

The wolf, a pure breed, looking animal, a silky thick coat of silver and black. Looking thin and fit, about the size of an Alsatian dog until he snarled. His fangs looked over sized to the rest of him.

The cross breed Doberman Rottweiler was big and bulky, maybe two stone heavier and four inches higher at the shoulder with a head the size of a big shovel, a massive ugly thing that looked like it had come out the machine the wrong way. He looked at the wolf with no hesitation. Gladiator was a good name for him

The wolf seemed a little timid, trotting from one side of the pit to the other. His head turned all the time towards his master. The big German Rottweiler seemed to bound across the pit. His head seemed to zig zag slightly and the first meet he had the wolf. But his mouth was not big like his Doberman mother. His massive head was like his father the Rottweiler, smallish mouth with stompy teeth that sank into the wolfs shoulders, the thick shaggy coat was too thick. The wolf let out a low little scream. That quickly stopped. The blood matted in the wolfs thick coat, but the thick stompy like teeth of the Rottweiler did not penetrate the thick furry coat deep enough for a kill. He had the wolf down. There was a lot of blood. 'Roll, roll' shouted his master.

Many masters of fighting dogs would teach and learn his prized animal tricks and moves like a circus man would teach his animals.

The wolf was in pain but he obeyed. As he rolled, the Rottweiler rolled also. The wolfs jaws was now right underneath of the Dobermans head. His long fangs went deep into to the soft throat and neck of his opponent. 'Don't let go, you've got him, bite and pull' shouted his master.

The big Doberman could not back off. He screamed like a hare that had been snapped by a greyhound, his legs were kicking fast backwards and forwards.

Fiell shouted over to the owner 'do you want me to stop it? He's losing a lot of blood.'

The two owners was now in the pit with Fiell, and his brother Ted all over the far side. 'No let it fight on, it might get free, I've got good money riding on it.' Fiell looked disgusted with him; there was a couple of boos.

'Let him go' shouted the wolfs owner. The Wolf released its grip and backed off; his head went from side to side. He then slowly walked forward, he was the master. He was now the victor of the big Rottweiler's challenge, and he was going in for the kill.

The Rottweiler started to whimper, and turned showing fear of death. 'Get a leash on your wolf now Doffy' called Fiell. It came over to him and stood by his side like an Alsatian dog would. It was a wild champion. The back woods man put his arms around its neck. He was proud of him.

'That's not sport that's slaughter. You could have stopped it when I asked. The dogs now done for, dying' said Fiell, to the owner. 'I trained and fed that useless piece of shit for six months, and I've lost a handful of money in it.' He looked down, it lay there bleeding, it's neck half out.

He took two kicks at it. There was several boo's. 'Do what you want with it' he said. Fiell walked over, drew his revolver and fired once behind the dog's ear. 'Don't you ever come here again, not even as a spectator, now get out' said Fiell holding up his hands. 'The winner, by an outright attack shamrock the wolf' shouted Fiell.

'What a fight it would be the Staffy Penkridge, and the wolf' shouted several men. 'Yes it would' shouted Fiell, knowing it would be a packed meeting for his place. 'But that's up to the owners' shouted Fiell encouraging the future fight. 'In three weeks we'll fight the wolf, my Staffy needs a rest' shouted Tennessee Bill.

'We accept that challenge with a one hundred dollar private bet on top of the purse' shouted the mountain man. 'I'm not missing it' said one man, 'I'll be here too' said his friend.

Fiell held up his hands walking around the pit. 'So we have a top of the bill big fight in three weeks, and now for the main event of the night: Unbeaten five times champion Ben.' 'Who challenges any dog from anywhere?'

Ben was as big as a full grown lion, taking two men all their time to hold him on a long chain, 'whatever kind of dog is it' said Tex to Fiell. It had a deep growl. It stood the height of a Great Dane, but half the weight again. It was dark brown with white blaze, and a head the size of a young cow. It was a powerful animal, most have weighed well over twenty stone. 'We'll fight any dog and give two to one on the money. Four hundred dollars to two hundred' shouted Fiell. There were no takers; no one wanted to risk their dog against Ben.

Fiell walked over to the owner. 'He's too well known, you're going to have to take him a long way away and change his name.' 'What is it? Asked Adam leaning over the rail. 'You won't see another like him' said Byow-Johnny, the owner. His father is a french Bordeaux and South African ridgeback. His mother a bullmastiff.' Tex looked at Adam. 'If that attacked you, you'd never stop it with a hunting knife. You'd need a gun' said Adam. 'Any takers, any takers, come on gents' shouted Fiell. Four or five minutes passed, 'okay we'll have two reserves in.' Everyone moaned and grumbled.

'I say old chap, you've got a challenger' shouted the old English sea captain, walking down through the crowd. He had a very heavily built bulldog under his arm. 'You've got to be kidding me' shouted Ben's owner, Byow-Johnny.

'I kid you not sir, this is an English bulldog. Some of the men pushed through to look at it. Very few had seen one in the flesh. He's carrying it under his arm said one man. 'Ben will kill that the first meeting.' 'You're on' said Ben's owner. 'Now hold on, that big brute is twice the weight, and size two to one is not enough.'

'I've got two hundred dollars and I am wanting five hundred to my two hundred. Private on top of the piers. Ben's owner looked at his friend, who nodded. They counted up the five hundred giving it to Fiell and the captain did the same.

'And what's the fight going to be, what rules? Asked Fiell. 'To the death' said Byow-Johnny. 'So be it, to the death' said the English sea captain. 'And what's his name?' asked Fiell. 'He's called Dassy Boy.' 'Not much of a name for a gladiator' said Byow-Johnny.

'Listen up gents, we all know Ben and he's a champion. The English bulldog, we have never seen his like before. A gladiator called Dassy Boy. No rules, it's a fight to the death.' There were some laughs as the captain put his dog down holding him on a slip lead. He was sniffing and grunting.

'What do you make of it? Looks more like a fat pet' said Tex. 'I just don't know. He's built like a bull, supposed to be a great fighter, but that other dog he'd fight a lion. They're giving to two to one on Ben to win, it'll be a long fight, or over very quick.' 'You betting?' asked Tex. 'Yes I'll have twenty on Ben' said Adam. Seeing the other dog, Ben was going wild. He'd had a lot of fights and he knew what he was in the pit for. Seeing the size of the bulldog he was very confident.

'What do you think of it, I've never seen one before' said Byow-Johnny. 'Neither have I' said Fiell.

The captain slipped the lead. The bulldog just stood there. 'Take your time Dassy Boy, let him come, good boy' he patted the bulldog, who sniffed, grunted, then farted. You could have heard a whisper. 'Steady now Ben' said his owner, arms around his neck while the handlers slipped the chain over his head. Both owners were now out the pit. 'Go for it Ben', he came across the pit like a train. The bulldog just stood his ground and stepped to one side, as Ben went head first into the earth wall.

Dassy-Boy just sniffed and trotted to the far side off the pit, moving to left and then the right as the Staffy had done. Ben had tried this three times and he was now very wild. Dassy Boy just stood there snorting when's he gonna fight shouted Byow Johnny.

Big heavy Ben was now a little out of breath as he came in for the fourth time. Dassy Boy short little buckled front legs dropped. As Ben went over the top off him. Dassy Boys teeth sank deep into Bens belly and looked as Ben was jumping high trying to get him off but the bulldogs jaws was locked. He was small but very heavy and Ben could not get him off, as they hit the ground Dassy Boy rolled and rolled. Ben had to go with him then they separated. Ben was holling as Dassy Boy just spat the lump of flesh out.

No one was cheering or shouting. Everyone was just watching. They all know it was not over. Ben was hurt and out of breath, but a champion. Dassy Boy stepped to one side. He snapped and locked around Bens tail, as he was cowering at it, Ben came round in an half circle as he did Dassy Boy looked harder snapping Ben's tail. Ben was bleeding bad, as his teeth sank into the back of Dassy Boys neck, and he started to shake him. But he was a very heavy little dog. 'You've got him now Ben, bite, bite to your hardest.' He'd have killed most dogs, but Dassy Boys neck was thick rolls and layers of fat, and thick muscle. Ben's teeth could not go in far enough for a kill. There was blood coming out of Dassy Boys neck both sides.

But he just stood there letting Ben bite. He then started to roll. Ben would not let loose, so he had to roll with him. They hit the earth wall, Dassy Boys stompy little front feet started to scratch and dig forward. It looked like he was finished. 'You've got him, he's dying' shouted Byow Johnny.

But Bens face, his nose and eyes was going further into the earth wall. He was having difficulty in breathing. His mouth was full and his nose was pushed in to the earth wall. His eye was blind with dirt. Both dogs' front legs was now kicking. Ben had to let go, as he did Dassy Boy went underneath, his jaws opened wide round Bens throat, then they locked. After four minutes Ben's confidence and champion ability was gone. His eyes was staring from side to side quickly. As Dassy Boy was ripping and pulling. The blood was pumping out of Ben's neck, and he was letting out a muffled whimper. It was fear of death.

'Stop the fight, stop it now, he's killing Ben. He's killing him' 'Can't do that Johnny, you wanted it to the death.' Johnny looked at the old sea captain. 'It will cost you another one hundred my boy for me to call it off, you wanted to the death. You'd better talk fast alright' Johnny answered 'alright I'll pay.'

Fiell went over with the iron bar, 'that won't be necessary' said the captain. Dassy Boy it's me, come on old boy, let go now, it's captain.' He patted him on the head. 'It's captain.' Hearing his master's voice he released his grip and stepped back. Captain put the slip lead on him, the champion Ben was now over the far side. He turned, Dassy sniffed and took a step forward. Ben whimpered with fear and turned quickly. 'He's finished Johnny, what will you do with him?' asked Fiell. 'I'll keep him for stud' said Byow Johnny. The captain proudly paraded

Dassy Boy around the pit to cheers and clapping. 'How long?' asked Tex. 'Twenty minutes' answered Adam. 'Best dog fight i've seen.' There were others saying the same. 'He's a true gladiator that bulldog, first one I've seen fight' said Tex.

Just then the owner of the Staffy Penkridge lad climbed down into the pit. 'I am Tennessee Bill' he said, reaching out his right hand. 'Yes the master of the game Staffy' said captain shaking hands.

'Penkridge's sisters three years old just in to season, last week, would you put your bulldog to her for me?' 'I'll pay.' 'Of course you will and what champions the pops would be you see Tennessee Bill. 'These massive big mix breed dogs that you's are breeding are really attack dogs, and strong to guard. They don't have the fighting qualities, they are not professional fighting dogs. Now what you are wanting to breed British bulldogs with Staffordshire bull. Both are top fighting dogs, the pups, they will be the best of the best. I want the pick of the litter and one hundred dollars.'

'It's a deal, I'll pay you now.' 'No tomorrow is alright' 'Pick me up at my ship tomorrow twelve o'clock, it's the big one SS Great Britain.'

'Another beer before we go' said Tex, offering Adam a cigar. They both stood there looking around enjoying the smoke when Fiell walked over.

'Well gents did you enjoy it, they're usually very gory. But I did enjoy your fights, very fair, except for the Doberman Great Dane, that you had to shoot. Yes there's always a bad apple in every barrel were all after money but we love our dogs, enjoy the sport, and know when to stop a fight. No one likes that man. He did not care about his dog.' 'I know you I've seen you here before it's young Johy. I didn't recognize you without the beard, and you English man Mister Boswell. How you dress, speak, an English gentleman if ever I've seen one.' 'Thank you.' 'You put on a good show.' 'Once a month we have a pit fight, man to man, no weapons, fist, feet, no rules, go as you please and five minute rounds. One left standing, fight to a finish, three fights in the one night and we have a doctor there.' 'That's my sort of fights' said Adam as they climbed into a cab. 'See you tomorrow' said Fiell. 'If we're still here, we'll come, were travelling to Glen Parva.' 'Yes I've heard of it, better class small town. Could be a bit quiet for you.'

'Is that so, why don't you bring your business down there?' said Adam. 'You're a man of the world, looks like you've got money, why don't you start one there?' 'See you tomorrow if we're still here' said Tex.

'Where to?' said the cabby. 'Mississippi Princess and just give us a run through your main area, my friends new here.' 'Very good sir' just giving the horse a quick flip with his whip. Adam turned and looked back as they headed for the steam boat.

'Some nice shops and restaurants, it's definitely half French. I suppose the docks and ships bring and take a lot of trade.' 'Big trade, big money, but it's slowed down a bit. No slaves brought in and no selling of them, and no labour for two meals and a bed; they now get paid. We will have to find more trade' said the cab driver. 'You's will have to start producing and selling what you have around, you's have the docks, there's no end of wood it's everywhere' said Adam. 'Makes a heap of sense' said Tex.

As they walked up the gang plank Adam smiled as he looked at Tex. 'There's that loud country jazz is it you call it?' 'There's lots of names for it.' 'You seemed to like it' answered Tex.

Adam looked at the big bales of cotton as they got off the gang plank to the top deck. There was a half cast black young man playing a guitar and singing Memphis Tennessee is home sweet home to me. 'Nice atmosphere' said Adam as he followed Tex through the tables. Just four steps that went up onto a higher level with a banister rail running the full length that separated it from the casino area. 'If Glen Parva doesn't suit me, I'll be back here.' There were eight tables with cloths on. 'I'll have a steak rare with whatever goes with it and a beer.' 'And you sir?' said the waiter. 'Do you have fish trout?' 'No sir but we do have salmon.' 'I'll have one filleted well cooked, mushrooms and whatever goes with it, and bring me a glass half beer and half lemonade with it please.'

'Do you always say please?' asked Tex. 'Most times' answered Adam getting up and changing his table to look down at the gambling tables below. Tex told him there was two roulette tables, a dice game in a cage and some card tables, with a long bar across the back wall. 'It's bigger than i thought it would be, it's got quite a lot of character.'

Tex gave him a quick sideways glance. 'I suppose that's a new way of saying it's okay' answered Tex sitting down.

'Those four women are well beautiful, doesn't sound enough are they?' 'Yes they're Crell' said Tex. 'They were quarter black, maybe something else, flashing eyes, white teeth and raven black hair. 'Are they on?' 'Yes they are' interrupted Tex, 'and have their own cabins.' 'And what's the charge?' 'I believe it's ten and twenty for the night.' 'That one with the red carnation in her hair, she's worth thirty dollars' said Adam as the barmaid placed the drinks on the table. Five minutes passed and the Crell girl with the red carnation in her hair came over. She was standing by the table smiling down at Adam.

'I am Rosetta. I believe you think i am worth thirty dollars Senor.' Adam looked straight at her, 'you are more beautiful close up than from afar. Yes, every penny of it. I am Adam' getting up and pulling out a chair for her. 'Waiter a bottle of champagne please. You'll dine with me Rosetta?' Tex gave him a quick glance. He's got some style. 'Looks like it's going to cost me thirty as well instead of 20.' 'Your friend in the yellow dress, would you wave her over?' asked Tex. 'Adam I'll have a lobster.' 'Darling you have whatever you want, and how old are you Rosetta?' 'I am seventeen Mister Adam.' 'That's great, I am not superstitious.' They all laughed. 'Better have another bottle' said Tex, 'and how old are you Mister Adam?' 'I am 26.' 'Ooh la la such a change, a young gentleman' said Rosetta.

'You have a french accent.' 'So i've been told my father was french, my mother half cast. Have you seen France?' 'Yes Paris, Nice, Monty Carlo. I loved it, had four months there. Here comes your bottle of bubbly Tex. Let the good times roll. Let's have more music. I like this old Memphis' said Adam. 'And I like your company' said Tex.

Two Days Later

Adam glanced around the carriage, the seats were like a park bench except for the loose thick cushions that was thrown on them. The walls were just painted, a narrow fold up table between the seats. They had been transferred to another train and coaches, the engine had needed another wheel. Memphis and Little Rock was gone, this was called the Texicana Cruiser, the so called cruiser a rust bucket thought Adam. They had changed trains. 'This is a let down from the New York Flyer and the Kentucky Rocket' said Adam. 'It's still a lot roomier and comfort than a stage coach' answered Tex. 'Texicana looked wild and rough, you live there long?' asked Adam looking out the window. 'No I spend time there. 'As you say it's wild and rough'. 'I've been on this rough train so many times, I don't really notice it but you're right, it is a mess compared to the others.'

'Look at that' said Adam, 'that's unusual, they were just a mile out of Texicana' pointing to the two flags, the state flag is flying level with the stars and stripes I've noticed as you enter or leave a state, the stars and stripes are always higher than the state flag but here both are flying level.

What you've gotta realize about Texas, were not level with other states, were above them. Texas the lone star state, the biggest and power fullest state in the US' said Tex with pride in his voice.

Texicana - 'So how does it earn its money?' 'Regular small cattle sales and a Coppermine.' ' So it has regular work' said Adam. 'Yeah low paid, a lot of Mex there' answered Tex. ' How much track left is there before we get to Aberline?' 'Maybe 600-650. 'First we've got a settlement, they call it Dallas, right now biggest town in Texas, is Fort Worth.

'So how did you sleep last night?' 'On this old train?' 'Not too good I slept better the night before in Memphis on that river boat.' 'I'll bet you didn't sleep much' said Tex with a big smile. 'So what did you think of Memphis?' 'It's got the lot, great place. I'd have liked a week in it' answered Adam.

Kicking off his shoes and lying back on the seat with his back leaning against the window as he gazed out through the opposite window at the vast open prairie, no hedges, no roads, no villages, just a few scattered farms, open prairie, it just kept going in every direction as far as the eye could see. 'I thought Yorkshire was open, you could drop it in this corner of Texas' he said aloud. 'Is Yorkshire in Scotland?' asked Tex. 'No it's the biggest county in England. Did you stay in Yorkshire?' 'Yes, used to have six to seven months every year and be away all summer travelling we had about five to six years there. That's where me and my brother Layton was educated, we learned so much, so quick, a different way of life, we mixed and grew up with titled people, Lords and Ladies there, and met the young Queen Victoria.' 'No kidding, that must have been something. Why don't you tell me about it?' 'You wouldn't believe it.' 'Try me and see' said Tex. Adam was finding it difficult to get Yorkshire out of his mind and when he actually met the young Queen Victoria.

CHAPTER EIGHT- A VERY ROYAL VISITOR CALLS

Now early October it was a little cold, the early morning sun was shining but there was not a lot of heat from it, the three boys had been hedgehog hunting, now being the best time as they had finished breeding. I found a run over here amongst the dead leaves, said Walter. The brothers Adam and Layton walked over to have a look, he's getting good. You're becoming a gentleman gypsy, said Layton. You's two are becoming that as well, answered Walter. You could be right I never thought of it like that, said Adam. I lost the trail, then slowly brushing away some fallen fresh leaves, I picked the trail up again.

'We don't need a Jack Russell dog with you along. It was now the right time of the year for hedgehog hunting as they were now getting nests finished to go into hibernation for the winter. The other half of the year they were on the run and breeding. It was considered bad by the gypsies, wrong to hunt them down and kill them. Even though they was considered good food.

Here's the nest said Layton starting to pull it apart with 2 thick sticks, the hedgehog was curled up in a tight ball, his prickles or spines now standing up. This is where a good Jack Russell would come to a stop; he could find the nest and would eagerly start pulling it apart his nose bleeding, he could do nothing with it just stand there and bark. Adam held the thick sack open while Layton rolled it in with the 2 sticks, that makes three, if we can just find another one that will make a nice supper for all, said Walter.

Another hour had passed and they had found another one, they had taken it in turns carrying the sack and holding it out because of the spines protruding out of the sack. They had gone deeper into the forest than they thought. Making their way back they would give the sack a good shake now and then which would stop the hedgehogs from eating through it, even though the sack was in another sack. The first time Walter had gone hedgehog hunting with the brothers was 2 years ago, and he put the hedgehogs they caught that night in a wooden garden shed, the next morning they had eaten a hole right through it and gone.

A coach heavily decorated with gold Guilt was slowly coming up the drive, who could that be, asked Layton. Walter started to slowly walk forward the 2 brothers following. As the sun caught its gold guilt work there was a gold crown sitting on the roof. It looked something out of a Fairy Tale. Yes it's a royal, look at the gold crown sitting on the roof; well does that mean there's a royal in it asked Layton? It certainly does, answered Walter as the coach came to a stop in front of the steps. Getting hold of Adam's arm, we're in no fit state to be seen, we need to get cleaned up. Let us watch from a distance then, said Layton. There were five pair of mounted guards to the back of the coach and five pair to the front.

The guard that sat up front alongside of the driver jumped down, reaching underneath the side of the coach, a step was slid out. 4 guards dismounted, 2 standing on either side, there breast plates gleaming as the sun caught them. The 2 guards that stood on the end of the coach jumped down, each one holding a back wheel, so as to keep the coach still. The Captain of the guards walked up the steps, knocking hard on the door twice, the heavy door swung open, the butler Jeeves looked at the Captain of the guards. He stepped to one side giving Jeeves a slight piss taking smile.

Jeeves looked at the crest on the coach door, My God, it's the Queen. Now you've discovered that, run along like a good chap and tell your master that the Queen of England is here. 'Of course Sir. Good Morning my lord and lady, the young queen is here to pay you a visit said the Captain. Sir John and Lady Florence walked side by side down the steps. The guard that had pulled out the step turned the door handle, opening it wide. Sir John stepped forward giving a low and humble bow, your loyal subject Lord Sir John Bates, your Majesty, he said holding her hand to help her out of the coach. Lady Florence stepped forward giving a low curtsy, Welcome to Essington Manor, your majesty. The queen looking out over the grounds.

Jeeves! Yes Sir John, tell the gilly to make arrangements for the coach and horses, and you make arrangements with the captain of the guard. It's so pleasant to see you again Lord John, and you look so happy Lady Florence. This is my companion and lady in waiting lady Beatrice. Sir John smiled, looks to be an old spinster about sixty, not much company for the young Queen thought sir John.

The Queen walked up the steps holding sir johns hand. At the top he let go of her hand, walking inside she started to slowly look around at the soiled tatty hanging flags, and the slightly damage shields and swords that decorated the walls over the large fireplace hung lord john's coat of arms. A plaque underneath read 'Fortune favors the brave' She smiled looking away and then back at Sir John, I feel very much at home here my lord john. Thank you we are honored, our home is your home for as long as you wish to stay,' do you have any guards? No my queen, I am no longer in service, I have only servants.

I am travelling different parts of my kingdom at random. She stopped in front of a painting that must have been 9ft long by 5ft deep it was a battle scene. A young officer was kneeling, there were wounded soldiers, many dead including the enemy, a small cannon lay on its side dead horses in the distance, the Union Jack flag was flying with several holes in it, there was a small group of soldiers standing at one side looking on in a woe as the king, is uniform torn and dirty was knighting the young wounded officer. Underneath on a plaque were the words, knighted in the field of battle.

What a brilliant scene Lord John, Yes ma-am, your great-great grandfather and my great grandfather, they had fought side by side. She looked to the captain standing behind her, it's families like this that keeps this little country great, you may go to your men. Is there too many here for you lord john? Not at all Ma'am there are many spare rooms and stables. I would point out you are now on your own and should always have a guard, I have you Lord John. That you do, my Queen.

On a gold chain around her neck hung a gold whistle with a pink coral handle, putting it to her lips she blew 2 loud blasts, there was suddenly five guards coming through the doorway, 2 withdrawn swords, 3 with pistols she gave 1 long blast and they turned and went. Very good I like it,' said Sir John. And how have you been Lady Florence?' it's been over a year since i have seen you last, Yes your majesty it was at your coronation. I may be staying 2 nights. Oh I am so pleased to have you here your majesty, shall we have tea and cakes?' I do have some lovely cakes, one is a gypsy cake similar to a Welsh scone, richer in flavor, made with milk many currants and raisins well-cooked split and buttered. It does sound good who gave you the recipe lady Florence?' the gypsies cook them for me.

You jest with me, I jest not your majesty, we have three families of gypsies who stay in our grounds. How exciting I have heard much about them, some call them Romanies and some call them gypsies, which is it?' Well your majesty we call them Romany gypsies which I am told is the proper name. 'And how long have you had them here?' Nearly four years Ma-am. The queen got up and walked over to the window, you have a nice view and lovely grounds, i do like your colours in this room blue and silver. Yes we call it the blue room Ma-am said Sir John.

Do tell me more about the gypsies, they are my subjects as well you know. Well they have been here so long and we all seem to get along so well they are actually our friends, singers, dancers, musicians. They entertain at our parties. Is it true that they can tell fortunes?' Well your majesty there is many that aren't gypsies, that try but the real ones can. There is a clairvoyant stargazer, fully gifted, in the family. I would like to meet with them, speak with them and maybe seek the future. I have many advisors who has loyal smiles to my face and some that wish otherwise behind my back. These people that you have here they have nothing to gain, and would be honest with me, a stargazer it sounds exciting. She may be young, but she knows so much thought Sir John.

Just a slip of a girl about twenty and so shrewd thought Lady Florence. I can ask them to come in sometime. No, no Lady Florence I would like to see them in their own natural way. Just then the door opened and lady Elizabeth walked in holding a riding crop. Oh Aunt Florence I've had a lovely morning riding down to the village, a glass of wine at the inn and riding back with Jack, she suddenly stopped looking at the Queen, oh please excuse my manners, I am Lady Elizabeth Hilton and you are? You don't remember, you was at my coronation over a year ago with your aunt here, said the young queen smiling. Suddenly realizing who she was lady Elizabeth placed her hand over her mouth and gave a very low curtsy.

Forgive me your majesty for not recognizing you. Come and sit next to me. This Jack I suppose he is your beau?' well yes your majesty he is, I am older than him by four years, he is just twenty. 'I am twenty.' answered the queen. Lady Elizabeth went to say something and pulled it back. The queen smiled, i like people to be themselves and not look for appropriate words when in my company. Well you seem so young to rule three quarters of the world your majesty. I am but i never asked for the job, you know I would rather be a titled young lady like you, to do what i like and go where I pleased. She suddenly turned, Please excuse me lord john and lady Florence I did not mean to neglect you. No, no not at all your majesty we have a arrangements to see to. I am so pleased I have found someone my own age to spend time with, said the young queen. Sir John and his wife smiled nodding to each other, he gave a bow and Lady Florence a curtsey, and then they both left.

So you like riding Elizabeth? It is also my favourite sport; do tell me do the young people have any hunt or riding balls? Yes we do they're quite good fun. Lady Beatrice, said the queen, maybe you would like to join lady Florence? Of course your majesty she answered getting up. As the doors opened Lady Elizabeth noticed a guard standing either side, it's so good to have someone my own age to talk to, I feel the same your majesty. Now Elizabeth you must tell me what the young people are doing in this part of England. Would you like me to ring for tea and cakes your majesty? Oh please do.

Isaac and Nelson were slowly walking around the coach admiring it, vater the doosters of sunakai booty a drey the tister, said Isaac (Look at the lots of gold work on this coach) The 2 guards that usually sit on back of the coach was polishing the panels with a soft cloth. 'Can we have a look inside? Said Nelson. Of course you can but don't go inside answered one of them opening both doors wide. The seats either side and door panels was a beige duskin hide, deeply buttoned, the roof was lined in a cream silk, the panels pleated and buttoned. The heavy plate glass windows had a 2 inch beveled edge right around with the initials 'VR' carved in script in the bottom corner. Nelson turned to the guard that had opened the doors. This coach it carries the young queens initials, that's right Victoria reign, she is inside he answered. Isaac was leaning in the coach admiring the interior.

Father, said Nelson pulling on his arm, this is the queens' coach and she is in the house. The guard smiled at Nelson, 'In between these panels is a hard thin sheet steel, a sword or musket ball will not penetrate it, and the small glass windows is nearly two inch plate. Isaac nodded, not sure what he meant.

Having heard the news, Delly made the 2 boys quickly wash and change, everyone sat around the fire hoping they would get a look at the young queen. 'I expect she will want to be duckered all women do (her fortune told)', said Manx Nellie

Five of the cavalry guards suddenly appeared their horses were saddled up and they rode off over the open fields. Another five appeared and they also rode off in the opposite way. Lady Elizabeth came walking out from the house into the back cobble yard, there was a smartly dressed young lady at her side. They were walking over to the gypsy wagons in the far corner. That will be the young queen that's with lady Elizabeth, said Isaac. 'Let us all act normal and well mannered, and boys do not speak to the queen only if she speaks to you. The 2 boys nodded looking excited.

Everyone was dressed in fresh clean clothes, as the 2 young ladies walked across the courtyard 2 of the cavalry guards appeared in the doorway, another 2 standing in a far corner making themselves as less inconspicuous as possible. As the queen approached the fire all stood up. Young Adam and Layton was surprised that they had done this for no one had told them to, the sudden presence of your Queen was overpowering, as she stood there both bowed their heads for two seconds, then looking straight at the queen, smiling. She stepped forward reaching out and leveling Layton's untidy hair. 2 rough boys. I should imaging, she said to nobody in particular. Yes, your majesty they are my boys and they can be a handful, said Nelson bowing, he then called his grandfather old Byron over, introducing him as the elder of the family.

Old Byron introduced all his family to the Queen. Manx Nelly stepped forward curtsying, 'You will be the fortune teller?' 'With all due respect your majesty, I am a clairvoyant stargazer.' 'I am told they are rare' said the Queen. 'That is up for you to judge my Queen'. And so I will' answered the Queen.

I have given an audience to some so called fortune tellers and tarot readers; they pick your brains using what you have told them, said the queen. Your majesty without throwing you obvious compliments you are a very astute young lady, for your age. I like how you speak, you are humble and know your place, but you are not afraid to speak out on what you know and give an honest opinion. I would like a reading before nightfall. I will be honored my queen to give you my best, answered Manx Nellie curtsying.

Old Tom was coming out of the stables walking between 2 horses holding them by their bridles. Cupping his hand he helped Lady Isobel into the saddle, then glancing at the queen he took a step back, hesitating. Isaac quickly stepped forwards bowing. Let me my queen I will be honored, he said. She placed her left foot in his cupped hands and her left hand on his shoulder, then went into the saddle with a little spring. Isaac held the young queens left foot as he placed it into the stirrup. You are a people with a mind of your own, said the queen.

Jack had gone over and sat on the front board of one of the living wagons, he was finding it difficult to take in. the lady he was courting was actually keeping company with the Queen of England, My god he said under his breath, she is the power fullest human being on the planet. They sat side saddle on the horses whispering and having a little laugh with each other. Jack shouted Elizabeth, you can keep me waiting but not the queen, Jack jumped down walking over quickly, 'Please excuse this your majesty, Elizabeth did not tell me I was to ride with you's said Jack giving a slight bow. The queen just smiled, that big horse you are on is high spirited and will take a lot of handling your majesty. Yes I know I chose him, I ride three times a week. Old tom was just coming out of the stables with Jack's horse. Putting his fingers to his mouth he let out a short sharp whistle, his horse came at a fast trot, Jack's left hand gripped the saddle and reins as his right hand came hard down on the horse's rump.

The fast trot suddenly became a gallop running alongside he lifted both feet off the ground, his left hand pulling himself up as his two feet left the ground , now in the saddle going full pelt at the five barred gate the far end of the courtyard and cleared it.

The Queen hit the rump of her horse twice with the riding crop, the big high spirited horse took off at a gallop across the courtyard as it leapt for the gate, her left foot in the stirrup was pushed forward as she leaned well back, the horses hooves hit the ground with a loud thud, still leaning well back she pulled hard on the reins, turning the big horse towards Jack. You may be Queen, but you are some young lady on a horse, and how quickly you turned him.' The Queen smiled, he looked into her eyes then her mouth, then quickly looked away, Please excuse me your majesty, I forget that you are Queen.' 'I maybe Queen, but also a young woman. Thank you for the compliment Jack.'

Elizabeth was sat on her horse waiting. 'You could be in trouble, said the queen with a smile. Jack trotted over and opened the gate for Elizabeth. A titled lady seems not enough. I don't know what you mean, stammered Jack. 'I saw you flirting with the Queen, not waiting for an answer, she trotted off. The queen turned to look at Elizabeth, 'He's quite a horseman isn't he?' and good looking in a rough untidy sort of way, Yes your majesty, answered Elizabeth. The queen had a slight smile as she answered. I jest with you Elizabeth, don't be jealous'. They both laughed.

Jack had held back, he could see they were talking and laughing, he had occasionally noticed in the far distance, back and front, horse guards. Yes, they're always there.

'I suppose there's never any real privacy is there? You must get tired of it' said Jack. Elizabeth glancing at him, how easily he speaks to the queen. 'And how about you Elizabeth when you're going to York or Lincoln, do you have a guard?' 'Not really your majesty, I am with my uncle and aunt and sometimes Jack. On odd occasions I do go with Jack and his father when they buy and sell horses and other various things at sales.'

You know I have everything except, the Queen paused. 'Privacy and freedom' said Jack. 'Really Jack' said Elizabeth looking straight at him. 'Are all gypsies like you?' asked the Queen. 'I don't know what you mean, your majesty.'

'You don't hesitate or look for words you just say what you feel.' Jack just smiled, 'I think so Ma'am.' 'You would make an honest courtier', said the queen. 'I will sometimes go out horking with Jacks gran selling a polish called daub and find her a customer to have their fortune told. 'How exciting, you live in 2 worlds Elizabeth, one day in the future I will live in just Jacks world. 'And we will travel; in a vardo, a gypsy caravan.

'So you will leave the life you've been born into?' Yes I will, answered Elizabeth looking away. You have a slight Scottish accent.' 'Yes your majesty, my family's castle is at Kilmarnock, my cousin lives there.'

'Your majesty, you make this England great, said Jack. That is the third time today the word great has been used, when I get back to

London I will have it declared throughout the empire and the world. That it is not Britain it is Great Britain. And you can alter the name of a country just as you wish, asked Jack. Yes, just as I wish, he stared at her. Your word your majesty is not to be questioned, but to be obeyed.' 'Your good with words Jack, you would make a good courtier.'

'There is a big oak over there' said Jack going in his saddle bag and giving Elizabeth a Welsh bed rug. 'Thank you', he gave a quick nod to the queen then turned his horse to Elizabeth. 'I will see you later.' 'Of course darling Jack.'

He was sat in front of the fire with a mug of tea all the family there, no one had bothered about work, it was far too important an occasion. 'You're very quiet Jack. 'It's hard to understand that one person can have so much power, she's going to change the name of Britain to Great Britain because great impresses her. 'My god she's only about twenty, younger than Elizabeth, said Isaac. She has that authority, born in her you can sense it and feel it when you are in her company, and yet so easy to speak to, said Jack.

We are fortunate to have such a queen, such a majesty, in some countries they would not bother to even look at us, never mid to talk friendly to us, said Isaac, she seems a lovely girl and I am looking forward to duckering her tonight, said Manx Nellie. She then took two long thin pale green leaves out of her pinny pocket and rubbed them in her hand until they became a dust. Then pouring it into her tea. I will be having a good sleep this afternoon, do not wake me, I want to be strong and alert for the young queens reading tonight, said Manx Nellie.

It's so exciting and romantic; Elizabeth, but you will have a hard life. 'Not really your majesty. When we are alone you may call me Victoria. I already live part of a Gypsy life. They are different aren't they Yes your majesty, their ways and culture, they are very clean, maybe overdo it a little. Really, answered the queen. 'Yes they will not have a dog in the home, it must stay outside in a kennel, also must have its own eating bowls.

One day as Isaac was scraping the leftovers to Fawn the greyhound, it licked the plate and he broke the plate, will not wash their dish cloths or table clothes with clothes that they wear, they are washed in a separate bowl and hung on a different clothes line, all using china, as its own bowl to be washed in. And there is so many, many different things and ways they do. For instance, if a man is buying or selling a woman should not interrupt when men are dealing. 'Really, answered the queen. A woman that doesn't abide by their clean house rules, they consider being dirty in the home and they have a name for it is called mockadee. , And you will do all these things, and more asked the Queen, yes majesty, I mean Victoria.

'I will be his wife, there is many smart eligible young men of title and wealth' said the Queen. 'I do hope you know what you're doing.' Elizabeth nodded and looked away. 'You are very astute Victoria, I will consider all that you tell me. I do worry; I fear my family will disown me. Yes that may be so, answered the queen. Elizabeth stopped and looked away; say what it was I don't mind. 'Do you have a beau, your.. I mean Victoria. They have been trying to marry me off, I don't know how many times. 'You're only twenty aren't you? No I am not quite twenty yet, and do you have a beau?

The young queen threw her head back and laughed, she's so full of fun and life, thought Elizabeth. I do have my eye on one, he is quite handsome, a distant relation. I am pleased for you Victoria, you are so young for such responsibilities. 'Well I had no choice, it is my duty, brought up to expect it, produce an heir for the throne. Many times I would like to be like you, free to do as I wished. I like your company Elizabeth, you would make a good lady in waiting. 'I would love it but I would miss my beau. 'I could command it if I so wished, said the queen with a smile. Elizabeth looked down and never answered. 'I only jest with you. 'I will admit Victoria I would love to have a month at the great castle Windsor.

'So let us say, a month, Christmas and New Year', answered the Queen. 'Thank you Victoria. I like your gold bangle, I hear they are the latest thing and called a charm bangle. That is right I had this one sent from Germany they are called a Lucky Charm Bangle' said the Queen taking it off. 'The elephant, and this is Windsor castle, it's very heavy.' Elizabeth then reached out fastening the clasp and safety chain back on the queen's wrist. The idea with these is to have a charm as a present on special occasions, birthdays or Christmas.

'I would like one, I will suggest to Jack just a thin gold chain with a locket similar to yours to start. As they talked the queen took out a silver flat flask of apple juice with 2 telescopic opening silver cups.

'Now tell me about this clairvoyant stargazer. I have had on odd occasion's astronomers and tarot readings. I have heard aunt Florence say Manx Nellie is the best and she has seen a lot of them. 'It sounds exciting, as she told you yours yet Elizabeth? No she hasn't I prefer to let things come and go as god intended it to be, answered Elizabeth. 'Are you very religious?. 'Well not really Victoria, I go to church, weddings, funerals and the odd Sunday, and of course say my prayers. 'But you Victoria you are the defender of the faith aren't you? 'Yes, I am a Christian queen and i represent the Christian faith.

You say you have a beau in mind, does he know you- are- erm. Come along say it. 'Does he know you are after him? The queen laughed, no he doesn't yet, he is very handsome, he won't know until it's too late, they both laughed. You are such good company Elizabeth, I could do with you staying at Windsor, a few months after Christmas. They maybe the stronger of the 2 sexes but we are the cunning and brainiest. Poor Jack, I hypnotize him you know? And what will he say about you not being home for Christmas, enquired the Queen? Well it's a royal command; I can't really refuse can I?' 'Of course not Elizabeth it would mean the tower, they both laughed. You know Victoria I really enjoy your company too, I don't have many young friends here unless it's a party.

The boys emptied the hedgehog bag into a metal chest. In a side room off the stables, how did you get on boys? Very good father we got four. They looked to be about 2-three years old. I'll kill and clean them now, they're fine hochie whichies (fine hedgehogs) said Nelson as he reached inside his wagon coming out with a round iron bar about fifteen inches long as thick as your thumb. I am off to get cleaned up said Walter walking away. He didn't like seeing them killed but he did like the rare taste, you could say a delicacy like slightly sweet pork. But some say a bit too greasy, whereas pork is very dry. Hedgehog being a slightly strong tasting meat like pheasant.

The metal chest stood in the corner, Layton lifted the clasp throwing the lid back, then tipping the chest on its side, one hedgehog rolled out and remained still. Layton shut the lid, it was still in a ball, being a self protected animal there is no way you could handle them, you could just not pick one up.

Nelson went over to the hedgehog, placing a foot on its back, he applied pressure rolling it back and forth, then pressing a little harder and rolling it back and forth again, its head popped out then went back in, the second time it stayed out longer, that's when nelson struck, hard and fast just once across the back of the head, it was dead. And then it would open up, uncurl, bleeding from the mouth. Keeping a foot on it then with a very sharp knife, it would be taken across all of its back and down the sides, the blade would be hot, when it lost its heat it would be put back in the fire and then a second knife used; when finished there would be no bristles, maybe just the odd small one. It would then look like a tiny pig with a very humped back.

Carrying them out in the sack, Nelson put 2 at a time on an iron rod, running through them from mouth to rear end, turning them slowly, high over the fire for five minutes, this cleaning them, then placing them on a board and scraping them thoroughly removing any debris and burnt parts of the skin, it was then clean. Placing the sharp knife on the hump back and using the iron bar to strike it, split in 2 halves, the guts washed clean and given to the dog. Then a bowl of slightly salted water and the halves of the hedgehog would be thoroughly washed then left on a plate to dry till the next day. The next evening, they would be spit roasted about 8" above the fire. Being a rich strong meat, half of one was usually enough for one person, once cooked they would be left to go cold all day and on a plate with a few small boiled potatoes with the skin on that had also been left to go cold, it made a very tasty supper, this was a meal to look forward to as they could only be eaten for four maybe five months of the year.

You would be completely cut off from the life you know, another world, it would be very hard, no parties, fine clothes, you would be a lot better if Sir john gave Jack a well-paid job, horses or game keeping. We have been through all of that and he did not want it he would not have a job, he would feel belittled, he is his own man. That's how they are, answered Elizabeth, and he wants to travel, he is missing his own natural life and says they are spending too much time herein one place. You want to give it a lot of thought, maybe an extra few months at Windsor with me, would let your mind clear, help you to think more clearly.

'I would like the break, to see London again and a few parties, what will Jack say, will he allow it, these gypsy men are different. You must love him a lot, said the queen. 'And where are you going next? Asked Elizabeth, changing the conversation. I will have another day here as I am enjoying it and then we will be on our way. I am not supposed to say where, they have a new meaning and they call it security. 'I understand your majesty. We will probably have another three stops down this side of the country then its London and Windsor.

Next year I will tour Carlisle, Lancaster, Worcester and Bath, so as to know the Lords and shields I can call on, loyal to the crown. 'You see Elizabeth it is not me or any Monarch after me it is the crown, and what it represents, we Royals represent the crown and that is England and the British Empire. On rare occasions there may be little squabbles over land but when a foreign power or danger threatens our country England, Wales, Scotland, Northern Ireland, the Royal Lincoln magna carter, we are all British and we all stand as one, the lords of this country, men with titles like your uncle, they are the stones in the crown. Loyal beyond question I could place five hundred men under him against 2000 and if I gave the order stand, he would stand with the last man because of what he is, because of what is in him and what he comes from more than 1500 years we have beaten everything that has come at us, this little country rules three quarters of the world and it will now be known as Great Britain because it is great. She stopped, looked away, and then back, her hearts in her job, the royals are bred and brought up to it, thought Elizabeth.

What a speech that would be, truly Victoria you will be a monarch to be remembered. 'Thank you Elizabeth. Knowing you are going to be a monarch you are taught many things by teachers even professors, from childhood, my father would tell me, only one thing beats the book and that is the real thing, the teachers and professors did not know of the real thing, he did, because he was the real thing and there for me to learn from.

The late dinner finished, the queen and Elizabeth walked out of the back entrance. 'That pheasant was delicious especially the sauce. The sauce was made by Jacks grandmother, said Elizabeth. They supply most of the game as they are good hunters, rabbits, hares, pheasants. They actually live off the land. I think it would be quite an experience to live their life in one of their caravans for a couple of months in the summer, said the Queen. They have a saying your majesty 'we are born free, as free as the birds in the sky, as free as the wind that blows, we are born free' 'very appropriate, I may have my minstrel compose a song of that, answered the queen.

It was gone eight o'clock, the young queen looked left then right, she could see the usual five guards at each end of the long courtyard, they were not in uniform, keeping themselves as inconspicuous as possible, they would be changed by another ten halfway through the night, and another ten around the outside perimeter of the manor. 'You must feel very safe, your majesty. 'I do, my father used to say when out and about you can't have too many guards, you never know where or who is your enemy. As they approached the fire, all stood up, she smiled glancing around. 'Please be seated, said the queen motioning with her hand.

You are old Byron the elder?' 'Yes I am your majesty' he said, giving a bow. You must have done and seen a lot in your life? 'Yes I have young queen, we are so honored, how you walk amongst us. 'You are an unusual people and of course you are my subjects, that is why I show an interest. 'Good evening Captain Jamesy, also to your sergeant Jacky, they were both Scots.

The queen being seated they both sat down. Elizabeth noticed each had a pair of pistols in his belt. Are you comfortable? Our hosts have looked after us well your majesty, answered the captain. Lady Elizabeth whispered in the queen's ear. That is the famous gypsy cake is it?'

'Yes Ma-am, it is very filling answered the captain. Louisa, Old Byron's wife stepped forward, making the mistake of bowing instead of curtsying. The queen smiled a little, Your majesty would you like to try a piece?' Yes I would, said the Queen. The large black iron pan that had hung over the fire sat on a wood box. Louisa cut the large flat cake into four pieces. Placing the largest warm piece on a plate,, then splitting it and buttering each piece, then cutting a small piece off and eating it to show it was pure and clean, then holding the plate out to the queen .

15 minutes had passed then taking out a handkerchief she wiped her mouth and hands. That was delicious, if I had known it was so good I would have eaten less pheasant, said the queen. Then offering the plate with the last half to Elizabeth, who quickly accepted it.

Manx Nellie sat on top of the steps between the shafts of the wagon. 'Good evening your majesty, I have been waiting for your visit. Big Jacky got up and walked over to the wagon, he held out his hand to help the queen up the steps, his coat opened showing the brace of pistols in his belt. Allow me my queen.

She glanced around the inside at the highly polished mahogany interior, the glass beveled cupboards in each corner, with a small star carved in the centre and a heavy beveled edge. The 2 small windows, one each side of the top half door, the carpet was embossed Grosvenor Wilton, a blue carved glass angel lamp was bolted on either side wall.

Its fit for a queen, said the young queen with a smile. Thank you your majesty. It's nice to have the best when you can, a good answer Manx Nellie. The queen sat at one side of the table, Manx Nellie on the other side. And what reading do you do, asked the queen. One hand or both is silver, the crystal reading is paper money. And what of the tarot card readings? Enquired the queen. Our family does not do tarot cards they are of the devil and easy to fake. 'Yes I see and you are a star reader a clairvoyant? I am, the stars, stardust and the rings between them, answered Manx Nellie.

'What do I call you, enquired the queen. Manx Nellie hesitated for a few seconds. Most clients always call her Mother, how could she possibly ask the queen to call her mother. Just call me Nellie, she answered. The Young Queen sensed something about her hesitation and answer. Then bringing the crystal and it's stand out, then placing it in the centre of the table. Place the paper money under it Ma-am. 'I don't carry money' 'Wait a moment she said standing up and opening the top half of the door. Captain James she said quite loudly. Yes, your majesty, he answered standing up from the fire. Four or five strides and he was there at the bottom of the steps. 'Do you have any paper money?. Yes your majesty, taking a pound note out of his wallet, thank you, I'll see you get it back, said the queen. Please place it under the crystal said Manx Nellie, lifting the black ebony stand. I want you to forget about matters of state, or your thoughts or opinion of me. Place your hands on the crystal for a few minutes and just clear your mind, then remove your hands.

Manx Nellie had previously thought about this reading, she had had a 2 hour afternoon sleep, a wash, and change and felt really fresh, then putting out of her mind the importance of the young queen. She would be just another young lady, Manx Nellie lifted the queen's hands off the crystal and held them for a few seconds. I am calm, relaxed and at ease, said the young queen. That is good, whatever questions you want to ask, also whatever is said in this wagon when you walk out it will stay in here, not even my husband will know of your reading. 'So Nellie you don't call it a séance, no young lady it is a reading between those of the rings of the outer planets and stars and I have been gifted with the ability to read that there are very few that is born with the gift.

Nellie turned her attention to the crystal, there are many high titles that would like to have the importance of being next to you, even to have their full say, they know that cannot be and there is jealousy. 'You have many protectors, still be careful who you put your trust in. never show all your feelings, a lot can be hid behind a smile or a cough. 'Thank you Nellie that is how my father would speak to me. 'What of Scotland and Wales? She asked. Yes the Scots said Nellie staring into the crystal. The stardust in between the rings that moves around the planets, the little people there so small they float and move in and out of the stardust. How wonderful do they have wings like fairies? Yes they do they are very tiny. Four or five could stand on your hand, they know all and see all, because they have a view, an oversight on everything in our down on or plant, they live till four, five times our age and pass their knowledge on again. They are looking at you, smiling, some are even bowing, they know who you are, even in the vast distances of space and they are very choosy who they receive.

May I call you Victoria. 'Yes please do' It makes us more closer and removes barriers, said Manx Nellie. Scotland a proud strong people, slow to accept friendship, Nellie was staring deeper into the crystal as she was speaking, they are very loyal once you have their friendship, and you must go more than halfway to win them over, but once they are your friend, they are a friend for life, I can see that you will do well to have a summer palace, in Scotland Scone near Perth. No leave Scone with he who has it, where the crowning stone is kept. Please do not interrupt, the queen looked down like a child, not used to being chastised then she was back to Queen Victoria.

Where then, she asked. A summer palace and around it, full of game, for you and your husband, a big asset, and you must wear your tartan regularly for them.

You have heard the request, the queen's request, I wait for the answers now, little people, we respect you and we wait for the answers. Nellie sat back, waiting and staring then looked up at the queen, your beau will be a distant relation from another country, dark and good looking, and you will be married in less than 1 year, in the month of February. 'Oh how wonderful, will he love me?' Yes, very much. The little people they are waving flags and dancing, you will have many children. 'How many? Asked the young queen. I am not really sure it's seven or eight said Manx Nellie. Scotland will become very loyal and in years to come there will be a Scottish lady who will become the English Queen and her name will be – Nellie hesitated for a moment, no I, yes it is Mary she answered. A titled lady from a Castle, oh how exciting, never ever have I met a fortune teller, the queen suddenly stopped, staring at Nellie, her eyes were half the size again and staring straight ahead, her head went right back and still staring at the wagon roof, no more young queen, it is dangerous for me please. Throw that black cloth over the crystal now.

The queen looked in a cupboard and found a glass she had noticed the water can on the front board with its polished brass bands, she held the glass of water to Nellie's mouth, twenty seconds had past and Manx Nellie was back with her again. She started to stand up I really enjoyed it as much as you my Queen, I'll make us a nice cup of tea,' No no Nellie, just relax, tell me where the things are and I will make the tea. 'But you are the queen, Yes, I am and that does not mean I am useless, and know only things of entertainment and state matters. I must see you again Nellie, never have I met one like you before I have heard there are genuine fortune tellers at the resort called Blackpool . Yes your majesty, most of them are my husband, Isaac's cousins. And you are called Manx Nellie? Yes I am, and from the Isle of Mann. I am a Manx Boswell. You say your name with a pride Nellie, Yes majesty it is the oldest and most well-known gypsy name in Britain, many scholars say it is the royal gypsy name. My people have been on the island Isle of Man for some years. I have not seen the island yet, said the queen, looking closely at the thin crown Derby china cup she was drinking from. Also the jewelry that Manx Nellie wore and how she was dressed. Noticing her mannerisms.

'Your people are different than what I thought they would be'. One only needs to be in your company for an hour, hear you speak, and one can sense you are something different. Elizabeth has told me a lot about you, I like your earrings what are they?' They are half Canadian gold dollars, , with a gold maple leaf on each side, I had them made, Nellie smiled looking at the queens charm bangle. I have heard of these charm bangles that's a heavy chain, I might start one said Nellie. They talked and laughed for half an hour. Nellie? Yes my queen what is it, will you give me another reading tomorrow night, as we are leaving the next morning? Of course I will my queen I enjoyed the reading as much has you have.

Nellie placed pen and ink on the table and the pound note that had been placed under the crystal, will you sign or initial that for me Victoria? I never want to get rid of it. The queen lifted her head giving a little laugh, and then signing it. 'You Romany gypsy people, I do enjoy your company, you are different, I don't know what. 'I call you Victoria again because I left something out when I went dizzy, it was the last things the little people whispered to me. Yes, said the queen excited. Except for another English queen over a century into the future, you will be the longest reigning queen in the world. And who will that queen be Nellie?' It will be a daughter of the titled lady from Forfar who will become queen, and my husband, you did not ask about your husband? Nellie hesitating for a few seconds, you know Victoria sometimes it's not good to know too much. Manx Nellie reached out giving the queens hand a little squeeze. I can now call you majesty again. The queen smiled, I do hope you now feel better Nellie?' I am fine your majesty. you are so at ease, even with a Monarch, said the young queen.

'Tell me Nellie your family, their health, wealth and future, each one of you could tell it, for each of you'. No my queen it does not work that way, I do not know if it is the rings of the planets or the little people, whatever but it is definitely not allowed for a family member to read another family member, it just does not work not even for a cousin. It comes to an end because of the blood line. I have really tried several times and nothing happens, however, it does work for in laws as long as there are no blood ties to the actual stargazer. Your second in command Jack, is Scottish. Yes Nelly why? He is dark, heavy built. I feel he has gypsy blood? I do not know Nelly, but when I see him with your people, maybe he is a Scottish gypsy. He is a smart big man said Nelly. Yes they call him the big yin.

It was 9:30 the next morning, the young queen sat at the table with Sir John, speaking about royal matters of state and loyalty of Yorkshire and Lincolnshire. The Scottish Captain Jamesy was sat on the opposite side of the table with a map laid out, He was always near the queen, the most trusted, the most loyal, thought Sir John. None of the gypsy families had gone to work as they know it was the last day of the queen's visit, they had all enjoyed the time off and the excitement of the young queen's visit and her company. Jack was brushing his horse down and constantly blowing out to keep the floating hairs away from his face. She has enjoyed seeing and knowing of you first hand and of your culture. She is seeing Manx Nellie again tonight for another reading. They leave in the morning, where to?' asked Jack. She did not say answered Elizabeth. She could see by his mannerisms that Jack was in a bad mood. She had told him last night of the Christmas holiday at Windsor with the queen for a month. I know you cannot refuse the queen, no one can, but a month, said Jack

Elizabeth dare not say it could possibly be 2 or even three months. 'I suppose you will be at royal parties and dances with young toffs, smelling of ladies scent with a lace hanky hanging out of their sleeve?' She started to laugh, Jack I would swear you are jealous, I have no choice, it's a command. And what if she should command you to be her personal lady in waiting?' Elizabeth looked away, he's very quick she thought it's like he can see through me. She looked back, straight at him, she knows we are courting, and I don't think she would keep me away too long from my beau. Her answer seemed to satisfy him and he was now more at ease, what does your family say about this, about you being at Windsor and London for a month? It's with the Queen, they say it's an honor, I should have known better than to ask, replied Jack. Don't spoil it for me Jack, it's not for three months, it's an honor.

He threw the blanket over the horse, then the saddle, I ride alone today. I have to think, you have me chasing my tail woman. He turned, pulled her to him rather roughly, giving her a long kiss, then pushed her back. I worry about you in London, something inside of me is saying it is your world calling to you. I could lose you and I can do nothing.'

'Where are you going Jack? .There is a farmer I need to see. 2 shotguns sticking out of the bag tied to his saddle. You're dealing today?' Yes, i hope to there is a fine mare and foal, and the farmer is interested in a pair of good shotguns. Leading the horse out of the stables, then climbing into the saddle. He looked at her, don't you make a fool of me Elizabeth because I would never forgive you.

The day had passed very slowly, so did the last night of the young queen's visit. It was early morning, 7:30. Layton and Adam sat by the stick fire with their granddad. 'I do miss the fun of puvving the grays at rarty (night), (putting the horses in and out of the fields) and getting them out the fields the next (soler) morning, said Layton to his granddad. We have now been settled in one place too long, just going away for three or four months in summer. I am pleased you are getting a good education but you are starting to miss out on some of your own ways of life', said Isaac, and that's not good, when you will be living as a gypsy.

Nellie and Delly was up, the large black iron frying pan hung over the fire, full of home cured bacon, sizzling and popping as it was turned with the long fork. Elizabeth came walking straight over to Jack, looking at Delly, she smiled, 'I hope there's enough in the pan, I could just eat a bacon sandwich, of course young lady, answered Delly. Elizabeth looked over towards the field, the mare and foal was in, I see you had a deal Jack, the foal is lovely. 'I'll sell the mare at Doncaster market next month, they are making big money down there and i will keep the foal with the other foals and sell them next spring, said Jack.

She went over to Manx Nellie, Good Morning Aunt Nellie, her majesty sends a message to you. 'And what might that be Lady Elizabeth?' 'After you have eaten your breakfast you are all to put on your best clothes and you aren't Nelly with all your jewelry. 'What can this be? Maybe she has brought some titled lady for a reading? No I don't think so, no one is more important than the queen, said Nellie out loud.

Another hour had passed, all stood looking on the royal coach that stood in the courtyard with four white horses coupled up to it, the queen came walking out with lady Florence and her lady in waiting following behind. Then came 2 men carrying camera equipment. Manx Nellie walked forward to meet the queen, she gave a low curtsey, 'Good morning your majesty. Delly and Louisa came forward doing the same. The queen held out her hand to Manx Nellie. 'I am so very glad we stopped here for a few days and never went down to Nottingham, should I require your services in the future Nellie, I can get you through Lord John can't I?' Of course my queen. Now I have something for you, I noticed the framed fortune telling signs round the back of your wagon, she clapped her hands and 2 men came forward carrying a tripod each, mounting large cameras on them. These pictures you will hang by your signs and they will draw people in.

What a wonderful idea, said old Louisa, the queen picked up Nellie's hand then standing closer Nellie who was holding the queens hand as if reading her palm, several other photos were taken with the rest of the gypsy family.

Manx Nellie would have the photograph of her with the queen in a thin brass frame with 2 hooks screwed at the top corners. The picture would take centre place of the other pictures, after this she became known as the royal gypsy.

I am Mister - - - Mister Jones, Mister Jones he repeated, bowing to the queen. 'You will send 2 sets for my gypsy friends, 2 sets to Lord John and 2 sets for myself. 'Of course, your majesty. Send all of them to Lord John. 'Now what do I owe you Mister Jones, that is alright your majesty, it is our pleasure. 'Do I have permission to put them in my window?' No put them in a photo album in your studio, and people will come in to see them.' The young queen then got in the coach with her companion.

Manx Nellie came over to the coach and gave the queen a folded up and knotted table cloth. The queen opened it to find several pieces of buttered gypsy cake. 'Oh thank you Nellie, she said. Nellie then reached in and placed something in the queen's hand. The young queen undid the lavender scented lace handkerchief in it was one of Manx Nelly's Canadian dollar earrings with the Maple leaf on each side, she looked at it closely then placing it back in the lace handkerchief, folding it several times and putting it in her bag. 'I thought you might like this your majesty, a lucky gypsy charm for your bangle', Oh thank you Nellie what a lovely story to tell to my friends.

The young queen leaned out of the window to look at the gypsy family who was all rowed up, each smiling, 'and what will you do today? She asked. Isaac stepped forward 'nothing my young queen we have not the want to work or go this day, your presence has filled our day. His words seemed to touch her, even the 2 young boys stood cap in hand smiling. Old Byron held his cap up then looked up at the rest of the men to do the same costy bock he said quite loud. They all repeated it. She looked at Nellie? It means 'Good Luck majesty

The queen then removed her glove, giving Nellie's hand a little squeeze, 'God Bless you and your family Nellie' and may he look after you my queen. Nellie's eyes filled up a little, she gave a quick curtsy, turned and walked away.

CHAPTER NINE – ABERLINE

There was a sudden jolt as the train finally came to a stop, Tex just sat there his expression was blank. Suddenly realizing where he was, some story, it would make a book, 'I do believe it because it's so ridiculous and you tell it without any hesitation, I believe it.' Adam never answered. 'Have you ever shot anyone?' repeated Tex. 'Well yes I did. I shot a man and badly wounded him, a dual in Paris over a lady, and killed a man in a duel over a card game, in Berlin.' 'Oh so you're not quite as civilized as I thought. In Paris, France hey? A dual? It sounds very well bred and civilized. In these here parts, there's no seconds, no counting how many paces. It's who gets it out the fastest and shoots straight' said Tex. 'It's ten paces, you only have one shot each you're told take aim, then you both fire exactly at the same time, it sounds too civilized and very deadly' said Tex.

'End of the Atlantic track from New York to Aberline, end of the line' the attendant repeated walking down the corridor.

The train will stay tonight, Saturday, and tomorrow, Sunday, then going back Monday morning 10 o clock. 'Thank god were here'. It'll take a month to get that clickety click track out of my brain', said Adam as he reached up for his two cases. He looked at the size of Adam's two cases. 'you've certainly brought enough stuff' he said, unloosening his shoulder holster and fitting it to his belt.

Glancing at Tex's gun holster the face was trimmed away where the trigger was. It was well worn. 'It looks a fast rig'. Tex smiled and shook his head. 'Have I said something wrong?' asked Adam. 'No offence meant, it's just for a dude, you have all the right sayings.' Adam noticed one of the men coming out of his cases with a gun. Another with a large hunting knife similar to the one Tex had on the opposite hip from his gun. 'Looks like everyone's going to war, must be a dangerous town'

'Looks worse than it really is. you see a man just likes to know he's got some sort of back up when he needs it, let's say protection, something he can rely on, very little law compared to big civilized towns this is new territory out here won't be really civilized for who knows how long, sometimes however quiet you are, trouble can find you. You'll have a gun I suppose?' 'Yes and a rifle' 'Are you putting it on?' 'No I'll see how things go' answered Adam.

Dropping his case on the platform. 'What's wrong?' asked Tex.' 'I'll carry one for you.' 'That's okay. The town must be over two hundred yards. 'What have you got in them lead or gold?' 'Some lead, two pistols, two rifles, and the rest is my stuff. A teenage boy came over with a Barrow. 'Take your cases sir?' As they went down the main street, Adam being well dressed, the boy following with his cases on the wheelbarrow. It might have looked alright in some big city. Aberline was another thing.

'Who's your girlfriend Tex?' someone shouted. They went up three steps. Adam looked at the sign. 'Summer Breeze Hotel 'Welcome Mr Steve.' Ann come and see who's here, his wife came in from the kitchen, a blond woman about forty, long time no see, glad to see you're back Tex, must be six months 'Howdy Bill, this here is Adam Boswell, a friend, were needing a room each.' Excuse me a minute gents interrupted a well dressed man. 'Mr Schultz I don't really want to sell my hotel, we've spent seven years building it up, from a three roomed guest house to an eight room hotel it's a very good offer a generous offer you've made me but I prefer to keep the business a pile of money like that I would spend a lot and gamble the rest, then I would neither have business or money'. 'That makes good sense to me, said Tex. No one's asking you your opinion Tex Steve. I am trying to buy this business. 'No offence meant to you Dutch. 'If I was wanting any business advice I wouldn't be looking to you for it, and it's Mr Schultz.

He turned around; his hand was on the door handle. 'Good evening gents.' Adam had noticed Mr Dutch Schultz had a short 38. special naval Colt with mahogany handles sitting high in a cross draw holster. There goes a very dangerous man always ready to meet trouble more than halfway, said Bill. He looked very arrogant, full of his own importance, said Adam

'Sorry Mr Steve, only got one room left but there are two separate beds in it.' Tex looked at Adam. 'Suits me Tex, when's the next Stage to Glen Parva?' 'Supposed to be Monday morning' answered Bill. 'What do we owe you?'

'Tonight and Sunday night, breakfasts both mornings, it'll be four dollars each.' 'Your prices have gone we'll up' said Tex. 'That's right Mr Steve, its weekend, and I'm still cheaper than the lone star hotel.' 'Okay' said Tex' 'Thank you sir' said the hotel owner.

Adam looked around the room it looked clean and simple, stripping to the waist he started to wash. Tex glanced at Adams back then looked away.

Dropping two pinches of salt into the cup of water then dipping the end of the towel into it and rubbing his teeth with it, finally taking 2 mouthfuls gargling twice and spitting out.

As Adam picked up his shirt off the chair, the cross and chain Esmeralda had given him fell out of his pocket, he Bent down and picked it up, his thoughts going back to Cambridge settlement, a nice quiet place, a village that would become a nice town. Maybe I should have stayed there, too small he thought has he put the chain and cross around his neck for the first time.

'That's nice Adam, I didn't know you was religious. I'm not really, a gypsy girl took it off her neck and gave it to me. 'Nice thing to do,' said Tex. Man that's some nasty scars on your back, 'Yes a so called gentleman horse whipped me, I was just 13. 'You'll have to tell me about that sometime, sounds interesting, said Tex, as he went into his bag coming out with soap and a razor. 'What time does the stagecoach leave tomorrow.' Tex never answered for a minute, giving the razor a fast shake in the bowl of water several times. 'It's usually about ten, but it's not tomorrow, it's Monday and there's usually a supply wagon with it they usually put 2 on at the same time, a second stagecoach that is. There's safety in numbers.

'Tex if I ask you something personal not sarcastic, I ask it has a friend. 'Well sarcastic, I don't rightly know about sarcastic, you've got a way of saying things, just say what's on your mind.' 'When you was near that Dutch Schultz I could notice a fear, Tex put down the razor and then looking at Adam. 'You're quick, you know I do private bodyguard jobs, there is a US Senator, I think I told you about him, Steven Evon'. Yes you did, answered Adam. 'Well there's been two attempts on his life, and he won't go anywhere of importance without two bodyguards he's important, could be trying for President within the next five or six years.

There's a private lawman like myself Mississippi Georgie Dur-an, handles himself well fast with a side gun even though he's getting on a bit. Six or seven months ago we had to go to Washington for a week with this Steven Evon and his wife Clarice, there in their room, me and Mississippi is in a separate room on either side of them.

The next evening we were at a table next to them in this posh restaurant. When he went for a piss one of us would even have to go with him. At the end of the night we was leaving the restaurant as we got towards the entrance two men started a fight. Me and Mississippi could see it was a put up moody fight then they went for their guns, it was a four gun shoot out, we got both of them. 'So where's the problem then Tex?. You give me your word this will go no further. You have my word, said Adam .

'That Dutch Schultz he has no family just a nephew, his sisters Boy, looks the spit of Dutch and they even named him after him.' He was one of the paid assassins to gun down Steven Evon and his wife, as I said. It was a four gun shoot out, lead flying everywhere, two bystanders was wounded, one killed. This young Dutch was hit three times and he died within ten minutes. Mississippi George reckons we both got him.

Now his Uncle Dutch Schultz that you just met, has swore to kill the two body guards. Nobody knows me in Washington, I've only been there once before. Mississippi George has even worked for the President a few times, been there many times, a lot of people know him around Washington.

Dutch Schultz has put up a re-ward of 2000 dollars to anyone who knows where Mississippi George is, also 2000 dollars re-ward to anyone who can identify the other bodyguard, being me and where he hangs out. 'Did he get this Mississippi George?' 'No way! Mississippi George let out fast for Canada, he's not scared but he has 2 daughters to consider.

'So how good how fast is this Dutch Schultz? He's a cold blooded killer, no woman, wife, or kids. He's put seven or eight men in the cemetery, I don't want to have a go at him. He'll come after your family to get to you. 'I don't blame you or Mississippi George, said Adam. Well why don't you get out Tex it's a very big country?' I've lived here in Texas all my life, not having some would be run me out, no way! You don't know, someone might take care of him for you one day said Adam.

Tex had a wash changed his shirt, then checked the window Bolts Before they left. The hotel owner met them at the Reception desk. 'Would you like to sign in gentlemen?' Adam handed Tex the pen. Joe Steve (Tex) of Glen Parva.' 'Adam Boswell of New York' he said, looking Adam up and down. 'You've come a long way sir, are you a Banker or a Lawyer Mr Boswell?' 'I'm neither, just here to see Texas' answered Adam.

'I noticed the door to our room has a clasp, is the lock Broke?' do you have a padlock?' 'I do sir for all the rooms.' People carry a lot of things so I use padlocks. 'I'd like that lock put on' said Tex. 'I'll see to it sir, and here's the keys, the Big ones to the front door. It's locked at eight o clock. I'll give you a knock in the morning. Breakfast eight till nine thirty.'

Adam was taking his time slowly looking round. As they walked up the long wide street, at the top it went across in a T, halfway went a street to the left and one to the right, then a second one to the right. Half way up on the left was a Saloon called The Palace. It was nearly 8 o'clock, all the shops was closed. Adam looked down at the dirt road, then at the Buildings, which was wood planking. The first two feet were cemented stones and rocks. Some of the roofs was corrugated metal sheeting, most was wood shingles. There were only two Brick

Buildings in the town. The Bank and the Sherriff's office with a jail adjoining. 'It's like a step Back into the past' he said. 'No kidding' answered Tex. 'The cafes over there' he said, pointing across the street.

As they crossed the street Adam looked at the sign, Mediterranean Café, a short fat Greek man welcomed them. 'Table over here sir near the window.' 'Thanks' said Tex, noticing Adam had taken his hat off he did the same. 'It must be five -six months I last seen you Mr Tex.' 'Yes it's a while, what's cooking tonight?' 'We've got the all-day breakfast, ham and eggs, ash brown, sirloin or rump steak and there's beef stew.'

'Hold on their fella, I'll try one of them drinks as well' said Tex. A man and wife further down the restaurant were just leaving. 'Your quarter change Sir.' 'That's okay.' 'Thank you Mister Johnston.' 'Well aren't you going to say hello?' 'I'll Be a son of a gun, if it's not Tex Steve, didn't recognize you without the beard and no hat. Look whose here honey.' Tex stood up to shake hands with the young man. 'Sit for a few minutes' he said, moving the hats. 'This here is Johnny Johnstone and his wife Maud from The Lazy Wye. Meet a new friend of mine, Adam Boswell from New York.'

The couple sat down. 'You have some very rich and important friends Tex, John Parva and the Senator Steve Evon, and Charlie Watson, the owner of The Last Chance Saloon at Glen Parva, and now this Mr Boswell of New York.' 'I can assure you I'm neither rich nor important' said Adam. 'We have a spread, a small cattle ranch about six miles out of town.' 'And what's small round these parts?' asked Adam. 'Oh it's only 900 acres, just my young brother, and father in law. It's easily handled with the three of us.' 'How have things been?' asked Tex. 'Cattle business is good, I bought two young Scottish Highland bulls, John Parva's been breeding them into his herd over a year now. Cold weather doesn't seem to bother them, and if it's rocky or poor grass, they can take it, they're hard animals from Scotland, England. These Hereford animals we have, pack a lot of Beef. Put the two together, it'll be a new strain.'

'Sounds interesting, what will you call them?' asked Adam. 'Texas Longhorns' answered Jonny. 'I bet they were dear.' '800 dollars.' 'Man that's a lot of dollars 800 for just two pieces of beef, should have been a lot dearer but they were shipped over with John Parva's.' 'They'll be a new strain, hard for winter and heavy for selling.' 'It was good of John letting you have them.'

'Yes he is a very nice gent, I was with him and his wife Angelina weeks ago in New York, said Adam, ready to impress as always. Just then the meals and drinks came. 'We'll leave you gents now, don't want to be too late getting the wife back home, Saturday night, there could be trouble. There was a shooting two weeks back, one killed and a knife fight. 'Maybe I should have stayed in New York' joked Adam, standing up to shake hands with Jonny and his wife.

Outside was a horse and wagon half full of supplies. Jonny put his rifle under the other arm to shake hands with Adam. 'A pleasure to have met you and your wife Jonny.' 'Likewise Mr Boswell, A few minutes passed, Adam looked at Tex 'they seem to be nice decent people.' 'You're a good judge, they are, you certainly impress people don't you Adam, the way you dress and speak. What race are you, anyway? You're dark for English, you look Italian? 'Oh that's right you told me you are a Romany Gypsy. 'How many countries do you say you've seen? Adam thought about things quickly, some time or another it would come out what he was, there were so many different people here, it would make no difference, thought Adam, and Tex seemed genuine. 'I'm not really sure, probably eight or nine. But you know Tex when I look at this America, most of the different countries and people here, no wonder they call it the New World. I can't be the judge of that, born and bred here in Texas, he answered.

Starting to cut a piece of steak, then scraping some onions and a piece of mushroom on it. 'It's nice the sauce or gravy I'm pleased I tried it', he said. 'How is it sir, does it suit you?' asked the café owner. 'Best I've had for a long time,' answered Tex. It's tender you must have beat it on a wooden block, asked Adam. 'That's right sir, we have to down here in Texas, the beef can be tough, it's out there for who knows how many years'.' You cook a good meal, no complaints' said Adam.' Thank you sir'.

'It made sense how Johnny was taking his wife home early, most men would have left her while he had a few drinks and a gamble in the saloon', said Adam, placing his knife and fork down. 'You finished already? Asked Tex. 'No, just taking a rest, it's too good to hurry.

'You know Adam this is not London or New York, there's no way you can just drop a woman at a café for 2 hours, well you have a gamble and a few drinks, you could get a couple of drunken drifters, red necks, see her sitting on her own, come in, drag her out to the prairie, just do what they want, leave her for the Coyotes, it has happened there's thousands of square miles out there, they can just disappear. 'Yes I see what you mean Tex; I noticed he had no side gun carried a rifle. You've got to have protection out here of some sort, we call it back up, we grew up with it.

Tex looked up, pushing his plate away, 'that sure hit the spot'. Hit the spot repeated Adam, I enjoyed it. 'You can tell me all about the civilized world, and I can learn you about this New World. 'If you went in one of them two saloons without a gun there would be other men without a gun, probably four out of ten, some like a knife'. 'Most townsmen if they're carrying a gun it's a light small caliber in a shoulder holster, but men that's passing through, drifters, red necks (cowboys), they all carry a Colt or a rifle'. 'No one travels this country without protection; it's too wild and very big.

Adam looked at Tex, I'm a gypsy. 'No kidding,' said Tex. 'Truth 'My people go back many hundreds and hundreds of years, you can trace them down through the lands and kingdoms in Europe. You can find them fortune telling even in the bible. We originate from Babylon, Egypt and came down through many countries, India, Spain, The Mediterranean over the centuries.

'I've heard different stories, about your people, some call you the wandering Egyptians?' 'And you have your own language, don't you?' Adam smiled. 'Yes we do. This new lands made up of many people's from most countries, and over the next hundred years or so, there will be thousands more people come here. It needs a handful of Gypsy families in this vast country. 'Let's say, to give it some quality and character', said Adam smiling.

'You don't speak low bred'. 'No offence meant' said Tex, pushing his plate further away. 'You're dress, how you speak, that big gold ring, you seem to have money.' Are you having me on are you really a Romany gypsy, it's hard to believe. 'That's because some people associate us with tinkers and field workers, it is so easy to blame any wrong doing on the Romany gypsy that was here the last few weeks and has moved on this week. 'When in London I went into a library I traced my mother and fathers people back 200 hundred years ago, to the late 1600's they first came to England, from The Mediterranean, but all gypsy people, their ancestors, originally come from Babylon. When they first landed in England, there were only 10-12 families.

In Scotland, Edinburgh two men were hung for stealing horses and they wasn't even in Edinburgh at the time, they were nearly forty miles away in a place called Berwick-On-Tweed, on the Scottish border it is convenient to blame things on the moving gypsy, they are regularly blamed, for things they have not done. 'Is it true you're woman can read the future Clairvoyant?' As Tex finished his drink watching how tidy the knife and fork lay, side by side on Adams empty plate.

Just then the café owner placed two slices of apple pie and cream on the table. 'No thanks, I'm full, said Adam. 'Some can, they have a genuine talent a gift handed down to them, and some can't but they try and manage to get a living out of it. We must stop now Tex we could probably go on for hours on the subject; I'd like to see what the saloons are like out here, I'm fancying a gamble. '2 dollars and 60 cents please Mister Steve. Tex placed a dollar and 2 quarters on the table, Adam placed one dollar and a fifty cent piece down.

As they stood outside on the planked side walk (pavement) Tex took out the makings and rolled a cigarette. 'You want to try one?' 'Why not, then lighting it up and having a few drawers at it. 'What do you think of it? 'Not a lot, answered Adam. 'You want one of these?' I've been smoking yours for two days. 'I enjoyed that drink, tasty, what do you call it again? 'A shandy' beer and lemonade mixed answered Adam, It's good with a meal. You're not in New York or London now, out here, it's whisky or beer, but I will admit it was nice with a meal'.

Holding his case open, there was three left, then putting the long thin cigar between his teeth. Tex lit both of them up, then taking the case out of Adam's hand. It's heavy, I like the small gold initials in the centre, you've got style 'What did you think of the meal, is it as good as the big cities?' 'Yes it was I enjoyed it. Again Adam slowly looked back down the long street. The only 2 brick buildings in town were the sheriff's office, adjoining jail and the bank on the opposite side; all the other buildings. The first 2 feet were stones and boulders cemented together, then wooden planking. 'Well what do you think?' asked Tex. He had seen Adam looking around as they walked. It's like a step back into the past. 'Yes so you said before', said Tex

As they walked slowly up the street Adam noticed most of the best buildings were painted white or pale grey. The main street was long and very wide. It's not as big as I thought it would be. 'I wouldn't call it a town, a big village what's behind the street right at the top a livery stables and school? There's 2 saloons Yellow Sky and Grand Canyon, answered Tex.

'What about that saloon? Said Adam pointing, 'Well that one's not really a saloon, mostly a whorehouse, it's very posh, the palace, whisky in there is very good, real Scottish malt. The Yellow Sky at the top of the street's ok, card games roulette, music, it's got the lot.' 'I've worked in there a few times and the Grand Canyon is across the street. 'Well let's give it a whirl, said Adam. Tex smiled 'Yeah' let's give it a whirl, whatever that means.

As they walked up the steps onto the planked sidewalk (pavement) some 3ft off the ground. On the left hand side near the bat wing doors was a large coloured poster nailed to the wall. Texas yearly state Fair to be held in Glen Parva July 3rd, 4th and 5th Independence Day Celebration. 'Is this a regular thing, said Adam pointing to the poster. Yes, It's a yearly event been going on the last ten years usually held in a different town, in Texas each time, brings a lot of visitors and trade to the town. It's the yearly state fair for the full state of Texas, I don't suppose you've been to one.

Quite a few, we've been having them for hundreds of years back home and many gypsy families go to them as a holiday. Appleby horse fair Mussel burgh champion trotting near Edinburgh. There's Nottingham Goose Fir, Barnstable in Devon. Stop, you've convinced me you Brits had them first, tell me about them. 'There's bare knuckle gypsy fighting, jumping, horse dealing, songs, outside parties nearly all night, pigs on a spit, horse trotting, dancing, fortune telling for the on lookers, young people courting, I must stop Tex it would take me an hour to tell you about that. You said a goose fair? You're not kidding me do they really sell geese there, asked Tex, Adam just smiled let's get a few drinks and see where the action is.

Following Tex through the two bat wing doors, and slowly looking around. The sides were panelled in several different types of wood that was varnished, it was a nice effect. The roof painted a very light grey which had a tint of yellow from the smoke. It was big and went well back. There were 4 wagon wheels hanging from the roof beams, each one had 5 paraffin lamps on it that lit the place up like daylight. A piano over in the far corner it was banging out that new song 'oh those golden slippers'. A second man in a bowler hat sitting on a small barrel was keeping time with a fiddle. Two ladies were singing, they looked on the wrong side of forty. There was quite a bit of smoke as they made their way through to the back where the card games were, Adam noticed a roulette table.

'What'll it be?' 'I'll have a beer'. 'Long time no see Tex, said the barman where you been hiding these days?' 'I've been working away a lot.' 'I'll have three fingers of whisky, the best one, and two beers', said Tex looking around. 'Through here Adam. This is where it's all happening' he said, carrying his two drinks.

Adam followed Tex through the tables. 'It's bigger than I thought?' 'It's okay I've been in a lot worse.' answered Tex. Considering it was early four of the five gambling tables was busy. Brag, two playing, Poker the Black Jack was slow; the only thing bringing the men to it was the pretty young blonde in a very low cut dress. Adam slowed down as he past. I'd rather be on here than on my horse.' said Tex 'I'll Bet she's not a minute over eighteen' she's stunning, said Adam. 'What's stunning?' asked Tex.

Adam thought about it for a minute then just shook his head. Tex smiled, you Brits don't even know your own language. 'Poker's over here'. 'I'll join you for a while, roulettes my game' answered Adam.

'Too many rules, numbers and combinations for me, never could understand it all' answered Tex. 'Got room for 2 more' he asked, pulling up a chair. They joined a poker game, nearly an hour had past. Adam was losing about fifteen dollars, But Tex was losing over fifty, he was on his sixth whisky, and second beer. Adam wanted to tell him heavy drinking and gambling doesn't mix, But somehow he just couldn't get it across to him in front of a table full of players.

There card table was next to the roulette, Adam had been watching it for the last fifteen minutes trying to memorize the croupiers words which wasn't easy when playing poker. 'Number ten, evens, on the black, he heard,' 'Deal me out I'm going to have a look at the Roulette, you alright Tex?' I'm okay,' he said dragging his words a little, raising his right hand to scratch his forehead to cover a quick little wink. As Adam got up he gave Tex a nod.

Adam smiled standing over by the roulette wheel. This was his game. There were only four players around the roulette table. Most of the men didn't seem to show a lot of interest, it was mostly cards, there was also caged dice. . It was a nice clean table with a cross on the top of the wheel, being a Monte Carlo wheel. 'Do you mind me glancing at your card?' asked Adam. 'Not at all fellow,' answered the man sat at the roulette table. Turning around he handed Adam the card with many rows of squares numbered, some of them penciled in. 'Thanks mate, you from England, that's right said Adam, reaching out and placing the card back down in front of the man. There had been nine blacks in a row. Adam quickly walked outside the saloon taking a 500 dollar wad out of one of the pockets of his money belt. By the time he had got back to the table the ball was spinning as the wheel turned the opposite way. 'Place your bets please, place your bets now, round it goes, where she stops nobody knows,'

Should have known you was fooling, Tex. 'You was playing possum, said the cow hand, throwing in his hand. Tex had played drunk and it had paid off. 'Come to Tex,' he said pulling in the big kitty with both hands. Adam quickly reached over and placed 25 dollars on the red. '25 dollars cash bet on the red,' the croupier, taking the cash and replacing it with a chip. 'that's a pony on the red sir.' The little white ball was now slowing down. Adam reached out again to place a small bet on the zero. No more bets please, no more bets,' said the croupier. The little white ball was bouncing now slowly from one slot to another, then stopped, it's black again, 'Number fifteen on the black, he said pulling all the winnings in with both arms, then dropping the cash down a slot in the table.

There was a Mexican standing at the opposite side of the table he looked angry has he had just lost fifty dollars. 'That wheel's a jinx, there's a jinx on it. 'Three bets, that makes one hundred dollar it has taken off me'. He placed twenty dollars in chips on the red square, being his fourth bet. 'Just a fool, a gringo fool' said the Mex out loud seeing Adam smiling, after losing.

Adam reached out and placed fifty dollars on the red, the croupier replaced the notes with 2 chips, 'That's fifty on the red sir.' The man sitting in front of him turned around, 'That zeros not come up for I don't know how long, not seen it all night. It's a good safety bet at 35 to 1'. As he had just bet ten dollars on a half split bet on the numbers, and five dollars on a column bet then another five on zero. 'Place your bets gents, roulette's the name of the game, place your bets. Round she goes, where it stops nobody knows.' There was now only four players left, including Adam. The Mex banged the edge of the table in temper 'Please don't bang the table Sir, you could jar the wheel.'

'You have had a hundred dollar of my money, I'll do what I want', he said, banging the table again. Suddenly, there was a man stood at the side of him, Adam had seen the man, he had nodded to Tex when they came in 'you've been asked not to bang the table Sir, so don't do it. You understand?' He was wearing a badge like Tex had. The Mex looked at the peacekeepers badge noticing he wore two guns, the holsters tied down. 'Okay okay Signore Americano, law man. I understand.' The name of game, it's roulette, last bets' 'we know it's roulette you idiot' growled the Mex. 'No more bets gents, no more bets.' The little ball had slowed down, jumping again across the slots. Clickety-click clickety-click click, click then it stopped. The winner, and it's black again, evens, number 20 on black. The Mex was getting wild, losing again. The Americano, the gringo, happy to lose his money. 'A fool, just a fool' said the Mex. Be careful young fella I think he's Common Charro and he's not on his own warned the man in front of Adam, who had lent him his card, thanks mate. Adam was getting a little annoyed as the Mex was pointing at him and others could hear the Mex. Adam looked down at the card, 'ten straight blacks' ' it's got to be red this time, if not it should be next time. As he reached over and placed 180 dollars on the red to clear his losses and win a hundred dollars, Adam glanced down at the card.

It had 50 squares, three quarters of them was marked, not one showing a zero. The man in front of Adam placed ten dollars on it. It's showed no zeroes all night, must be due any time. 'You could be right friend.' 'What's the limit on zero?' 'thirty five to one, it pays out at thirty five to 1 as all the numbers do,' answered the croupier. Thank you said Adam then reaching over and placing the limit of thirty five dollars on the zero. The croupier was now looking a little nervous; The Mex was staring and pointing his finger at him, as if it was all the croupiers' fault, he was losing. The white ball was now spinning around fast, as the wheel went the opposite way.

The bet was now going quickly through Adam's mind. He had just bet 180 dollars, which would clear one hundred dollars profit, he glanced down at the card a second time. 'thirty five dollars bet on zero, if red comes up, I'll be a hundred dollars in front, if zero comes up, he paused for a few seconds, I'll laugh all the way back to the hotel. 'Come on zero', he said loudly, forget red I want zero.' The man that was seated in front of Adam stood up. The roulette area it had gone quiet 'You can do it little white ball it's time for zero we've never seen you all night, he said quite loud. Around the roulette table it was silent. The Croupier looked up. 'You are right gents, 100% right, it is zero. The house takes all bets except for zero, and pays half back to any even money bets, said the croupier, counting fifty dollar chips, then slowly pushing the 2 stake across the table to Adam and of course your stake money back sir. All who had bet red, got half of their money back, it was even money bet. There had been no bets on odds or evens, or highs or lows. Just a few numbers. By now a small crowd had gathered around the table. The Mex looked at his money, he had 180 dollars left, he reached out and placed a hundred dollars on the red square. 'So how much have you won? I am not sure Tex, about nine hundred dollars', answered Adam.

Tex counted up 140 dollars profit, he put 40 dollars back in his pocket, then holding up the hundred dollars. Adam, what now?' 'Put it on red and shout it home.' 'Place your bets gents, it's Roulette. At this two men that were stood watching placed a bet each on the red, Adams mind was now going over it very fast. 'I'm well in front with the zero bet, but I am losing 260 dollars on the even money red bets' he thought. 'Croupier, what's the limit on an even money Bet?' '300 dollars sir', he answered looking up, as he was stacking the piles of chips. 'Only 300 dollars, it's usually a 500 dollar limit, everywhere,' said Adam. 'I don't make the rules sir, the limit is 300 and if you look on the Back wall all the gambling rules are up there.'

A bald headed man was now standing about twenty feet away on the opposite side of the table, it was Dutch Schultz with the Navy Colt Special in a crosse drawer black leather holster, immaculately dressed, tailored suit with a diamond horse shoe tie pin in a silk cravat. This maximum bet should be 500 not 300, I've been betting too high for another double up, if I do win it will be only forty dollars profit, it's a silly bet, 300 to win forty.' 'Even then it could come Black again, thought Adam.

Come on fella, you're going to miss the bet, get it on,' said the man sitting in front, turning around, 'it's no good friend the 300 dollar limit as beat me before the ball rolls. 'Man that's tough because it's one good bet'. 'You bet the 300, and push over 100 to me, I'll bet it for you, with my bet,' Adam looked down at the 2 50 dollar chips in his hand. Suddenly the croupier coughed loudly, then staring at Adam and slightly shaking his head from one side to the other. His eyes turned quickly towards the bald headed man, then back to Adam. 'Please don't pass the money to your friend; you will get me in serious trouble, lamed and probably the sack,' Adam pocketed his chips, then folded a 10 dollar bill twice, reaching over he pushed it into the croupiers breast shirt pocket. I've had a very good night' said Adam, 'thank you Mr? 'Adam Boswell. 'Thank you Mr Boswell you're a gentleman

'Place your bets gents, place your bets. Tex placed the one hundred dollars on the red square. At this, two men that was watching placed bets on the red. The croupier looked around there was a lot of money riding on red, and very little on anything else. He could see his boss looking over again, and giving him 2 nods as if to say 'Get it finished quickly'. There was more men looking over. Some were putting their hands in their pockets, to get money out. The wheel is spinning. No more bets gents repeated the Croupier. Adam stood watching. When the odds are against them they try to carve you up. The wheel hasn't even slowed down and he's shouting no more bets.

The gent in front of Adam stood up. 'Come on red, don't you let me down, you've been hiding too long – come on red!' 'It's going to be red' said someone in a whisper. As the ball finally found its slot the croupier reached out his hand on top of the cross to stop the wheel spinning. 'It's on the red gents, it's the colour you all wanted, and the Yellow Sky always pays out'. Yellow Sky honors all winning bets, it's twenty three on the red winner.

'You unlucky red, you should've come up two spins ago, said the Mex, as he picked up his winnings, then drawing his Colt and firing it twice into the floor boards. 'Cool it Mex, and holster that iron'. 'It's okay folks, it's okay, just the Mex letting off a little steam' said the peacemaker loudly.

Adam turned and walked away with Tex and Bill the Barber. 'Cash me in' he said, stacking his chips up on the counter. 'You finishing already? It's your night.

Aren't you going on?' said Tex. 'It's been a very good night, and it's time to walk away, I am about nine hundred dollars in front' said

Adam counting his chips, 'I've gone back before a few times and lost the lot, so now is the time to walk away' answered Adam.

'I'm about 300 dollars in front, 'I'll hang on in there for a while. I might walk back over with you later on for a few more spins' said Bill.

Adam waved the old man over that was clearing the glasses up off the tables. Yes sir?' he asked. Adam placed a 10 dollar bill on the table. 'Two large jugs of beer, and a bottle of whisky, tell them it's the good stuff for Tex Steve, and have yourself one.' 'Thank you sir' he said. Tex stood up, I need some smokes 'a what do you call them there cigars that you get?'. 'Kings Panatela's'. Adam Boswell' he said, putting out his right hand. 'My name's Billy Hibb, I am the Barber in Glen Parva. Are you from England?' 'No Scotland.' 'Well I suppose it's all one isn't it?' said Bill.

Adam was going to explain, and then changed his mind. Tex came back over with three packets of cigars. The old man came back with the tray of drinks. Adam unscrewed the lid. 'It smells familiar' he said with a smile looking at Tex, then getting up. He came back from the bar with a small jug of orange juice. The old man placed some coins in front of Adam. 'Have you had a drink yourself?'. 'I kept the money for a whiskey later on sir.' Adam glanced at the old man. His clothes were worn out. The heels of his boots was well over and cracked at the front. He must be seventy, thought Adam.

'That's okay old timer, it's your tip.' Adam poured himself a drink. I've got a few clothes that's gone a bit tight for me, and a pair of shoes if you can use them that is.' 'I sure can sir I live in the back, thank you very much' he said, then walking away. 'Years ago he was a well to do business man, he owned the other general store. His teenage girl died of pneumonia. He only had the one. She was everything to him. He took to drinking and gambling. His wife ran off with some fella. He went through everything he had' said Bill. 'Bad way for a man to end up' answered Adam.

'Hey foolish laughing dude, why you wear that silly hat? Said the Mex loudly pointing to Adam's Bowler Hat' 'Let it go Adam, I think they're common charo's' said Bill. Yeah so you said, They're wearing guns, all four of them' said Tex. Adam nodded in agreement. 'Hey fool dude, why you wear that silly hat?' Adam ignored him, pouring a little orange juice into Tex's whiskey. 'See what you think. Tex closed his eyes, shook his head just once slowly. 'That is one nice drink fella. You start to feel the fire a minute or so after it's gone down' then emptying the last of the glass. Tex poured Adam and Bill one each. 'I'll make this the last one for me. 'It's usually beer for me, I don't drink spirits.' Tex then filled his own glass and lifted it. 'Here's to friends, new ones and old ones' he said, raising his glass. 'I'll drink to that' said Adam, touching his glass to Bill and Tex's glass.

Adam was enjoying himself. He liked these frontier men, rough and ready something like his own people. 'I have to agree, it does taste nice, nothing like an I don't know what, but it's nice' said Bill.

'Hey you fool, why you not answering me? I ask you about your silly hat, gringo fool?' Adam drank half of his drink, and then took two big puffs of his cigar looking at the glowing end. 'Why you not answer me fool dude? You afraid to talk to a real man, is that what it is?' 'I am here to enjoy the night with friends said Adam. 'I don't think he's going to let it go. He wants trouble' said Tex. 'Well if that's what he wants, I'm gonna give him plenty' said Adam. Billy Hibb looked at Tex, his eyebrows going up as if to say, this Adam is very confident

'Are you frightened like a woman is that why you wear a silly hat and talk so different?' I speak English, what you're trying to do. There was five or six men drinking at the Bar. They quickly moved away. Adam stood up and smiled at the Mex, 'Hey low life 'Chummer mandes Bull Mex. 'What does that mean?' he asked. 'Kiss my arse. That's what it means' answered Adam. 'This could be a bad night' said Tex, having a puff of his cigar and sitting back. Some of the card games had stopped and the players had moved over by the walls. The place had suddenly gone a lot quieter. The clickety click of the roulette wheel could now be heard more loudly. 'No more bets please' said the Croupier. He opened his mouth to repeat it, but when he looked round, he said nothing. Taking a draw on his cigar Adam then smiled, 'I am your gypsy boy and you've found just what you're looking for.'

Adam had quickly weighed the Mex up. He was big enough, a good 2 stone overweight, about 6ft. Two Bandoliers of bullets cress cross his chest. A big 44 colt on his hip, probably, in his late 30s. Adam stood up. 'You're a low life mongrel.' Tex glanced at his friend, Wally the Peacemaker. Wally shook his head from side to side, as if to say this is not a drunken brawl. It is a challenge and the dude is taking it up. It is an unwritten law of the west, a challenge is a very private matter, for nobody to interfere with. Not even a law man. The Mex smiled. He would easily beat this dude he thought. He was from a big city and would know very little about gun play. I will have another notch on my gun, and I will be the fast gun tonight he thought.

'Can you use a gun dude?' Adam opened his coat wide. 'I don't have any weapons, I'm unarmed' he said loudly. 'I cannot allow this insult to pass by. I am going to kill you, white eye' His right hand opened and closed twice. Wally took 2 steps forward then stopped. 'There'll be no shooting down of any unarmed men in this saloon tonight'. Tex stood up, holding his coat back, his badge showing. 'I'll second that.' 'No way will I allow this insult to pass by' said the Mex. 'Is that so? You're just a bucket of shit' said Adam, taking his coat off and throwing it on a chair, then taking 2 puffs of his cigar. 'Fight' said Bill. 'Fight' said some other man at the next table. By the tone of their voice they seemed happy to watch a fist fight then a gun fight, which can be finished and over too quick 'There's been enough talk. 'Get the gun off and let's see what you've got' said Adam as he shaped up.

With his thumb and index finger the Mex slowly took his colt out of its holster laying it on the bar top. 'And here's where we see if Adam's bite is as good as his bark' thought Tex with a smile. Adam had his fists deliberately a little low. The Mex came in throwing 2 punches a left and a right. Adam eased his head back from the left , the right grazed his forehead. Adam shook his head twice taking a step back then moving around the Mex, jabbing at his head with a few fast straight rights, to bring him round onto his left, being his best punch. Adam seemed to stumble. Lowering his guard as he did taking the half cigar out of his mouth. Maybe it was for real or the come on for the Mex?

As the Mex threw a straight right. Adam eased his head back the fist went sailing by missing his jaw by some three or four inches.

Adam brought his left over the top of the outstretched right arm stubbing and twisting the red end of his cigar in the Mex's right ear. He let out a low scream. There was a smell of burning flesh his hand was brushing backwards and forwards fast, several times across his burnt ear.

Adam quickly stepped forward placing his left hand behind Mex's right shoulder, pulling him forward, as he punched two low hard rights into Mex's stomach, he doubled up dropping to his knees. His burnt ear throbbing and smarting, his stomach ached. He glanced towards his friends.

One of the other three Mex's went to step forward. 'His hand sneaking towards the gun, leave it be, said Arby, the big peacemaker. His fingers tapping the face of his gun holster. 'On your feet low life' said Adam, taking three steps back giving the Mex room to get up. As he got to his feet his right hand suddenly reached down pulling a hunting knife out the side of his boot. 'I'll cut your white man's heart out and eat it' he said, making several criss cross slashes in mid air. 'My God, He looks mean said Billy Hibb the barber. At least I know what I am.' Your mother was a cross bred Squaw whore for the soldiers' and you don't know who or what you are. Adam had succeeded getting the Mex into a wild rage. He was starting to circle Adam with the knife.

Billy Hibb sent a folded razor sliding down the bar top. 'Cut his ears off '. 'Thanks Bill, but I've been here before' answered Adam. Tex looked on not knowing what to make of it. He knew Adam hadn't been in the Yellow Sky Saloon before. He was now moving from side to side as the Mex was slowly circling him to attack.

Adam eased his head back as the blade went passed missing his face by some three inches. He then grabbed the outstretched wrist gripping it tight, turning it. He jumped, then bringing the edge of his left hand hard down in a chop. The outstretched elbow snapped like a twig. Wrenching the knife out of his hand, Adam brought it down hard, the Blade sinking into the Mex's right shoulder, it had happened so fast, seeing the knife sticking out of his shoulder. Then came the pain he felt the blood trickling down his side. The point of the blade protruded down out of his armpit. 'You're just as well to have it all' said Adam, as he hit down hard on the top of the handle. The last three inches of blade went down to the hilt.

Adam kicked the back of Mex's right leg hard, he hit the floor with a heavy thud, the pain seem to have started everywhere. He lay there cowering back, blood running down his side, not knowing what to expect next, 'You're just a bucket of shits,' said Adam turning to walk away.

Suddenly one of the other three was on his back. The man's wrist around Adams neck, his 2 hands gripping together very tightly. Adam was gasping. He lifted his left foot high, bringing it down as hard as he could, three, four times his heavy heel sinking into the man's toes. The grip slackened then suddenly he felt a finger either side in his mouth trying to rip his mouth apart. He quickly placed one hand on top of his own head and the other underneath his chin giving his jaws maximum power as he clenched his teeth, the ends of the two index fingers snapped off as he spat them out.

The saloon dog under the back table rushed forward taking one of the bloody fingers in its mouth back under the table, then chewing on it. Tex looked away feeling a little sick. The man stood looking at his hands, half of his 2 first fingers missing, tears running down his cheeks. Adam grabbed him by the shirt front measuring him he hit him really hard. The man's right eyebrow seemed to split, the heavy gold ring had opened him up. 'He's finished' said Tex. 'I'm not', said Adam gripping him by the shirt front, 'try a Glasgy kiss, he then let him drop to the floor.

One day Gringo, one day you English rubbish I will see find you and I will enjoy killing you, he was in such a state he was sobbing as he looked at his fingers, blood was trickling out of his split eyebrow. One of the other 2 stepped forward, his face dark with anger, eyes flashing. 'You white eye Gringo, theses are my cousins' pointing to the 1 on the floor, the other one getting up off his knees holding a dish cloth tightly round his fingers, look what you've done. 'You have crippled my 2 cousins for life you must die now white eye.'

His fingers were just stroking his gun holster. Adam froze. He felt more fear than any other time in his life. This is no circus routine. It's for real. He thought there was about twenty feet between them, no way can i get to him this man is going to gun me down, thought Adam, and he's taking his time, sweat was trickling down the side of Adams face.

'Hey ugly slap leather.' There was only 35 to forty feet between them, when Orby, the big law man made his play. The Mex's gun had just cleared leather, when Big Orbs colt 44 went off like a canon. The Mex seemed to walk backwards two, three small steps, then fell face down. He was dead before he hit the floor, the neat hole in the front of his chest was nothing like the ugly hole in his back, you could have put your four fingers in it. Orby gave the big colt a twirl, landing it in the holster.

'How about you? You got anything on your mind fella?' He said to the last one. 'Not me Senior Orby, I am no relation' he said with fear in his voice. Tex stood up slowly took his Colt out of the holster with his finger and thumb, laying it on the table. You Know I never did like your lot, like my friend has said, you're a bucket of shit, all of you. Maybe you'd like to try me without a gun. 'Not with you Senor Tex Steve, I've seen you fight, not this time. 'No your time will be when it's three to 1 or down some side alley, said Tex, pushing his colt back in the holster

The one with the missing fingers was leaning on the bar holding a blood soaked bandana to his split eyebrow. The colt revolver that was still on the bar top, his hand had been slowly creeping towards it. Tex smiled. 'When your hand touches that six gun fella, you'll be in hell with your loud mouth friend, now either go for it or step away, Tex's fingers was just touching the side of his gun holster, the man quickly moved away. Adam walked over unloaded the Colt, then leaving it empty on the bar top.

Two men came forward, taking the body out to the back room. One came back with a mop and bucket of water, quickly cleaning up the floor. The saloon was now coming back to life. People were talking again. 'Place your bets please gents, place your bets' said the Croupier, the music had started up. My god everything's back to normal thought Adam slowly looking around as if coming out of a bad dream. He could smell the gun powder there was still a little gun smoke high in the air. One dead on the floor, the other with a knife buried in his shoulder and the third crippled up. The Elephant and Castle and the Gaubles is nothing to this frontier town he thought 'See what I mean about wearing a gun?' said Tex. Adam just nodded. 'Take him in the back room' said the Doctor to the fourth Mex. The Doc had come forward with his black bag, that seemed to go everywhere with him. The fourth one helped carry him through to the back room.

They laid him on one of the couches, both stained with blood as the Doctor slowly pulled the blade out of Mex's shoulder, he passed out. The blood trickled faster, soaking the couch where he laid. 'Hold his arm up high, that's it.' The Doc poured pure alcohol spirit into the gash then pressed a white thick cream in it to clog it up, opening a small tin, he choose a needle which was readily threaded with cat gut. Then pouring some alcohol spirit over it and quickly put four stitches in the wound. As the gut pulled it close together the white cream oozing out, the doctor patted it, placing a thick pad of white lint on the wound. 'Now keep his arm tight to his side, I'll clean and stitch the top wound, then I can get it all bandaged up.' 'Will he be able to ride tonight?' asked the other Mex. 'If he does, he'll bleed to death.' 'Take him to a room upstairs, give him a couple of double whiskeys. Just leave him. He needs a good night sleep. I'll see him tomorrow about eleven o'clock and clean the wounds again and apply new dressings to them. See he gets a good breakfast as well. His arm is also broke at the elbow' said the Doctor.

'You going to splint it then Doc?' asked the fourth Mex. 'If I do, he'll never bend it again, the joints broke, I'll just bandage it. If it's left he'll be able to half bend it. He really needs a specialist hospital in one of the big cities.' 'I don't think that will happen Doctor. He does not have that kind of money.' 'In that case I doubt if your friends arm will be the same. That dude sure made it look easy how he handled your 2 friends. 'Well that's it all done and finished for now. No disrespect. If you can settle me up, because many just ride out of town and I don't get paid.' 'How much is it doctor?' 'It's 50 dollars now and 25 dollars in the morning.' 'That's dear doctor 75 dollars.' 'It was very dear for my college education and medical school. If I don't get paid, I won't be seeing him in the morning.' 'There's your 50 dollars doctor, thank you.' Now let's see this split eyebrow and I'm going to have to burn the end of those fingers and that will be another 50 dollars

Are you alright now Adam? You've lost that tan, gone a little grey' joked Tex. Life seems so cheap out here. I thank you friend, you risked your own life for me. He was going to gun me down. I thank you Bill for the razor' said Adam, as he placed it in front of Bill. Then pouring himself a large whiskey. Orby Baa the Peacemaker came over. 'Nice play Orb, I swear you're getting faster.' This is a friend of mine, Adam Boswell from New York, this is Orby Baa' He's a contract law officer like myself. Adam glanced at the badge. Unusual name, Orby? It's really Albert. Adam looked at the size of his hands, must be about 6ft four" and 18 stone, are all the Texans big he asked, looking at Orby then Tex, they all laughed. Thank you for what you've done said Adam, shaking hands. 'That's okay Mr Boswell that's my job. 'You sure can have a fight as you know Tex both of you will have to make a signed statement tomorrow for the Sheriff. I'll go witness for you. "So will I' said Bill.

'So what's it been like this last few weeks?' asked Tex. 'Quiet enough till you lot got here' joked Orby. 'One knife fight. Cowboy stabbed in the leg, the other in the arm over a card game as usual. Sheriff took them in and fined them 30 dollars each for disturbing the peace.' Mr Boswell. My name's Adam. You made a big mistake.' 'Is that right?' 'What mistake did I make? ' You bet your bottom dollar you and Tex did, you should have killed all of them. 'I think Orbys right, they'll be back, could be five weeks, five years, they don't let it go that lot. Could be plenty with them when they come too, said Bill

'I noticed when you challenged him, you never gave him any time to make a decision' said Adam. 'I already made the decision, He was gonna kill an unarmed man, it was a fair challenge. I told him to draw if he wanted to think about it. That's up to him said Orby. When it's a challenge out here you gotta get it out fast and put it away slow' said Tex. Adam glanced at Orby then Tex, I've made some good friends out here. Thank you lord, he was surprised that he had said that used to hearing his mother Delly say it, when help came. 'What did you say? Asked Orby. Oh I just said thank you Lord for pulling me through that and my new friends.

Are you religious? Asked Orby. 'Not really just used to hearing my mother say it. 'You'll get along with my wife, she's religious answered Orby

'This here is new territory and I doubt if it will be civilized for fifty or sixty years, maybe more, said Bill putting the razor back in his coat pocket.'

Adam stood up pouring himself a large whiskey. You going, asked Tex. I need some fresh air, he answered, knocking his double whiskey straight Back. 'Take your time man, we'll be here or back on the tables.' Adam picked up the large jug and filled his Beer glass taking it with him. Tex looked at him has he was walking away. He's not used to it out here, we've grown up with all this. 'You're right answered Bill.

'He can have a good fight, he has an unusual way of fighting, said Orby. He is an unusual fella , said Bill

Adam stood looking across the street; two men had taken their coats off to have a fight. They had just come out of the Grand Canyon saloon. Adam sat down on the bench, took a mouth full of beer then lit a cigar. Several men had come out to watch the fight. After only five or six minutes the so called fight had turned into a wrestling then kicking the onlookers laughed and went back in the saloon. The 2 men was now up on their feet, they stopped wrestling they seemed to have no idea as they were now trying to kick each other, one of them suddenly pulled a knife, the other turned and ran down the street as fast as he could. Putting the knife back in its sheath the man went over, picked up the other mans coat and started to go through the pockets.

Adam turned his head in disgust then looking back at the coloured poster. Texas yearly state fair, 3rd ,4th and 5th July. Shooting, boxing, horse riding, running, etc. prizes and refreshments to be held in Glen Parva all are welcome. Might be interesting, he thought about what Tex had advised him twice, ' that he should have some Back up, looks like he's right, said Adam softly turning from the poster. 'I wonder if it's anything like our fairs, Mussel Burgh and Appleby. 'Must be a big fair if it covers all Texas. Sitting back, then taking a deep puff on his thin cigar.

Adam was thinking about Esmeralda 's brothers at New Cambridge, they had said to him there are 2 gypsy families at Glen Parva, I do hope so it would be nice to know, some of my own people are there.

'You okay? said Tex squeezing his shoulder slightly, Adam looked up. Yeah I'm okay, you know Tex I could be dead if i had been on my own. 'No I don't think so. Orby Barr would have still stepped in, he knew you was unharmed, it did help us all being there, it gave some back up, answered Tex sitting down. 'Are you saying if you and Billy hadn't have been there with Orby they would have had a go at a lawman. Listen Adam, Orby and me we are contract, and we don't have the authority of a real sheriff or Marshall, them comancheros they wouldn't have give a shit, they'd shoot you down then ride out and nobody wants to get involved. It's a good job there was a few with you.

It's nice out here, cool. 'You were going to tell me something about your back being scarred. It's a long story, answered Adam. That's okay I've brought my beer with me and I got to thinking about what you said, going back to the tables and losing it all.

CHAPTER TEN– A ROUGH DAYS HUNTING

'It was afternoon the three boys Walter, Layton and Adam had taken Fawn the Big lurcher dog hunting and taken their catapults with them. Fawn had killed three rabbits and the boys had managed to shoot two pheasants. We are having a good day's sport, look there's a big (Caningra) a hare, said Layton. Walter wetting his finger then holding it up, 'if we go to the left, he won't pick up our scent and we can come up behind him. 'You're learning well said Adam. Yes and so are you's with your reading and writing they were now only about sixty yards from the hare when its big ears went down and it squatted. Fawn was pulling hard, now said Walter, slip him now,

Adam let go of one end of the slip lead. Go Fawn Go!!! Shouted the three boys running after the dog. It was a big field and flat, it was the start of a good chase. It had gone on for the past ten minutes; the hare kept gaining distance on each turn leaving Fawn that little bit further each time, then the big powerful lurcher would make up the distance again and again. He was a powerful young hare, but no match for Fawn.' What a good day we are having, shouted Layton. The hare suddenly turned and was coming back alongside of the hedge that separated the two fields Fawn had closed the gap and the hare knew the dog was close. It went through the hedge into the next field, as it did the powerful lurcher went up and over the low hedge, only four or five strides and he was on the hare. There was a low muffled scream as Fawns powerful jaws broke its neck and the cause was over.

The boys climbed over the five barred gate into the next field. Adam picked up the hare 'good boy fawn you've done well he said, as the boys gathered round the dog patting him, he seemed to like the praise, he would push his long nose under their hand for more attention from the boys. That was a very good course said Layton, Yes it was a long one, fifteen minutes, replied Walter. The Boys looked up they could hear horse hooves getting louder, a rider was coming up fast. He came to a stop alongside the boys. 'That hare and those pheasants is a day's poaching on my land you three young scallywags, I know you you're Lord John Bates' grandson, he's become the laughing stock of Yorkshire, encouraging gypsies to live on his estate.

'Sir these rabbits and two pheasants was all killed in them next fields, Rascliffe Estate, not here, the hare was chased from the next field into this one. 'Don't you dare answer me back you young raggle taggle scum, he shouted at Adam. 'We are telling you the truth sir why won't you listen, said Walter. 'This is my land, not Sir John Bates'. 'Now you get home, right now!' he said, pointing his riding whip at Walter.

I'm going to punish your two poaching friends, at that he started to lash out at Adam. the thin leather plaited whip with the whale bone centre cut through Adam's shirt, he then turned to Layton and lashed him across his forehead, then turning back to Adam again.

'You devil leave them alone they have done nothing wrong, shouted Walter. Adam's hands were protecting his head as his back was taking the lashes; his shirt was now very bloody. Layton pulled out his catapult loading it with a metal ball. No for gods sake don't you'll kill him, shouted Walter. He needs it, said Layton. Walter bending and picking up a big stone, he threw it hard, hitting the rider in the bottom of his back putting him off balance, he wobbled in the saddle.

Layton went underneath the horse coming out the other side; he pulled the stirrup forward, the man's foot now out of it. One hand slapped the rump of the horse hard, the other pushed the man's heel up in the air as the horse shot away the rider fell to the ground on his back with a heavy thud. He was slightly dazed. The two boys quickly jumped on top punching with both fists as hard as they could.' Let him have it good, shouted Walter, he deserves it.'

Leaving the game behind the boys helped Adam, one of his arms over each of their shoulders, half walking half running away as quick as they could. They turned and could see the man slowly getting back into the saddle then riding off. As they came into the cobbled yard, Lady Florence was stood talking to Dellie.

'My god what has happened to my boys, said Delly looking at Layton's forehead then Adam's shirt soaked in blood. She went a little faint. Lady Florence ran into the house. The Gilly and the footman following her back, they carried Adam into a downstairs small bedroom.

Dellie and Manx Nellie had been sponging his back clean. The bowl of warm water had a little salt in it, it had now turned red. The nasty welt across Layton's forehead seemed to go through his eyebrow. You're a very lucky boy you could have lost your eye, said Sir John who had came into the room.

Then turning to the footman, 'bring logs, pile them over in the corner this room will need to be kept warm day and night, the boy is starting to shiver, it could turn to pneumonia.

Isaac, Nelson and Byron had just got back from being at a horse sale. Layton finished telling them what had happened. My Boy you'll carry them scars for the rest of your life said Adams father. When i get the man that did this he'll have some scars, said Isaac. I'll go for a doctor said Nelson. I have already sent my gilly on the fastest horse to bring our doctor here, answered Sir John.

Nelson and Dellie had been bathing Adams back and keeping the fire burning. Adam had stopped trembling and his temperature had gone down a bit, with the folded damp cloth on his forehead. On the floor was a bowl half full of warm water with a little vinegar in it. Dellie had been taking the folded cloth off his forehead every fifteen minutes or so wetting it in the bowl, wringing it out then replacing it on his forehead keeping his temperature down. Nelson gave him a second askit powder he had also mixed a second hot toddy, whiskey, brown sugar and hot water. About twenty minutes went by and there was a knock at the door. The doctor came in carrying his black bag. He thoroughly examined Adam, also taking his temperature and blood pressure. 'Well Doctor?' asked Nelson. Quite a beating for a boy to take, there's no bones broken, you've done the right thing keeping him warm and bathing his head, keeping the temperature down and the hot toddy good old fashioned remedy. You can now leave the askit powders and give him two of these pills every four hours it will keep the pain down.

If the agers come back, shivering and trembling, you can give him another hot toddy, just a single; finish with the bathing now. 'You've done well putting a little salt in the water, now i want you to very gently smooth this ointment over his back, warm it in front of the fire and your hands, also tomorrow afternoon, leaving it to dry in. keep him on his side this ointment will stop any festering and poison setting in, he then turned to Layton, 'has that cut been washed?' 'Yes doctor with warm water with salt in it said Dellie also you young man, gently smooth some of this cream into that cut now and tomorrow afternoon. It's your eyebrow that saved you losing your eye. 'Thank you doctor, said Layton.

It took you long enough to get here, said Sir John. It could not be helped Sir John I was on another call to the man that done this to these boys, who might that be? Asked Isaac. Cederick mendip answered the doctor. It looks like the boys have given nearly has good as they got from Mendip. 'And how is that? Asked Sir John. 'His nose is broken, a tooth is snapped off, his lips are badly split and one of his eyebrows is split also a nasty bruise on his Back.

Good enough for him,' said Nelson looking at Adam and Layton's bruised knuckles and the gold buckle ring that each boy wore. He sent for the police, they was there taking a statement when i was tending his wounds. He's put in a charge against the boys for poaching on his land then attacking and wounding him. I should imagine the police will be here in the morning. 'I have told you nothing sir john I don't want to be involved in any way with this man. 'Thank you I understand, answered Sir John.

'What do I owe you good doctor?' asked Nelson. 'That's alright he sends me a Bill every month for his services for everyone in this house. I take it you'll be back to see the boy again, asked Nelson. Well if they're still here, answered the doctor. They'll be here, you come tomorrow, said Sir John, have a safe journey back.' 'Thank you, a good night to all here, replacing the empty cup on the sideboard he left.

All the men stood outside with a mug of tea. We will have to praster- avree (make a run for it) said old Byron then looking at Sir John and repeating the words in English. Adams wounds are too open and the cold night could turn his chill to pneumonia, we would be risking his life. And it is admitting guilt when there is none, said Nelson. We must plan what has to be done this Cedrerick Mendip he is an evil and powerful man, owns several farms and a timber yard, he's got money and influence but not well liked. If he can't bribe or cheat he terrorizes, answered Sir John.

Nelson looked at his watch it's eleven thirty i'll go back in. Later on me and Dellie will sit up for the rest of the night to see to young Adam. I am worried about this, when it comes to law and court we will be no match for this Mendip man, I am with you's all the way, let us all get some sleep, who knows what tomorrow will bring, Goodnight gentlemen, said Sir John.

It was a full moon as Nelson and his father Isaac stood by the fire, Byron sat on a stool, he had said very little. Over the next few days we must all do whatever we can, said Nelson holding his hands out over the fire. Yes my boy, Sir John is a good friend and he likes our people but rappa is dustow than parney (blood is thicker than water) and blood always comes first. It could be Dewster –Cheres (Lots of time) in Staraburn – (Prison) we have very little rights. It's lucky we have Sir John with us otherwise they would just do what they like with us.

Nelson glanced up from the fire to look at his grandfather old Byron. 'What you say is true grandfather, old Byron nodded as he lit his pipe, you see my boy, being educated with a professor, hunting with a lord, and living alongside of these people for years we enjoy it, we learn because we're quick to learn, but can we live in two worlds at the same time?' Grandfather I don't like being humble. I can do it to get my living but after that I think myself as good as anybody else, said Nelson

Yes my boy, that's the tachnu rumney chell rappa adre-lesty (that's the real Romany gypsy blood in you). You know son it's the same with me I love to play the rye (the gentleman). When I'm with Sir John I have no trouble in speaking to him on a level, I respect him for what he is but I don't feel beneath him, I strongly believe that attitude is bred in us from way back in those far Eastern or Mediterranean countries, said Isaac.

Some of the original oldest gypsy families, they had titled blood, illegitimate but it was there. A dark pretty gypsy girl dancing, if it is a Lord or even a Prince when the blood runs hot a man is a man there was nothing could be done against such powerful people. It was rare. When it happened. But it did. The grandmother would say it was hers born late in marriage in her late forty's and the child's mother would become her older sister to hide the shame, they would be cast out of the kingdom. A lord or prince feeling guilty would follow the wagons would give a small bag of gold coins to help bring the child up and that self-importance of pride that is where it comes from in the breeding down from the generations. What is in the blood will come out, gypsy pride.

'Tell me, what is the oldest gypsy name you know of grandfather?' or name Boswell, which was originally Bosvell, but they altered it like many gypsy families did, when the Boswells, Shaws and Lees first came to England they were called the Egyptians. 'Thank you grandfather I have learnt more this night from you.

After the prayers they sang a hymn, then all getting up and pushing the padded poufys back under the chairs. 'Let us trust in the Lord, said Nelson. ''Amen to that' said Sir John

The Butler stood waiting as they came out of the chapel room, he walked over to Nelson. There are two policemen waiting. The butler walked ahead of them opening the door. 'Thank you Jeeves that will be all said Sir John. The two policemen stood up with their helmets under their arm. Good morning my Lord. Good morning to you Tom and your constable. It's not a pleasant visit i am here for my lord. The maid brought a trolley in with toasted teacakes on. The sergeant slowly looked around at so many people in the room.

'Be at ease Tom the boys, you are here about this is their family, they are my friends. The women got up and left the room. The Sergeant had been writing everything down for some twenty minutes and that is everything, the truth master Layton, 'Yes it is sir, he answered, and of course Walter your grandson will confirm Layton's story, 'Yes sergeant he will, I would now like to see the injured boy said the sergeant.

Adam's mother pulled the thin cotton sheet off him. The two police officers slowly looked from one to the other.' My God he's only a boy said the sergeant. If he'd have not stopped he would have killed him, said the constable. He did not stop, we stopped him sir, said Layton.

Can you see out of that eye, yes sir i can. We obviously can't take your brother Adam in; we will have to come back for him when he's more well to travel. 'My God, said Isaac, they're going to put them in starbrn (jail) and they're only boys. You'll be leaving with us now Layton, said the sergeant. Dellie was standing at the door and burst into tears. 'I suppose it will be the junior prison at York, Tom. Yes it will, answered the sergeant.

I want you to speak to the prison governor, the boys are to have extra blankets and food, whatever they need, Tell him who has made this request and i can be generous. 'Very good my lord I understand. Please step away I have to put the handcuffs on the boy. Isaac looked at Layton, I have not seen Fawn, where is he my boy? He's dead old grandfather, that devil shot him twice with his pistol. 'That would be the lurcher you spoke of said the sergeant taking out his pencil and note book again.

The next court hearing is the case for the two gypsy boys is to be included. Sir John had managed to keep Adam out of prison for five or six days with a strong letter from the doctor and a hundred pounds bail money but they would not release Layton on bail as well, knowing they were gypsies there was a chance that they would run.

As they walked out of the court hearing Nelson stopped, looking at Sir John, it doesn't look good does it?' 'I must admit it looks bad for both of your boys.' answered Sir John

Cederick Mendip looked over to Sir John's group; he was some ten yards away. Old Byron took out his pipe and walked over. 'Excuse me sir, have you got a light he asked. Reaching in his pocket and coming out with a box of matches. Keep them gypo; I wouldn't want to soil my pocket after you handling them.' I want to say something to you and I want you to listen because I will only say it once. 'My two grandsons they are only boys, I am not bothered about them doing a few months, we are a hard people, but if they go down for years, I will put a steel ball bearing in the back of your head, I will kill you, I am nearly eighty, I've had a good life and I have nothing to lose, as sure as it's going to get dark tonight, I will kill you it could be 5-6 weeks after the sentencing but you'll get it, you're messing with the wrong people, said Old Byron.

Cederick Mendip took two steps back and waved a police officer over. 'This gypsy has just threatened to kill me. Old Byron turned looking up a lot more bent over than he was, taking out a box of matches from his pocket. 'I only asked him for a light officer and he gave me this box of matches. 'That's alright old man just move on said the police officer. 'Did he mean that? Nelson and Isaac never answered Sir John.

They walked over to the tea room and joined the women. I don't think your lawyer looks man enough for the prosecution, said Manx Nellie. Oh he is a good barrister, but I have heard of a new young QC in Sheffield, only about forty, he very rarely loses a case. 'What is a QC asked Isaac. It means Queens Councilor; it is as high as a lawyer can go, answered Nellie. He would be very expensive, answered Sir John.

Manx Nellie put down her cup, get him Sir John he is needed, we have money and plenty of good jewelry. 'Sir John? Yes Nellie what is it? Can you wire your letter to him today, your title and standing will have a lot of pull, and he can book this case in. Yes I will do that, he answered. This Manx Nellie has brains as well as good looks thought Sir John.

On the sixth day the sergeant and his constable were back this time for Adam. Sergeant? Yes my lord, tell the prison governor we will expect Adam to be in the same cell as his Brother and both of them are to have whatever they need and I will call and see him after this is all over.

Also the doctor will have to call on my son to see how is wounds are healing, said Nelson. It will all be carried out to your wishes my lord and to your wishes Mr. Boswell. Thank you Tom, answered Sir John. Nelson just nodded twice.

The Butler knocked twice and then opened the door, My Lord, there is a Mr. Tommy Bee the QC, he is in the reception room. Thank you jeeves, tell the footmen to take coffee and biscuits in we will all be in there soon.

I am pleased to meet you QC Tommy Bee you have quite a reputation, I am Lord Sir John Bates, they shook hands and then sir john introduced him to Nelson, Isaac and old Byron.

'I have sent for the young gentleman in question and my grandson Walter. Five minutes past and then Walter and Adam came into the room. Tommy Bee had finished his second coffee in between taking notes, each boy went through it the second time, Adam took off his shirt, the seven long cuts he had were now turning to yellow green scabs. 'Not a nice sight to see but it is to your advantage and I will want the jury and court to see your back. There was a knock on the door, 'Yes Jeeves what is it?' the two police officers my lord; they are waiting for Master Adam.

If any of you have any friends in the surrounding villages even York, casually see them, see what you can dig up on this Cederick Mendip said Tommy Bee, looking from one to the other. The locals would not want to be involved with me, a big lawyer from the city, they would feel sorry for the boys' parents and grandparents, you are an astute people see what you can find out every little will help. 'If he's a well-liked and respected man I want the case tried out of this area, I would prefer another town another court. But if he's a cad, badly respected, then I want the case to be tried in this area. I think I am going to enjoy having a go at this child beater.

Lord John, You move in high circles, and never know what you may learn that may help. He then stood up shaking hands with all the men. 'You are very welcome to stay here as long as you wish.' Thank you me lord I prefer to be alone where i can study the case, I will be staying in the village hotel for two or three days. And I will send my assistant out round here for a few days to do some ground work it will cost you a lot les then my time.

I will make a point of casually calling in to see Judge Bill Bailey, he is an old friend of mine, said Tommy Bee with a crafty smile. Manx Nellie sat back weighing this young lawyer up, his beige cavalry twill jacket trimmed in brown suede, dark brown handmade leather shoes trimmed in suede, a silk cravat with a diamond tie pin and a very heavy pale gold wedding ring. Well he certainly looks what he is, thought Manx Nellie.

'I am going to try and get this case into crown court, the opposition will be pleased with that, crown means a custodial sentence if there has been violence. 'Is that wise? 'Asked Sir John. I think so, it would be a custodial sentence anyway if we lose, but the advantage of a jury, they are just working class ordinary people, many would have young grandsons and sympathise. 'My job is to win them over with friendliness and most of all, truth. I have no titles and come from a working class family myself, and has regards to this Mr. Mendip, let's kid him along let him have all his say, give him enough rope and he'll hang himself, and the boys can appear frightened young boys in court that has been bullied by this overpowering man. We need to win the jury to our side.

Mr. Bee, Yes Missus Manx Nellie, do you mind me asking, have you any gypsy blood in your back breeding. 'I don't think so Ma'am but granny was very friendly with the gypsy boys when she was young they all had a little laugh.

So young Master Walter you dazed and knocked him off balance with a stone and Layton pulled his foot out of the strap?' 'Yes Sir that's how we got him out of the saddle. 'Lord Bates, said Tommy Bee turning, if you let your grandson go up as well being involved with the fight, the chances of a custodial sentence would be very slim being who he is. 'You see if one gets off they would all get off, it would look more of a self-defense. That's what it was, said the two boys nearly all at the same time.

And if it went bad would, could Walter go down as well asked Sir John. I'm afraid so but with him being who he is it would only be a fifteen percent chance, answered Tommy Bee. We can't go down that road, if the worse did happen it would ruin young Walter. One day he will be Lord Bates and Sir Walter and of course will go to Harrow, with a prison sentence for violence it would tarnish his name, title and reputation. But I was involved granddad and we are not just friends we are like three brothers. Very well then Walter, I will let you just give evidence, not to be really involved.

I need to go to the prison to speak with the other young man. Now if i can speak to the parents, say whatever you wish we have no secrets from our friends, said Nelson. I don't like bringing this up but it has to be agreed, my expenses in court is twenty five to thirty pounds a day and out of court interviews etc is fifteen pounds a day plus hotels and all other expenses, an assistant to help five pounds a day, plus paperwork. Putch so booty luva assa (ask how much money altogether) said Dellie to her husband. Let Mandy Rocca to the rye (let me speak to the gentleman) said Manx Nellie.

Manx Nellie held up her hand, 'please excuse me interrupting I am the boys grandmother what would the total bill roughly be?' I can't rightly tell you that ma'am. I take it you expect to be paid. 'Indeed I do ma'am. So we will need to know roughly how much we need to find. 'That's a fair request, said Sir John. Well it will be expensive said Tommy Bee looking at Manx Nellie. '£220 - £250 - pounds for the total'. 'That is expensive, said Nelson and Isaac nearly at the same time, but we can pay you.

Of course I would need a retainer of £100 pounds to make a start. Tommy Bee, Yes me Lord I will guarantee your bill will be met, that my friends will pay you, just make sure you get the boys off. Very good me lord, he answered. Now that is done there is a second thing I have to go through with you. This is not an open and shut case that the boys will get off, so I do have to show you or tell you the possibilities the bad side.

Because Master Adam has had a very bad whipping by law it does not mean he is innocent, I will speak bluntly because I know what is ahead. 'Right we have a local well known business man who finds two gypsy boys poaching on his land with a hunting dog, with game, even encouraging a local Lords grandson into this. He, Mr. Mendip is then attacked and beaten badly by these two young gypsy ruffians, and he has to protect himself with his riding whip, and even has to shoot the vicious dog, that went for him, then after a beating he has to flee in fear. 'And of course he contacts the police so as these ruffians don't come to his house, how does that sound?

Nobody said a word for nearly half a minute. It sounds ghastly and very untrue said Sir John breaking the silence, Mr. Tommy Bee had been looking out of the window, he turned beautiful grounds. Well gentleman that's how it will sound. 'You're supposed to be the best lawyer in this part of England, said Nelson. Thank you for the compliment, but I don't have a magic wand, I can only do my best and QC's don't like losing cases. We lose reputation if we do. I need ammunition and plenty of it i can't fire blanks, we don't want a half decision, a full win and the boys would go free.

Mr. Tommy Bee, yes Mr. Boswell. 'What is the worst that can happen to my two grandsons, are you sure you don't want to just find out how it goes, the worst might not happen. 'We would like to know, said Isaac. 'If guilty of the charges, they can be sent to a boy's borstal working prison until they are sixteen, then put into the navy for three years.

'How about if Sir John got them out on a big bail, we could then just disappear', 'well I did not hear that'. If this man is as bad has we've been told he could possibly put out a big private reward and if they got you, you would do time as well and the boys would do a lot more time. Legally this man has been attacked so he has the ball at his feet, and so was my 2 young grandsons. He will say he was defending himself, said Tommy Bee with all respect Mr. Boswell you's don't really belong anywhere, you's are known to be fighters and you have, he suddenly stopped. 'No rights' interrupted Sir John. 'Yes I suppose that is true, said Tommy Bee. We will all meet here in four days, ten o'clock Friday morning. Sir John i need the prison warden's name and what he likes, whisky or cigars. If you's find out anything of importance and you want me to know before we meet here i will be staying at The Red Lion in the village, you can get me in the evenings. I take it Me Lord you will be giving a character reference for the boys, 'Indeed I will, answered Sir John.

When getting testimonies off any people you know it must be genuine, do not offer a bribe, if it got out it would cause a lot of trouble. So until Friday I wish you's all goodnight.

Old Byron and Louisa was in their wagon, they looked really worried as the old people were having a brandy with some hot water and a little brown sugar in it. The fire had just been built for the night. Nelson left, Dellie was with Adam, then got up and walked out. They looked very worried. I'd give every penny i've got including wagons horses, jewelry, everything if my two boys was out and we were going down that road, we could work hard and start again, I know how you feel my son, said Isaac

Good Morning to you Joseph, and good morning to you, said the blacksmith, they were in the small town of Essingbold about five miles from Rascliffe village. 'I will have a nice horse for sale next week. 'That is good news we will come and look at it and make you a good cash offer for it or a deal? 'We have 2 nice pistols, a shot gun, and a few good fishing rods and some catapults.

Sounds good Isaac, I'll have a look at your rods and catapults. 'You look very worried Nelson, we've heard about your boys, in fact the whole town has'. Doris! Yes husband, bring a brew for my friends, thank you for your sympathy Joseph.

'I've told people that the boys they don't have to poach game, they're always with Young Walter and they have the run of Lord John's estate, we all know that said Joseph. 'What's this horse like, asked Nelson, not wanting to look too eager for news? Fifteen hands, very quiet mare, fully broke in and pulls a trap, comes from an old retired lady. That sounds good.

So you were saying about my boys Joseph, all your family is well got around these parts, and has i have said we are with you, this Mendip he's definitely got it in for your people, be careful, he'll get your boys put down if he can, there is very bad things about him. Such has?' asked Isaac. I won't say no more. 'Do you know Fred and June Watson?' 'No I can't say I do but her name rings a bell, I think she sees our women for fortune telling, answered Nelson. 'Bring me a pencil and piece of paper wife. Isaac and Nelson got up and lit their pipes having a look round the workshop while he wrote the letter.

'Now go out of Essingbold on Husthwaite Road, about two miles, the fourth on your right, it's a big farm, 'Badger Acres' , ask for Fred give him this letter he may be able to help you. 'Thank you Joseph, you're a friend.

Nice place, kept very tidy said Isaac as they approached the house, a short thick set man of about forty came walking out of a big double barn. Nelson pulled on the right rein guiding the horse from the house. And what can I do for you two gents?' Are you Fred Watson? 'I am he answered, as Nelson gave him the letter, leaning against the barn he read it through quickly. He then reached out to shake hands with them; I have seen thee once or twice at Thirsk and York horse sale.

Come into the house, June make a brew we have visitors, sweet cider would be better said Isaac. Nelson gave his father a quick stare for his cheek. I will help thee if i can, sit down, said Fred in his Yorkshire accent. My father passed away some six years ago and left me this place, three hundred acres of good bonnie land but no buildings, and the house badly in need of repair. I was only 26 and just out of the Merchant Navy, having been reared on this farm, I knows about farming.

This Cederick Mendip tried to buy the farm off me for the second time, he owns the two next door, he said he would be a friend to me let me have wood, materials, whatever to build two big barns and repair all the house inside and out. As you know he sells all that stuff. A good six months had gone by and then I had a bill from him for nearly seven hundred pounds, such an amount, I knew it was wrong I went to see him and I knew it was under five hundred he had told me there was no hurry for me to pay him, I could pay him a bit now and then, three weeks later another bill. If I didn't pay him within one month the debt bailiffs were coming in to put us out and take our farm also he had sent more stuff than we really needed. I managed to get the money off the bank by leaving my deeds with them. I and my wife have worked like slaves this last four years another year and it will be paid, and we had to pay the bank 15%.

So that's what he is a piece of rubbish, he was trying to steal my farm. Thanks Fred, that will help, said Nelson, we are not feared of him nor his 2 henchmen, I'll face them up with a double barrel 12 bore. I would give a character reference to a court for you. 'There's something you should know, he hates your people.

There is a big open lay by between his two farms and mine, no man's land, there was a gypsy family on it, with a wagon and tent, friendly people, a boy of about eighteen and a pretty daughter about fourteen. He would often stop to talk to her when passing, and the young girl would be left home to do her housework while the others were out, he called by one day and raped her twice.

That night the boy and father went to his farm with a gun a sword and a can of paraffin burnt half of his house down and one of his buildings. He managed to get away. He has family up at Darlington, the father and son they was tried for attempted murder and was transported to Australia the woman sold everything she had for her and her girl to go out and try and find her husband and son, and he got off with it. A nasty story, said Isaac If you or your lawyer could get to see the police records it would prove this, it happened three years ago. He will he's a QC said Isaac.

June came down the stairs with a coat over her arm, then went over and spoke to her husband as I told you Nelson I was in the Merchant

Navy I was issued with an overcoat, sort of a best coat when in town off ship. Never hardly used it and you're about the size I used to be is it any use to you. Nelson looked at it a ¾ length lightweight navy blue Melton. Thank you Joseph it fits nicely, a good quality. I don't know about these buttons, everyone's got an anchor carved on it, nice quality, said Isaac.

Nelson and his father Isaac did not realise, just by chance some years later this coat would be the start of one of the best convincers for selling continental rugs and wall tapestries and it would be Nelson who would start it and Adam would help, it was started at Blackpool. Some would call it 'The Jacket' others they would call it 'The bag' it would be a money spinner as usual you needed a greedy customer.

Isaac and Nelson turned as they drove away to wave to Fred and his wife, nice people said Isaac looking at his watch, it's three o'clock 'What do you think if we can get a copy of the trial and what Mendip done to that gypsy family, I'll bet that lawyer could.' 'So we will tell this full story to Tommy Bee,' said Nelson

Byron came over and undone the harness then turning the horse out to graze. The women were pleased when they heard what the men had found out. And how did you do? asked Nelson.

Are you going to tell Tommy Bee about this? The outside table was laid, young Walter came over, 'can Mandy hol (can I eat) with you he asked. Of course you can said Nelson. I think he's becoming a gypsy. He will have to get a lot more sun on him, said his grandmother Lady Florence. Lady Elizabeth stood by the wagon wheel her hand in Jacks. I worry a lot what is going to happen to them said Lady Florence. Don't worry because love can overcome, can conquer all said Manx Nellie. There was three loud knocks on the study door. Yes, come in! Oh I am pleased it's you Isaac, is there any news of today.

Good News, Sir John, we spent time today over at Essingwold, this Medip is not a liked man around these parts, tried to steal a man's farm off him and ruined a gypsy family, Isaac telling him both stories. 'Yes I remember something about that said Sir John, we was not here we were away in France for a month, he's no good, he's a bounder we need to bring him too book, said Sir John picking up one of the decanters. 'You'll have a large brandy of course?' Isaac nodded he couldn't help smiling; these gentry have such a way with them he thought. Anything else, Isaac.

Tommy Bee put down his whiskey glass looking straight at Judge Bill Bailey, thank you for seeing me without an appointment Bill, that's alright i wasn't doing anything this afternoon, would you like to stay for evening dinner. 'What is it? Asked Tommy Bee. Jones. Yes Sir, run along like a good chap and find out what is for dinner. Very good sir. You've done well Tommy, even spoke about in London. Lovely place you've got here Bill, thank you. It has eight bedrooms, five of them are en suite, a billiards/snooker room stables, forty eight acres in all; servants house at the rear coach house, only 3 miles out of town

I am telling you all this because I am putting the place up for sale in three months, heart's playing up a little, going to retire, I play a lot of this new sport, golf. Yes, I've been told that you go up to Scotland now and then, yes that's right Tommy.

'We've brought a little four bedroom cottage sitting in 2 acres of land at St. Andrews, retiring there it's a lovely place to live.' 'You know I might be interested in this place Bill, what are you asking for it? 7,000 pounds. It's a vast amount of money, I would have to sell my house in Sheffield, it would only be the deposit down on this place, I'd like it, the wife loves horses. Beg your pardon Sir, it's lamb chops, kidneys and veg, Sounds too good to miss, said Tommy Bee. Mr. Bee will be joining us, will that be all? Asked the butler. 'Jones, run along like a good chap and bring two bottles of that sparkling South African wine,' 'Very good Sir.'

So Bill what do you think of these Romany gypsies or whatever they are? They seem to be genuine, and have a good name around here, answered the judge. If i ask for a character witness on this man Cederick Mendip, would you approve it? Yes within reason Tommy but don't overdo it, the jury has to make the decision not me. I do feel sorry for these boys and this man Mendip seems to be a bad one a cad, if what I have heard is true, he's very racial and that's not British is it old chap.'

I'm thinking about your house as I'm talking to you, I would like to bring my wife along to see it when this case is all finished. I think we both know this Mendip is no good and I would say a big thank you, if they work free, a new set of golf clubs to go to Scotland with, just give these boys a chance. Thank you Tommy I will do all that I can but the prosecuting barrister as not been very helpful. Thank you Bill for what you are doing and we won't come out and see you until this case is over. A good idea. Jones, are you there Jones, push along the chops and kidneys old boy we're hungry.' Very good sir.

Good Morning Mr. Bee, said the butler, Good Morning Jeeves, can you inform me lord and the Boswell family that I am here. Very good Sir. Jeeves showed him in to the blue room, a footman followed Jeeves, all the chairs were formed into a half circle. As the room filled he looked around. Sir John had that English bulldog style and attitude, but this Timmy Bee was not fooled by it. He could see the old Lord was just as worried as everybody else. Tommy Bee dismissed with going round shaking hands with everyone except Fred Watson and his wife. Good Morning all I would like to say thank you to Mr. Fred Watson and your good lady for both of you coming here this morning. It could possibly overflow into the next day with it being a jury trial. A maid came in pushing a trolley with several pots of tea on and crockery underneath. A good two hours had passed.

I have been through everything thoroughly with each of you. I will ask the boys exactly what happened and Master Walter will back it up as a witness only. The boys will show their scars and Lord Bates will give a testimony and we will read out the list, 5 upstanding local people's testimonies on behalf of the gypsy family, and then i will ask Mr. Fred Watson to personally give his testimony.

Now I would say to all of you don't drag your testimony out, strong points, not opinion, clear and short will penetrate, just follow me I will lead you. Missus Dellie Boswell you will take clean clothes and shoes to the boys the day before the trial. Yes I will sir.

Locals were surprised that the flogging of two gypsy youths had got as far as a jury and crown court, the charge was grievous bodily harm and wounding with intent to Mister. Cederick Mendip an upright citizen and business man of Essingbold, with no mention of the gypsy boys, as it was taken for granted they would be going down for such a crime.

CHAPTER ELEVEN - IN THE NICK

Nelson looked out of the window there was a 2 horse coach pulled up at the back entrance. Adams coat was around his shoulders, as his hands were handcuffed, he walked between the 2 police officers he stood just level with their shoulders. Jeeves rushed forward and opened the door, looking down at Adam, a lot of water had gone under the bridge so to speak since he had first met the gypsy family, he had grown to like and respect them, 'Good luck, Master Adam I hope all turns out well for you, Thank you Jeeves so do I. The coach had no side doors or windows, just one door in the back. Nelson walked out with them. The sergeant helped Adam to get into the coach. Nelson poked his head inside, it was a prison on wheels so to speak, bars on either side, also the roof and floor, thin steel, covered over with wood both sides. On the back door was a gold crown underneath, in script the words 'Black Mariah' Nelson put his arm around Adam giving him a hug, Don't worry son, we have Sir John behind us and this top QC Tommy Bee. You and your brother will come through it alright.

I'm used to taking criminals in, not boys; I am only doing my job sir. I know Sergeant I know answered Nelson. Dellie stood at the window, Manx Nellie had an arm around her. The door with the iron bars suddenly slammed and the lock was turned twice and then the outer heavy wooden door, the lock turning twice also. Young Adam stared out of the small square window, his father Nelson felt very bad about it, in fact ready to cry. He turned and walked away. A few minutes had passed and Nelson turned to look again, the black Mariah was nearly at the end of the driveway. 'Is there anywhere we can be equal, are we to always be so down trodden' said Nelson

Adam stood watching the black coach being parked over by the stables to the left of the big gates, 2 prison officers looked down at him, Adam Boswell are you any relation to that other gypsy boy Boswell that we have in here?' Yes he is my brother. It's yes sir, or boss, do you understand?' I did not know sir' Well you know now don't you?'

Right hold this bag open, 2 blankets, 2 pillows, a pair of half worn out shoes, 2 shirts with some buttons missing off them and 2 pair of socks which is about half finished, also 2 vests and 2 pair of pants. As they get dirty, you wash them out yourself and hang them in your cell, have you got that?' Yes Sir, do not let any of the other prisoners pinch them replacements can take a long, long time, till you are allocated from here to another prison. Have you got all that?' Yes I have sir' Now go into that cubicle over there, strip, wash and change into some of those prison clothes, there is a cardboard box in there, put the clothes and shoes you have on, in it. 'Do you understand me?' 'Yes Sir I do'

They went across the courtyard to the 2 adjoining buildings, each one had three rows of windows, Adam dropped the heavy kit bag, pick it up now, said one of the officers, I can't carry it sir over my shoulder, may back has been cut. Lift your shirt and let me see, said one of the officers that looks very nasty, I'll carry it for you. After a few minutes they stopped, it was just getting dark, as Adam stood there looking around the yard, the 2 police officers had the makings out and was rolling a cigarette each. Adam felt a little chill go through him, it's not a pretty sight is it young fella, no it's not sir answered Adam. The wall around the prison was some 30ft high it had several rows of broken bottles pressed into the cement at the top.

I am used to living out in the open sir' You shouldn't break the law then and be a young ruffian should you? Yes Sir, not bothering to explain why he was in prison.

He went up three flights of stairs reaching the top floor, the long corridor was some 250ft long, with a small gas light at either end and 1 in the middle, it wasn't a nice place to be, was dimly lit and a little cold. Adam stared down it and then looked up at the officers, this little holiday will make a man of you, Adam never answered.

Three quarter way down they stopped, one officer at the front of him, one at the back, the key in the lock turned twice, the heavy door was kicked open it hit the inside wall with a bang, he stood there on the step looking in, then was suddenly pushed hard. 'In you go young villain', he landed on his hands and knees, the big kit bag that was full of stuff was thrown in landing alongside him then the door slammed shut and the key turned twice, Adam stood up, there was some light, the moon was trying to shine through the small dirty window. Adam looked around the nearly dark cell, you alright fella, Adam looked up on the top bunk bed was a young black man. Yes thanks my name's Adam, my names Donald he said reaching out his right hand. Adam put his foot on the corner of the bed and reached up for the bar that went across the 12" by 9" window.

'Nice view isn't it, lovely said Adam. Just 12ft away was a brick wall. Adam was pleased he had someone to talk to, there's some matches on the table and a candle, said Donald. About half an hour had passed; Adam had shown him his back and told him all about it. Hope you gave it to him good, said Donald. We made a good mess of him that's why we're in here. You say the other gypsy boy is on this floor. That's right about four or five cells back. So what are you in for Donald?' Burglary with violence, I already done three years in a borstel prison for boys, they didn't want me in the merchant navy, why I don't know?'

So what did you do for a living Donald, what sort of job did you have? Nothing in particular I was just anybody's dog for a bone,' have you got any bacca?' No I haven't I don't smoke, answered Adam. My family will be coming in to see me, I'll ask for some off my father and grandfather for you, thank you that would be really appreciated.

'So are you a gypsy, yes said Adam. What is your full name then? It's Donald O'flynn. Unusual name for a coloured man, I don't know who my father was, the man that ran the orphanage him and his wife were Irish and they gave me their name, I never did see my father, and my mother dropped me off at the orphanage when i was 2 years old, I have had to fight all my life to survive. 'Can you fight?' asked Adam. I am the hardest man in this nick, answered Donald. 'Pleased to meet you, I am Adam Boswell' answered Adam looking at him. It seems gypsies aren't the only people that's looked down on and has to fight to survive.

'Don't worry about it young Boswell.' 'You just let me know if anyone messes you about, and I'll stand up for you fella. Thanks Donald. You are young to be in here, they are very keen on deporting people, it's a lot cheaper than keeping them in prison for years, said Donald.

'Do you think we will go down, asked Adam, after telling him all of it, you're no different than me, no rights, and you get little respect, with that Lord as your friend and a top lawyer as well I think you will walk free. How long before your trial?' I don't know answered Adam laying back on the bed. 'How about you?' My trial is not for another 6 weeks, they've put it back for more evidence, I' just hoping and praying I get deported to one of the colonies, Australia or the Americas. I could make a brand new start, but if i go down after doing time before for thieving and fighting I might get ten years. Adam looked at him feeling sorry, you'll get deported Donald they don't want to feed you and look after you for ten years.' 'I hope you're right.'

Adam sat back staring up at the ceiling, stood up he could just reach up and touch it. It was curved like a horse wagon roof, very dusty with cobwebs in the corners. He seemed to toss and turn some of the night, getting little sleep; it was a night of mixed thoughts. He could suddenly hear doors being banged open and the rattling of keys. Donald just sat on the edge of his bed waiting. Adam was stood up in the centre of the small cell ready to be out. The key was suddenly; in the lock turning, then the door was thrown back, as it hit the wall Adam stepped forward up onto the step, which was the corridor floor.

You're a bit keen, back there i say, back, said the jail officer prodding him with his truncheon in the stomach, he stepped back into the centre of the cell. 'Now all step forward shouted one of the officers, As Adam stepped up Donald pushed him to one side and they stood side by side, Adam was looking to the left and then to the right. Layton it's me your brother Adam. Layton turned his head he had never been so happy for a long time. It's good to hear you my brother he said.

There was seven or eight men between them. 'There'll be no talking or shouting in the corridor or you'll go back in your cell for the rest of the day, said a loud aggressive voice. They walked slowly forward coming into a hall; there was a long counter with three men serving on the other side. Adam noticed a pile of stainless steel trays thrown on the floor in the corner, as they went forward each man picked one up, he was going through them one after another as there was dried food still left on them in places.

Hey Boswell, you're too fussy, take the next tray or get back to your cell. Adam picked one up and started to rub it clean with the sleeve of his shirt then looking at the meals that was being served, 1 slice of fried bacon half raw, a boiled potato, a sausage and 1 round of bread showing mould on one of the corners.

Stopping he walked over to Layton to start talking, not here said Layton over his shoulder, we'll be put back in the cells with no breakfast see you in the exercise yard. There was a stainless steel churn over in the corner with what looked to be full of hot coloured water. Adam plunged the tin mug into it and then continued to follow Donald back to the cell. Let's hope the midday meal is a lot better than this and some proper hot tea, this is like piss and nearly cold. Donald looked at him with a smile, that's your tea, the only sort of tea you're going to get, and the midday meal does not exist there is none. Your next meal is at six o'clock and that's it till the morning. Two meals a day, maybe a cup of hot soup with 2 pieces of bread for breakfast some days. An hour had passed and Adam was taken with Donald back to the food hall.

Donald was glad of the company and the help. It was a big hall to mop up for one man. There's four pieces of bread left over here, said Adam walking over. He folded one in half putting it in his pocket, the other one he broke the side off that was moldy and started to eat it.

On the trot, pick em up; pick your feet up there. There was 2 doorways that the men were coming out into the exercise yard. Layton was already out, Adam walked over and threw his arms around him, It's good to see you my brother, I feel like I've been in here six weeks not six days, 'How is your back? The smarting has stopped it has now scabbed up and is itching. The doctor is supposed to be coming to see me in two days so we will get some news on what is happening, said Adam, giving Layton the folded round of bread.

Keep walking there; keep walking, it's supposed to be your exercise said one of the prison guards. Adam looked around the yard, then at the 2 buildings each with three floors, there must be over three hundred men in this yard, but there didn't seem that many for breakfast. There's 2 separate halls we eat in, said Layton.

He could sense Adam was in a bad mood, so what's happening then my brother? They've got us a top lawyer finding out what they can about that devil with the whip. This is what's called an allocation prison; they send you from here to where you're going to do your time, said Layton. Adam looked at his younger brother, who cares what type of prison it is, it stinks, the foods swill, I'm telling you what's happening to get us out and you're telling me about this shithole. Layton looked away he knew Adam had enough, he's on a short fuse I do hope he's not having any trouble in here

No good you losing your temper with me Adam, the first three days are the worst, after that you'll get used to it' Adam looked sideways at him then looked away annoyed. Then turning back to look him straight in the face, you' don't seem to know how serious this is the lawyer said we could do three or four years, maybe more and then more time in the merchant navy'

Dad's cousin Benny was in the Navy joked Layton. Dad's cousin Benny was a three quarter bred gorger so he would enjoy the navy wouldn't he; didn't know any better. Gypsies don't join the navy, we travel.' Adam started to walk away, Layton walked after him eating the piece of bread. We shouldn't even be in here we're under sixteen said Adam.

There are fifteen other boys in here as well as us, the borstel house for boys out of town is full, this is the main Yorkshire prison, said Layton. So it could be three or four years in jail then another three years in the navy said Layton now looking a little frightened. What about Walter he asked, he's okay they're keeping him out of it because of who he is. He is going to go witness for us.

Adam could see Layton looked a little frightened. So Layton we could go to prison for up to five years and then in the navy like cousin Benny for another three years, why aren't you laughing about it?' Layton turned away and then looked back. 'Why don't you shut your mouth Adam, I'm sick of hearing it?' You've just got here and well it's not my fault

'So how long before the court case how much longer in here?'

'I don't know everything. You've woke up. Don't take it out on me, you shut your mouth, I was only having a joke. It's not a good time to joke, you look scared now Layton. I didn't mean to frighten you.' said Adam. I'm a gypsy boy, I don't scare easy, and I can take it, who said I'm frightened said Layton, shaking his head a couple of times and looking straight at Adam.

They slowed down walking over to a corner, we've been going around and around this yard so fast, I don't know how many times and I'm panting a little said Adam. I know it's like sheep you just keep following everybody around.' 'There's some of the other boys, and that big one he's sixteen, they call him Barton no one likes him, he's the bully of the boys in here, he's set about quite a few, everyone backs down to him. You had a go at him yet?' asked Adam. Yes I did, a stand up fight and then a wrestling fight the second time, how did it go, he's too strong. You're new so he'll be over to you soon. Good, I'm looking forward to it, ready for a good fight. He'll know he's had a go when he comes to me.' answered Adam.

Layton looked sideways at his brother he could tell he was in a bad mood. Adam would give this Barton the hardest fight he'd had for a long time, thought Layton. As Barton came walking over he had a swagger with him, a few other boys stood back watching, knowing there would be a fight. 'My brother tells me you're the tear away in this shit hole. 'Oh so you're another gypo, that's right low life, I can fight like a horse kicking.' Adam took two steps back you're messing with the wrong type of people lowlife, we don't scare easy, we don't back down, and somehow we always win.

Layton?' Yes brother when Mandy dells him with the shurra, lesty and mandy gellin delling with both vasters (when I hit him with the head we both go in together with both fists punching) So what does that mean asked Barton?' 'It means we're going to give it to you good.' 'That's not fair.' said Barton. You're about two years older and three stone heavier so that'll even it up, said Adam. Layton stepped back clinching his fists. I'm ready Adam get it started. No, no let's leave it I don't want trouble. Adam steeped up close to him twisting him by his jumper 'are you sure about that?' 'Because we're already to go.' 'When you see me or my brother coming you better step aside, cause you'll get it good off both of us. Barton never answered he just nodded his head twice and looked the other way.

One of the prison officers was coming across the yard. You could be in trouble gypo, said Barton with a snigger. Listen low life whatever trouble we're in, you will be in more, when it's finished and over, you'll get plenty of trouble in the far corner of the yard or in the toilet block, and if you're out before us, I've got plenty of people outside that can see to you, you're messing with the wrong type of people'. Barton went quite, looked down and walked away

You Boswell brothers follow me' yes sir we're right behind you. The prison officer knocked twice and then opened the wardens' door then going in, standing behind the brothers. The governor looked them up and down, both boys stood up straight, so you're the Boswell boys? Yes sir. This is Mister. Tommy Bee your lawyer, or should I say QC. How is your back now Adam? It's sore sir and started to scab up. You will be Layton? Yes sir I am.

The boys glanced at the warden's desk on the far end, by the wall there was a bottle of Bristol Sherry, and a five pound notes folded under one bottle. This Tommy Bees got the level on the warden thought Adam.

Now young men you follow the prison officer, we have a few special rooms for waiting cases. Yes sir, thank you sir said the two boys as if they did not know the governor was on the take. The room was as big as three cells, 2 separate beds, a fire with coal and logs, table and chairs, books and cards. Layton walked over to the big window and looking through the bars, we can see the street and shops in the distance. Adam looked at Tommy Bee, there's not much money can't do or buy is there?' 'I notice you've got the warden leveled.' ''Yes five pounds and 2 bottles.' said Layton.

Please boys, keep that to yourself. Of course Mister Bee we don't want to be thrown back in the cells again, said Adam. Tommy Bee just looked at them for a few seconds saying nothing. They're only boys, but so astute he thought. He placed a cardboard box on the table. Layton lifted the lid; there was a full chicken, some cake in the pan, and crusty bread, also 2 bottles of lemonade. Looks like Christmas to me, said Layton. Your parents can visit you twice if they wish, instead of once. 'Thank you Mister Tommy Bee for what you do for us,' said both of the boys nearly at the same time.

They sat at the table eating, drinking and discussing the case with Tommy Bee for about twenty minutes. That's about it then boys, he said standing up, the doctor will be in tomorrow to look at your back, thank you again Mister Bee for the treatment we are getting , sad Adam.

Well really it's your fathers' money and Lord Johns influence I just hope it's all worthwhile said Tommy Bee. I have a friend that smokes do you have any tobacco?' asked Layton. No I don't, he opened a silver cigarette case with his initials in gold in the centre. I like that it's very classy, said Adam. He gave Layton 2 long thin cigars. Mister Bee there's plenty time left we'd like to go back into the exercise yard if that is alright. The boys followed Tommy Bee back down the corridor there was another 5 special prison rooms, being 3 each side. Special cells like ours I suppose? Yes I believe so answered Tommy Bee. The warden does alright out of it doesn't he. Please keep your voice down Adam. The boys followed Tommy Bee into the warden's office again.

I would just like to say thank you sir for your kindness and what you're doing for us, said Layton and Adam giving the impression they knew nothing of his private affairs. That's alright young man we are not all racial, but please keep it to yourselves about your new cell. After your exercise one of the prison officers will always show you back up here.

The boys walked straight over to Donald. Adam gave him a chicken leg and a piece of cake in the pan. When Donald had finished eating Layton then gave him the 2 cigars and told him of Barton's bullying. As Layton was talking to him Adam looked at Donald, he wasn't so tall about 5ft ten, but the width of him and the size of his hands, he looked awesome, I'll bet the police officers show him respect, thought Adam.

After listening to Layton Donald waved Barton over, he looked a little scared as he was coming over. Donald stood there staring into his face, now listen shit for brains, I'm the hardest man in this nick, yes I know you are answered Barton, You're going to be in big trouble do you get my drift, I understand I understand Barton repeated. 'Don't you worry Donald I will spread it around, that you're the hard man.' 'I don't, I'm not worried, and it's you, the bully boy that needs to worry. 'I want you to understand these 2 gypsy boys are my friends, personal friends, you even look at them the wrong way and I'll break your 2 arms, you just leave them alone, you understand? Donald prodded Barton's Chest; Barton just nodded his head you can go now. Barton quickly walked away fear on his face.

Donald put one of the cigars in his mouth I know what it's like to be picked on and badly treated bullied because of what you are. You boys just let me know if you get any trouble off anyone, said Donald lighting the cigar and walking away. The 2 brothers looked at each other and smiled, I think you made a very good job of that,' said Adam. 'I definitely did, Granny Nellie couldn't have done it any better.' said Layton.

CHAPTER TWELVE - RETURN TO ABERLINE

So where did you do your time, and did your friend Donald get transported? I will finish it for you another time. We've been out here nearly an hour, it's getting chilly, said Adam, standing up.

'That's a nice weapon, not to heavy well balanced and accurate.' 'And just how do you know all that?' asked Tex. 'By the SW on the side of the hammer, I've got one, used it quite a while. Bill took it out of the shoulder holster, handing it to Adam, Nickel plated engraved barrel with ribbed feathered top mother of pearl handles and double barrelled. 'It's now a collector's pistol, a limited edition, one of two thousand because that is all they made,' said Adam opening the six chambers and closing it again, then pressing the safety catch down. He twirled it forward fast several times then back finally a fast sideways twirl; all of a sudden he had the barrel in his hand, giving it handle first to bill.

Orby and Tex looked from one to the other. 'I'm surprised you don't carry a gun Mister Boswell' said Orby. Just call me Adam. 'You say it's one of two thousand, a collector's piece?' said Bill the barber, taking off the safety, then holstering it again. Tex poured Orby a whiskey with a dash of orange juice. 'Well what do you think of it?' he asked. 'I'll try another' answered Orby.

'Yes I bought mine at Rigby's of London, had to wait 3 months to get it. Fine weapon.' 'My two sons bought this one for my birthday three years ago. Mine was 15 pounds, that's about 60 dollars.' One in that condition you'd pay maybe ninety dollars now.

'That's a lot of dollars for one hand gun' said Orby. You're Smoking these fine cigars, very expensive guns how you're dressed. You must be a rich man.' said Orby. 'I'm a long way from being rich. I just like the best when I've got the money. That makes sense, said Tex. What's the girls like in the Palace?' asked Adam 'Two's about fifty odds, had more fun than I've had bacon sandwiches, and I've had a lot of bacon sandwiches' said Bill. They all laughed. 'There's two nice young things in their 20s, make an old man feel young, and a young man wore out.' 'Is that right? What's the charge?' asked Adam. '5 dollars for a short time, 10 dollars for the night, and they're very, very busy. Cowboys, High plains man, drifters, passing through.'

'Too busy for me' said Adam, 'I'll pass on it.' 'You might be making the right decision,' said Orby. I wonder what they do with all the money when they're old, said Tex. In London when they get to about fifty they buy a guest house in Brighton. And where's Brighton? Oh it's a nice resort 40-50 miles from London'. 'What's a resort?' asked Orby.

'A seaside town.' Answered Adam. There's a gal in Texicana, and I always have a day with her when I'm there. She's a widow of forty, very smart. I am going to have to level with her and tell her it's no go, I'm already married. She's nice but things like that on your mind can slow you down in my business, when you think or hesitate, you can get very dead.' Said Tex

'You could be right there, cause I sometimes think about it, said Orby. Married, four kids, the moneys very good. 20 dollars a day. It's mostly nights. It's always around 60-80 dollars in a week 'That's good money' said Adam. 'Trouble is I get the same chat, nag every Sunday morning when we're leaving the house to go to church. 'We've got a nice house'. We've got money in the bank, a family. Why don't you pack this job up? But it's so easy. Where else am I going to earn, that kind of money without hiring my gun.

Bill glanced at him, he had never seen his friend worried before about his job. 'You know Orby, you're 50, you've got four kids, three boys, and a daughter Louisa's probably right, get out while you're in front. You ought to buy a nice little ranch,' said Bill.

'Could you, your wife and family live fifteen or twenty miles out on a prairie, coming into town just once every 3 weeks for supplies? I've lived it, a lonely life' said Tex. 'What do you think Adam?' 'I think as Tex said, you're a gun fighter, your mind only needs to wander for a few seconds at the wrong time. Your family would have no father. There's plenty of businesses in a town, especially a new town like Glen Parva, move down there, start a shop. There are two of you, to run it. Think of something that's needed. You'll get no messing from anybody. You'll have the reputation of being a hard case.'

I'll think about that, it makes sense, Glen Parva's a nice place. It's Sunday, go to meeting tomorrow at the church, after you're all welcome. I'm inviting you back for Sunday dinner' said Orby. 'Leave me out the church Orby, I'm a gambler and occasionally a whorer. 'Are you married Bill?' asked Adam. 'I was. She passed away with consumption 7 years ago, answered Bill.

'Oh well I suppose I'll go to church with you. It might make me say my prayers more' said Bill. 'How about you Adam?' 'I will if you's are going, why not.' 'The bottles empty Orby, it's your shout' said Tex. 'Just a beer for me' said Adam.

'So you're from New York?' said Orby. 'Only this last five months.' 'I'm really from Scotland. My mother came from a place called Forfar.' Said Orby. 'I know it. It's about twenty miles from Perth and Dundee. 'So you come off Scottish people like Tex then? asked Adam' . All of a sudden a shot gun went off. 'It's in the Rising Sun across the street.' 'Is it a rough place?' asked Adam. 'It's been quiet for some weeks now. I work there now and then. Who's the trouble shooter over there these days?' asked Tex. 'An Irish fella, has a side gun, but uses a very short shot gun, answered Orby.'

Adam looked over at the bat wing doors, she looked a little frightened, probably heard the gun fire he thought. The old timer who waited on the tables was standing next to her, waving. 'She's pretty' said Tex, 'too young for you' said Adam. 'I think I'd better keep you company'. 'You don't miss a trick do you?' said Tex. There was quite a few eyes on her. 'Good evening ma'am, what can I do for you?' said Tex touching his Stetson. Adam just stood there looking out over her shoulder. She glanced at him twice whilst she was speaking to Tex. This old gentleman told me you're the main guard so I came out for a walk and I thought I was just as well to find out about the stage coach tomorrow.

'Not tomorrow ma'am, they don't travel on Sunday's. It'll be Monday. Where are you staying anyway?' 'I'm in the Summer Breeze Hotel, we was going to stay in the big hotel but I heard it was noisy and sometimes dangerous.' 'You picked a nice quiet place. That's where we're staying, Answered Tex'

There was suddenly 2 pistol shots, then a shotgun blast then all was quiet. 'My god it's like a human jungle. Is it always like this?' she asked. 'Only once in a while, sometimes months' said Tex. 'What time does the Stage leave Monday?' 'It's usually around 10.30. I don't suppose you're wanting to come in here?' 'Not really, I'll just go back now. I have a book I am reading.'

Adam's eyes looked into hers as she turned. She was more beautiful close up than afar, he thought. She glanced quickly away. The city bowler hat he wore was cocked slightly to one side, his tanned skin showing his white teeth off, he removed his hat, his black curly hair hung over the top of his ears, I am Adam Boswell from Scotland and you are? Angelina Sinata from Sicily, she answered. I've been to Rome, a lovely place, also Naples that wasn't so nice, I've never been to Sicily. You're a long way from home ma'am.' 'That is true, but America will now be my home.' Adam smiled 'were all from everywhere out here? No wonder they call it the new world. Would you like us to walk with you, back to your lodgings?' Adam's got the chat with the ladies thought Tex. 'Thank you I would appreciate that'.

As they went down the dry dusty road, she walked between them. The Sheriff was walking up fast, fastening his gun belt. 'Hello there Tex, I heard gunfire.' 'It's in the Rising Sun.' 'I'm on my own; Tex looked at Andy Watson, the Sheriff. He knew what was coming,

I need backup, I'm on my own, got no deputies, 2 brothers they both left for California Gold fields 'I'll make the bill out for 2 nights, 40 dollars, I wouldn't let you down anyway Andy, said Tex. Pinning his badge back on as he turned to Angelina

'Don't worry miss, Adam will see you back to the lodgings.' 'Thank you Senior.' She hesitated, 'Tex ma'am.' 'I thank you Senior Tex and for escorting me back, and you Mr Boswell' she said, putting her arm through his. 'Call me Adam.' 'I am Angelina-Sinata.' 'I'll see you later.' Tex said, Adam then noticing the low cut crochet lace across her cleavage. Adam could see the top of her tanned breasts rising and falling when she breathed deeply. Her long black hair hung at the back tied with a velvet ribbon her complexion was slightly tanned. Adam was having difficulty not putting his arm around her waist as they walked.

'You've come a long way from Sicily Miss Sinata.' 'We've both come a long way, she answered' They said no more for the next eight or nine minutes. They stood in front of the Summer Breeze. 'I'll see you inside. A town like this, you should not be out alone at night' said Adam unlocking the front door, he held it open for her to go through first, he could see she liked that. 'Thank you Senior Boswell, I mean Adam.' she said, stepping inside, 'would you like a coffee before you go upstairs?' She hesitated for a moment, then smiled 'why not?' she answered. Adam stood by the reception then rang the small brass bell. The owner came out looking at the clock on the wall, a little annoyed. Adam smiled, placing a silver dollar on the signing in book. 'Can we have a pot of coffee?' The hotel owner picked the dollar up smiling. 'Of course Mister Boswell, of course' he said showing them through to the dining room.

'So you was on the train from Texicana ?' 'Yes we joined up to the Texicana line from across country, the Boston line.' I came straight out from New York, how do you find this country Adam?' He hesitated then poured her coffee first. 'Help yourself' he said, pushing the cream jug and sugar bowl towards her. 'I find it so big, vast, no hedges, I've never seen such open areas before.' 'Yes that's how I would describe it, my country Sicily it is small; I think you could put it in the state of Texas.' 'Yes and Scotland with it.' answered Adam.

'So if you don't mind me asking, what are you doing all these thousands of miles across the sea?' 'It's a long story, my Father died back home, he was the Don of our county.' 'Yes' said Adam, she could tell he did not understand what she had told him. 'Do you know what a Don is?' 'No I don't' he answered. 'A Don is like Spanish or English Lord, but in Sicily they are many times more powerful. They still have the power and authority, just like hundreds of years ago. It's not just a title, the men that work or do his bidding are usually loyal on to death, they kiss his hand and follow him.' 'And what does he do for them in return?'. 'As he can call and really depend on them, they can call on him and he will stand by them, with his power, authority and wealth, they become part of a family, not just a job and boss.'

'Like a brotherhood' said Adam? yes but they don't play brotherhood she said, tapping his Masonic ring with her index finger, they live it to the death if need be.' She's very sharp, and has an air of importance about her' he thought. 'Sicily is as big as Ireland, it has 25 Dons. When my father died, my uncle, being his younger brother took over title, his lands and businesses. His loyalty and character did not come up to my fathers. He let the family name down badly. A lot were cheated, some disappeared, and some had accidents. Most of the businesses and land was sold up. He gave 10 percent to his eldest son, my cousin. We were given 10% if you could call it a share, which was ours, then he left with a fortune, mostly in gold and came to Texas 2 years ago.'

'But surely; the authorities, the courts?' 'Do you not understand Adam, they held many of the court judge's and top men in their pocket. Adam could see she was glad to be telling someone her troubles. 'My Uncle Marshall Manuel Sinata sold up and paid some off, it was either take what he offered, or expect an accident. He had very little honour. He was excluded from the table of 25, where the Dons of Sicily sit. His eldest son, my cousin is now trying to strengthen the good name to what it used to be, and build up what little he has. The family estate was big , it took my great grandfathers 4 generations to build that up, many businesses and farms, all we got was 10%, we should have had 50% at least, it was my father's.'

'It's been a long day for you Miss Sinata.' 'Thank you, I've bored you with my problems. 'No you haven't and we will talk again. It's nice to talk to someone, she said. He walked her to the foot of the stairs, she had probably been used to men bowing and being humble. But that was not his way, he had left that behind many years ago, he felt equal to her.

'You must finish this story for me another day Miss Sinata, I am a good listener,.' He could sense it had taken a big weight off her mind to talk about it. He thought of his grandmother Manx Nelly, a top duckerer, star gazer. She would have pulled big money off this young lady, thought Adam. 'And you Senior Boswell.' Call me Adam. you must tell me your story one day.' 'Yes I am a gambler, a wheeler dealer,

'I'd like to make a bet, everyone who comes to this new world has a story to tell, answered Adam.

Still holding her hand he turned slightly to stand in front of her. Looking at her mouth, then their eyes met, she had a slight smile as she looked away, then gazed back into his eyes. His hand lifted her chin up then very softly kissed her on the side of her nose, then the corner of her mouth, then really kissing her she did not pull away, her mouth opened slightly and her arms went around his neck, they were pressed close together as they kissed again, it was a long kiss, she weakly tried to pull his left hand away, then let him continue, then finally stepped back looking at him, 'I must go', Goodnight Adam, she said slightly out of breath. she was stood at the top of the stairs. I'll see you tomorrow, he said, she did not answer, just smiled and nodded twice. He turned then opening the door.

As he walked back down the street, he had mixed feelings about Angelina Sinata, she was beautiful. One part of him was pleased how quickly she had responded to him and he felt he would get a lot further with her, but yet another part of him felt a little disappointed that she had let him have his way so quick. She is beautiful and well spoken. That little country, those 25 Dons and their families would be about the closest thing to royalty that would be there. I'd like to hold her, and slowly melt her, then take her to my bed he thought as he walked back up the street.

I'd like to know more about where my family came from. Scotland, Glasgow, said Tex, as they sat at the breakfast table drinking coffee. 'Well it's big, it's the third biggest city in the country, they make ships there at Clydebank, and they also make sewing machines, that go all over the world, mainly metal work. It's bigger than New York, Washington put together. I never would have thought it was that big, said Tex

'Is it classy like Paris? 'No it's a big old working area, similar to Birmingham, and it's getting bigger every year. There are posh, nice parts, Hamilton, Bothwell, Uddingston, on the other side of Glasgow. "Is it true they're a fighting breed?' asked Tex. 'They are that, they will never back down, even when outnumbered, the Glasgow men are not big, the big Scottish men come from up north, Inverness and the Highlands' said Adam, as the breakfasts was placed in front of them. No thanks just have another coffee and a small bacon sandwich, said Adam. Have you been to Church much? Asked Tex' 'Weddings and funerals, how about you? 'Very little.' 'It's nice to go, you feel you can talk to god better in church.' 'That's a good point, I never thought about that before' answered Adam, 'You gonna show us how to shoot?' he asked.

'That's right Tex; this dude will give you and your friends an education in sharp shooting today.' 'You think you're good don't you?' Adam put down his coffee cup and looked straight at Tex. 'No Tex, I know I'm good.'

As they came out of the Church, Adam slowly looked around, it was just the same as before, they went in several clusters of people stood talking and smiling. The women looking at each other's clothes, it seems as much of a social event as praying to God he thought. The Catholic Priest stood at the entrance, shaking hands with some of the congregation coming out 'I enjoyed the sermon Father Frank, the word you gave on sin' said Louis, Orby's wife. 'Yes Missus Baa. If all the guns and whiskey were taken out of Aberline, there would be a lot less sin in it. I've seen you before' he said, shaking hands with Tex. 'Yes I have visited your church once or twice before sir' said Tex.

'You must call him Father Frederick, as we all do' said Louis. 'That's right' said the Priest. 'Nice seeing you again Father Frederick' said Tex. 'And this young man, I have not seen you before, you're new to Aberline, and you have no gun.' 'That's right sir, I don't wear a gun' said Adam, shaking hands with the Priest. 'No young man, it's Father Frederick.' 'With respect, I have 2 fathers, and that's enough.' 'And aren't you a lucky young man, who are your 2 fathers?' 'My father who sired me and my father god in heaven sir.' The Priest smiled then turned, ignoring Adam to shake hands with Orby. As he finished buckling on his gun belt then looking up a little embarrassed.

'You know honey 'I have to be armed at all times, he said rushing after her. I've got a few enemies; it's what I do for a living isn't it?' 'Shucks she knew that when she married him' said Tex, as they took their time, leaving a gap between themselves and Orby's family. Adam looked at his pocket watch, 1 o'clock. 'God it's hot, like the south of France, but this is a dry heat.' said Adam as they walked over to the other side of the street, into the shade. Orby and his family were now at the bottom of the long main street.

A large oblong terrine was placed in the centre of the table. It was filled with chicken legs and wings. Another two with roast potatoes and corn on the cob. 'It smells delicious' said Adam. 'Would you like to say grace?' said Louis to her husband. They all bowed their heads. 'Oh lord we thank you for the meal you put before us, our home and our friends, Amen.'

The heavy terrine was sliding around the long table, all taking a good share, then replacing the large lid. Louis rushed back and forth from the kitchen, placing the vegetables on the table. Leanne waas helping her. Orby placed the full plates in front of the children who sat at a separate table. 'So you don't like to call a holy man father Mister Boswell?' asked Louis. 'It's nice what a difference in home cooking to café food' said Adam. He was trying to avoid a conversation on religion or the priest. This man's so hospitable, welcoming me into his home and I barely know him, thought Adam.

'You never answered my question Mister Boswell.' Adam looked up giving his favorite smile, but this time it did not work. 'Well ma'am Missus Baa, I suppose it's how I've been brought up. The priest is probably doing a good job in a wild open town like this.' 'He's not probably, he does do a good job Mister Boswell.'

Tex and Bill the barber glanced at Orby. She's had more than her say' thought Tex. 'Honey Adam's new to things round here. Give him a chance.' 'Have you been to church many times Mister Boswell' she asked. I am going to have to give some answers he thought. 'Yes I have, St Pauls in London, Notre Dame in Paris, the Vatican, and St Peters in Rome, St Mary's Cathedral in Edinburgh, and quite a few other ones, as I have travelled a lot of the world. Not that I am religious in any way. But I had to see them when I was there.'

Tex looked away smiling. That's my friend Adam, always gives a good impression he thought. 'And you've been to all those lovely places, Cathedrals?' 'Yes ma'am.' 'They must have been, really something to see, yes they was.' 'So what is your opinion of calling a holy man father?' Adam thought for a minute, taking a second sip of his coffee. He only knew a little about the bible, as his father Nelson would tell him a few things even though Adam and Layton had read very little of it. 'What can I say Ma'am, if I have offended you, or your beliefs in any way, I apologise.' 'You haven't Mister Boswell, I'm just curious about your thoughts on religion regarding a priest.

I don't know as I have any religion, I have respect for any man of god, a vicar, a priest, whatever. I just don't agree calling any man holy father, they are men and only god is the holy father and Jesus the son and that's where it stops with me.' 'You are wrong Mister Boswell.

Adam got up from the table looking at her bible on the sideboard. 'Can you show me where it says I must call a priest father and I will believe you, she looked away not answering. Thank you for the meal, it was very nice.' He took out his cigar case. 'Excuse me; I'm going for a smoke.'

He turned and walked out of the house. She's very religious' said Orby, taking one of Adam's cigars. 'She's a very good cook and a good wife, your homes spotless.' The 4 of them turned right at the end of the side road making their way back up Main Street. Adam looked slowly around as they walked up the street with its dirt road. It was probably a hundred feet wide. The sidewalk or pavement was made of wood boards, some 3 feet off the ground. Nearly everything was wood, as if the people who lived there wasn't really sure if they were permanently staying there or moving on, thought Adam, used to seeing brick buildings and stone pavements.

'You're very quiet' said Orby. 'I was just looking and thinking, what makes people, families leave a beautiful city like Perth or Bristol, and come out here half way across the world. 'You tell us why you've come out here as well' asked Bill. Adam hesitated, 'a good question. 'I suppose change, to leave many old ways behind, a new start, in a new world. I know you feel more' said Tex. Adam looked at him I think this country has got a lot of growing to do, because there's so much of it that's not been touched.

'I feel I want to be part of it, to truly belong here'. You're not humble, you're equal, free to do and say whatever you feel. It's the country of the future, said Adam. 'That was quite a speech and you speak so well.' Said Orby. 'You should take up politics, if you want to be somebody. You could do it there. You've been around.' said Bill. You know, I just don't know, the European way, I've always lived here.' said Tex. Maybe in a hundred years it will all be the same as Europe, said Bill. Adam smiled, I don't think so, but who cares anyway, we won't be here in a hundred years', they all laughed.

'Were glad to have you here' said Bill. 'I'll second that, said Tex. They came to the Sheriff's office. The bank was right across the road. They were the only 2 fully brick built buildings in town. Bill banged on the door, come to report the shooting and knife fight last night in the Yellow Sky Saloon' said Tex.

'Yes you told me the biggest half of it last night. I understand you're a witness to it all Bill.' 'That's right Sheriff, this here is a new friend of ours, Adam Boswell from London and New York' said Tex. 'Pleased to meet you Sheriff.' 'Likewise Mister Boswell' said Andy, shaking hands with Adam. 'I hear you made very short work of 2 common charos last night, a good job Orby and Tex was there. I see you don't wear a gun Mister Boswell. You need to get one, and get some practice in with it. This isn't London.' 'So I've noticed, I do have 2 pistols, a 38 and a 32.' 'Is that so Mister Boswell?' said the Sheriff with a smile looking at Tex.

'Well as I've said, you need to get plenty of practice in and buy an holster to put one of your guns in, this bottom half of Texas can be wild and dangerous, especially for a tender foot from the city.' Adam was getting annoyed. 'You know Sheriff because I don't wear cowboy boots and a 45 on my hip, doesn't mean to say I'm a city idiot. I was brought up mostly in open country, and I can handle a gun and a horse, as good as most western men.' 'That's quite a mouthful for a dude, said the Sheriff.'

Adam looked past the Sheriff, there was 7 tin coffee cups on a shelf. He took 3 of them. 'There's no rail to sit them on here in town, said the Sheriff. Adam' smiled as he looked at one of the tin coffee mugs. It was at least twice the size of a whiskey glass. 'that's alright Sheriff, we'll just throw them up in the air' said Adam, giving one to Bill. 'Pace out 35 strides down there Bill then stop, and when we say up, throw it up as high as you can. 8 out of 10 men out here can take one of them cups off a fence post at that distance. That's a 100 ft away in mid air, dropping fast with a hand gun. It's only one in 50 could do it, said the Sheriff

'You're right.' said Tex. To hit a cup dropping fast in mid air with a hand gun at over 100 feet away'. Tex was looking at him things going through his mind. 'You always seem to have a surprise for me don't you?' he thought. 'And you can do this or you wouldn't have suggested it' thought Tex looking at Adam.

'You go first' said the Sheriff. Tex took out his colt, checked it, and then held it at arm's length, his hand moving slowly like a pendulum from left to right. 'Up' shouted Tex. He fired twice, the cup fell to the ground untouched. 'It's a fool thing to hit, that at a hundred feet away, spinning in mid air with a hand gun.' 'it's the distance, you're not standing underneath of it' said Orby. 'The speed it's falling at as well', said Tex 'Try again, Wait! Let it reach its highest point and then shoot. 'I'm ready up' shouted Tex. The tin mug seemed to stand still in mid air for barely half a second before it started to fall quickly. Tex fired twice, his second bullet hit the cup passing straight through it, sending it down the street.

'Nice shooting Tex' said Orby. 'Thanks for the advice Adam.' The Sherriff let off 2 fast shots, the last bullet just clipped the top rim of the tin cup. 'There was suddenly clapping from a small crowd of men on each side of the street. 'How about you Bill, would you like me to throw one up for you?' 'that's okay, I wouldn't be nowhere near fast enough. Orby Baa tried, the tin mug was at its highest when his second bullet went straight through it, he turned to Adam, thanks for the advice' Adam walked over to Bill, 'can I lend your gun?' 'Of course you can' said Bill. 'This guns new to me, I just want a trial shot' said Adam, walking round the back of the Sheriff's office. The bullet had been right on target, but it had dropped 3/4".

'Nice gun Bill, you need better ammo, it's tight, you haven't used it much'. Orby gave Tex a quick glance. 'No I haven't, just one box of shells for practice.' 'Right Adam, let's see what you can do.' 'Why not, let's give it a whirl' said Adam. 'Yeah give it a whirl, whatever that is' said Tex with a smile.

As Bill picked up the cup, 'Wait a minute' said Adam, giving another one to Orby. 'Dudes going to show us up, as you would say Tex, you bet your bottom dollar I am, said Adam.' 'You'd need a shot gun to hit 2 at that distance in mid air at the same time' said one onlooker. 'I'll bet you 5 dollars he doesn't do it' it's a bet, but I want 2-1 said his friend.

Adam gave Tex a quick wink and pulled out some money then counted out 1 hundred dollars, 'I've got 1 hundred dollars that says I can do it' said Adam, putting on a slight hesitation in his voice. Bill held the money up. I've got fifty dollars says he can do it, shouted Tex. It was covered in a matter of four or five minutes. Bill stood on one side of the street, Tex on the other. 'Get ready' said Tex waiting for Adam to lift his gun. The gun stayed at his side as he shouted 'up', he fired twice from the hip. Each cup landed down the street. There was no applause, no talk, they all just stood staring at Adam, 'a very lucky shot that last one, you only just hit it.'

Adam turned around, there was a thin well-dressed bald headed man of about forty five, the one that was in the Saloon. 'I'm Dutch Schultz the owner of the Yellow Sky Saloon. I seen your fight last night, and you had a big win on the roulette, now you seem to be the crack shot of Aberline. You're a new comer and you're making quite an impression.' Tex slightly shook his head side to side, glancing at Adam as if to say watch it.

Adam didn't like this man's sarcastic tone. 'Maybe you're right the second cup, might have been a better shot.' Bill the little cockney barber gave Adam a sly wink. 'Here's your money, 2 hundred dollars.' 'You want me to try again Mister Dutch and maybe you'd like a side bet.

Tex glanced at Adam. 'Or do you want to have a go Mister Dutch, I see you're wearing a gun.' 'I don't shoot at tin cans and bottles. I'm the fastest gun in Texas, never been beat' Adam noticed no one corrected him on his claim. 'As regards for that lousy 2 hundred dollars.' 'So you'd like to make it a bigger bet then Mister Dutch. 'A bigger bet, I can buy and sell you, there's 2 hundred dollars here' said Adam handing it to Bill, 'put your money where your mouth is Mister Dutch.'

'The dude wants to shoot for 2 hundred dollars now' said one of the lookers on. 'that's a big bet on one shoot off said another one. There was suddenly a silence. Now everyone was looking at Dutch and he knew it. 'I'm one of the biggest men in this town and this dude, this nobody is pulling me to pieces in front of all these men' he thought. 'I'm not bothered about a 2 hundred dollar bet' he said, taking 10, 20 dollar bills out of his fat wallet and handing it to Bill.

Adam looked at Tex on one side of the street and then at Bill on the other. 'Up' he shouted. He fired twice from the hip. Each tin cup seemed to dance in mid air as the bullet passed through it, the cups landing further down the street. There was a loud applause. Tex and Bill walked over to Adam. 'I take it all back, all the joking, piss taking, I've never seen such shooting before' said Tex. Bill stood there just nodding in agreement. Dutch had no praise of any kind, his face was dark with anger, giving the revolver several spins either way then a fast sideways spin, the barrel was suddenly in Adam's hand, as he offered it back to Bill. Orby Baa put out his right hand, you're good, the best shot I've seen, but are you fast, he asked?

Adam turned. 'I apologise Mister Dutch, I did not give you a chance to win your two hundred dollars bet back.' Adam then held up the four hundred dollars, his own two hundred and Dutch's two hundred. 'Do you want to go up again Mister Dutch?' Double, 'you're a lucky fella you're not wearing a gun Mister Boswell, I rarely get taken for a fool, and I'm not in the habit of giving money away.' 'Nobody is taking you for a fool Mister Dutch. It was a bet, I won and you lost, it was as simple as that, now I show you respect Mister Dutch I've just given you the chance to bet again, to double me up, that's respect.'

Dutch hesitated for a moment, thinking about what Adam had said, he had mentioned that he showed me respect, and they all had heard it, that was good he thought. 'There will be another time Mister Boswell, there will be another time' he repeated looking at Adam then turning. 'There's always another time, let us both look forward to it, good day to you Mister Dutch.' that was close said Tex under his breath,

The owner of the Mediterranean Café came over. 'Mister Boswell I won 20 dollars on you, you sure can shoot.' As they turned around to walk away, Adam waved to the onlookers. They all quickly waved back. 'Well they'll be talking about you tonight' said Tex. 'Oh this story will be told many times' said Bill, 'and I think it will grow a bit each time.'

Adam signed a statement, his signature under Bills, Tex's, and also Orby. 'you made a big mistake Mister Boswell-Adam.' 'what's that Sheriff?' 'Yous should have killed them, common charo's, you obviously don't know what they are. They are bad, bad people, and if they see you, it will start again, and that goes for you as well Tex.' Said the Sheriff

Adam felt happy as he walked back to the lodgings. He had made some good friends, a few troublemakers, and money it just seems to come to me. Maybe Aberlines meant for me. 'No' he said under his breath. 'I won't change my mind, I'll go to Glen Parva as planned. If it's not what I thought, I can always come back to Aberline.'

He went up the stairs, unlocked his door, threw his hat on a chair, took his boots and shirt off and lay down on the bed. About an hour had passed, when there was a loud knock on the door. 'Who's there?' he said. 'it's Tex.' Adam got up and pulled the bolt back, opening the door.

So what did you find out about the Italian beauty and the old lady with her?' 'Her name is Angelina Sinata. She's from Sicily, and the old lady is her mother' said Adam, telling Tex all that she had told him. 'She must be worried to tell so much of her life to a stranger.' 'that's what I thought Tex, but everyone's a stranger when you're new out here. I suppose you have to befriend somebody.'

Her story, it just doesn't seem to ring true. This uncle of hers sounds bad stuff. What's his name?' Marshall Manuel Sinata.' 'I've heard of him' said Tex quickly. 'Some sort of Italian or spanish lord, only been out here about 2 years, bought several big ranches up, and those that wouldn't sell got burnt out. He's bad news, definitely on that.' 'So where is his place then?' 'Does he live around here?' asked Adam 'No he's somewhere between Glen Parva and the New Mexico area. His place is not as big as the fish of John Parva's, but it's big enough and he seems to want it to be a lot bigger, and he's started to show interest in the silver mines' said Tex.

There was thunder then suddenly a heavy downpour started. It was hitting the corrugated metal sheeted roof so hard, it was bouncing off of it. It could even be heard through the interior wood panelling of the roof. 'Sounds nice, like when I used to live in an horse drawn wagon, you could lay in bed and hear it. It would send you to sleep' said Adam. 'I don't know about that, it sounds like it's going to come through the roof if it gets any harder'. 'They'll be plenty of people happy about it, there's been no rain in these parts for about seven or eight weeks, said Tex. 'No wonder everything's so cracked and dried up, said Adam. 'That's nothing, 3 years ago, there was no rain for over 6 months, It just got hotter, cattle dying, losing calves, crops just withering up, streams going down to a little trickle. Around Fort Worth and Aberline half way and nearly down to Glen Parva. It was very hard times, many went broke, sold up and left with very little.'

Tex went in his bag and came out with an oil skinned coat. 'Do you think this rain will be on long?' asked Adam. 'I've seen it last a week. This is too early in the year for that. It'll probably finish some time tomorrow, or the next day.' Adam went in one of his two cases. The hunting knife that had been a present, he pushed it underneath the coats bringing out an old overcoat he had. Tex reached out picking up Adams bowler hat, It looks very posh, Dunn's of Oxford Street London, said Tex reading the gold stamp on the leather sweat band inside . No good to you out here, you need a broad brim for the sun. Looks nice in town though as they went down the stairs, the clock on the reception wall chimed, a short tune, then struck 7 bells.

'Evening gents' said the hotel owner. 'Evening Bill' said Tex. 'Would you like a coffee, maybe a sandwich in the breakfast room?' 'No thanks, I had a big dinner, coffee will do fine.' 'None for me Bill, I wanna leave some room, I'm drinking tonight' said Tex. 'How you can shoot Mister Boswell, I'm surprised you don't wear a gun, no offence meant that is.' 'I've never had cause to wear a gun.' 'Out west nearly everyone does, even most of the ladies carry a gun' answered, the hotel owner

They went through to the dining room, we haven't been formally introduced, but were a long way from civilization.' 'I am Mrs Sinata, a mazarra meaning a dons wife. This is my daughter, I believe you have already met.' Good evening, said Tex, touching his hat, Adam did the same, they sat down two tables away. Tex leaned forward. 'They ought to call her Sinatra Icicle.' 'I agree' whispered Adam with a smile. Just then Bill the hotel owner came in placing the tray of coffee on the table. 'I believe you're the main guard' said the old lady, tapping the empty chair with her stick for attention. 'Yes I am' answered Tex, turning around. 'What time does the stage coach leave tomorrow, and is it a dangerous trip?' 'The stage leaves about 10, 10.30, on its own it can sometimes be dangerous. But it usually has a second stage or sometimes a wagon travelling with it carrying goods.

The more there is the more guns, less chance of trouble, Well ma'am. 'I am not ma'am, I am a Mazarina, a Dons wife.' 'There's no titles out here in this part of the world.' 'Very well you may call me ma'am then.' Her daughter looked down at her feet, a little embarrassed. Adam looked away.

'And how far is Glen Parva, she asked, about 280 miles from here.' 'My god, are we ever going to get there? This Texas must be big.' 'Well up to now ma'am it's the biggest state in America, they say it's well over a thousand miles long, and nearly the same across. That's a lot bigger than Britain, said Adam. 'Is there any settlements or towns to stop over, or do we stay out in open country?' asked Adam. 'There is an old fort, about half way, it's now a big settlement, and there will still be a few nights in open country. In winter, there are only 3-4 stagecoaches. It's very cold, sometimes snow. In summer weather, there's usually a stagecoach every 2 weeks, there has to be to carry the US Mail. So now you've got it all ladies. One last thing, does either of you ladies have a pistol?'

She went in her big bag under the table and came out with a pearl handled British webley 38 service revolver and a long thin open and shut lock knife. 'You're well prepared' said Tex, 'I am a Mazarina, a Dons wife.' Adam looked at her so cold and hard then he realized what a Dons wife was. 'You are Costa Nosta then' he asked. 'that's right young man I am.' 'And you Angelina Sinata?' 'I am what I am' she answered. 'And what's all that mean?' asked Tex. Adam gave him a quick hard stare. I always carry a gun, said Susan, going into her bag and coming out with a 2 shot 44 Dillinger. 'I don't have a gun' said Angelina. 'I'll go to the general store in the morning, and pick one out for you' said Adam. 'Thank you Senior Boswell, you don't even wear a gun, what would you know about guns?' said the old lady. 'He is the best shot in all Texas' said Tex.

'So Senior Tex I am told you are a guard, a private lawman, and you, what is your profession?' 'I'll buy and sell anything I can pay for, I'm a horse dealer, a wheeler dealer, a gambler.' 'And your gun Senior Boswell?' Asked Mrs Sinata. 'I have never hired my gun' Adam paused, 'yet' he said. Adam's gaze went from Angelina's mouth back to her eyes. She quickly looked away then glanced back. The old lady gave a little cough. 'Angelina, will you pour me another cup of tea, and a slice of cake?'

Adam turned, then pouring himself a coffee, he started to discuss things about tomorrow's journey with Tex. 'I noticed on the bank board it reads Fortworth Trust Bank, Aberline and Glen Parva.' 'that's right Adam, it's the same bank in all 3 towns. Fortworth is the main bank. There's one here in Aberline, and one in Glen Parva. I believe Glen Parva could be getting a second bank. The town is getting the nickname of Silver City, and I think a new bank could be getting started with the silver dealers.' 'There must be good prospects there for a frontier town to start a second bank' said Adam. 'Well there's so much silver coming out of them mines. Are they prosperous mines?' asked Adam.

A really good vane is as thick as a pencil. But the strikes in them hills at the back of Glen Parva, the vanes are as thick as your thumb, and it just keeps coming out. The quality is said to be very good. That what isn't sold to the US Mint is going over to England. Why you asking about the banks anyway Adam? 'Well I'm carrying money with me, and you say on odd times there is hold ups.' He liked Tex a lot and he had helped save his life. Adam was carrying big money with him, in fact everything he had. He was dubious about telling anyone how much. Friends can sometimes think otherwise, big money can make a difference to men's principals. Adam had had a sharp upbringing.

'If I open an account, put most of what I've got in, I can get what I want out in Glen Parva.' 'That's good thinking Adam, that's my bank and I can draw money out here if I need it, because they know me and they have my signature with my own little mark by it. It would be silly to take all you've got on a stage coach.' 'Another coffee?' asked Adam as he poured himself one. 'No thanks, I'm off to the saloon' answered Tex.

'Young man' said the old lady, tapping the empty chair with her stick. 'Yes ma'am' answered Tex turning around. 'I may have some work for both of you at Glen Parva, gun work and I will pay very well.' 'If it's good pay, I'll be interested' answered Tex. 'And you Mister Boswell?' 'I'm always interested in money, but I would need to know what was involved.' Tex got up, see you tomorrow ladies, goodnight.' He touched the brim of his Stetson as he turned to leave. 'This rain Mister Tex, it sounds like it's going to come through the roof. Does it always rain so hard?' 'Not always ma'am, only when there's been a dry spell. I believe they've had no rain now for 7 weeks.' 'Yes I see, I wondered why everything was so dried up. Do you think it will be raining so hard tomorrow?' 'I doubt it very much. It's too early in the year, probably stop tonight or tomorrow. This rain will make a late start, goodnight again said Tex.

Adam stood up, drained his coffee mug, has he placed it on the table then turned, 'good evening ma'am and it's been nice seeing you again Angelina. 'Thank you, good evening Mister Boswell' she answered with a slight smile. The old lady just nodded as the door closed her mother looked at her 'good evening Mister Boswell, thank you Mister Boswell, is it? I've seen how you look at him, a horse dealer, a gambler, and there's something about him, I think I've seen his type before somewhere. He is handsome in a rough sort of a way, but I want a lot better for you one day.' 'There are no courtiers or gentlemen out here mother. It's a rough new country, and the men are rough. I'm not seriously interested in anyone right now.' 'I am pleased to hear it' said her mother, turning her head and looking away annoyed.

The rain was still coming down hard. 'Just look at them' said Adam, pointing up the street. People were shouting and jumping up and down in the rain. The dry dusty road was now getting muddy. 'It's keeping it up hard' said Tex sitting down on one of the chairs under the porch, then pulling out his cigars. Offering one to Adam' nearly 7 weeks, no wonder how dry everything is, they must really need this' said Adam blowing out smoke then sitting down. 'it's needed for animals, crops, rivers going low. This can be a very hot part of the world, said Tex.

You've come a long way to buy a few horses and do some gambling, I'll bet you've got something up your sleeve. Maybe buying 2 or 3 ranches and turning them into a big spread, said Tex. 'I've only got enough to buy one, I come off a race of nomads, wanderers, we've always been on the road, travel is our way of life. I was told by John Parva the vast wealth in silver and ranching and how busy Glen Parva is he said it could possibly grow into another San Francisco, I'm young enough to grow with it.' Build a business up now and again then sell it on for 3-4 times the amount, I've seen it done in London and Edinburgh. Maybe end up one day with a really big hotel casino, the biggest in all Texas and breed the best horses as well.

'You think big Adam, and good with a gun too, you could maybe make your mark in Glen Parva, 'Tell me when are you going to start wearing a gun, because trouble seems to follow you?' 'I don't know I've been thinking about it. My younger brother will be out here next year. Is he as good with a gun as you?' He's an harder man than me, there's not much in it. We never did get round to finding out who's really the best with a gun.

Tell me about the gypsies in Glen Parva. Not enough time, said Tex throwing the cigar stub into the road. 'I'm off for a drink and a gamble, are you coming?' 'No I'll sit here for a while.' 'There's only 2 you'll find me.' Adam watched as Tex's boots left imprints in the muddy road. The heavy downpour started to ease off just a little, as he closed his eyes and leaned back in the chair. The rain seemed to play a constant tune on the porch tin roof.

He thought about Angelina Sinata. The hotel they had brought in Glen Parva, Tex had said it was probably the biggest in Texas, what a casino and restaurant it would make if the right man had the running of it and maybe an extension, a theatre, welcoming acts from cities, a small auction sale of various things once every three months, he had seen big hotels run like that, Glen Parva will grow, especially when the railway comes, and I intend to grow with it.' He said soflty. Angelina, she is beautiful, he thought. Good business sense and manners would win the old lady over. What would his family think of such a marriage, They would lose respect for him. His hand went to the cross and chain that hung around his neck that Esmeralda had given him. She was what he was, there was nothing to learn her, he was only in her company less than an hour and he wanted her for his woman, if only she was in Glen Parva but she's not he thought. He had been with women before but never felt this way. New Cambridge was a thousand miles away, he did intend to see her again it could be less than a year as he let go of the small cross.

The things he had seen, and places he had been, especially London and Monte Carlo. 'I can do it, maybe two years, I would be a full partner, and as she got too old, I could buy her out. What of Esmeralda's brothers? Knife men? Then there's the old mafia lady with that Webley 38 in her bag. I would be walking on thin ice. I will bring Esmeralda, my gypsy girl, to Glen Parva.' He whispered, holding the cross again; I have said a year to Esmeralda. And what of Angelina? She is beautiful here and now. An old gypsy saying 'when breads put in your mouth you've got to chew it'. He whispered.

CHAPTER THIRTEEN - THE TRIAL

All be upstanding for Judge William Bailey who will be addressed as Me Lord, thank you. Everyone be seated. The Crown versus erm these 2 brothers, Adam and Layton Boswell the charge of attacking and grievously wounding with intent Mr. Cederick Mendip of Essingbold. So Master Adam Boswell, you say the dog cleared the hedge and killed the hare that had gone through into Mr Cederick Mendips land and you then attacked him on his own land, and you were attacked by him, is all this as stated?'. Yes sir, I mean not really that's not how it happened, he did attack us first. And you master Layton Boswell, yes me lord that is correct, and you Master Walter Bates, Yes me lord that is what happened. 'We will see you may proceed Mr. Bee

'Good Morning' said Tommy Bee to the jury and good morning to you my lord, giving a slight bow to the judge and then the jury which they all seemed to appreciate. So the youths only entered the field to get the hare and the dog back, we are really looking at school boys, out for a day's sport, not hardened poachers, just boys that had permission to hunt nearly a thousand acres of Lord Johns three adjoining farms, they did not need to poach the next farm did they. He was looking from one to the other as he walked along the jury some nodded in reply.

He was dressed plain and simple in a tweed sports coat the heavy gold wedding ring had been replaced by a thin one the silk cravat and the diamond tie pin. The handmade skin shoes also, the heavy gold cufflinks had disappeared. He was now nicely but plainly dressed, not the flamboyant man about town, his accent was normal, not an Oxford or Cambridge University accent, and the working class jury liked what they saw and heard.

So me Lord you say you yourself often go hunting with these boys and their father. 'That is correct, answered Sir John, these boys and their family has been on my land nearly five years and I find them a good and genuine people, answered Sir John. Thank you said Tommy Bee sitting down. The prosecuting barrister stood up, my lord Sir John I put it to you the boys could not find enough game on your land, which they regularly hunt, so they went into Mr. Mendips adjoining fields as they have probably done before which you have overlooked.

'Are you standing there calling me a liar Sir? no one from my house or my estate has ever been on this man's land. 'Don't you dare stand there insulting me, my ancestors fought alongside of the king and was knighted in battle nearly 150 years ago, when you and this man Mendip didn't know who or what you came from. Thank you lord John that will be all, said the practicing barrister, slightly embarrassed.

Mr. Fred Watson was then asked up. Place your hand on the bible and take the oath, Mr Watson, said the judge. You are Mr. Fred Watson and a neighbour of Mr. Cederick Mendip, is that right sir? Asked Tommy Bee. Yes it is, I would first say I have known the gypsy family in question and of them for nearly four years and I find them to be decent and honest folk. Tommy Bee paused for a few seconds to let that sink into the jury and can i ask you Mr Watson what do you know of your neighbour Mr Cederick Mendip? Is he upstanding as well?

He is a crook, very dishonest. The prosecuting barrister held up his hand. 'That is an error me lord it needs to be struck from the record, it is taking Mr Mendips character away with hearsay. Thank you, said the judge looking at the prosecuting barrister, we will dismiss that comment that is if Mr Fred Watsons testimony has no proof to his statement, otherwise it will be added to the records, said the judge glancing at Tommy Bee knowing that there was proof.

Mr Fred Watson quickly told of the crooked deal showing demands and payment receipts, quickly telling the story of how Mr Mendip had tried to ruin him and get him off his farm. He then went on and told the story of Mr Mendips rape on the 14 year gypsy girl, the opposition held up his hand, standing up out of his seat, 'there is no proof of this me lord' and this incident has nothing to do with this case trying to tarnish Mr. Mendips character again.

Tommy Bee then stepped forward slightly bowing to the judge then the jury which wasn't really necessary, they seemed to like it. 'Make it quick Mr. Bee we are getting away from the point in question, said Judge Bailey looking over his glass Tommy Bee's assistant gave a copy of the unproved rape charge, the files and the transporting of the gypsy man and his son to Tommy Bee and a copy for the judge and the prosecuting barrister. Tommy Bee then slowly walked the length of the jury I think this proves without a doubt the type of man this Cederick Mendip is. The prosecuting barrister stood up then throwing his pencil hard at the table, 'whatever on earth does this incident five years ago have to do with this case today, nothing was proven against Mr. Mendip, my lord, he said quite loudly.

The judge glanced at Tommy Bee, saying quite loud I think Mr. Bee the prosecuting barrister states five years ago this terrible thing that happened, not an incident, a brutal rape attack on a young girl 13-14 as little to do with these two boys today. This copy I have in my hand of the trial and the disgraceful transporting of the father and brother of the young girl to Australia and the so called story of the tramp which was never seen or even heard of was a made up story. Whoever brutally raped that little girl twice, he needs jail and the key thrown away, was there a tramp? Said Judge Bailey glancing at Mr. Mendip.

The prosecuting barrister noticed how uneasy Cederick Mendip looked. He then glanced at the judge. Tommy Bee placed his hand over his mouth to hide is expression as he smiled.

Tommy Bee then asked the two boys up. Layton showed the scars on his head and then Adam removed his shirt, the jury gasped. This is what a 6ft man sitting on a horse done to two young boys, a racial attack by a so called gentleman, he then turned to look at the jury. If they were your sons or grandsons, what would you feel towards this man, he even shot the dog. The prosecuting barrister put up his hand, me lord he is leading the jury. The judge glanced at Tommy Bee, you must stop addressing the jury so personally, so directly. I am sorry me lord I am only telling it as it was, you must stop this opinion, 'yes my lord.

These boys are now your witnesses to question said Tommy Bee looking at the prosecuting barrister. He approached the two boys pointing at them. I put it to you boys, you started to attack Mr Cederick Mendip first knowing you was on his land. No sir, we didn't. We only have your word for that, said the barrister in an angry tone of voice waving them back to their seats, the boys looked a little frightened as Tommy Bee had previously instructed, it went down well with the jury. Tommy Bee stood up and walked into the centre of the courtroom and addressed the judge. 'My Lord, can we please call Lord Johns grandson Walter as a witness.

Now young man, you are Sir Lord John's grandson is that right? Yes that is right sir. 'Can you please tell us in your own words who attacked who and what happened? Yes Sir. This man came riding up in a furious mood accused us of poaching on his land; he then shot the dog twice, then started to thrash the two Boswell boys, Adam and Layton with his riding whip. The horse reared up and he was thrown to the ground, the boys pounced upon him and started to fight back. He then got up scrambled to his feet, got on his horse and rode off like the coward he was. Lord John nodded to his grandson and smiled as if to say you have done well. This witness is now yours to question said Tommy Bee. I have no more questions, said the prosecuting barrister looking a little annoyed.

The judge slowly looked all around and then putting his watch back on the desk, it is now 3:45 and I think the witnesses and the trial of attack and defense is now completed, so that is just leaving the prosecuting barrister and Mr. Bees final summing up and of course most important of all, you the Jury's decision, so we are going to adjourn for today and we will all be back in court tomorrow morning at 10 o'clock. 'I say to you the jury you are not to discuss this with anybody and we will have your decision tomorrow'. He then looked at the two prison officers. 'Please take the boys back down. His gavel, the mallet hit the block quite hard, , 'court is now closed'

So what do you think father, asked Nelson, it looks good this Tommy Bee is worth his money , he can say in five words what most men need ten, and he has a nice way of slipping things in, but how many of the jury of twelve likes or hates gypsies and how many are frightened of Mister. Mendip, we do not know, tomorrow will tell.

All the Boswell family sat around the outside fire that night each with his or her hands together each praying or asking in his own way, twenty minutes had passed when Nelson stood up, the leading prayer was up to him because it was his sons. Holding both his hands up, he then looked up, the stars were so bright, oh my god the father of us all, and father of our lord Jesus who was crucified for our sins, i pray to you this night and i pray justly we're in the right my god, my 2 sons only boys was protecting themselves, I ask you my god in your son Jesus name help us all in our hour of need, show mercy, in your own way may it be in or out of court, i throw out my love and sacrifice to you an unconditional love whichever way this ends up I say to you right now, my wife Dellie will never ducker, fortune tell again, as long as she is with me as I know you do not agree with this and it states clearly in your bible that you do not agree with this, I give this to you my god, not as a deal but as a show of my love and honesty to you, I say to you now my god we are the closest people on this earth, to your chosen people, the Jews, maybe that is why we are so persecuted like they are. I reach out my hand to you like a child does to a parent to wait and receive, have mercy my god. Nelson just stood there in silence, then one hand still held up, his other hand gripped the lapel of his coat and tore it straight down, a sign similar to the Jews, a sign of obedience; repent and all followed him saying 'Amen. Then there were quite little prayers from the rest of the family

Isaac looked at his wife, Manx Nellie; she looked away, then at the fire, saying nothing. His horse dealing was really a side line, she was the earner and very good at what she did, duckering (fortune telling). Isaac looked at his son Nelson, nodded and stared back at the fire. Nellie looked up at her son Nelson, smiled and looked at the fire again, she would not make false promises to god, that she could not keep, and her husband Isaac knew that.

The next morning the boys sat in the dock, all the Boswell family were there looking clean, well dressed and shoes polished, the 2 boys looked at their family, proud of them, smiling. I would like Mister. Cederick Mendip to take the stand please, said Tommy Bee. Please step forward Mister. Mendip and take the oath said the judge looking over his glasses.

'Now Mister. Mendip it is my job to question you said Tommy Bee. I will lead you then it is up to you to just say 'yes' or 'no' and that way keeps it plain and simple doesn't it. Mr Mendip just nodded. Tommy Bee glanced at the jury. Now you saw the three boys on your land, Adam, Walter and Layton, were they in the distance or close, when you first seen them asked Tommy Bee. 'Yes that it so' they were in the distance with pheasants and a hare that had just been killed on my land.

'So you say you seen the dog kill the hare and game on your land. 'How sir did it jump in the air? No they were probably shot. So Mr Mendip you now say probably you did not see them and there were no guns. I say to you sir, you did not know because you did not see the pheasants killed, they was shot with a catapult on Sir Johns land, not your land sir.

Did you see the dog jump the hedge and kill the hare on your land?' Yes I did it was on my land. 'I say to you sir, a greyhound chases rabbits and hares, course them, is the correct word …… not jumping hedges, it only goes over an hedge whereas a hare goes through it, and that hare was chased through it from Sir Johns field and the dog then jumped the hedge and killed it.

It did not course it on your land. Me lord, where is all this nonsense going, the hare was killed on Mr Mendips land, said the prosecuting barrister.

The judge looked over his glass, 'you win one Mr Bee and you lose one, the pheasants were killed on Sir Johns land and the hare on Mr Mendips. Thank you me lord I'll continue. 'This was on your land sir is that right or wrong?' Yes Mister. Bee that is correct? And you rode up to them Sir and told them they were poaching on your land? And you said how wrong they were, and they needed a lesson, then they started to attack you, so you say, is that correct?

Yes Mister. Bee it is, these young boys they deliberately attacked me, is that correct. 'Yes Mr. Bee it is correct.' Tommy Bee was silent for five seconds. 'I say to you Mister Mendip you are a liar, a racial liar sir.'

You could have heard a pin drop, the judge looked over his glasses. Come, Come Mr. Bee, you go too far sir, this is a Crown Court, not a public house, I think not me lord. I have the highest respect for your position, and the crown behind you.' said Tommy Bee, giving a bow. When he's finished with this act, what proof does he have of his

203

slandering statement to Mr. Mendip, said the prosecuting barrister. Well Mister. Bee, he gives you a challenge and you will need to put up or shut up! Said the judge looking to Mr. Mendip and the barrister who nodded back in agreement to the judge, now his friend Tommy Bee somehow had the ability to beat the barrister, but did he have proof to make such a statement stick?

Tommy Bee walked slowly across the courtroom floor hands in pockets, then turning from the jury to look at Mr. Mendip, you have just said and agreed that you were in the distance and rode over to them, not those to you, these boys have been charged with intent that is deliberately going running to you and attacking you. He looked at the judge then the prosecuting barrister.

Tommy Bee looked over to the clerk, who was taking it down in shorthand. That is so, said the clerk. So Mr. Mendip you are a liar sir, because you rode over, you went to them, and attacked them, the boys was supposed to go to you and rip you out of the saddle a heavily built man over 6ft sitting up high on a horse 2 young school boys is supposed to have got hold of you and ripped you out of the saddle, you insult or intelligence sir, that is impossible. So you are a liar again Mr. Mendip, a racial liar.

You was lashing out with your whip and shouting at them, the boys were screaming in pain and shouting back, frightened, with all this going on your horse reared up and you were thrown to the ground, because Lord Johns grandson who is a witness said you were thrown out of your saddle. Tommy stopped for 5 seconds looking around, the prosecuting barrister looked at Mister Mendip then looked away, he then looked at Tommy Bee. He's the best I've seen he said under his breath.

Adam just stood there his shirt undone hanging around his waist has practiced in the blue room, proof, these 2 school boys had to pounce on you when you came off the horse to protect themselves from a racial child beater, a heavy built man over 6ft with a whip, another three or four minutes and this boy could have been dead. These boys have many wrote out and signed character references, said Tommy Bee waving a handful of paper, how many do you have Sir from local people?' I don't need a reference against a band of dirty gyp he suddenly stopped. Yes Mr. Mendip why don't you finish it, gypsies said Tommy Bee. Just 2 young gypsy boys wanting a fair crack of the whip, 'Here, here!' shouted two or three.

Slowly, walking from the jury, then stopping halfway in the room saying nothing for three or four seconds, then pointing his finger at Mister. Mendip. You are the one that should be in the dock being tried, not 2 school boys, he then turned to look at the judge, then the jury, he just stood there for a few seconds, I have finished with him, my Lord. Tommy Bee, you ought to be on the stage, thought Judge Bailey, looking over to the prosecuting barrister 'do you know wish to add your closing remarks sir.'

The Barrister looked at Cederick Mendip then looked away, then looking at the jury he said; 'I show you twelve local people respect. What is truth or what is lies, is up to you to judge, not myself, not Mr. Tommy Bee, not even judge Bailey, it is you who must make the decision were these youths guilty or not guilty as charged of willfully attacking Mr. Mendip on his own land and physically wounding him, 'yes' or 'no', I rest my case, he sat down. Tommy Bee glanced over at the barrister and the barrister gave Tommy Bee a surprised glance and then looked down. Tommy Bee realised the barrister had lost a lot of respect for Mister Cederick Mendip and he could have put up a stronger finishing remark against the boys if he had wished to .

It looks good, we have a ninety percent chance of winning thought Tommy Bee. There was a silence for five or six seconds, the judge slowly looked all around, then at the prosecuting barrister, under the circumstances what has been proved and admitted by Mister. Mendip answering Mr. Tommy Bees questions. I am now striking the charge of intent from this case, there was several yes's and a few amen's from court. The judge hit the block hard once with his gavel, 'silence please' you the jury will adjourn for up to two hours, there is tea, coffee and sandwiches, there are also toilets, you have two hours to study it and come back with your decision of guilty or not guilty and it must be a majority count.

Tommy Bee stood with Nelson and Isaac, they noticed Cederick Mendip giving a nasty stare to some of the jury how they quickly looked away, frightened of him. The 2 hours seemed like 2 day, they sat in the small café across the street from the court and Nelson had never stopped eating from when he went in, for when he was very worried, he would constantly eat and his wife Dellie just looked at him shaking her head slowly. 'What do you think said Dellie to her mother-in-law. Manx Nellie emptied the cup then slowly looking at Dellie by what we can see and hear I would say the boys have won. That little chap Tommy Bee he tied the prosecutor and Mr. Mendip in knots. I think the boys will be home tonight.

There was only a quarter of an hour to go as they walked through the double doors and up the stairs to the courtroom. All be upstanding for judge William Bailey who will be addressed as me Lord, he sat down slowly looking all around, and looked over at the usher 'please bring in the jury' Mr. Mendip who was sat on his own one chair from the prosecuting barrister, the judge looked all around. This is the final part of the trial it is now in session, I will have no interruptions or outbursts, bring forth the accused. The 2 boys stood in the dock with a police constable on either side, they looked a little tired and frightened, the 2 days court session had obviously taken it out of them. The judge looked at the jury prey tell me who is the spokesman for the twelve.

A short fat man stood up, my Lord, I am Charles Chris butcher shop owner of York, the judge looked over his glasses at the spokesman, 'has you know I have previously dropped the charge of intent. Yes me lord that is good, answered the spokesman. 'Now Mr. Charles Chris I would like you to speak up loud and clear. Me Lord the charge was attacking and wounding Mister. Cederick Mendip, and causing grievous bodily harm on his own land, we the jury by a decision count find the 2 boys in question guilty as charged but would ask for leniency considering their age and the case. Manx Nellie was now holding Dellie, her arm right around her waist, Dellie had an handkerchief to her mouth to stifle the sobbing, thank you Mister. Charles Chris there was a tone of disappointment in the judge's voice, pray tell us Mister. Charles Chris. I am not wanting or trying to divert the jury's decision, but under the circumstances and evidence of the statements of Mr. Mendip, how did you come to such a decision.

Me Lord, we realise they were not poaching with a thousand acres of Lord Johns estate to hunt and with the lords grandson with them, we find them not guilty of poaching, but we do find them guilty as charged of attacking and viscously wounding Mr. Mendip on his own land as was stated, and as was charged that is how we find them guilty, my lord. Thank you Mir Charles Chris you may now sit down. The Judge looked at the boys then quickly glanced at Tommy Bee.

The 2 boys looked at the judge not knowing what to expect, he could see they were frightened as they looked over to their family as if for help. The judge then looked at Mr Cederick Mendip, you will take that sarcastic smile off your face sir, or I well have you charged for disrespect of court. 'Well boys, thank you for standing. First, considering the character and no previous convictions your age your sentence will be the most lenient I can give for viciously attacking and wounding, the sentence is from three to ten years, you will serve three years in a boys borstel prison at least fifty miles from where you live, also when the sentence is finished you would then normally do 1 to five years in the merchant navy as a cabin boy, this will be only 1 year this is the least I can give you that is the set amount of a four years sentence to serve because of your age, you will be held at the Queens pleasure, and should there be any new evidence, a retrial would be allowed.

Oh my God, four years they are only boys and were just protecting themselves I-I Dellie just collapsed to the floor, four years repeated Manx Nellie. She had to steady herself between 2 chairs. Nelson bent down to see to his wife, Isaac, Old Byron and young Jack said nothing they just stood there, Shame, shame on you, you devil shouted some woman at Cederick Mendip.

The judge looked at the 2 police officers, take the boys down and back to the prison, the court seemed to empty very quickly. As they walked towards the stairs old Byron seemed to walk in a diagonal line which took him closer to Cederick Mendip, he stopped and looked at him straight in the face, you're a dead man walking' within 5 weeks you will be dead, you won't know what day or how 'Did you hear that, what that old gypo said to me? The prosecuting barrister turned to look at Cederick Mendip. No I didn't hear very much of it, you see, you are messing with a different type of people, in fact with their children, they have a different culture and ways, trying to live in our world. Last time they nearly got burnt alive. 'You want to watch your back Mr Mendip.' He turned, to walk away.

Sir John looked at Isaac, it's just an hasty threat isn't it Isaac, he would not, would he?' Look what he did to that other gypsy family, he just can't keep getting away with it. Sir John they are only boys and in the right and have to go to jail, my father is the elder so it is his job, if he was not here i would be the elder and that would make it my job, he is still a very good shot with a catapult loaded with a lead ball. My god Isaac it would be murder, not as far as we are concerned it would be justice, gypsy justice. We have tried the gorger way, it will now have to go our way, the gypsy way.' 'Tell me why 5 weeks?' asked Sir John, 'It will give him time to go back and say he lied.' 'Yes of course it would then be a retrial wouldn't it. But I don't think he will do that, well that's his problem.' said Isaac. 'And it will be the last problem he will have on this earth.'

CHAPTER FOURTEEN – THE QUEEN AND THE GYPSY EARRING

<u>One Week Later</u>

The next morning the gypsy family all sat around the fire except for Adam and Layton who were in jail, there was little talk about where to hork and where they were going to go, in fact you would think there had been a death in the family. All sat with a cup of tea and a egg and bacon sandwich, young Walter sat with them, having his second breakfast. 'Well I think we will all make a fresh start on Monday. We have only had a few days off because of the boys. Yes a new start, a good idea.' said Nelson. As Adam had been in jail 12 days, and Layton 18, the family was still having difficulty accepting it.

Walter, Walter, yes grandfather I hear you. Sir John was stood in the doorway; the teacher is here for your lessons. Walter stood up, finishing his mug of tea. There was still half of his egg and bacon sandwich left, he walked into the stables, Smokey the greyhound bitch was in the far byre, 2 old blankets was thrown on top of the straw, she had four pups, all sucking at her teats, Walter walked forward with his hand held out slowly as Nelson had showed him, then stroked her head, not touching the pups. Hello old girl, you look very tired. As he held out the half-eaten sandwich, she stood up, 2 of the pups still hanging from her, taking it off of him her tail giving a slight wag, the pups was now ten weeks old. Fawn was the father of them, Nelson walked in standing beside Walter. They're now getting too big for her'.

And how will they be fed and trained, Uncle Nelson, ask young Walter. 'A mongrel is hard and can take a hard bringing up but a well-bred animal has to be looked after and brought up on the best, and properly trained or it will just be a well-bred fool, these pups they come off good stock so they need to have the best, build them up strong, cooked off cuts of meat and tripe, rabbit, all cooked and then mixed half and half with baby biscuits three times a week, eventually 4 times, with just biscuits the rest of the week. Three eggs whisked with warm milk, and when there's no chill in the air taken out into the field to play and run with their mother, then later to chase after a stuffed rabbits skin on a long string behind a bicycle.' Is that how you trained Fawn?' Yes it was, what then Uncle Nelson tell me more. Well when they are six, seven months old let them have a small meal now and then of raw rabbit or hare, then at nine months old they go out, just one at a time with their mother to run alongside or behind her to let them taste a fresh kill; finally allowed to hunt alongside her as they got bigger. She would turn a rabbit or a young hare and the pup would kill it. No food the day before, they course and kill better when hungry.

Nelson heard something and turned, good Morning Sir John' so with all that would there be anything else asked Sir John. Oh Yes, you get out of a good bred hunting dog or horse what you put into it, answered Nelson as he walked out of the stables. It's a shame the boys aren't here, they would enjoy it all. I will miss them said Walter. Nelson looked at Walter then away, yes we will all miss them. Just you on your own young Walter you will have a lot to do, exercising and helping with these young dogs.' We have to go out to look for a living, you will learn a lot.' said Nelson. 'I'll enjoy it Uncle Nelson.' Then he ran to the house. He's a lovely boy thought nelson, but why was it we always have to take the shit end of the stick, he said under his breath thinking of Adam and Layton in jail. 'What was that, asked Sir John, Oh nothing, just thinking out loud?

Sir John sat by the fire, holding one hand out for the heat, the other hand held a mug of tea, you know nelson I have seen quite a few litters over the years, and the biggest is usually a dog but this litter it's a bitch and she's massive. That's why there was only four instead of six or seven.' answered Nelson. 'Er... is that why you've chose the bitch asked Sir John. With your permission, yes that is what we agreed on.' said Nelson. I think she's nicely marked, all fawn like the father and Smokey grey tail and socks like the mother, and what will you call her? I'm not really sure Sir John; Layton suggested Smokey Fawn, yes it's appropriate, answered Sir John.

Nelson broke three eggs into a large jug, then pouring in 2 pints of milk and whisking it all up for five minutes he then poured it into a bowl. As the four pups eagerly started to lap it, the mother managed to get her head in between to get her share.

'We'll take them out in the field it's going to be a warm day.' Said Nelson. 'I'll leave it to you; I have things about the estate...' He stood back from the fire. Sir John? Yes Manx Nellie what is it? He answered handing her the empty mug. What exactly does the Queens pleasure really mean; he hesitated wanting to keep the answer simple and easy to understand as all around the fire was listening. 'In unusual cases where there is a lot doubt if her majesty so wishes there can be a re-trial she has the power to pardon immediately, setting them free'. And does that include a death sentence. Oh yes, her word is unquestioned. The power of life and death, said Jack; who was always bewildered by the power of the throne.

She represents the crown, she is the jewel in the crown, and the crown answers to no one only god. The most powerful organisation or constitution on earth, it has been here over 1500 years and it will always be here, said Sir John. There was a silence from the gypsy family.

Sir John? I want to see the young Queen, said Manx Nellie. He smiled shaking his head. Do you know what you are saying, what you are asking? She sits in state seeing to many important things not riding round the countryside like you may think. I understand that, Please find out if she is in England. I will tell Tom the gilly to go to the post office in the village, they will wire London and we will be told where the flag flies, St James' Palace or Windsor, she could even be in Scotland or Wales, but we will have the answer in about an hour.

Sir John then stopped turned around to look at Manx Nellie, 'you people never cease to amaze me.' What do you hope to do, he asked. We have tried the educated gorger way, all the fine words, we will now try our way, as they say the astute way. Does astute mean, to be cunning like a fox, asked Isaac. Yes that's right my husband, answered Manx Nellie. 'And if that way fails that will be an end to it? answered Sir John.

There is always another way when a life or freedom is at stake, we just cannot say that's the end of it, it's not our way, said Isaac. Even a prison warden, a greedy man, £100 pound in gold coins. A man only says no when it's not enough, and that would be enough, more than enough. That would be a fortune to a man with a wage.

Sir John turned to look at Isaac. Don't bring any trouble to Rascliffe Hall. If we have to get them out our way, we will be 100 miles from Rascliffe Hall, answered Isaac. He was surprised Sir John was so blunt. Would he be the same if it was young Walter?

Tom the Gilly had been to the village post office twice. They all walked over eager to hear any news. This time nobody seemed to be interested or impressed with the splendour of the blue room. A trolley full of various cakes was brought in which nobody again was interested in, but they did have a cup of tea.

Sir John walked slowly backwards and forwards as he spoke Lady Eleanor has been in touch by cable wire with her majesties secretary Sir William Miller who I know, the Queen is in meetings for about 2 weeks with various Prime Ministers and Ambassadors of South Africa, Canada, and other counties of the commonwealth. You say Sir John, some 2 weeks where is she staying?' asked Manx Nellie. Not looking very impressed with the importance of the Commonwealth meetings, Sir John never answered, just looking out of the large bay window at his vast lawns and flower arrangements, looking slightly annoyed with it all. Manx Nellie patted the top of the table twice, the heavy gold ring hit the wood table top, it broke the silence like a pistol shot. 'My 2 grandsons are in jail doing 4 years, yours is home with you,' 'steady Nellie.' Said Isaac.

Sir John looked around, Nellie intended to have her say, I am not the least bit interested Sir John in what Prime Ministers or Ambassadors are doing in London, I am not even interested in the Commonwealth, let those who are in charge look after it. I asked you a question, please give me an answer. 'Very well Nellie the young Queen is in residence at royal Windsor castle. The meetings will take 2 weeks, she usually sees one a day, sometimes two. 'What you do is up to you personally I wouldn't dream of going there, you won't even get in, you'll make a fool of yourself. I've done that a few times, once more won't hurt, you see sir john I am more interested in my 2 young grandsons that are locked in prison for just protecting themselves and I am not wanting to see my father in law old Byron hung for murder, because he will see to that man for what he did. He is the head of our family our ways are not yours Sir John.

The Next Day

It was 7:30 in the morning as the coach pulled up in front of York Railway Station. Tom the gilly jumped down then tying a rein from each horses bridle to the hitching rail, the door swung open and Isaac stepped down, then holding his wife's hand as her foot found the step. I'll hang on a while Isaac and see you off. It had been 3 quarters of an hour journey from Essington Hall to York station. Everything was damp and covered in dew, I hope the coffee and tea room is open, said Tom as he took their travelling bag. Isaac walked up to the flap above the counter and tapped on it, a few minutes passed and then he tapped again. A red faced man stared out at him, 'can't you read the signs' we're not open until eight o'clock, then slamming the flap shut. Isaac tapped the flap again, 'what is it now, said the red faced man. 'I can't read, said Isaac.

The clerk looked him up and down, nice suit, heavy gold watch chain across his waistcoat, handmade polished shoes. Obviously a sarcastic gentleman thought the clerk, and aren't you the funny one. He answered, slamming the flap shut again. Tom just smiled following Isaac through into the tea room.

I'll have 2 eggs on toast please, and you Nellie, yes Isaac make mine the same. Isaac turned, 'do have some breakfast Tom, 'thank you I will have the same.' 'That's three double eggs on toast and three coffees please miss. Isaac placed a florin 2 shilling piece on the counter. Thanks Isaac, answered Tom. Isaac glanced at him, you can read can't you Tom?' Yes i can. We're catching the tartan arrow from Aberdeen to London, stops here at 8:30 but we do not know what changes we have to do. Could you please find out for us and write it on a piece of paper' Tom turned, you can read Nellie, yes I can no problem Tom, just get it all wrote out for me, answered Nellie.

Looking around the café starting to get busy, the platform benches was filling up outside. 'Must be a busy train this, it goes through quite a few cities before it gets to the capital, from Aberdeen to London about 450 miles, said Tom. Pushing his plate away he then got up. He was soon back, 'You don't need the paper there are no changes it goes straight through from Union Street Aberdeen to Euston Station London and you get into London about seven o'clock, that's about twelve hours'. 'You'll stop at four or five cities before you get to London, said Tom turning to look out the window at his coach and pair of horses.

They walked out onto the platform. 'Don't be disappointed if you don't get an audience with the Queen, i think your chances will be very slim, said Tom. It's the first time I've seen it said Tom as they looked at the engine, it was enormous the biggest Stevenson train built, in fact the biggest train engine in the world. There was a pair of them, its sister train went from Glasgow down to Bristol and then on to Plymouth whereas this one went from Aberdeen to London. There were seven carriages behind it and it was said that it could keep up 45 miles an hour on the flat all day. They walked out onto the platform and stood looking at the engine it was painted a deep Brunswick green with a tartan stripe running though the centre, just below was the words 'Tartan Arrow' Tom shook hands first with Isaac and then Manx Nellie then walking towards the exit. He turned, 'Good luck to both of you'.

If it hadn't have been a mercy trip for the 2 grandsons they would have enjoyed it, seeing the countryside and so many villages, thought Tom it was a few years since Isaac had been on a train from Scotland down to Slough near London to his sisters funeral.

They had been travelling for about three and a half hours when the train started to slow down pulling into Nottingham. The going now was straight and somewhat flat, and the train was keeping up its maximum speed. Isaac was looking at the 2 thick small tickets that the conductor had just punched a square hole in one with a pair of pliers. Put them in your pocket, if you keep playing with them you might lose them and we will have to pay again. Lesty keep rockering to mandy as if mandy is a tickner and mandy will dell lesty (You keep speaking to me like I am a child and I will hit you) you need to show me more respect. Manx Nellie looked out the window saying nothing. 'That's right keep vartering a drey duvver evya and rockering che chi to mandy (that's right keep looking out that window and say nothing to me). Manx Nellie glanced at the 2 couples that were sitting with them in the compartment and they just looked away, knowing nothing of the short conversation. Probably thinking Isaac and his wife was either Greek, Italian or even Turkish.

Manx Nellie suddenly realised she was showing her husband little respect. I am sorry my husband that I do not show you enough respect, please forgive me' he just nodded giving her a stare and then looking out of the window.

It wasn't easy when you were a man amongst men, and your wife was a good getter even earning a lot more than you. When in company it was always flash Manx Nellie, she had the name for being a big getter. The 2 best in the country was Blackpool Daisy Smith; she used to be Old Byron's mother-in-law, and Manx Nellie. Looking out the window Isaac started to think back when they had pulled down from Scotland down to Slough after the funeral. There was only three or four other gypsy families on the field, Bucklands, London, Shaws, and Smiths. It was the Smiths that Isaacs's sister had married into.

The other twelve or fourteen families was all travelers, most of them friendly people and very hard working, most spoke with a London accent, some went out getting scrap, some had stalls on the markets. They spoke with a slang knowing very little gypsy rumness. In the pub one night 2 of the men had been very cheeky to Isaac and one had stepped outside to sort it out, he put the 2 of them away in 10-12 minutes, he was very annoyed as he walked back in the pub. I am Isaac Boswell, I'm from Scotland.' he said quite loud. They had not realised who he was, no one took up his challenge. No surrender until there's only one left standing.

That night Nellie looked at his bruised knuckles and a few blood speckles on his shirt. 'You've been fighting again, was it with the gorgers in the kitchema (public house) Yes I put 2 of them away, it was 2 travelling men.

Isaac had been just having a few horse deals now and then, and going to the odd horse auction, he didn't need to work too hard or rush too much, maybe three days a week was enough, as his wife Nelly was one of the top fortune tellers in the country. The traveling women, those that did go out, hawked lace or flowers from the basket, some trying to ducker, this is what usually caused jealousy for Isaac, him and Nellie had always had the very best of everything, he had always money to spend and did little work. His two best suits were tailor made, their jewelry was very heavy and they ate and drank out of Royal Crown Derby neither seemed to do any hard work, he was one of the few to have such a wife.

'Nellie I am going to start out to work, real work, I'll need to buy a big Shire horse and a big heavily built wagon with strong high sides. I am going on the scrap. 'Well my husband you know where the luvva's (monies) kept under the woodress (bed) take what you want and buy whatever you need, you don't have to work you know.'

The next day he had brought a big Shire horse and a heavily built wagon from a brewery, he now had to find a joiner, to get high strong sides on it. He went out horking for a full week, at the back of their living wagon was a big heap of scrap, cookers, copper boilers, a few brass pipes, and a few lead pipings, etc, and quite a lot of iron. He spent the next week hammering and chiseling the non-ferrous metal off the steel and iron and at the end of the second week there was 3 full loads.

Some of the travelling men had passed remarks on how well he had done, in an area that had been so well horked for scrap. He called business, plumbers, builders, gas fitters, always managing to see the yard foreman. He would buy £2 worth, and push 10 shillings into the foreman's hand, got him a good load at the right price. He would say that me saying thank you is all well and good, but thank you does not pay the bills, have this for yourself for helping me out, not many refused. He had a way of putting it to them and he would come out of that yard with a good load that was not seen by the manager behind the high sides of the wagon

He sat in the living wagon counting his money up, it's good Nellie, better than I thought, £35 pounds profit for the 2 weeks. If I could keep that up every 2 weeks while you're covering all the home expenses, just look what I could save. She looked at him not wanting to hurt his feelings, you have done well Isaac probably better than some of the other men on here, that does scrap all the time She picked up one of his hands, 'just look at the state your hands are in all cut and scared, you used to shave every morning and would not wear the same shirt 2 days on the run, you shave now only twice a week and keep the same shirt on for three or four days as you're so tired. 'If I was amongst some of our family rumney chells (gypsies). I would be ladged (ashamed), as if I had let you down, you have earned £35 I have earned £55. You don't have to work like a collier down the pit, I can keep you like a gentleman, and when we leave here I want it to stop, and go back to your horse dealing, you don't need to do it, a gypsy woman can do it and do it easy, we're bred to it.

He turned slowly from looking out the train window. I'm sorry Nellie, how I snapped at you you're a good wife. No it was my fault I must stop speaking to you like that. I believe there is a dining car let us get chumney to holl (something to eat) and a cup of peermengra (cup of tea). Isaac glanced at her bag on the seat, fetch lestys gunna (fetch your bag) there's chaws (thieves) about.

Having enjoyed a light snack, and a pot of tea, he went and sat by the open window and lit his pipe. We're passing some nice towns, I have never seen before, we have been around York too long it's time we had a move'. You're right Isaac we have done well they're nearly five years, but money is not everything. I've been thinking if we can't get the boys out of starraban (jail) we will have to move close to where they are jailed at, so as we can go see them and also you will have to see the warden and see if he will take a back hander so as you can take proper food into the boys and we can see them regularly, it's bad enough that they're in starraban (jail) but only seeing their family every three months it would break their heart. 'Don't worry Nellie if you can't see the queen, I'll get them out somehow'. Money finds a greedy man.

Manx Nellie woke up Mandys gellin to the muttering tan (I am going to the toilet) Isaac stood up then following her, pushing open the door he glanced inside then stood back to let his wife go in. He stood looking out of the window at the open countryside.

Back in their compartment Isaac looked at his watch, we've been travelling about eight hours, I feel like I've been locked in this compartment for two days, Sir John was telling me in the new world America they travel on these trains for more than a week at one time'. Sounds impossible however big is America, you could go on one of these trains from Inverness down to Plymouth in 2 days and that's more than three quarters of this country. So just how big is America? I'd love to visit it one day, said Nellie.

The attendant pulled the sliding door back, tickets please' how much longer to London asked Isaac, pushing the 2 tickets back in his waistcoat pocket. Seven or eight miles we're at Northampton, more shoes made there than any other city in the world, is that right? said Isaac. There's a shoe factory at the bottom of every street, answered the ticket conductor. 'To answer your question after Northampton we stop at Oxford then it's straight in to London, 2 and a half, maybe three hours. 'Thank you, said Isaac. It's been a long journey Nellie it would have taken a good three days with horses and coaches, yes but these things don't stop, and they keep the speed up all the time', you've been very quiet Isaac what have you been thinking about? I've been thinking about Northampton the city of shoe factories, they'll probably be loads of seconds to be bought there cheap. The problem would be the journey back with them.

Nellie smiled, you could take big boxes full to the railway station and travel with them and you'd have them back In York in one day. 'How about Blackpool in the summer, I could have a big stall on the promenade, yes you could answered Nellie, looking out of the window. The train had stopped and the platform was three or four people deep waiting to board the train, just above their head was a sign hanging on 2 chains. Isaac pointed to it, Northampton, said Nellie. People was coming into their compartment, Isaac stood up to let a woman holding a baby have his seat, thank you sir' said the young man that was with her.

There was an elderly gentleman sat facing them, very well dressed with long grey sideburns and moustache, holding a black ebony stick that had a carved silver handle , he tapped Isaacs arm do excuse me' I don't mean to be rude but I could not help overhearing you and your good lady with your idea about shoes. 'I am Latchey, my family have made shoes for over sixty years and we own three shoe factories in Northampton, my card sir' 'and what can I do for you? asked Isaac. 'We get quite a few seconds, not faulty quality, the stitching just a little crooked or some of the lace holes out of line, they are very good quality for London High street shops, you will appreciate with three factories, we sometimes get pushed for storage if you would be interested, don't worry about the prices. 'thank you very much sir, my name is Isaac Boswell he answered holding out his hand. 'I am pleased to meet you answered Latchey, as they shook hands then taking out a fountain pen and asking Isaac for the card back then writing on the back of it.

Now you know who to ask for, my son John who is sales manager. Isaac looked at it making out to read it which he couldn't then pushing it in his waistcoat pocket.' By the way Isaac I do like to see good manners, it shows good breeding. I couldn't get up myself for the young lady, my leg it's an old war wound. 'If we do have any dealings I don't deal in bank draughts it's all ready cash with me, said Isaac. The old gentleman smiled, say no more Isaac we will both profit well from this encounter. Yes we could have passed like ships in the night, said Isaac. Manx Nellie smiling she had heard Sir John use that expression several times, she gave Isaac a short quick look and a smile, then looking out of the window. Isaac felt pleased with himself he knew she had been impressed by how he had handled himself with Latchey.

Over an hour had passed and the train was now slowing down, the young lady with the baby stood up, thank you sir, please have your seat back. Latchey then stood up; Isaac could see he was putting a lot of pressure on his stick as he rose from his seat. 'It's been a pleasure to meet you Isaac'. 'Likewise!.' 'Do you travel on these trains a lot? 'Oh yes it's the only way, no horse problems and it's so fast.

There was a sudden jolt as the train pulled out of Oxford station Isaac felt in his waistcoat pocket then handed the card to Nellie, 'what does it say he asked.

The porter was walking up and down the platform with his shouting funnel, "Euston station London!" he shouted repeating it twice. The passengers were embarking from the train coaches on either side. It's the size of a village said Isaac as he looked around at four or five shops, a café and a pub, I'll be back in 2 minutes don't go away he said, walking towards the gents toilets. Nellie just stood there, she thought it best not to go looking around as the station was so crowded. Right Nellie let us see about a cab to Windsor. There was 2 exits out of the station they walked towards the nearest one. There was a row of some 8 or 9 cabs that went from one entrance down to the other with sitting benches here and there by the wall. If you go to the far end sir, that's where they leave from. 'thank you answered Isaac walking away.

Now cabbie we want to go to Windsor. 'You're going to find it a long and expensive trip, why is that, asked Isaac. Well you're in the centre of the city royal Windsor is out of London some 8 or 9 miles' are you telling us it is all town from here to Windsor? well ma'am yes it is, there's factories here and there and lots of houses, a few farms, a couple of villages, then you're in Windsor. 'So how big is London then? Asked Isaac. From one side right through to the other, about sixteen to seventeen miles, you'll do a lot better if you catch the Bristol train, it stops halfway between Windsor and Slough. Thank you cabbie, you're very welcome ma'am. Over there sir platform four, leaves in about ten minutes said the clerk in the ticket kiosk.

They sat back in the thick padded seats, we have been gone from Essington Hall all day and we're still not there' I could have drank a pint and a double malt. There just wasn't time Isaac, let's just get there I'm very tired', said Nellie. Eight o'clock train to Bristol, stopping at Slough-Windsor, Reading, Swindon then Bristol leaving in five minutes, shouted the man with the funnel.

The cab stopped in the centre of Windsor, and where now sir?' a small clean hotel please, answered Isaac. The room was clean and

217

simple, with 1 double and 1 single bed. I could do with a drink before bed, I am not hungry are you?' No just tired Isaac, I'll come down with you, see if they have a lounge Isaac I don't want to go into a bar.

'A pint of your best ale and a double malt whisky miss, said Isaac lighting his pipe. Nellie sipped at her Bristol Sherry. Fifteen minutes had passed both of Isaacs glasses were empty, he was like most scotch men a hard drinker, I'll have the same again please miss, 'no more for me Isaac this is enough, her glass was still half full. Isaac put a half crown piece (2 shillings and sixpence on the bar top) and have one yourself miss. 'Thank you sir, and what time is breakfast, asked Isaac, Eight till ten sir. Give us a loud knock at 8:30. 'Very good sir, she smiled leaning over the table to pick the empty glasses up, her half unbuttoned blouse was bulging, she came back again. You're three pence short sir, Isaac looked at his loose change giving her a silver three pence piece. He couldn't help having a second look. Nellie looked a little annoyed, you know the only way an ugly woman can get a man's attentions is by showing her body', looking at the bar maid then getting up to leave.

Isaac looked at the loose change in his hand, 2 pints, 2 double whiskeys a sherry and half a beer for the bar maid. 2 shillings and 9 pence, that's just ridiculous, 'what do you expect you are in London, answered Nellie. They both had a good night's sleep. The proprietor of the hotel came over to their table, 'is the breakfast to your liking sir? Yes everything is fine you're looking after us well, we may need a second night we are not sure yet. 'Very good sir, pay for last night and we will hold your room till 11 o'clock. 'How do we get to the castle?' asked Nellie. The hotel proprietor smiled, Oh yes it was dark when you arrived, just walk out the hotel, you can't miss it'. The small hotel was situated down a side street, they walked down the three steps and onto the pavement, then looking left and right, seeing just houses with a few shops, the road was obviously leading out of town. Looking left again, they then looked up, it overshadowed the little town like a mountain. As they came to the end of the street, there it was, Windsor Castle, light grey stone, looking so clean, big and important.

Looking left then right they could see the town, shops and houses that went right around the castle, the hard stone road, some twenty feet wide as they walked along the pavement, then stopped in front of a shop, looking over at the castle. It makes Essington Hall look like a house, said Isaac. The Union Jack is flying; she's in, said Nellie pointing to the highest tower. Isaac could detect hesitation or a slight lack of confidence in Nellie's voice, it was very rare.

They both just stood there for a minute staring. This was one of the most important buildings in the world. They looked at each other, was this an impossible task thought each one, not saying anything to the other.

This is the last card I have to play and it's MY ace', said Manx Nellie. As they walked across the road she walked over to a bench and sat down Isaac sat beside her, she put her hands together and bowed her head. Isaac did the same, somehow he felt a little uncomfortable, he very rarely prayed it was usually for thanks now, it was to ask. Forgive me my lord god I am not offering any deals to you this day, and I am not worthy, I am a sinner, I ask nothing for myself. He continued in his illiterate and true conversation which was the only way he knew. 6-7 minutes passed then Manx Nellie stood up looking at the height and importance of Windsor Castle, my husband, our mission is just and true, Isaac was lost for words and just nodded

I think walking up on foot; we are not going to look very important are we? That's right Nellie we need the finest coach and horses we can find. They walked back across the road, 'excuse me constable where is the best Hackney hire service round here, 'well we have 2 one is just ordinary but the other is very posh, J.W.Browns, out of Windsor on the Slough Road, it's a good mile and a half walk, thank you constable.

The cab pulled up outside of J.W Brown and Sons. Isaac got out first holding Nellie's hand, he stood back looking at the Silver and grey coach with Navy Blue wheels, the spokes was taken out in gold leaf to match the double gold belly band that ran the full length of the coach.

Can I help you Sir I am James Brown Junior, this is Manx Nellie, she is over here from the Isle of Mann, Nellie stepped forward going into her bag and coming out with a photograph of herself holding the Queens hand. 'So as you can see we are over here for the Commonwealth and Ambassadors meetings. 'Yes ma'am this rig is the best we have, usually for weddings and you are lucky it is available today. Pulled by a pair of grey horses, I'd like four pulling it, it would be more impressive, said Isaac. 'The only double pair we have is four matching whites.' Sounds nice, how much asked Isaac. The full rig has to be back here for six o'clock, no later, and the driver is in very smart uniform as well, it would be six pounds for the full day. 'That's dear, young man, I can supply you with a plain rig, taxi type, and driver for the full day, £3-10 shillings. 'Nellie looked at Isaac, her eyes turned to the grey coach then back to him, she did not want to interrupt her husband when buying or dealing as it was the wrong thing for a gypsy woman to do. Get it ready, we will take it now, said Isaac.

It seemed a long way round the castle they finally came to the main entrance. The 2 high gates were closed. Two guards both stood at ease, each with a rifle. 'Do you mind if I talk Isaac, they may show more manners and respect to a woman, Isaac just smiled and nodded. The driver jumped down, opening the coach door, removed his hat, gave a slight bow, then holding Manx Nellies hand as her foot felt for the coach step. We're putting on a good show, thought Isaac

Good Morning to you guard, good morning ma'am and what can I do for you? I am here to see the young Queen and where is your pass ma'am, there was no answer, and I am Prince Albert he answered with a smile. Be very careful how you speak, show manners and respect, you could possibly ruin a future promotion for yourself young man, answered Nellie. I can go to the post office and wire the Queens secretary Sir William Miller who I know well. All I ask is to see your superior. I know the young Queen is busy seeing Prime Ministers and ambassadors from other countries. The young sergeant looked at her now more serious. You would be very surprised at what I know and who I am, and I don't take kindly to being kept standing at this gate'.

Nellie had now got her confidence and was speaking with an air of importance, which seemed to come so easy when she needed to do it, going in her bag coming out with the photograph of herself holding the Queens hand, please excuse my remarks ma'am we get all sorts of people coming up to these gates, handing her the photograph back.

If you would instruct your driver to pull the coach over to that siding I'll find the major who is in charge of the castle guards and security'. As I don't have the authority to allow you into the grounds so you may have a short wait. Fifteen minutes past and the young sergeant was back, 'the major will see you and give you his decision ma'am, if you would both please follow me.'

Isaac looked around the long room there were 2 tables in the centre with some ten or twelve chairs. In the corner on a table, stood a long glass canister full of water with a tap at the bottom and a tray full of glasses. Isaac walked over to the fireplace tapping his pipe then refilling it, the long inner wall had a row of windows nearly from one end to the other that looked out onto the cobbled courtyard. 'What do you think Nellie he asked standing beside the open window smoking his pipe. A lot depends upon this officer that we are waiting to see. 'Yes, you're right it's all or nothing, answered Isaac. She glanced out of the window 2 guards were standing at ease each with a rifle some sixty or seventy feet away, giving them privacy but having them in view all the time.

Some twenty minutes had passed which seemed like two hours. The young sergeant opened the door then standing to one side as the officer went in first. I am Major Percy Tay, of Leicester regiment, now just what is all this about? I am Isaac Boswell and this is my wife Manx Nellie, from the Isle of Mann answered Isaac putting out his right hand.

Nellie did the same then remaining seated, letting the major now he wasn't as important as he thought, as you have probably guessed by my title I am Manx Nellie, Ambassador from the Isle of Man, opening her bag then showing him the photograph of herself with the Queen. 'You will appreciate Major Tay we have came a long way and it was a last minute decision I made to come. 'My meeting is of the highest importance and very private. The Major sat down I understand, he answered. 'What I am asking of you is for you to just give the young Queen a message. I am not being foolish enough to ask to see her, without her asking for me first with how busy she is, but my message is of the highest importance.'

'What is the message, asked the major, taking out a small notebook and pencil then turning to the sergeant, 'you can wait outside sergeant until I am finished' the sergeant then stamped his foot and saluted. Isaac looked the other way, if it had been any harder his foot would have gone through the floorboards thought Isaac. Nellie then went in her bag coming out with a lace handkerchief smelling of lavender, the major opened it then folded it again putting it in his breast pocket with the note. I have seen this somewhere before he said. 'When you give it to the Queen, if she has her charm bangle on, glance at it. Now I know where I have seen it he answered. That's right major, there is only 2, they were both mine and I gave one to the young Queen has a present. 'You may have a long wait ma'am, but I will get your message to her majesty, you can depend on that. He answered as he stood up. Thank you Major, said Nellie staying seated

He walked over to the young sergeant that was waiting, 'you've done well sergeant you have used wisdom in calling me here and I will mention you in my report. 'Keep this meeting to yourself, yes sir thank you sir. They could be here quite a while, see that a tray of tea and cakes is taken to them, 'yes sir, at once sir.

'What do you think Nellie, were in, and i think it's looking good, but if she's forgotten all about us we could be in borey tugness (big trouble) with this major, answered Isaac. Nellie looked at her husband and nodded, this was no Mayor, Sir or Lord, they was conning their
way in, to see but the Queen of England, she had hesitation in her voice when she spoke, I have done no wrong only gave an impression, a very strong impression Nellie, I am worried. 'Don't be my husband she may

be the Queen of England and half the world but she is a lovely young lady with a big heart, she will see us if not she will laugh at our cheek.

Over an hour had passed when the Major came back, 'good news Manx Nellie she will see you, her meetings for today will be finished at three o'clock and she will see you at four, we thank you Major Percy Tay and we will be at the gates for a quarter to four. He turned hesitating as he stood in the doorway, 'yes Major?' asked Nellie, her head held high. 'Will you mention me to the Queen, I did try hard for you. 'Of course I will mention you Major, you have done well, answered Nellie. He looked down slightly embarrassed, thank you he answered, and then closed the door.

Nellie and Isaac looked at each other smiling; we must never mention this outside our family, said Isaac. Not to worry my husband no one would ever believe it anyway.

They walked slowly back to the coach escorted by the young sergeant, then hurried back to the hotel to keep the room on for another night; finally dismissing the coach driver until 3:30. Windsor or Royal Windsor has it has now been called was just a small town, with a row of shops and houses and a few businesses that faced the castle going right around it with some three rows deep of houses, with a few small hotels and 2 cafes it had grown quite a bit since the young Queen had chosen Windsor for its peace and quiet, staying in it more often than Kensington Palace, probably because it was out of the biggest city in the world offering a lot more peace and quiet.

They passed three quarter of an hour looking in a few shops, as they entered the park there was a three wheeled bicycle with a big box bolted across the front, on either side was wrote' stop me and buy one' home made Italian ice cream wrote underneath. The man was just emptying a bag of ice cubes around the 2 metal containers of ice cream, come Nellie said Isaac walking towards the ice cream man. '2 of your cones please how much will that be? 2 pennies please. It's a beautiful park said Isaac looking at the large flower beds of many colours then staring at the cricket field over to the right side, and in the distance there was a gang of men working in the fields. It's big said Isaac yes it's going to be a lot bigger it's being extended again into those fields and beyond. The young Queen and her husband Prince Albert often come horse riding here. When it is finished it will be named as Royal Windsor Great Park, very interesting said Manx Nellie, then walking away with Isaac.

They had been back to the hotel, having had a rest washed and tidied up the coach and horses waited outside for them. They stood in front of the gates, a new sergeant questioned them then looking at the pass the

Major had gave them. Major Percy Tay was waiting for them on the other side of the gates, Good afternoon ma'am Manx Nellie and to you sir. 'Thank you Major Percy, said Nellie giving him a mischievous look and smile which the major seemed to appreciate.

He was in his early fifty's standing about 6ft 2 looking very fit thought Manx Nellie, Excuse me a moment Major, Isaac just dismissed the coach driver. We won't want him no more today. I'll enjoy the walk back to the hotel. Please excuse me for 2 minutes said Isaac walking quickly towards the long waiting room with the toilets in.

They first crossed the main big cobbled yard, which was steep, then going through a long hall, taking them into another smaller cobbled yard, finally standing in front of the centre tower. It must be nearly a 100ft said Isaac looking up. '110 actually.' answered the major, I would think it just about impossible to take it, said Isaac. A hundred years ago you would be right, but with modern dynamite and now gelignite cannons that can fire a mile it would be a long hard fight, but it could be taken.

The major then gave 2 slow knocks and 2 fast ones a small flap some 6" x 6" opened. 'Who goes there be identified, it is I Major Percy Tay. Isaac noticed the steel plate door, the other side was heavy oak, the inner guard stepped to one side saluting. These people are visitors to her majesty, very good sir. 2 more guards from an inner archway stepped forward each had no rifle but a large service revolver on one side and a short sword on the other.

They both saluted then with a very light stamp of the foot. 'Please follow me sir, there was one at the front and 1 at the rear, as they walked through 2 corridors which had several doors on either side, then up just fifteen steps, the back wall went in a half circle with just four doors. At either end of the half circle stood 2 guards standing at ease, one from each end came forward, saluted the major, then turned and went back to their place. Isaac noticed at the back of each pair of guards were several steps going up then a thick steel plate door with rows of bolts. I suppose that goes to more floors?' No just one big floor, right at the top, it's not used these days, it was originally built for a last stand to hold a siege off, answered the Major.

They stood for four or five seconds, you can leave now you are dismissed, said the major to the escort guards. Ignoring their salute he turned. Now Isaac this is important, when you meet her majesty, you do not offer an hand shake unless she does, do not walk in front and you do not sit when she is standing. Also you give a short bow when you meet her and when you are leaving you give a short bow before you turn your back to walk away, and you address her as your majesty after that you may call her ma'am. 'I'll try to remember it all said Isaac.

The major knocked twice and then stood back to let Nellie go through first, she turned to look at Isaac as if to say we've done it' he just smiled back. The room was smaller than Isaac thought it would be, about 30ft square with a door on either side, also an open fire place at either end. The major gave a low bow, Manx Nellie and her husband Isaac is here. The young queen was sat by the fire, she looked up, you may leave major, all is well I am with friends'. His hand was on the door handle major Tay, yes ma'am he answered as he turned. You have done well so as your young sergeant you have both made a wise decision. 'I thank you ma'am, making a slight bow and looking very pleased he then glanced at Nellie. She smiled and could sense a thank you from him.

It must be coming up for 2 years, Manx Nellie. And I remember you, you are Isaac aren't you? Yes my queen I mean your majesty, that is alright. You must be tired your majesty as you have been seeing people all day. The queen stood up then held up her hand, 'enough' it is very rare I allow an audience as such as this and if it had not been you, you would have not got past the major, but I am pleased you are here Nellie, I have an astronomer and several courtiers they are all supposed to be my advisors, I am never really sure if I fully employ them or not, as they seem to live so very high on their salary.

First you're saying in your note your family is in deep distress, the sentencing of 2 teenage boys, you must now tell me all Nellie. She tried to make a start then stopped, suddenly bursting into tears and going down on her knees, Oh my Queen!, my queen! You are the only one we can now turn to, that has the power to correct that which is wrong. She then stopped just sobbing a little. The young queen bent down taking hold of Nellie's hands, come now Nell you must tell me all. Isaac gave a slight bow, turned and walked over to the outer wall. There was 2 long windows, heavy plate glass with a floral patterned wrought iron hinged gate bolted to the inner thick wall. Nellie stood up looking straight at the queen then looking down, now Nell wipe your eyes and tell me all.

Isaac noticed a row of oil paintings along the opposite wall each in a carved frame with a plate at the bottom of each one. You can read Isaac? No my queen, he answered a little embarrassed, the queen then glanced at her lady in waiting, putting down her embroidery lady Helena got up. Nellie smiled looking away. You speak with your eyes your majesty, maybe like a gypsy answered the queen. Nellie never answered just nodded. She knows so much and about so many things and so young thought Nellie. These pictures Isaac are some of the countries that belong to the British Empire, she spoke very softly explaining a little about each country as they went along the row of paintings. In these past fifteen or twenty minutes i have learnt a lot, thank you lady Helena said Isaac, then returning to the window.

The queen held out her hand pointing to a chair, her lady in waiting got up, going to a decanter and glasses on a tray, then poured three glasses of red wine giving one first to the queen, then Nellie, last of all Isaac. Do have one yourself Lady Helena said the queen. Thank you majesty. Then walking over to a far corner and picking up her embroidery again. Isaac was very impressed with the view, he was at the far window most of the little town of Windsor seemed to surround the castle and the mass of London in the distance, he sipped his wine, then placing the Stewart crystal glass on the deep stone recess of the window.

Now Nellie if I so wish I can find out within the hour by wire , so before you tell me everything there must be no exaggeration, it must be exactly as it is, if I find it not so, I will be finished with you for good and you will wish you never seen me. 'Isaac said the queen raising her voice, yes ma'am he answered walking over, you may smoke your pipe if you wish, the bottom 2 corners of the window opens and do take that high chair over with you. Thank you ma'am he answered. Nellie was now telling the queen in full detail of it all, Isaac glanced over he could see by the young queen's expression she was getting very annoyed.

He turned slightly so as not to look over any more, another ten minutes had past. The young queen stood up, the lady in waiting coughed twice. Nellie was already standing; Isaac also took the hint, the queen paced slowly back and forth. Please, all be seated, she said. 'What of the Magna Carter, she said quite loudly looking around. Isaac looked down at his feet for three or four seconds then looked up, he did not know what or where of the Magna Carter or what it was. 'This would be gentleman, this scoundrel that he is will know of the Magna Carter said the queen. A dreadful story of racial bullying of a quiet people, assault on boys, a rape of a young girl; all this and being allowed to get away with it. I will not allow it in my kingdom this wrong will be put right and this scoundrel brought to book, she clapped her hands, Lady Eleanor send for my scribe, yes your majesty.

Lady Eleanor walked to the door opening it, then speaking to one of the guards. And what of Lady Elizabeth, how is she and is she still courting your son?' No your majesty it is my eldest grandson Jack. Yes I remember him riding with Lady Elizabeth and myself. A fine horse man if I remember.

They are still courting and so much in love ma'am. Nellie could sense the queen was still in a bad mood, how quick she spoke. That is good she must make up her mind what she wants, she was good company for me that winter and Christmas, but I am now married more than a year, yes I know ma'am, and are you? yes Nellie I am very happy and as you foreseen for me it was a distant relative, my third cousin. I am happy for you my queen.

You, your people speak so openly, so direct, cutting through, she stopped, smiled. I do hope you have brought your crystal with you Nellie. Of course, your majesty, of course. There was a sudden knock on the door. Lady Eleanor glanced at the queen who just nodded. The scribe came in bowing twice, a little man called Jimmy the Scribe who originated from Wolverhampton. Shutting the door lady Eleanor returned to her embroidery. Now Jim sit down I have 2 important letters for you to write. Yes your majesty he answered undoing the strings on his case, and placing some royal headed cream parchments, also ink and feathered quills on the table. The first one is to be addressed to the prosecuting Piscal of York, Isaac will give you his name, and the second one is to QC Judge William Bailey, also of York. Very good your majesty answered Jim, unscrewing the silver cap on the ink jar, then choosing a writing quill, the queen stood up they all did the same. Please all stay seated she slowly walked back and forth as she dictated the 2 letters some fifteen minutes had passed, then Jim sprinkling each one with a fine dust and blowing them off.

The queen slowly read each one then signing them Q-Victoria-R. Then opening a drawer and coming out with a large heavy gold ring that had a carved crest on the square top. Jim the scribe had been holding a square stick of red wax slowly turning it over the candle flame, then letting several hot drops of wax fall on the parchment just below each signature. The queen then pressed the ~ring lightly once on the top of each warm blob of wax.' there it is done and no one can undo it said the queen looking at Nellie then Isaac. 'I have dated them for 4 days time which gives my personal secretary and QC plenty of time to see it is all correct what you say.

Jim then quickly rolled up each parchment one into the other, then pushing it down into a leather tube with a strapped top. 'Will there be anything else ma'am? 'Yes Jim can I borrow a pound note off you, a pound repeated the scribe, surprise in his voice. Yes Jim as you know I don't carry money. Going through his purse twice he looked up, I have a sovereign ma'am. No Jim as I have told you it must be paper money, then opening the wallet side of his purse, he looked at the 2 folded pound notes, and he slowly placed one on the table looking at the queen. She smiled do not worry Jim I shall see that you get it back, yes ma'am, then taking several steps backwards he bowed, turned and walked to the door.

Everything was suddenly silent, Nellie glanced over at her husband he was sat on the high chair gazing at the view and smoking his pipe. Nellie then looked slowly into the queen's eyes and smiled, holding out both hands, the queen placed her hands in Nellies.

Nellie had been occasionally glancing at the top of her nose, each side near the eyes, you are expecting my queen, whispered Nellie. However do you know? I am not sure myself whispered the queen. Oh Albert will be so pleased, if it's a boy? If not will I have a boy next time? asked the queen excited. The crystal will tell us all whispered Nellie.

Lady Eleanor!" said the queen standing up, they all stood up, please be seated she said. Now Lady Eleanor please take our guest Isaac to the games room. Isaac, 'yes my queen, there is billiards and the new game snooker, cards, darts all sorts of games and drinks, you will enjoy it. 'Thank you.' he bowed and walked to the door. And Isaac if you feel uncomfortable with Lady Eleanor she will call for one of the guards to keep you company.

She glanced at Nellie giving her a little smile, and Lady Eleanor? Yes your majesty, if you could ask for a nice selection of cold meats and salads. She suddenly stopped glancing at Isaac. Apple juice? Ma'am. Have it brought in about an hour's time and we will all eat. 'Yes your majesty she answered giving a quick curtsy.

Isaac hesitated at the door then turned walking back. He stopped giving a bow, you are our queen and half the world's queen, born with unequalled power, a champion to the weak and under privileged. Victoria queen of queens. She stood up holding out her hand, thank you Isaac, what you have just said in minutes there are courtiers and MP''s who could not do that in 2 or three days he bowed then turned, the heavy door closed. Now Nellie it has been a long time since i last seen you, my Albert will be so pleased. Nellie placed her bag on the chair, reaching into it then placing the black ebony stand and crystal ball on the table.

One week later

The large trap pulled by 2 horses was halfway up the long drive. When they all stood on the entrance steps. Tom the gilly stepped forward to hold the 2 horses' bridles. Young Walter was the first to welcome them, he just rushed forward throwing his arms round Layton and then Adam, kissed each one on the cheek, I have missed you so much; it's been like five months, not five weeks. 'Kill the fatted calf the boys are back said Sir John as they walked into the great hall. Jeeves the butler stepped forward, 'Welcome back, Welcome Home Master Adam and Master Layton. Thank you Jeeves answered the 2 boys nearly at the same time.

More good news said Sir John placing the empty cup on the saucer, then reaching out for a second beef sandwich. And what might that be asked Isaac. They were all sat in the blue room, several tables joined together. Jeeves the butler and tom the gilly sat at a different table. 'That scoundrel Cederick Mendip has gone on the run, on the run repeated Isaac. 'Yes he was taken into custody on 2 charges, lying under oath in crown court, attempted manslaughter on 2 youths, 2 very serious charges and he had to put up his 2 farms, timber yard and house. He has recently cleaned his bank out and all his ready cash and it was said he had quite a bit of gold coin. They say he has left for the South of Ireland', none of the gypsy family seemed surprised. They knew how easy it was to go back and forth to Ireland without papers. Well you don't seem very surprised? said Sir John.

Finishing her tea Nellie looked up, the Queen told me he would pay for his wrong doings and Judge Bailey said he would be looking at a long sentence in Dartmoor. That's a terrible place it's ruined quite a few men. They'll find him in Ireland and bring him back, said Sir John. I don't think so, travel papers in Ireland are very slack compared to ours, you don't need them. Fifty pounds in cash or gold coins is big money in the right Captains hand, I'd lay a bet he'll soon be on a ship bound for Canada or the Americas, answered Nelson.

Long run the fox but caught at last, he'll get what's coming to him in one of these new wild countries especially Australia, with his pockets full of money said Isaac. He's got to get there first, a rich man travelling on his own, four weeks at sea with a ship full of immigrants and a greedy captain he could very easily end up with the fishes. You're probably right Nelson, said Sir John.

CHAPTER FIFTEEN – LADY AND THE GYPSY

York county fair, Thursday, Friday and Saturday, July 10th, 11th, 12th, wrestling, bare knuckle boxing, racing, jumping, shooting, etc. flower display, refreshments tent, many stalls.

Well done Adam, well done, you went straight through it with no mistakes. 'You done very well, you're just about as good as Layton, said Sir John. So I'm still the best then. Sir John smiled, looking at the tall thin youth. 'Not at everything Layton answered Sir John. They were out for the day in York with Walter and his grandfather Sir John. Five years had passed since they had first met Lord Sir John Bates when they were pulled with the gypsy living wagons on his land, being a large lay by some three miles from Rascliffe Hall. When there was no horse dealing involving Sir Johns farms, he would recommend them to other land owners for horse dealing. The first winter Sir John asked them to pull in the big cobbled yard at the back of the manor house. They had back-end and winter five months every year just travelling in spring and summer.

All in all the gypsy family, they had done quite well, the woman, granny Nellie and their mother Delly had built up a good few regular customers and reputation for duckering (palmistry) mostly farmers wives and friends of Sir John and his wife Lady Florence.

The two brothers Adam and Layton had grown up with young Walter over the last five years. They had had a good lunch at the Copper Kettle in York, all sat quiet as Layton drove the open trap the twelve miles back to Rascliffe Hall. As the boys lifted the goods out of the back of the trap, Jack came walking over, 'you know you two boys are living the life of two young gentlemen, day out in York , calling at the gun shop, dinner in the café, walk around town. If you aren't careful you're going to lose a lot of what you are.' Just what do you mean Jack?' interrupted Layton. 'I'll tell you what I mean very soon Wally will be off to boarding college then university. He'll come home ready to run this mansion and estate, a young Gentleman.

'He's right boys' said old Byron, their great-granddad standing over to one side. Maybe two days a week living the better life is enough, and the other days your own way of life, with your father or granddad Isaac. 'You see boys you're not gonna run an estate one day. 'You have your own natural life to learn and live. Their father Nelson had been whittling some wooden flowers for the women to hawk and sell. Young Walter liked to watch has Nelson pulled and turned the straight stick across the sharp hooked blade of the knife resting on his knee. The shaved heads were making a lovely flower head. Four small bowls yellow, blue, red and green paint each being three quarters full for the flower heads to be dipped in. On the table also were two small tins of paint one silver and one gold with two tiny brushes and this was for the stems of the flowers.

Adam and Layton glanced at their father then back at each other feeling a little uncomfortable for he had been off all day with Jack and Granddad Isaac, looking for horse dealing. They realised that they should have been doing the flowers, and not their father doing them when he got home.

Adam spoke up first, 'I'm sorry Father'. Old granddad Byron is right, we should be doing our work first', I am sorry as well father. I will always put my work first, said Layton. Nelson put down the finished flower then looked up, you both are what you are, and what you come from', you are picking up ways and doing things of another life, a gorger life. 'A very high class gorger life.' 'You both now speak a little different, I should say posh and that is good, but you must never forget what you are, you have not been born a gentleman you will have to get your living moving about, wheeling and dealing, and never lose the deep cunning and shrewd ways that god has given you. 'Look at Walter he is the future Lord of this vast estate. The biggest in all Yorkshire.

Walter sat with his legs crossed on a Welsh bed rug on the ground by the stick fire with Jack. There was a large plate with two rabbits jointed up into pieces that had been spit cooked over the open fire, and a second plate full of crusty bread. 'You see how young Walter has picked up some of our ways, so you have picked up not some but many of his and of course the knowledge and education this old professor has been learning you, the difference is one day Walter will become Sir Walter and a Lord and you will probably stay what you are. 'I'm not saying it won't be useful, it will.'

Walter threw the nearly finished rabbit leg to the greyhound dog, maybe not he said, wiping the grease off his mouth with the back of his hand. 'I speak to you with respect Uncle Nelson. When a young gypsy man or girl spoke to an older person of their own type they always addressed them as uncle or aunt even when they was no relation and even if they was in their company for the first time, it was showing respect and good upbringing. And this was the gypsy way which Walter had picked up, I am listening young sir, said Nelson.

'You don't know what they may become in life.' They both now have a good education, what standard of knowledge and wisdom they have now; in a year they could probably train in the future for a degree. And please don't call me young sir that is for the servants I am Walter and you are Uncle Nelson. 'Maybe in a new land Walter, like the Americas or Australia where there is no' - Nelson stopped. 'No stately homes and titles' interrupted Walter. Adam and Layton smiled. Walter was getting quick with the answers, not all titled families are as nice as yours,' said nelson.

Old Byron gave his grandson Nelson a quick glance straight in the eyes, then looking away. It couldn't have been more than three seconds. It was as good as a three or four minute conversation. Nelson smiled, we are all changing, all learning different ways, he said. Adam and Layton sat down by the fire; their mother came over placing three mugs of lemonade down by them, then came back with a plate that had more pieces of spit cooked rabbit, scooping them onto the big plate. 'Tuck in boys there's plenty here' she said.

Six years ago when old Byron's family had first been pulled on the lay-by with the living wagons, they had been coursing and hunting with Sir John some days later the women had been invited up to the manor house to give readings, fortune telling (duckering) for Sir Johns wife Lady Florence and their friends.

The start of that winter was cold and wet. Sir John had insisted that they pulled their living wagons over in the corner of the big cobbled yard at the back of the manor house. Life had become more comfortable for old Byron's family, no more walking over a filed or putting up a makeshift frame with a sheet around it. There were two separate toilets, one at either end of the stables. No more going down to a stream and filling a large can full of water then pouring it through a linen cloth to stop dirt and insects.

By the stables in the cobbled yard was a water trough with a water pump only two presses down on the handle filled a large jug with water. There was a seven acre field at the back of the manor house and Sir John would not allow any crops grown so close to the big house but he did allow his gypsy friends to turn a few horses out now and then that they had brought. All in all Sir Johns family had become very friendly and familiar with the Romany family and both families had found true friends.

'You look tired mother', said Layton. 'I am me and your granny Nelly has been helping all day in the big house.' 'I thought it was all finished yesterday'. 'No there was still a lot to do.' 'Aunt Delly, asked Walter, have you made any cake in the pan (gypsy cake) 'Yes I have and there's been enough mixed for three trays full for tonight, I thought you men might like a few pieces now', she answered with a smile.

Gypsy cake as it was called first started was mainly pastry that was usually left over in a large enamel bowl from making tarts. Rather than throw what was left away, quite few more handfuls of flour, and a handful of currants and raisins were thrown in, 2 large spoons of butter added then some full cream milk added and two eggs; never watered down milk that was the gorger way, always full cream. Always a heavy iron frying pan, not a tin tray, it had a ring on the top of its hooped handle and hung over the open stick fire. The thick pastry was poured nearly covering the pan, being turned over several times when the edges were slightly burnt it was taken out and cut into several pieces then split open and buttered, somewhat like a very large welsh scone in appearance, more lighter and richer in flavor, and because of the full cream milk, a very light flour was used, being cooked in a thick iron pan over an outside fire, 'it had flavor of its own'. 'I wonder why the men seemed to like them more than the women,' 'It's always been like that,' answered Louisa, old Byron's wife.

Walter would be fifteen in two weeks. Adam was his junior by six months, and Layton was just 12 months younger than Adam. The private tutor had tried really hard with Adam and Layton some days they came into the classes he would give them an extra hour as they only had three days a week of schooling. The gypsy boys did not like the gorger school. Sir John had told their father and grandfather it would help them quite a lot in their future life. So they had been made to keep the lessons up. The old tutor was amazed at the quickness of the brothers. He had said it was like they had an extra sense. Delly threw Walter a wet flannel then a towel, 'Wipe your hands and mouth or your granny Florence will be going onto you.

Isaac sat in front of the fire in the small study with Sir John who was drinking a large Brandy with a dash of lemonade. Isaac had a large malt whisky with a dash of orange juice. 'My grandsons will miss young Walter when he goes to boarding school, they have become more like three brothers than friends. 'Yes', said Lady Florence, 'he has become more rough and ready, and a damn good shot with a catapult, and hunter said Sir John.

'And my two grandsons have lost some of their roughness, answered Isaac' 'Gentleman gypsies', said Lady Florence with a little laugh. 'Your grandson Adam is only fourteen and can shoot better than I can with a pistol.' 'Yes he's better than all of us, it's uncanny he doesn't even take aim just points and fires, said Isaac.

'I've just picked this up today from the gun shop in York, said Sir John. Isaac opened the polished walnut box, then taking out the pistol, 'I have never seen one quite like this. I've heard of the American Colt revolver' Sir John held his hand out for the gun. It is called a Colt Revolver and they are made in America, you flick back this clip and the chamber is open ready to load, it holds six bullets, which are loaded into the chambers, it then fires six shots one straight after the other without reloading. 'What a pistol, and such balance, beautiful how the top of the barrel is ribbed and engraved, just like your Purdy shotgun, Yes this one was especially made for me'. 'I would like to try it out'. I thought you might Isaac, one afternoon we will have some target practice and invite your grandson Adam'. They are usually 44 caliber they are big and heavy, I ordered this one in a 38 caliber and had to wait three months for it.' 'I would like to give my old pair of 32 caliber pistols, two shots over and under, one to Adam and one to Layton and my 38. to young Jack as a gesture of my friendship to the three boys, I know Adam and Layton are sensible boys, but I will ask their father first, I know he would only let them use the pistols when he was with them,' that's very nice of you Sir John', said Isaac, then handing the gun back.

Well Isaac, now you have taken your royal arch side degree of the ark and dove. You are now a fully Royal Arch Free Mason. 'Yes I have enjoyed going with you to the various lodges in Yorkshire. Sir John had always felt safe when he had Isaac along with him. The big towns and cities in Yorkshire were many miles apart and could be rough at night. It's very good you've been to my family Sir John. You're a gentleman Isaac maybe not by birth but in many other ways.'

Walter will miss your two grandsons when he goes away to College. 'They will miss him as well.' 'Isaac, as I have told you, when we're on our own do drop the sir, i know it is a show of respect, save it for when we are in company.' 'And where will he go from Gloucester?' 'He will do three years at Gloucester College coming home for the holidays, then four years at Harrow'. His father and myself having been at Harrow his name is on the role so it is a straight walk in for him.' Isaac looked away, annoyed. 'What is it?' asked Sir John, He will leave as a boy of just fifteen, and won't be back home until he is twenty one, answered Isaac, emptying his glass. Their only son, lovely people, titled, but still gorgers, no common sense; thought Isaac.

Sir John pushed the whisky decanter across the table, then taking two cigars out of the box. 'I can see you don't agree, he said. 'Do you want me to speak to please you or do you want me to say what I think? Speak the truth as you have always done, said Sir John. 'Your only son Walter died when he was 23, because of college and university you lost him', 'That's right, beaten and stabbed to death by two thieves and his so called friends ran off and left him, just cowards.' 'Yes that was your only son, now you're sending your only grandson Walter away for seven or eight years, you will then be into your 60's, I hope you live a long life, but if you don't you won't see much of him as well will you?' Sir John drew deeply on his cigar and looked away.

'Knowing who built the pyramids, who were the King of Spain two hundred years ago, does he really need this to run the estate?' Sir John poured himself another brandy and relit his cigar. 'If you were me what would you do?' 'I would want to keep him near to me, after losing my only son so young, you'll lose a lot of him when he gets married one day.' 'You don't understand Isaac, college and university, he would have degrees. If he so wanted he could probably go forward and train to become a doctor or a lawyer.' If it was me I would get another teacher in with a lot more knowledge than the one you have, for say, two extra years. Then let young Walter work with yourself and your estate manager, he would then have experience to help run this big estate without leaving here and still be well educated.'

'I'll talk to Florence about it, she's already upset about him leaving for so long, and it brings back memories about his father. You and all your family are invited to Florence's birthday party tonight.' Thank you John but I think we would be out of place, we will entertain your friends as gypsies know how. Sir John smiled, your women folk may think otherwise, answered Sir John.

2 Hours Later

It was now gone six and the guests were standing about admiring the flowers and making their way up the steps to the front of the great hall. As the horses and coaches were brought around to the back courtyard Nelson and Jack had been giving the drivers a hand with the horses. The drivers were seated at several tables in the courtyard. Two servant girls rushed back and forth from the kitchen with plates of food and jugs of ale for them.

Tables and chairs had been placed in various corners and alcoves in the great hall it was a lavish turnout, there was all sorts to choose from, pheasants, turkey, pieces of beef, pork and various cakes. It was the latest thing at banquets and parties to have a running buffet. As the couples and individuals came through the main entrance the butler would call out their names. A five piece group was softly playing.

Isaac and Nelson were sat at a table with some of the coach drivers. Layton came over, 'Granny Nellie wants to see you and it is important.' Each emptied his mug of beer and followed Layton over to the wagons.

'And just what are you doing?' asked Isaac. Nellie had her best dress laid out on the bed brushing it. 'I am dusting my dress off, I hope you're not going to tell me you're going to the party. 'Yes I am and not on my own, all of us have been invited, but not the children.' 'Lady Florence has insisted that we are guests at her party and she wants us to entertain her friends.' 'We have been getting ready for half an hour so you men had better get cleaned up and changed.' Nelson pulled his eldest son Jack to one side. 'We all know, and so does lady Florence and Sir John that you have been seeing Lady Elizabeth for quite a time now, if you dance and stay with her at the party too much, it could cause trouble, embarrassment to her family.' 'Father we love each other very much, what am i supposed to do?' 'Go and hide somewhere till all the gentry have gone home then court her again. 'She wants me to ask permission for marriage in the near future.'

Nelson shook his head from side to side. 'You know her family are titled people, they like you but would not give permission, look at the position you're putting Sir John and Lady Florence in, she is their niece and has been brought up here as a daughter. I would imagine she would be sent up to her cousins in Scotland so as you could not see here. 'You would never be accepted, just classed one step above a beggar or a tinker, you're just a gypsy not a titled gentleman. 'We are not children father, I am 21 and she is 24. I would say nothing to Sir John until your grandfather Isaac speaks to him as he is well in with him,' answered Nelson.

I think that would be a waste of time when he sees us walking together or horse riding, he does not like it when my arm is around her, we are alright as friends and that's where it is expected to stop father.' 'I couldn't have put it any better myself I'm pleased you are seeing sense my son you will find another and so will she, 'answered Nelson. Then putting down the razor and wiping the soapy bits off his face with a damp flannel. I don't want to find another and I couldn't care less, even if she was the queens' niece I am having her, I will take her and we will marry and that will be an end to it'. Nelson looked away he could see it was a waste of time. Jack was adamant about it.

The great hall was now full, little clusters of five or six people stood talking and drinking some sat at tables. The butler stood at the entrance to the great hall the two large oak doors were fastened back. He stabbed the wooden floor twice with his staff, then announced the Lord Mayor and Mayoress of York. Many turned to smile and nod, some of the men raising their hand, there was then some titled people from Nottingham.

Then came old Byron and Louisa standing in the entrance with Isaac and Manx Nellie behind, then Nelson and Dellie behind again. As the butler was going to announce them he looked a little uncomfortable, he banged the floor twice with his staff, Lords, Ladies and Gentlemen the

Romany Gypsy Boswell family, musicians, entertainers and clairvoyants, the hall went quiet for half a minute as many heads turned. The gypsy men had short soft leather boots trimmed in different coloured leather just above the ankle, with the belt buckles in silver and gold and the buttons were gold coins on their shirts. The women had long silk dresses to their ankles of many colours. Around Manx Nellie's waist hung a heavy gold chain with a mixture of two pound piece coins and twenty dollar coins they were all gold with a bracelet to match, in different colours of gold earrings to match. Old Louisa and Dellie were similar dressed but not has heavily laden with gold jewelry.

A servant footman escorted them to a round table that was sat halfway in an alcove. And is that what your father said? Is that his opinion? Elizabeth looked in a bad mood. Yes, It was, no way could we marry as others do, as there is such a big space between what we are and what we come from, answered Jack' 'So you're letting your father talk you out of us getting married. 'Of course not I love you this is a very good night for what we were going to do next month'. So I am changing it for tonight, 'Oh Jack, I'm so excited. We will leave tonight pack only two cases with everyday clothes, nothing too expensive remember you can't be seen wearing an overcoat at the party, bring only some of your jewelry you want, and your ready money not your bank book, you understand leave that. 'We will make it late in the night when they are all happy with wine.' She stood on her toes putting her arms around his neck and kissed him.

As she went to leave Jack pulled her back. 'We must go now, I will be missed. I will work with you Jack, we will get by and we will be together for always.' 'You must let me go now Jack they will be expecting to see me. 'Very well, I will go and tell Adam what to do and when'. Now remember Elizabeth it is the left hand side fourth window, the last one I will wait beneath it.' He then walked away to join his family.

The butler announcer stood in the doorway, then banged his staff hard three times on the wooden floor, 'My Lords, Ladies and Gentlemen please be upstanding for Sir John and the Lady of the party Lady Florence. All stood up lifting their glasses. 'Happy Birthday, Happy Birthday' repeated everybody lifting their glass as the band played the birthday song.

Nelson turned to speak to Jack, 'Just look at the splendor, how these people live, nearly like royalty they are the cream of the land, this is what she has been brought up to this is what she comes from, this is what she is leaving behind if she has you, you are asking a young titled lady to live in a gypsy wagon'. 'Father she loves me'. Sir John stepped back and stood to one side has Lady Florence stood in the entrance of the great hall, slowly waving to the left and right to all her friends. They then walked around the hall shaking hands and greeting people. Sir John waved over to the gypsy table then guiding Lady Florence to the table, 'I am so glad all your family have come tonight Isaac and I know you will enjoy the evening, and you're going to entertain us aren't' you?' 'Of course we are, we are pleased to entertain you Lady Florence, we are also your friends. She smiled you all look so, so flamboyant, your clothes, jewelry. She squeezed his hand then kissed Manx Nellie on the cheek, also greeting Nelson and Delly, you all look lovely and thank you for coming to my party.

Just then the band started up, Sir John holding Lady Florence's hand then walked onto the dance floor and started the first dance off it was a lively military two step, no one got on the floor until they had gone right around once. Manx Nellie and Delly sat back smiling, enjoying every minute of it. Three quarters of an hour had gone by when the Mayor and Mayoress came over to Lady Florence's table. 'Please sit for a while David, said Sir John standing up and motioning to the empty chairs at his table. I say John I rather like this running buffet thing you can eat what you want, when you want and go back again. 'Yes it's a new thing from France, said Sir John.

These Gypsies cut quite a dash, give your party some colour, said David. 'Yes they are lovely people they stay in the back court yard with their living wagons it's exciting we all learn from each other, ways and culture you know.' Said Lady Florence. Oh I don't think I could sleep in my bed at night with people like that in my grounds, I think not Betty. Every day we are in contact with each other, they're friends, true friends, lovely people, answered Lady Florence a little annoyed. Two hours had passed the waiters were carrying trays, going around with various bottles of wine, and some spirits, everyone was in a happy mood. The compare stood in front of the band that had suddenly stopped playing, My Lords, ladies and gentlemen the Romany gypsy entertainers. The full family stepped forward giving a slight bow to the left and right, then sitting down at a table to the left off the band.

Dellie stepped forward to the centre of the floor, the small band started to play very softly as she sang, for a small woman her voice filled the hall there wasn't a sound to be heard. When she finished the song there was a loud applause. As she turned to walk away many stood up, clapping shouting 'more' as the clapping died down she smiled nodding to the band for her second song.

Nelson walked forward and stood on the left with Isaac on the right as she sang the second song. They were harmonizing, sort of humming in tune very softly. At the end of the song they all bowed and walked back to their table. A few minutes passed then Isaac came forward carrying a thick oak chair, placing a velvet pad on his forehead then balancing it with one of the legs on his forehead. He walked right around the hall, then placing the chair on the floor. Dellie and Manx Nellie carried a short broad plank of wood, there was a part trimmed out for his neck as it sat across his shoulders then there was a second chair, each one on the plank. The women then sat on either end. Isaac stood up and placing a hand on either side he lifted the thick plank above his hand, full arms stretched with the women, one sat on either end of the plank. He then walked right around the great hall. When finished he bowed twice, there was a loud applause with many of the men commenting on his strength. The band suddenly went into a fast lively tune, Nelson and Jack came walking into the centre of the floor tapping as they walked.

Jack stepped to one side as Nelson started walking backwards, tap dancing, then walking forward again. Jack went into a slow tap dancing, a circle right around him. Nelson then stood still his left foot and then his right foot started floating outwards and backwards as if flying, first bucking and winging then heel and toe fast tapping in double time. American dancers called this bucking, winging heel and toe tap dancing. But the Mediterranean gypsies had altered this river dance to what it is now, more than a century before it got to America.

Nelson slowed down as Jack tapped his way alongside of him. Suddenly the three women, also Isaac and old Byron all stood in a half circle in front of the band clapping, pausing, then clapping again to the music as Nelson and Jack tap danced in double time, the sweat slowly trickled down their faces. Nelson and Jack were then slowly walking backwards tapping in time then stopped and bowed either side to the audience. The full hall, everyone was on their feet clapping some of them cheering. The family all holding hands, then started to sing, they all bowed and walked off the floor. Manx Nellie then walked forward onto the floor again as there was a low roll on the drums, she bowed smiling, then speaking at the top of her voice 'Born free, we're born free, as free as a river that flows, as free as the wind blows, as free as the birds of the air, no job no town can hold us, a born free race, to follow our star.' She bowed twice. It was a low clap, some standing up to clap her.

Then old Byron and Isaac came forward into the centre. Each had a button keyed accordion. Nelson and Jack each playing a violin in tune to the accordions it was Mediterranean Spanish music. The audience was slowly getting up, first one couple, then another dancing to the unusual music, it was like they just had to. Sir John then raised his glass and drank from it complimenting the gypsy family on their floor show.

Elizabeth could see Jack through the couples looking at his watch, twelve thirty he said to himself, dropping it back in his waistcoat pocket. Elizabeth looked at the blond young man standing over to her left. She walked over, 'Would you like to dance with me?' she asked. He was a bit taken back at the forwardness of her. 'I never dreamed that you thought of me like that Lady Elizabeth, 'he stammered. She did not answer, just smiled. Jack could see her in the distance, halfway down the hall; she was keeping well to the edge of the floor as they danced their way around. As she got closer Jack could see the smile on her face. When she was close she deliberately twirled around and stepped on Jacks foot. 'Now' she said. Then danced on, further round the floor she came to four steps, she turned letting go of the young man's hand walking towards the steps. He just stood there looking at her lost for words, she turned with a smile and said thank you for the dance.

Jack could see what had happened. 'She's got some nerve', he thought. As she went quickly up the steps. Jack stopped playing his violin, putting it down he turned, 'I love you farther', he said as he kissed him on the cheek then turned away taking his violin. Nelsons sharp mind had quickly put it altogether. 'You will need lovva (Money) 'I have all my money with me', answered Jack. 'I'll write you two letters, one to York post office and one to our family in Blackpool. He then stopped in front of Dellie his stepmother, 'I love you Dellie, he said as he kissed her on the cheek,' 'I love you too Jack,' she answered with a smile. He turned and walked away. She looked at her husband Nelson, her smile slowly disappeared, she could see a tear trickling down his cheek. She walked over to him. 'Oh Nelson, he will be so alone,' she said. 'They will have each other.' Let's hope and pray it works out for them, he answered.

Adam drove the trap quickly around to the side of the big house. Jack sat at his side, 'this is the window,' he said. Then standing on the seat and stretching up he tapped the glass two or three times. It opened, 'is that you Jack?' Yes it is,' he answered. She threw two cases out and Adam placed them in the back alongside of Jacks bag and violin case. He then leveled the two feather beds for Elizabeth to land on,' Jump' he said. She looked down from the window sill it was six to seven feet but it looked more like ten. 'Jump,' he said again. A little frightened she closed her eyes as she sat on the window sill then jumped.

Jack had an overcoat on with the collar turned up and an old trilby hat pulled low over his face. Elizabeth had a large thick shawl wrapped around her to hide her evening dress and a bonnet. With two horses pulling the trap it had gathered speed and there was another two tied to the back of the trap. At the end of the long drive they both turned to look back, Adam waved to them, then quickly walked back around the house. She put her arm through Jacks cuddling him. 'A new start and a new life,' she said. After three or four miles they pulled into a siding. Jack moved one of Elizabeth's cases over opening his lock knife he lifted part of a floor board, beneath it was a thick wood centre beam, and a dummy second beam next to it , part of it was hollow, 'give me your money and jewelry,' he said. She handed him a small bag that drew tight with a string. 'Put some of it on, but most of it leave in the bag,' he said.

Jack then took out his money, putting three quarters of it in her small bag and putting one quarter back in his pocket. He then pressed the small bag down into the gap pressing the board back over it with the cases and bedding on top of it. 'It's best not to keep all your eggs in one basket, 'he said whilst pushing the double barrel pistol back into his belt. 'If there's highway men, would you use it Jack?' Yes, if it was him or us,' I would use it without a second thought.

'So where are we going Jack?' 'Hereford, my sister Jane and her husband George travel that area, Gloucester, Cheltenham, Bristol, it's a nice country. 'Is it very far?' 'It's far enough, about a 160 miles. Tell me about it Jack, I haven't been very far, York, Doncaster and two summers in London. 'Well Hereford is a big clean farming town with a cathedral right in the centre of town, nice shops, and there's gypsies and travelers there, you'll like it'. They drove through the night letting the horses take their time at a steady canter. They had been travelling more than three hours when Jack pulled up into a siding and changed the two spare horses over. He could see Doncaster in the distance. 'Look' he said, pointing to the sky, 'a brand new day is just starting', 'its lovely Jack and the whole world is ahead of us'.

The rabbits were jumping down the far end of the lay by they had pulled into. On the far side of Doncaster there is a country pub, a tavern there, we can give the horses a break and have some breakfast. We're making very good time with two horses and a peer to change. They sat enjoying breakfast and a mug of tea, sitting close to the window so as jack could see his horses and trap. 'Inn keeper what do I owe you?' 'Two breakfasts, tea, a bag of pork sandwiches and two bottles of sweet cider to take with you, comes to one shilling and sixpence' he said.

'How far is Nottingham from here?' 'Nearly sixty miles,' answered the innkeeper. Elizabeth came back to the table. Jack noticed her lovely evening dress was gone and she was dressed in a tweed jacket and riding skirt to her ankles. 'Good you've changed into something less noticeable' he said, looking slowly up and down at the outfit a lightweight tweed, with the edges of the sleeves and lids of the pockets all trimmed in leather. Even the skirt matched leather trimmed slanting pockets. 'That's a very nice outfit, was it tailor made for you?' Yes it was she answered, as he admired the platted shows with smoked mother of pearl buttons Jack thought about what is father had told him. 'What's wrong?' asked Elizabeth. That outfit that you've got on would probably take me three months to save the price of it' I don't know if I can keep you in that style 'Don't be silly the clothes I have brought with me I will put them away for best, they will last years and I will wear some cheap ordinary clothes for everyday.' 'You can help me chose them, maybe gypsy style', they both laughed. He leaned over and gently kissed her.

They made the far side of Nottingham by 5: 30. She had slept a few times and he had changed the horses over again. Jack you're falling asleep again, it's dangerous you've been driving all day and half of last night.' 'That's alright you've taken a turn twice, answered Jack. We have made good time so please find somewhere to pull up, you worry me.' 'I'll pull in at the next inn for the night. That sign we've just passed says it's only four miles to Coalville. 'Have you been there Jack?' 'No I haven't, there will be an inn, there always is one each side of a town.

Tomorrow is a busy day; we will have to go through part of Birmingham. It's big isn't it Jack, yes it's next to London, then there's Glasgow, I've been to all three. 'It must be nice to see different places and live there for a while,' said Elizabeth. That place you've lived in it's like a small castle, I am worried if you will manage in a gypsy wagon.' 'You mean a Vardow? I've been picking up the Romany language over the last two years. 'I will soon fall into place, she said. Jack smiled looking away. 'You will always be a Lady, he whispered to himself. 'What did you say? 'Nothing just thinking out loud, look there's an inn up ahead we will stop there for the night.'

'Can I help you sir?' 'Yes two hot mugs of coffee, 2 small suppers, and we will need a room for the night and breakfast in the morning', 'Thank you sir, will you sign the night book?' Jack signed in as Mr. & Mrs Smith, his great grandmothers Louisa's name was Smith, she was a Blackpool Smith. 'And what do we owe you innkeeper?' 'Supper, breakfasts for two and a room for the night and livery for the horses, that will be three shillings and six pence,' if you have any drinks that's extra. Jack placed a silver half crown and a two shilling piece on the night book. 'This way Sir', he said, Jack was thinking of the four bunches of flowers he had seen in the trap that Adam had forgot to take out. Would you give me a lift out with the bags, my right wrist is a bit sore, he said. 'Of course sir.' following Jack outside, 'watch the flowers' said Jack as the man lifted the bags out. 'They're so beautiful and look so real, lovely colours, where did you buy them?' 'I didn't I'm a sales manager, my father owns the business, they're my samples, that's used to take orders with, they are now a month old and I will be getting new samples tomorrow or the next day when I get back.' 'And what happens to these when you get the new ones, do these go back into your warehouse?' 'Not really, it would be like taking coal back to the mine, the reps, that's me and 2 others have them after the month to do what we wish with, you could say a bonus. 'Do have a look at them said Jack getting them out before he had time to reply, Elizabeth opened her mouth to say something, Jack gave her a long stare and a smile, she took it and just smiled back. She just cocked her head on one side wondering what Jack was on about. 'My wife is an arranger for hotels and banquets, said Jack knowing she used to do all the flower arrangements in the big hall. She just picked the two big bunches up, blew them and gave them a little shake removing any dust.

Walking back into the inn, she then arranged two vases in the dining room and the other two in the lounge after getting rid of the dead flowers that was in them. 'They are absolutely lovely said the innkeeper, I would like to buy them, how much would they be?' 'I don't know you've looked after us so well, they are usually very expensive being all handmade and painted, just do us a small basket of sandwiches, a couple of bottles of lemonade for tomorrow and with tonight's bill back, we'll just call it all level. Jack noticed the innkeeper winch a little, 'Oh don't worry Mister Innkeeper I know there's another bunch in the cart over there, that ones for free 'Oh that will be fine, said the Innkeeper, smiling at Elizabeth; then getting the money out of the drawer under the signing in book. 'I'll be back soon said Jack as he went out the front door dropping the coins in his pocket. He thought it best to let him have the last bunch, he was going to sell them, but it now left the sale or deal good. He seemed a nice little man and Jack did not want to leave the deal in a wrong or greedy mood, the flowers cost him nothing anyway

As they sat in front of the fire the innkeeper came back with a tray it had two big mugs of coffee and a plate full of thick toast with several slices of fried sausage. 'That looks good', said Jack picking up the knife to butter the toast, the innkeeper then placed the keys on the table. 'Your room is number five Mr. Smith, he said. 'Where have you been Adam? She asked. 'To get our valuables out of the trap.' 'I enjoyed listening and watching how you sold the flowers to the innkeeper, you made it look so easy, like you was doing him a favour. 'That's how we get a living as we don't have much education,' the first thing you sell is yourself, keep your sales story simple and as honest as you can and don't push it, keep it happy.' 'Good stuff half sells itself.'

'We're not married you know', said Elizabeth, 'that's alright you have the bed and I will sleep on the floor', 'that will be hard for you', she said with a smile. 'Not to worry we will be married in Hereford as soon as possible. 'How far will we get to tomorrow?' 'Kidderminster, maybe Worcester and the third day we will be in Hereford early' answered Jack.

They stopped the next night in a small village called Lycinton near Worcester. Uncle John has a cousin near here, a place called Great Malvern, said Elizabeth pointing to a sign. 'I have been there', said Jack, not much good for horse dealing but the women done well there, hawking, and duckering (palmistry). 'Will I have to do that Jack? She asked with a smile. 'You'll be alright you'll pick it up, because you might have to keep the table going (shopping). 'I can earn money Jack, I have been out quite a few times with your granny Nellie, she is a clever woman I have learned from her' ' You must have known we was getting married before I did' he said, giving her a quick sideways glance. 'I have a gun your Uncle John gave me, I now need to find a good lurcher with a gun and a good lurcher dog you won't have too much shopping to find', I am good with fish as well.'

First you'll need to find a wagon as we have nothing to live in do we?' Don't worry my brother in law George sometimes as one for sale, or knows of one. She just nodded and cuddled into him. 'This is a very long steep hill', she said. 'Yes it's called Frumes Hill and it's over a mile, we are half way between Worcester and Hereford, I'll stop at the top and change the horses over and we can stretch our legs.'

There was a big open space either side of the road, at the top of Frumes Hill. 'What a lovely view Jack, we can see for miles and miles.' 'Yes you see all those farms in the valley on both sides of the road, they are hop farms, and you are now in hop country. 'Those vines I can see with the flowers on them creeping up and along the wires, are they hops?' 'Yes when they are ready to pick, there will be travelers in many of those farms, three or four families in each farm, with wagons and tents, they come back every year for the hop picking', 'do they earn good money Jack?' 'Yes it's a good living, but those who have big families, four or five children they're the ones that earn the big money,' 'Does your family do it?' 'No we haven't, why I don't know', we are more for dealing and the women selling and duckering (fortune telling).

When the hop picking is finished many of the travelers go down to Evesham, ready for the fruit picking. I know what you mean, in Scotland they do a lot of tatty picking (potatoes) she said. 'It feels so nice to be back on the road again, I feel free, 'I don't want to be tied I want to be with my own people, said Jack. 'I heard your great grandfather old Byron, one day he was saying the regular fortune telling and conveniences where the wagons stay at Rascliffe Hall are holding them there too long. He wants to travel again, and not just for the five or six months in the summer that you have been doing for the last five years, you see Elizabeth it's what we are it's what is in our blood.' 'We are born free, as free as the wind blows like the birds in the sky and wild animals in the fields, said Jack looking at her. She never answered but just smiled. The going was now a lot easier; the second half was all downhill.

The horses were now going at a slow trot as they came into Hereford. There was a large cattle market over on the right side. The railway station was also on the right then lots of shops with a big market hall. 'It looks to be a nice town, smaller than York. 'Yes it's a county town', As they turned passing the cathedral on the left then going over a bridge, There was now just a few shops and a long row of houses going out of town. 'What is it Jack, are you lost?' 'I don't know, it's a new stopping place and it is somewhere on this side of town. 'Whoa, whoa there said Jack, pulling on the reins. 'Excuse me sir, is this the Ross on Wye road?' 'It is young man where are you looking for? 'I think it's called Lacey Road where the gypsies stay. 'Oh you mean Holme lacey Road, it's the third on your left, about half a mile. There is a common at the bottom of the road, with a big rough pub, you will see all the caravans and tents over to the right as they are not allowed in the park area, keep an eye on your horses, they're gypsies you know.

Elizabeth laughed as Jack flicked the reins. 'Thank you sir', he shouted over his shoulder. 'I have never met this part of your family; I do hope I fit in?' 'Of course you will,' answered Jack looking at the row of houses as they turned left. 'They look very rough and scruffy, don't' they Jack, Yes this will be the roughest side of town; it must be for a gypsy site to be here. 'Do you always get treated like this?' Jack laughed 'Oh we're used to it we grew up with it, and in the playing fields the boys have to know how to fight to survive and as the years go by you love a fight.

It was a very big open field of about twelve acres with a few trees in places. The sign read Holme Lacey Common, there were patches of hard ground in places. Three quarters of the common was grass. 'Hello there', cushty divis is lesty a rumney chell (Hello there, it's a nice day are you a Romany gypsy) the man looked at him, smiled, then nodded. Elizabeth could see he did not fully understand Jack. 'I am looking for George Williams, I am his brother in law,' the man looked at the pistol handle showing under Jacks waistcoat and how well Elizabeth was dressed. He didn't know whether to believe Jack or not, maybe he had come looking for trouble, thought the man. 'I am a travelling Gadgey like yourself, my name is Jack Boswell I am not a collier or a gavver, (none traveler or policeman)' said Jack in the travelers cant (slang). The man pointed to a wagon and an open lot that was at the side of it. 'That's barwry-cowey' (good thing). said Jack to the man who nodded and walked on.

'He's not a gypsy like you is he Jack, he's different isn't he?' 'You're quick to notice little lady, they're travelers, they move about like we do, get scrap, some do farm work a few buy and sell like we do, but the women do not ducker (fortune tell) some hork goods. They are hardworking people, they are called travelers. 'He didn't understand your Romany language rumnus,' 'No, they know a little and pick it up being in our company they have a slang of their own it is called cant, a few of them know bits of our rumnus language and mix the two, very interesting Jack 'I suppose you could say they are something in between a gorger and a gypsy, said Elizabeth. Our people have only been in this country four generations, they were here when we got here. On very rare occasions we are now marrying into each other's people, answered Jack.

Elizabeth noticed the wagons and some tents they were not altogether, they were situated in little clusters with horses tethered near them; probably separate families or friends she thought. The travelers and gypsies covered barely a quarter of the common. It was four in the afternoon George and his wife Jane was not long home from work sat by the outside fire. A black smoked kettle hung on a kettle iron over the fire. George stood up 'Look Jane, if I'm not mistaken it's your brother Jack and he has someone with him.' 'That's them over there, said Jack.

The two men walked fast to meet each other both smiling then put their arms around one another, Jack kissed him on the cheek. Jane walked over, and kissed her brother, Elizabeth got down from the trap and just stood there, 'And who is the rawny (Lady) said George looking at Elizabeth. 'And just how do you know I am a rawny before I have even spoken?' by your clothes and style and your air of importance. It's called arrogance and posh, answered Elizabeth, they all laughed. 'This is my brother in law, and my sister Jane,' this is Lady Elizabeth.'

'Truth, you're not jesting.' said George. 'I jest not, she is a titled Lady, her grandfather was a Scottish Lord and we will be married here in Hereford as soon as possible. 'Welcome to the family said Jane, giving her a hug. They sat on a rug on the ground by the fire drinking tea. 'So how long have you been at this Lords mansion or castle, we have heard rumours. 'We have been pulled in the back courtyard over five years, just going out for a travel, in the summer months', said Jack. So you're becoming gorgers, joked George. 'My two younger brothers are having a good try at it, they have been getting well educated and even speak a little posh, George just shook his head slowly and looked away not knowing what to say.

Jane started to lift a table; George got up taking it off her and then carried it over, going back for some stools, then spreading a cloth out, plates and cutlery in the centre, a large salmon on a platter and a plate of boiled potatoes. There was also a plate full of bread and some butter and a large plate of boiled potatoes. 'Salmon looks good, said Jack. 'Yes, the river Wye is well stocked and good for Guddling fish' answered George. 'Just help yourself.' said Jane. 'I see Elizabeth has picked up some rumnus.' 'Yes she wants to be what I am, answered Jack. 'God help her then, said Jane, they all laughed.

'She loves me, she certainly must love you to leave a gentry life, answered George has he cut a thick slice of Salmon to go with his boiled potatoes. 'Has she got lots of money Jack? I don't know how much she's got, I haven't come empty handed, answered Elizabeth. 'I doubt if you'll ever be able to go back again, said George as he buttered a piece of crusty bread. 'It will all be okay once some time has gone by, time heals everything. Her Uncle Sir John is a very nice man and thinks a lot of our family, answered Jack as he glanced around. 'Jack, have you heard anything from Brother Steven?' 'We used to write now and then, but I have not heard from them for over a year, and I worry if they are alright' asked Jane. 'No, the letters stopped about a year ago' answered Jack. 'He knows letters will always get to Elizabeth's place for us,'

'Yes, it's the same with us, I have a gorger woman friend and she lets me use her address for letters to come.' 'don't worry Jane, they will be alright, I did hear from one of the Shaw's from Scotland; Steven and Maria was staying near Cooper, Fife, and they were going to Ireland with one of the Shaw family, that was last year.' She nodded, but still looked worried.

'How are Steven and Maria?' asked Elizabeth. 'My brother, he is the younger one, Jack and Layton. Dad had four sons; he is a bit of a loner. said Jane.

All the wagons and tents was down one end leaving most of the common open. Any rumney chells (gypsies) on here, asked Jack. Just two families, Robinsons and Smiths all the rest are travelers,' said George. 'Is it a quiet camp?' 'It's okay, everyone keeps themselves to themselves. Some weekends when there's been a lot of drinking and there's an argument usually a fight the next morning.' I think there's going to be a fight in the morning, it started last week but it didn't happen. I haven't seen a good fight for ages, said Jack 'That's a tidy little open lot you've got there. It's like the boys your younger brothers sleep in, said Elizabeth, this one is a lot better finished, said Jack looking at it then back at Elizabeth. The big living wagon about thirteen feet long was huge with a molly croft on top of the main roof with small side windows in it. Whereas the open lot was only three quarters the length lower with a green canvas hooped top roof stretched tight over the padded boards. I brought it to go again with. I am asking £45 for it as you can see it's a beauty, if you want it Jack have it at cost £35. As he walked over to it Elizabeth followed him, looking around it then inside. 'Would you be satisfied with it for this year? Until I get more money together I would want to buy a big wagon like George's for next spring. 'Yes I like it, you see Elizabeth I need to leave myself with money behind me, for expenses and dealing with horses or anything else. 'Do you mean keeping the table going like your mother and granny Nellie?' she said smiling.

Manx Nellie, there's a woman, said George looking up from eating. I'd lay money granny Nellie is one of the best getters amongst gypsies and travelling women in the country. For quite a few months on and off, when I was going out keeping your granny Nellie Company she was horking and duckering (fortune telling). I picked up quite a bit off her, i might not be much of a duckerer but i can sell flowers and daub (polish) very easily and I can talk very well to the gorger women explaining the daub and even arranging the flowers in their vases because our mansion is full of flower arrangements as you know.' And when I have finished selling and could see the mark or customer was interested in being duckered, I would fetch Granny Nellie over.

'I will keep our table going and buy you nice shirts and silk hankies (scarves). They all looked from one to the other. 'You never told me all that did you little lady, said Jack. 'You don't tell your man everything, especially if you have a few bars (pounds) put to one side. You've found quite a wife there, said George. I'm learning more about her every day, said Jack, glancing at her

The open lot was small inside compared to the wagons, a double bed across the back, standing high so as to leave plenty of packing space underneath. A half robe with a cupboard underneath, a hostess coal fire with a small oven adjoining it with a small lift up flap table bolted to the wall, either side a small seat. And of course there was the big kettle box across the back outside for storage of pots and pans. It'll be cramped and could do with a lot more cupboards in it, but it is nice and very well finished, I like it Jack' it would do us nicely all this year, the gold guilt lines on it outside gives it a lot of character by it. 'I'll have it, said Jack, coming out of his pocket with a small roll of money, counting out seven large white five pound notes. 'There's some luck back.' Said George, giving Jack a ten shilling note.

It's our first home and I know we are going to be happy, said Elizabeth. I am going out hawking tomorrow to a big village; I have my own horse and trap, said Jane, would you like to make a start with me tomorrow. 'So what do you hawk Jane?' 'I sell furniture posh dorb. I've hawked that with Granny Nelly many times, and found her a client to be duckered'. Jane looked up surprised, 'were you getting ready for when you would be married to Jack?' 'Yes that's right Jane.' Jack looked up. 'Woman, they're so, so cunning and crafty.' Jane and Elizabeth looked at each other and just smiled. 'No thank you Jane, Jack has to take me into town, I need some ordinary clothes, and we need everything, cutlery, china, pots and pans, blankets, everything.' He just looked and nodded taking it all in. George smiled, she's got you all sorted out already Jack. I am a gypsy man, what do I know about women's clothes, pots and pans and the like.' 'Not a lot but you did say my clothes are too posh, and we do need our own china, bedding and everything else, we have come with nothing,

'You're right' he said, going back in his pocket again and peeled off another white five pound note. 'I'll be expecting quite a bit of change, he said as he gave it to her. She could see he wasn't too pleased, so she handed him the five pound note back. 'You may need this for dealing, I haven't come empty handed, I can pay for all we need and still have some change'.

It's Friday tomorrow, I'll have the day off and go with you, and we can make a new start Monday. I know two very good second hand budicas (shops), said Jane. Elizabeth looked away, being what she was she had never worn second hand clothes. Jane noticed her expression had changed, smiling she said we always wash thoroughly second hand clothes. Even when we mong them (beg them); off rawnies (ladies), clothes that have gone too tight or had too long, I have often give them to gypsy women. I have brought money with me.' Said Elizabeth.

'I told you to leave your bank book at home, 'don't get annoyed darling Jack, he smiled you know when you talk like that to me he said, then looking away so 'where have you got the money from and how much?' I have £32.00 in cash as I have been drawing a bit out now and then whenever in York for this day, and i did leave my bank book as you told me'. 'Thirty two pounds is a lot of money for a woman to have. 'Don't you worry Jack I'll get all we need for the caravan, I mean the vardow (wagon) she said correcting herself including my new clothes. 'I will probably get everything we need for a lot less than ten pounds and still have money left to put in a stocking, and if ever you need it, you only need to ask, I have left all my jewelry except my gold cross with the little diamonds in, and my sapphire ring and gold bracelet, all the rest of my jewelry I have left back with the bank book.

Jack, do you want to work with me for a while say a week?' until you get yourself sorted out. Just what are you doing these days George? 'What we have always done, horse dealing around the farms and livery stables, it's good round here, there is a nice few villages and small towns, Ross-On-Wye and Ledbury Monmouth. There is a big cattle and horse sale in Abergavenny once a month, they give top prices for horses and it's a very good sale for old guns and fishing rods. You'd make top money off those two spare horses you have brought with you. 'I am not sure yet what I am keeping and what I am selling, I now deal in a bit of gold, also silver tea sets, said George. I have never done that but I would like to learn it with you, you're welcome.' it'll be thin round here for trade in the winter and hawking for the women, its farming country' said Jack. I go to Gloucester and Cheltenham for the winter. There's a big open yard there called the Hams it holds a good twenty families, 'I have never been there.' said Jack. 'It's about 40 miles from here, both towns are as big as Perth, and only five mile apart, plenty to go at for trade and loads of hawking for the women. 'We are still waiting for some tea, said George looking over at Jane. 'Sounds good then, said Jack. 'I've two men to see tomorrow about some guns and fishing rods, one of them has a silver tea set on a tray so you will see some silver trade as I will be trying to have him a swap, let the women see to what's needed and you come with me Jack, you might get some of the money back that you're out.' Sounds good to me I don't mind working with you, learning about silver for a week till I get the hang of it round here, said Jack.

What's happening about the sleeping arrangements, said Jane giving Jack a mischievous look. It's not cold I have two sheets we can run around the wagon, put one on the ground, we've got plenty of spare blankets, said George. 'So you'll be sleeping out under the wagon? I'll have the open lot for a few nights, hope you're not cold sleeping outside, said Elizabeth with a little smile. She has a nice friendly way with her thought George.

The night seemed to pass so quickly, George wanting to know all the news of Jan's family, for he had not seen none of them for a few years. He had only received four letters in this time, they had spent over a year at Blackpool. Her grandmother Manx Nellie and great grandmother Louisa both had dukkerer-pens (fortune telling shops) on Blackpool's busy promenade. Her stepmother Dellie refused one, she preferred to go out selling from her bag and duckering as the rents on the famous promenade, the Golden Mile were so high the gypsy women had to work in the shops six days a week from ten in the morning till ten at night. They would work all summer to cover the big rent and home shopping, the last eight weeks would be all profit, but it was a big profit!

George had not long been married and when the family left Blackpool to go back up to Scotland he and his new wife Jane travelled down to Worcester and Hereford with another young gypsy couple called the Bucklands, who came from Eversham front country. 'Do you know these people that's fighting tomorrow?' 'Yes they're on here I do know, he has to fight.' Is it over children or money?' asked Elizabeth. 'neither it's over honour, the man involved is about 25 been seeing a young widow women from Leadbury about ten miles away as there is a small camp there, he has taken her name away, been in the pub saying she's no good, that he has been having his way with her, very difficult to prove or disprove as she has been a married woman for three years and has a child, and lives back home with her people. 'You say people, do you mean her family?' asked Elizabeth. 'Yes said Jack giving her a stare for interrupting when men are speaking, she looked down for a few seconds as she knew Jack would tell her about it later.

'So continued George, he has been shouting his mouth off what a big man he is. 'He deserves it, said Jack. 'Oh he'll get it good, she's got no brothers but has two cousins and they're both good men, one of them is supposed to be a ring man, they'll be here in the morning. 'Sounds good to me, never seen a good fight for quite a while, the last one was two years ago when granddad Isaac fought the toughest man in York, at York Fair. 'How did granddad get on?' Asked George. 'He beat his man, it was a hard long fight, over twenty minutes, and he was bigger and about ten or twelve years younger than granddad. 'He should get a good hiding taking a young woman's name away said Jane to Elizabeth. 'Yes you're right', she answered, agreeing, but not sure about such matters.

I'll give you a hand' said George getting up, one canvas sheet was doubled and spread out on the ground under the living wagon, 2 thick Welsh bed rugs and 2 pillows was thrown on top, then the second sheet was stretched right around the bottom half of the wagon and tied. Won't you be cold Jack?' asked Elizabeth. It's early summer he'll be alright, there are a few families that can't afford a second wagon for their children and the boys have to sleep like that for a time till they can afford another one' Elizabeth shook her head, these men are so hard she thought thinking of how soft the young gentleman was that she used to know. 'I am tired said Jack looking at his watch, its 11:20. You both must be tired, none stop for three days, said Jane.

Elizabeth got up from the fire, standing in front of Jack, then putting her arms around his neck, 'Goodnight darling' she said then kissed him. 'Goodnight all, she said then turning. 'Oh its darling now is it?' said George with a smile. 'I'll probably sleep heavy, wake me up I don't want to miss the fight, said Jack. It was 6:30 when George reached in and pulled the bed rugs off Jack. 'Come on lazy bones, we'll see this fight, have some breakfast then get about our business'. Jack folded the two bed rugs then throwing them and the pillow over the shafts of the wagon to let the air blow through them. George had previously lit the fire and the black smoked kettle was hanging over it on the kettle iron. Jane started to make the tea. Jack was stripped to the waist, he walked over to a large oval shaped bowl that sat in a wooden frame, it was half full of water. Picking up a bar of soap and starting to wash. 'I have noticed you always wash outside, said Elizabeth. 'Yes even in winter, we break the ice with our fist, it wakes you up more quickly. He then pointed to a small square six by six feet framed tent, that is for you women and the men don't go near it, said George. Elizabeth smiled and nodded. It was ten past eight when three horse drawn carts pulled onto the common, there must have been eight or nine men on them as they pulled up in the centre of the area where all the living wagons was.

A tall man of about fifty walked forward, 'we are looking for a low life called Curly Boy Jackson, he spoke quite loud, you found him that's me came a short thick set slightly tanned young man with a mass of golden curly hair walked forward. 'So what excuse have you got for taking my girls name away, shouted the tall bald headed man. 'I was drunk and didn't know what I was saying, I apologise, I was drunk and it was wrong of me'. 'That's no good to my family and my girls name, now this morning you've got to take your medicine like a man. 'You've brought enough men with you, are you looking for a war?' 'They're here to see fair play and you'll get fair play.' came the answer.

You can bet your last shilling he'll get fair play, said a widow woman, of about fifty, being his mother, walking out of a ten by ten foot tent with a billock (curved small hedge chopper) in her hand. Seven or eight men came walking out of the other two tents and the two open lots to stand behind curly boy. 'We're too close to this for comfort', said Jack as there pitch was the next one to Curly boys place no more than eighty feet away. 'It's not a war, we are all family and we are just here to see it's a straight fight, one to one, came the answer. 'Keep well back you women, sit up on the front board of my wagon, said George. We're here for justice and honour said the tall bald headed man and we are not accepting any halfhearted apology, as if my daughter is some flatty or country girl. There's been enough talk who am I fighting, said curly boy pulling the thin jumper off over his head, walking back and forth with clenched fists and chest expanded. He looks like doing the job, whispered Elizabeth. George and Jack noticed the thickness of his forearms and wrists, 'I'll bet he can hit, said Jack, knowing that's what delivers a hard punch.

The biggest of the two cousins a hard looking tall partly bald headed man of about 40, stepped forward 'they call me one punch shanny, I am the man for you curly boy, I'm known to be the best man in all the hop country. Is it all in, go as you please or is it a straight fight, no kicking?' it's a straight go then said the tall bald headed man. 'you can take off that heavy gold ring, said curly glancing at the ring that had a square block top it must have been 2 ounces. 'It stays on, said Shanny. Curly boy's mothers hand went deep into her pinny pocket coming out with two heavy rings, a carved gold double-buckle ring and a square block silver ring. 'Well if that's how you like it two can play like that she said throwing the two rings to her son. He put one on each hand. Shanny immediately took the heavy gold ring off throwing it to his uncle curly boy then done the same.

'Let's see what you've got, said Shanny dancing about as if shadow boxing with a few fast punches in mid air. 'Looks good but they'll carry you off the camp, said Curly boy, he is shaping up like a ring man, he'll be good, said George. Curly boy was the first to go in, shanny being 4 or 5" taller stood at his full height his long arms held high. Curly was having it very difficult to get past Shannys long straight lefts and the odd right. This had now gone on for seven or eight minutes when Shanny hit him with a hard right, curlys nose busted and his top lip had been split with a previous punch, there was a lot of blood down his chest and stomach, you'd have thought he had been cut with a knife. Has he circled Shanny curly had got four or five punches into shanny only on his arms and shoulders they had been very hard punches, you could see this by how shannys guard had dropped slightly. Curly kicked off his shoes, he was now even lower being a very difficult target for punches to get past those big thick arms. That's it my boy, stay low, let him come to you, fight him your way, let him come shouted his mother. The width of curly and being so low he looked awesome as he kept going forward. You're bleeding like a stuck pig, said Shanny with a laugh. There wasn't a mark on him, the only blood on him was curlys.

Curly was taking a lot of punishment, you can't hit hard enough to stop me, you that's supposed to be the big one punch, one punch my arse, then taking another two straight lefts into the face. Curly then stepped in fast underneath of Shanny's long outstretched punch, his right hand went round Shannys waist grabbing his belt at the back, then pulling him forward, as he did he let two hard left hand punches go into shannys stomach, the man buckled at the knees, Curly then threw a hard right which missed his jaw hitting high above the ear. Shanny was down on one knee, panting, as he shook his head, his knuckles pressed to the ground to lean on, kneeling down on one knee. 'Get up, you can beat him, box him shouted his cousin. 'Hey you, with the mouth like my arse, you've got too much to say, when he's done, you have ego' shouted Curly. Half a minute had passed which had helped Shanny to get his wind back. He got up on his feet with a little spring, a show of confidence and fitness that he still had plenty left. As they sparred up again most of Shannys punches were hitting curlys forehead which didn't seem to bother him a lot.

Shanny suddenly reached out and grabbed Curly by his long hair, pulling him in, his other fist went for his head. Curly was moving has best he could from side to side, the punch glanced off his forehead. Curly gripped hard the wrist that held his hair, then suddenly dropping on his back with two feet up in the air, one in Shannys stomach the other on his chest. As he went down shanny went flying over the top of Curly. He turned sideways in mid air landing on his side with a heavy thud to the ground. 'I ought to kick your head off but I don't need to fight dirty to beat you, get up.'said Curly.

What's happened to the big one punch they've been fighting for over fifteen minutes, said George, his one punch is that big heavy ring that he's not got on', said Jack. Shanny was on his feet, curly stood his ground letting the tall man come in, he was coming in a lot slower and showing Curly respect for he had found out how hard curly could hit, his arms and shoulders were really aching from the punches and his stomach was sore 'Get to it Shanny, punch his face off, box him Shanny, come on man what are you waiting for,' shouted his cousin.

The fight had slowed down quite a bit when Curly stepped underneath a straight right got in close his powerful arms went around Shanny with his face pressed against Shannys shoulder and his chest was tight to shannys who was now finding it nearly impossible to punch. Curly started to pound a left then a right, another left then another right into shannys sides and kidneys. The tall man started to buckle at the knees. You've got him my boy, lay on harder, shouted his mother. Shanny's guard was high protecting his face. Curly took a step back, then he hit shanny twice with two hard punches, both to his chest. Shanny suddenly dropped to his knees and then fell face to the ground; you'd have thought someone had shot him. Curly took three steps back, his fists held high above his head, i'm the man today, Curly Boy Jackson, he shouted twice.

Shannys cousin and the tall bald headed man rushed forward and turned Shanny over, blood was now trickling out of the corner of his mouth and slowly running down his chin, his uncle ran his hands over shannys chest, he winced and pulled away moaning, 'he's got a busted rib, could even be two, we better get him to the hospital'.

You're not finished yet curly boy Jackson, it's not over, you've got me to fight next weekend, shouted Shannys cousin. I'll fight you now, give me fifteen minutes to get my second wind and I'll fight you now and beat you', because you're families are all shout and brag. 'We're taking Shanny to the hospital, answered his cousin. 'Hey long shanks, baldie, shouted Curlys mother to the girl's father. 'When you come next weekend bring your woman and I'll fight her. 'You've got too much mouth for a woman get back in your tent and do your housework. 'You come over here and I'll sink this billock in the top of your bald head. Curly looked at his mother smiling.

Considering Curly won the fight his face was badly bruised and cut, and lips split, yet Shanny who had lost the fight hadn't a mark on him said Elizabeth. 'What else?' asked Jane, 'A fair fight, very brutal and bloody, I wouldn't want to see my Jack in anything like that. 'I bet that Curly boy's mother is a bad old woman, 'so where's the justice, curly boy was in the wrong yet he still won, said Elizabeth ' I suppose you're right let's get the breakfast cooking, said Jack. I noticed you timed it, how long? Asked George '21 minutes, I thought it was a good fight, that Curly can hit.'

'Let's have breakfast then we'll get off I want to take that coloured horse, he pointed to a black and white mare tied behind his wagon, i think we can have a good trade for silver or a bit of gold coin, he seen the horses last week and likes it, very fair because I'd like to have a look around Hereford, No it's out on the Abergavenny Road, a farm about seven miles, answered George 'When you're round town Elizabeth getting what you need buy me something, said Jack. 'I'll do that darling' she answered. 'I noticed that big heavily built wagon and a young shire horse, you doing a bit of scrap as well' asked Jack. 'No, but I have a new thing going on Saturday. I had to deliver a load of compost horse manure for a farmer I know, to a big house for their roses. So I now do it every Saturday. I mix the manure with peat, and bag it up, goes well round the borry-ceers (big houses). I can get sixty bags on that wagon, at half a crown, that's about £8, I give the old farmer £1 a load and I bag it up myself one night in the week.' 'It's a new one, never heard of it before' said Jack. 'It's a nice £7 most weekends. But it's hard work. It's called compost. Come out with me and try it. You'll find it hard work loading and unloading, and calling the big houses all day. But it's good money. You don't always empty the full load every time.' 'Maybe that's why you only do it Saturdays' said Jack. 'It's no good during the week, most of the men are at work.' 'Thanks for the offer brother in law, its good money.'

Sir John was walking quickly across the cobbled yard he had a letter in his hand. Lady Florence was walking fast behind trying to keep up with her husband. Nelson could see he was in a bad mood. 'What do you know about this Nelson he said handing the letter to him. Nelson was very slowly reading it out aloud having difficulty with some of the words. Give it her man, it will take you a week said Sir John, snatching the two pages out of Nelsons hand and then reading it aloud.

Nelson and his wife Dellie just stood there as it was read out, did you know they was planning this, tell me the truth Nelson, don't you lie to me?' No I don't know, I did know they were seeing each other for a long while, so did you sir john, everyone here knew they was going out together, Sir John nodded in agreement, going out a flirtation, maybe a mild romance, but to run away. 'Maybe he's abducted her for a large ransom, said the butler standing behind Lady Florence, If you don't tell that low life lackey to walk away now I will break his jaw said Isaac. 'What do you think you are doing interfering this is private, get gone now man, right now, said Sir John. Isaac went to walk towards him, the butler turned and walked away very quickly.

'You know we brought her up from five years old, she's a daughter to us, Yes she is said Lady Florence wringing her hands has she looked down at her shoes. She would not tell me about it as if it was her secret and she would spend time, lots of time with Jacks gran Manx Nellie. We all seemed to get along so well didn't we, said Lady Florence, maybe too well? 'My god Nelson you must have some idea where they have gone, said Sir John. Truthfully I do not know and this letter is not Jack's writing it is too good for him. Lady Florence looked at Dellie

So she was really in love with Jack I thought it was a bit of fun a flirtation with a good looking young, just a gypsy boy, interrupted Sir John, then stopped. Yes just a gypsy boy, my grandson' said Isaac. Well they've eloped I do think it's romantic and exciting said Lady Florence to Dellie trying to cheer things up a bit. Romantic, exciting are you made women, her names gone for good, don't you realise that, who would want her now, stammered Sir John, She will be my sons wife, he may not be a rich landowners son with a lace handkerchief up his sleeve and smelling of scent, jacks a man and that's what some women want, even a Lady. She's left most of her jewelry and her bank book, my grandson probably told her to leave it, said Isaac. It's your sort that marry ladies for big money, dowries as you call it.

We marry because we love a young lady and want to be with her always, 'so do we' answered Lady Florence. Father you can't talk to Sir John like that, it's wrong, said Nelson. They're very much in love because they have left us all and gone to who knows where,' said Delly. 'They will send a letter to my cousins at Blackpool and they will then send it on to me.' And within less than 2 weeks I should be giving it to you,' said Nelson. I will have the country searched thoroughly and have the marriage annulled, I will find them' said Sir John.

'I will tell you our way Sir John, the gypsy way, said Isaac looking him straight in the eye. The more you search the further and the deeper they will go to ground because if a gypsy does not want to be found, you won't find him, he can just disappear, so be very careful what you do and how you hound them.' We have cousins in Ireland and the Continent. You hound them and chase them from one part of the country to another, we won't see them for years, please be patient and you will definitely receive a letter from them, and your letters will get to them, and in time they will come and see you but you hound them and you will spoil all of it, you must be patient.'

I don't seem to have much choice do I? Said Sir John. We are good company to hunt with, talk to and entertain, us older ones we know our place. But when you treat the young ones so friendly they forget their place and they think we are all equal. I respect you Sir John and will always be your friend. Sir John did not answer, he ignored Isaac, turning his back and walked away from him.

We have lived the gorger life too long, pack up we leave for Blackpool today, we will have the summer there and maybe the winter as well and the following spring maybe back up to Perth, we will send any letters to you that we get from Jack and Elizabeth, said old Byron, he looked angry, Sir John had dismissed his son Isaac, then turning to his 2 grandsons Adam and Layton. 'There will always be a hidden gap or a space, you are never really equal and that is because of what you are always remember that. Look what you've caused John and it has done no good has it? She shouted to him as he walked away, then turning to Nelly and Dell 'Please don't go, stop packing, they just smiled, ignored her and continued packing.

It was about 12:30 in the afternoon when the wagons pulled out. At the bottom end of the drive young Adam and Layton jumped down and waved for several minutes, then turned and ran after the wagons. Walter stood on the top of the steps, stopped waving as the last wagon went through the entrance out onto the road, he suddenly felt so alone, I wonder what you will see and do at Blackpool, he whispered.

CHAPTER SIXTEEN- STAGECOACH

Tex glanced at the parcel on the chair, 'what you got there Adam?' 'Oh just some clothes that's gone a bit too tight, also an old pair of shoes, I promised some stuff I didn't need for the old timer in the Yellow Sky saloon. There's a shop in town that buys old stuff if it's tidy.' Adam just nodded. As they came down the stairs the clock on the wall was chiming eight bells.

Good Morning ma'am and Angelina. Well let's hope it's going to be young man because it's still raining. Angelina smiled, nodded then glancing at her mother. They found a table 2 down from Angelina and her mother. Tex poured a coffee as they waited for breakfast, then glancing at the next table across. It's Malcolm, how is the whiskey business, the man turned, he had his coat off thrown over a chair. Adam noticed he had a nickel plated colt 44 with Mother of Pearl handles in a shoulder holster, everywhere you go there's guns he thought, it's okay cheap whiskey will always sell anyway or anywhere' You still trying to be a law man?' 'Sure am, answered Tex, pulling back his coat and showing the law badge that was pinned on his shirt, Adam glanced at Tex, and you? He said pointing a finger at Adam. 'You are new to these parts what do you do? Adam glanced at him, he had immediately taken a dislike to this man, and he thought him to be an arrogant show off.

'Oh I like a gamble and I'll buy and sell anything I can pay for if I can see a profit in it, especially horse trade.' 'Unusual accent, and where do you hail from?' 'I am from England, well Scotland and England and I have seen a lot of Europe.' 'So you're a wanderer then?' 'Yes that's right, my name is Adam Boswell', reaching out his right hand. 'I am Romany.' 'I'd have taken you for a Turk or Greek.' The handshake was over with very quickly. 'Romany, a Gypo, hey?' 'It takes all sorts to make this new world' answered Adam. 'My parents used to tell us about the gypsies. They steal, and some are dirty.' Tex looked away. The old lady coughed, giving Malcolm a long stare, then went back to her breakfast.

Adams face went dark; Angelina and her mother could see he was having difficulty keeping the lid on his temper. Adam put down his coffee cup, looking straight at Malcolm. 'A gypsy's floor is cleaner than a lot of people's tables. I don't have to steal, I can pay for what I want, and I don't have to be a yes sir. I am my own man.' 'Can you hear me ugly?' 'You've got a lot of mouth for a man that doesn't carry a gun. So if you can't shoot, can you fight Mr. Boswell?' 'Like a horse kicking', answered Adam. The old lady and Angelina looked away smiling. 'We heard about your fight Mr Boswell, how you beat 2 common charos' last night', said the old lady. 'Hoping it would stop a fight that looked like starting.'

'Ma'am, there's always some old drunk wanting to have a fight', said Malcolm.

'You're accents unusual', enquired Adam, turning as he picked up his coffee cup. 'I am a true American, born in Boston Massachusetts. My father and my mother are both German.' 'Hooray for you.' 'Your breakfast sir', interrupted the hotel owner, placing the two plates on the table. 'Excuse me I am hungry' said Adam turning, and then picking up his knife and fork. Tex leaned across to Adam, as he dipped the piece of bread in one of his eggs. 'Leave it Adam he's trouble, middle weight ring champion of Boston, also the state of Massachusetts, you won't get near him.' 'Thanks Tex. 'Don't want to fight a ring champion unless I have to.'

'Mr Boswell?' 'Yes? What is it?' answered Adam, putting his knife and fork down, and then looking up. 'When you get to Glen Parva, you'd better start wearing a gun because you'll need one. It can get rough.' Malcolm's index finger tapped his Colt 44. Adam slowly emptied his mouth. 'Leave it be fella. As far as I am concerned it's finished. When I fight there's no rules, no padded gloves or rings, I fight to win. I will use anything. I'll slit your throat with a broken plate; put this fork through your eye into your brain. I have been trained with Tibetan monks. I'll kill you, do you understand?' Adam stared at him as he spoke. Tex looked at Adam, then looked away, not knowing whether to believe him or not. Adam turned, 'my apologies ladies for what's happened, and thank you ma'am for what you've said.' 'It's not your fault Mr Boswell; he seems to look for trouble.

'How you've spoke to him, he'll have you' whispered Tex. Adam emptied his mouth, looking at Tex. 'In a ring or field, he would chop me to bits. In a bar, or this room, I would kill him in 5 minutes or less.' 'That's one thing about Gypo's they're always trying to put the frighteners into you, when you've finished you're breakfast Gypo, we'll go outside.' Tex gave Adam a quick stare as if to say I told you so. Adams left hand had slid under his breakfast plate; he pushed it up and forward very fast, as hard as he could into Malcolm's face. It broke into four or five pieces. 'Why wait to go outside you arrogant German bastard? You want trouble; I am going to give you plenty.' Malcolm's right eyebrow was cut and his nose was cut across the bridge. Adam's two hands now had him by the shirt front. As he pulled Malcolm towards him hard and fast, he turned his head to the left, then again to the right. 'Try a Glasgow kiss.' Malcolm's nose busted, and his top lip split. Adam's left foot kicked very hard to the back off Malcolm's right leg. Malcolm went down gasping. Adam then reached for the pot of coffee and emptied it over Malcolm's crotch. As he was shouting in pain, Adam had his knee on Malcolm's chest. His right hand still holding Malcolm by the throat, reaching out to the nearest table, taking a fork off it, then holding it just 2 inches from Malcolm's eye. 'I'll take your eye out.' 'No, no, for God's sake stop, I didn't mean it.' Adam pulled him up, the fork in his left hand was now under Malcolm's chin. 'On your toes' said Adam, as the blood was trickling down the fork, Malcolm was standing as tall as he could. Nobody in the breakfast room said a word. It all seemed to happen so quickly. Adam released him then kicked Malcolm hard up the area towards the door. 'On your way ugly.' Adam walked over to a mirror, there was egg and blood on his forehead off Malcolm's face. 'Excuse me' he said, so polite to the Hotel Owner, 'have you got a wet flannel and towel please? Also another breakfast and a pot of coffee, put any extras or damages on my bill.' Malcolm turned in the doorway, 'some time you're gonna have to wear a gun, and when you do you're dead meat.' Mrs Sinata glanced at Adam, smiling, and then looked away, quite a combination, sharp gypsy mind with an English man's education and manners, fights like a mafia man, she thought. 'Why is every ring tale bully picking me out?' 'They can tell how you look and talk different, but you are a dude', answered Tex. Just then a man came in, walking over to Tex. 'Sit down John, you want a coffee?' The man just nodded, looking down. 'Another cup over here' said Tex. 'I'm sorry to let you down Tex. I had a lot of drink last night, fell down, and broke my arm.' Tex looked up from pouring the coffee at John's bandaged arm. 'Hells Bells, you've dropped me right in the shit man. We're pulling out in less than 2 hours and there's not another spare driver that can handle a six in hand team with a loaded coach.'

Tex looked at Adam, 'I'll need help.'

Adam shook his head. 'I have never driven a six in hand, and loaded with passengers. I have handled a four in hand a few times.' 'Well I'll have to do the job myself' said Tex. 'Would you ride up top with me and take my place as shotgun guard? I'll sign you in. It's worth ten dollars a day for four days and free meals, and someone's got to do it, you'll get your fair back as well off Wells Fargo.'

'Why not, we've got to get there, and I don't like refusing money' said Adam.

It was still raining, but not has hard, as he put the parcel down on one of the porch chairs. Then turning his coat collar up, and pulling the brim of his Stetson hat lower, he walked up the long street. The dry dirt road was now nearly two inches of mud. The front and the side door of the Yellow sky saloon was locked. He walked down the alleyway, turning right, and found the back door slightly open. It was one big storage room, over in a far corner was a bed and sideboard. 'Good Morning. I have brought that stuff I promised.' He was sat at a table with a cup of coffee and 2 boiled eggs. 'That's very decent of you young fella, you're from England aren't you?', taking the parcel off Adam, and placing it on a packing crate, then undoing the string. There was a shirt, pair of boots, and an old coat. 'Thanks, I can use them.' 'That's alright old timer, finish your breakfast' said Adam, glancing around, and then sitting on the spare chair. Some of the paint was flaking away on the wood planking sides. This corner is obviously his home, thought Adam.

'I didn't always used to be like this. I was once well respected.' Adam could see the old man felt ashamed. His eyes had filled up a little as he spoke. 'You don't have to be rich to be respected' said Adam, looking away.

What a way for a man to end up after working all his life like this, he thought. He pulled out some money, and peeled off a five dollar bill. Then thinking of his old grandfather Isaac, how comfortably he lived, like a gentleman. His wife Manx Nellie, looked after him, but every wife is not like a gypsy wife. 'Take this', he said, adding a second five dollar bill. 'Get a tin of paint as well for this corner where you live, whatever.'

'Thank you young fella and you are?' 'Adam Boswell.' 'God bless you.'

'No old timer, may god bless you first. You need it more than I do.' Adam then took two cigars out of his case, placing one on the table, and lighting the other. 'You're a good man, Mr Boswell, you've got heart.' 'I'll see you again maybe' answered Adam, as he nodded, then went out the door.

The rain wasn't as heavy, now a constant drizzle. As Adam walked down the muddy street, he was finding it slow going. Crossing the street, he went up the three steps onto the sidewalk (pavement). Looking at his damp cigar, he threw it away, stamping his feet several times, and then wiping them on the thick sack. The little bell rang quite loud as he pushed opened the door of the hardware store.

'Good morning sir. You're my first customer today, and what can I do for you?' Adam took off his coat, throwing it over a chair, then his hat. 'It certainly can rain when it rains in these parts.' 'I have some hot coffee on the stove, would you like a cup?' 'Thanks, milk with two sugars.' 'Now Mr. Adam Boswell, what can I do for you?' 'You know my name.' 'Yes I saw you shoot yesterday. In fact the last time I seen anybody shoot like that. It must be three years ago, maybe four. A young gun slinger down Glen Parva, called "Sack Matthew". He could hit a silver dollar in mid air on the draw with a Colt.' 'That's good shooting on the draw' answered Adam. 'You're a pistol aero. Aren't you a gun hawk? No offence meant by that Mr Boswell.' Adam pulled his mouth back quickly from the hot tin cup. 'I have played the part for years now. That's what I am' he thought.

'First I want a waterproof three quarter length coat, size 44-46, and a four pint water canteen.' Adam was examining the metal canteen, canvass covered with a long strap. 'My name is John by the way, and I stock 2 waterproof coats. One at six dollars and one at ten dollars.' 'That's quite a difference in price' said Adam, trying the first one on. 'Yes sir. The six dollar, the one you have on, is heavy cotton twill waxed. The ten dollar one is a genuine Gloucester type oilskin.' Adam took the first one off trying on the oilskin. 'I'll take this one' he said, throwing it on a chair then walking over to a long glass cabinet that was full of various pistols. 'You keep a good stock.' 'Yes Sir, you need to. There's such a variety of weapons now.'

'I notice you're not wearing a side gun for a man that shoots so well. No offence meant. I have here a beauty, a 44. caliber colt peacemaker, six shot, mahogany handles, nickel plated, the most powerful handgun you can get, and filed down sights for a fast draw' he said, placing it on the glass counter.

'Too long, too big, and too heavy. What's the small caliber navy colt in the back corner?' 'You know your guns Mr Boswell. This one's known as the 'gamblers favourite.' The barrel is double rifled, not too heavy and accurate up to 40 yards, feathered rib top, 32 calibers with black ebony handles. It's one of the best' 'Yes it is a nice one, feels good, but the barrels too long.' 'Yes Sir, it's eight inches, but I do have one with a five inch barrel.' Reaching in a drawer below the counter, he pulled it out wrapped in grease proof paper. 'I've got a short range out the back if you want to try it out.' 'No that's okay. It's a new gun, small, not too heavy, and powerful. It's what I want' said Adam. 'You will need a holster, side or shoulder.' 'No thanks, it's for a lady' answered Adam. 'And a 200 box of shells, not black powder, the latest grains.' 'I have heard of grained powder but never seen it, just got powder, anything else?' asked the store keeper. 'Three boxes of those royals' said Adam, pointing to the thin cigars. 'You're a heavy smoker, fifteen Royals.' 'I am going down to Glen Parva, they have to last me maybe five days.'

'That's it. You do seem to keep a good stock of most things.' 'Just call me John' he answered, getting a piece of paper and a pencil. 'Half a gallon water canteen, five dollars, a coat ten dollars, 32 navy colt special forty dollars, box of 200 shells, 32 caliber, three boxes of five cigars eight dollars, tote 75 dollars cash.' '15 cigars Mr Boswell.' They may have to last me nearly a week. I'm on my way this morning to Glen Parva.' 'Yes, so you said Mr Boswell, a nice place, and a different class of people down there.'

'A lot nicer place than Aberline. There's trouble there now and then like all frontier towns. I think it will grow to be a class town' said John. 'You know John, I'm well known throughout several states' exaggerated Adam. 'I wouldn't doubt that Mr Boswell, how you shoot, and I thank you for your custom.'

'You're welcome, but thank you doesn't pay the bills does it John?' 'No you're right there. If I was to drop it now and again when I was in a competition shout out in conversation to other men that I get my ammo and guns from you, it would do you quite a bit of good.' 'It would that Mr Boswell.' 'There's 65 dollars cash' said Adam, placing it on the glass top. 'If it's no good, I can go elsewhere, no offence meant.' '10 dollars less.' 'I can just cover my cost at 65 dollars. Please take the goods, and please tell your friends. But don't tell them the prices I charged you.' Thank you and have a nice day Mr Boswell. 'Got the ten dollars back, I gave the old timer' said Adam under his breath as he went out.

The two stagecoaches pulled up in front of the Sheriff's office, one behind the other, Adam noticed two US mail bags was thrown under the front seat, also a big heavily loaded wagon behind again. Adam was giving Tex a hand throwing some of the luggage up on top, then helping to pack the boot at the rear.

Adam threw the last case up, then jumping up top, leveling the cases and bags. 'I say you up there, get my two bags packed.' Adam packed the small light one in between two bags. Then letting the case slip out of his hands, it landed in the mud with a thud, splashing over Malcolm's trousers. 'Thank you or please goes a long way' said Adam. 'Don't you forget, my name it's Malcolm Watson.' 'Your mouth is going to get you in a lot of trouble one day Mr Boswell.' 'I'm always in trouble' answered Adam. 'Don't forget to get a gun, and learn how to use it Mr Boswell, you're going to need it.' He deliberately pulled his coat back, showing the colt 44, then walking over to the second coach. Tex leaned over, 'you want to leave him alone, he's not what he looks. He's supposed to be fast with that gun.' 'Thanks Tex, they're all supposed to be fast and good. He's found out the hard way, everyone doesn't fight in a ring, and he needs to say thank you to the main upstairs that I don't wear a gun.' 'He's a nobody wanting to be somebody.' 'He's supposed to be fast. He's supposed to be a ring champion.' 'Who cares?' Tex could see Adam was losing it.

'This is a big stagecoach.' 'Everything out here is big' answered Tex. He smiled, looking down at Adam, standing ankle deep in mud. He's a paid up Wells Fargo passenger, thought Tex. 'I like your play Adam. When you come up front with me I'll sign you in. There's a Winchester rifle under the seat, and your fair will be refunded.' 'Sounds good to me' answered Adam.

One of the two dance hall girls had her dress held high, so not to get it muddy. She looked over to Adam and Tex. Adam smiled and walked over. As he picked her up, her two arms went around his neck. She seemed to hang on, taking her time, before getting into the coach. 'I am glad you are going to Glen Parva.' said Adam. Angelina turned her head looking annoyed. Her mother just smiled.

'I notice they separate the ladies.' 'That's right, some in each coach. If attacked, there are men to help them.' In the first coach was Angelina and her mother with Susan and her boy William, Bill the Barber, and Malcolm. In the other coach were the two dance hall girls, and two Christian evangelists, a salesman and an army officer.

Quite a few people were standing on either side of the street, to wave and cheer them off. The stagecoach went through every two weeks, only once a month in winter. Amongst them waving was Tex's friend Orby Baa, and his wife Lowy. Adam and Tex were on the leading coach. Tex stood up and flicked the reins hard. 'Move him out!' he shouted twice. 'Good luck Mr Boswell' shouted the hardware shopkeeper. John B, the Wagon Masters wife Seler stood waving to him. 'Love you John, have a safe trip.' He just smiled and nodded.

As they came up to the Yellow Sky saloon, the old timer, and the roulette croupier both waved to Adam. Dutch Schultz's top lip curled up in a little snarl. He turned, and went back into the saloon. 'You seem to have made quite a few friends' said Tex. 'He didn't seem too friendly did he?' said Adam. 'Well what do you expect? You took a good lump of money off him with the casino and the shoot off?' 'I have had good wins before, but never won so much money so quick', answered Adam.

'You were very lucky. You weren't wearing a holstered gun. That Dutch, he'd have insulted you, and then challenged you.' 'Would that have left me any choice?' 'Well out here if it's a challenge, you draw or apologise, crawl a little, and walk away with your tail between your legs. Some get so ashamed; they just get out of town.' 'Has he ever been beat, wounded?' 'No, out here nine out of ten gun fights, it's to the death. They say he's killed seven or eight men. You see a man like that, so full of hate, it's best to keep out of his way, 'then there's no problems.'

'I noticed you were bothered about him.' 'You don't miss much. I sometimes lose sleep over it' answered Tex. 'Anytime Tex, I'm a good listener. Is he really that good?' 'Oh there's no back shooting or drawing before challenged. He's a good shot, and fast. He just doesn't care; just doesn't value life. He recently became a silent partner in the Lone Star Saloon at Glen Parva. Let's hope we don't see too much of him' he said. Adam glancing sideways at Tex. He could sense there was something about Tex and this Dutch Schultz. Adam stood up and turned, looking back at Aberline.

The horses were keeping up a slow trot. Adam took out his cigar case, 'you want one?' 'That's a good idea. Light it up for me. My hands are full of reins.' 'How far do you think we'll get?' 'They're pulling weight 55 – 60 miles. We can't drive them too hard. When this drizzly rain finishes it will get hot. We'll have tonight out on the trail, then tomorrow morning, up and over table top plateau, and that's a hard, slow pull, then onto Fort Montrose for the second night.' Adam just nodded, looking out at the vast space on either side.

'Tell me about Montrose. How big is it?' 'What's the one like in Scotland? Asked Tex. 'Montrose in Scotland, it's halfway between two big cities, Dundee and Aberdeen, it's a nice little long seaside town. They play a lot of that new game.' 'Yes, I've heard of it, never seen it played.' said Tex. 'This Montrose here, is nothing like that. It used to be an army fort. The army moved out, went down about 70 miles past Glen Parva. Then Wells Fargo brought it, Fort Montrose that is, as a relay station for the stage coaches. It's become a rough settlement, gets all sorts there, mostly passing through, no law order or sheriff, one or two nights there is enough.' 'Is it nice country round it?' asked Adam. 'Big grass areas, a lot of dry bush, open range. A few bad wanted men, red-necks and drifters, use the fort now and then.'

'I was very surprised to hear Orby Baa is selling up and moving out of Aberline' continued Tex. 'Yes, I bet his wife lowey is well pleased. She didn't seem to like Aberline or Orbys job.' 'Let's hope there's a church there that suits her' answered Adam. 'You say it's about 280 miles, maybe 5 days.' 'No we'll do it in 4 days. It's just a long straight run, except for the plateau.' answered Tex.

Adam stood up, turning to look back at Aberline, it had now nearly disappeared. 'So what did you think of Aberline?' Asked Tex. Adam paused 'Friendly people, not a town, a big village in very nice open country, too many guns, wild, some of the characters bigger than life. Never seen anything like it, I like it out here, and I think my younger brother Layton will as well.' 'When you fight, you say whatever is around; you know how to use it.' Adam just nodded, then looking at Tex. 'I fight to win. I am really a gypsy bare knuckle fighter, but I was trained by a Tibetan monk and my grandfather, who was a gypsy bare knuckle champion. My grandfather told me to mix the two styles when I fight; you've got to give it to them really good!'

'Well Adam, I wouldn't bet on that with them common charos. It's not just a fight with them, it's something else.'

'You were going to tell me about that big sea town. What did you call it?' 'Oh you mean seaside, Blackpool?' 'That's right, and how you met up with the Wild West circus at Perth.' 'The gypsy horse fairs, fights, London – and'

'Hold on there Tex, we're going to Glen Parva not Australia.'

'I'll make a deal with you. You tell me about the gypsy family in Glen Parva, and I'll tell you about London.' 'You got a deal Adam.'

'Well as I told you, their name is Lee. They speak English, but it's well, a different accent.' 'Yes, that will be the Welsh gypsy's. There's some in Scotland and London as well; also there are Boswell's in South Wales' interrupted Adam.

'Are you going to keep cheeping in?' Adam just smiled, 'they're not as tanned as you, friendly, the lady tells fortunes, does a good trade, mostly the women folk go to her, there are a few men also.'

'I'd say she earns the most, the son, he's about twenty, not married, really likes the Mexican girls. His sister, she's about sixteen, seventeen, the most beautiful girl I have ever seen, and I've seen a lot.' 'I'll give you my opinion when I've seen her' said Adam. 'She helps her mother. There's always young cow hands wanting to have their hands read by her, but the old man, he will only let her tell the ladies fortunes.' 'That's how it is' Adam said smiling.

'You say they are originally Welsh Gypsy's, where is Welsh?' 'It's called Wales, a small country adjoining to England called Wales, North and South about 140 miles square' said Adam.

'It is small for a country' said Tex. 'So what does the man and son do?' asked Adam.

'They deal in horses, sometimes breed them. They have about seven or eight mares, and a stallion, grow most of their own vegetables.' 'Have they got a ranch?' 'No, it's a small holding like mine, about 12-14 acres, three miles out of town at the back of my place. They do have a horse drawn 2 gypsy wagons in Glen Parva they tell the fortunes from. I see them regularly.'

'Have they been in Glen Parva long?' 'Well when I came to town from our ranch five years ago, they were already there. I believe they've been in Glen Parva about 8-9 years, came out from England, well Wales I suppose, to Boston, then Texas, a stabeing, they call it deporting. They seem quiet people, keep themselves pretty much to themselves. He, the man says it was self-defense; a young toff came at him with a sword. The gypsy made a mess of him, but did not kill him, they deported the full family. I will introduce you to them.'

'Can they fight?' asked Adam. 'Well the old man, the father, he'll be 50-55. I've seen him have a go, he won't back down, no skill, he's good with a knife. The young man, I've seen him, he can fight and likes it. He wants to learn how to use a gun, but his parents are very strict, and doesn't want him to. He's not big, about five feet nine, only about thirteen stone. He's fast. Holds his hands high when he's sparring up.' 'Yes we all do' said Adam.

'What's this plateau?' 'It's about seven miles across by eighty miles long, has a spring and small lake in the centre, very hot during the day and cold at night, saves us 2 days not going round. A few Mex families live there. Not too bad going up, very steep going down the other side.' Over an hour had passed with no conversation. 'Got to go easy on these horses. It's a longer day tomorrow before we get to Fort Montrose.' It was now hard going for the horses, Adam jumped down, he was half walking, half running. He caught up with the leading horse grabbing its bridle, he started to pull. 'Come on old girl, belly to the ground.' He shouted 'pull! Pull!' As he was pulling at the bridle, encouraging the horse. It fell into step with the other front horse next to it; the man on the other side that was doing the same gave Adam a nod of thanks.

After ten minutes, the four back horses had now fell into step with the front pair. All six were now pulling as one. It had taken nearly forty minutes to get to the top. The second stage coach was not far behind. The big heavily loaded goods wagon was coming up a lot easier.

'I see the two front pair on the goods wagon is half bred shires.' 'That's right, they make the hard heavy pulling easier for the four behind.' 'You seem to know your horses don't you?' 'Just a little' answered Adam. 'We'll pull in a circle' shouted John, the wagon master.

All the horses were out of the harness, and tethered out for the night, a big fire had been started in the centre of the circle, and in twenty minutes, there was hot coffee, a large iron boiler was sitting low over the flames. 'You finding this hard going?' 'No I am right at home, I've lived like this all my life. Stew smells good' said Adam. Then Tex glanced at him smiling.

'You like your grub, don't you?' Answered Tex, looking at Adam, shaking his head. 'What's so funny?' asked Adam. 'Well you don't look so much the gypsy gentleman now' said Tex. They both laughed.

Malcolm, the whiskey salesman was standing over to one side of Tex, blowing his hot coffee and talking to John B the Wagon Master. 'Jews, Blacks, Chinese, now Gypo's, this country is going to be one big mess in twenty, thirty years from now.' 'Why don't you leave it alone' said John. Adam looked down at his boots and the bottom of his trousers covered in dry mud, running his hand over his face, he could feel the small dry mud speckles. 'I suppose you're right' 'Not much the gent now' smiling. 'Don't worry about it. There'll be hot water to have a wash.' 'I thought you'd have spare horses behind each coach for a changeover' said Adam. 'As I told you, there's not many about since the Civil War. They're now bringing good stock over from Ireland' answered Tex.

'Will we be leaving at day break?' asked Adam. 'Not that early. We just can't burn the horses out. They're pulling big weight. We'll start about 8.30, 9.00. Another sixty miles tomorrow will get us to Fort Montrose.' 'Halfway.'

'Is it a big fort? Many cavalry there?' 'No, as I told you, there used to be before the war, the soldiers just kept moving the Indians back fifty, sixty miles, each time the tribes lost braves. The soldiers had fire power, there were hundreds and hundreds of square miles of open land, so the Indians moved back.' 'And what about the Fort?' 'Oh it was closed, and another one started about seventy miles down passed Glen Parva. That was when Glen Parva was just a settlement, before the silver mines then they needed more land for settlers.'

'So I suppose the Indians being the real Americans were just pushed further and further back off their own land. So where did they end up?' Tex just nodded twice, and looked away, feeling uncomfortable how his British friend had put it. 'So Montrose is halfway, another two days from there, and it's Glen Parva?' said Adam. 'Thank god for that' said Angelina's mother, who was stood nearby. Tex turned to look at her, 'you've come a long, long way Ma'am. Are you buying a big ranch?' 'I am minding my own business' giving Tex a stare. Angelina looked away. 'Well you asked for that one' said Adam.

'I suppose you'll get to know it sooner or later. I have brought the Royal Hotel in Glen Parva.' Tex let out a low whistle. 'It is one of the biggest and best hotels in the state.' 'And what do you know about it Mr Tex?' 'Well ma'am, it is classy, has polished oak, and velvet reception, a big separate dining room, very good food, expensive place. It has about twenty bedrooms. Some have their own little Lounge, they call it a suite.' 'You seem to know a lot about it' answered Mrs Sinata. 'Yes ma'am, I've worked there a few times as a peace officer. No leather chaps, spurs, rifles or dogs allowed. Then there's another big separate square room, padded high back chairs, called Lounge it as waitress service.' 'Yes I've read about that on the survey papers' she answered. 'What is the gambling?' asked Angelina. 'In the long bar, poker card tables, black jack, roulette, small band, happy night girls, it has it all. There's only one roulette table, walnut, straight from New York. It's not a popular game out here. Too many rules and regulations to it. You see ma'am, there's only four or five out of every ten that can properly read and write.' 'I need to see who runs the gambling side. My husband was well into that. I only know a little of it'

'You're a gambler Mr Boswell. Do you know about roulette?' Adam was looking at the half moon diamond broach pinned to her scarf.

'There are three rows of twelve numbers, which are called columns, from 1 to 36, pays out 36 to 1. Two colours red or black, even money, three blocks of twelve called dozens 2 to 1 on, evens 1 to 18 and odds 19 to 36, even money bets. The 36 squares you can bet corners or splits on each one. Corners 8 to 1 splits 17 to 1 on, zero just one green square on the wheel clears the board. You can also bet on it 36 to 1. Then there's streets bets 6 line.'

'Enough, enough Mr Boswell, indeed it's too complicated. I have had a good education, and would not want to play it. It would give me a headache' 'Have you done any casino work?' Tex looked at Adam. 'Yes.' Is there anything he don't know? Thought Tex. 'A Monte Carlo wheel has a cross on the top, whereas the others hasn't.'

'I have worked a wheel when I was in Monte Carlo for a season' said Adam. 'He really only helped out for six-seven weeks, evenings, stacking chips and giving the croupier a break for thirty minutes, once a night, he could just do it.' 'And would you like to work casino roulette at my hotel Mr Boswell? Better someone I know, if only for a short time. You see I don't know what clever moves this Managers got going. You would be new.' Adam tried to not to look keen. 'I don't know ma'am' giving her his favourite smile. 'Call me Mrs Sinata.' 'We would need to talk money Mrs Sinata, and please call me Adam. But something has gone through my mind about your posh hotel big square lounge.' 'I have worked a wheel of fortune quite a lot.' 'Have you? What exactly is a wheel of fortune?'

'Well you could say it is a very simple to follow smaller watered down version of roulette, very easy to follow. There are no colours, columns, bets split, or the likes, there are only 20 numbers. It is a wheel as big as a cartwheel bolted to the wall, and the odds are set at ten to one, it is very simple and ladies like it as much as the men.' 'I think we might be able to arrange something Adam on a percentage basis. My place, your knowledge and skill, we will have to talk about it when we get there.' 'It would have to be straight and classy of course.' 'Sounds good' said Adam. 'Buying the hotel isn't the only reason I've come to Texas.' Adam gave no reply. He had won her over; she liked his style and his manners.

The hot bowls of stew were handed around. Adam looked down at the deep wheel lines in the damp ground. 'Heavy load!' He said to John, the wagon driver. 'It's a clock.' 'A clock? You're joking' answered Adam. 'No siree, it's in three parts, base, stem, and a large round clock at the top, must weigh about two ton. It stands twenty five feet tall.' Tex walked over to the wagon, and pulled the cover back, it was painted shiny black with embossed flowers, and leaves that ran up the sides. 'It's beautiful' said Tex, looking at the large face, with roman numerals. 'Whose is it?' 'It's John Parva's he's having it put up in the centre of town, a very nice gesture' said Adam. 'And just what is a gesture?' asked Tex. 'It err-, means a nice thought, a nice thing to do.' John B looked at Tex. He has a good education, speaks well. Tex just nodded.

One of the evangelists stood up, then walking over to the stage coach standing on the wagon wheel; he reached up for his guitar case.

The guitar hung around his neck as they both stood side by side in front of the fire. 'If you don't know the two songs, follow us, we will sing each one through the second time.'

'This is all we need on this miserable plateau at night' said someone. 'A couple of bible punching idiots.' 'I'll second that' said Malcolm, turning to the wagon guard.

'We are not wanting your money, just a little of your time.' 'Where's your dog collar and beads?' 'Are you a vicar or a priest?' 'We are neither. We hold no title. We are here to tell you Jesus loves you. He died for you' said the big one, Ringo.

The smaller one called Harry started to strum the guitar. 'This little light of mine, I'm going to let it shine. I won't let Satan put it out; I am going to let it shine.' They sang several versus.

Suzanne and her boy William joined in, singing and clapping. 'Jesus, who died, now glorified king of all kings.' The second song, it was a very touching song, and couldn't help but join in. Harry put his guitar down; taking a bible out of his pocket that looked like it had a lot of use. 'I am not going to preach for hours, ten minutes of your time is all I want.'

'The bible' he said quite loud, as he held it up. 'When you are born, you are named by it, and then baptized by it, married by it, and when you die, a few words is said over you from it. We must know it and believe it. It is God's word. There are many Prophets, many Pagan Gods, only one son of God (Jesus said, I am the way, the truth and life, no one comes to the Father, except through me). That's not me telling you that. It's in the holy bible, John 14 verse 5 and 6.' Harry held the bible up walking round the fire. 'Hallelujah means glory to god all over the world.' He then gave out another two scriptures.

'He's good' said Tex. 'Maybe God is using him.' 'I've seen ministers nearly twice his age not that good' said Adam. Even Malcolm and the Wagon Guard stood and listened.

Ringo now had the guitar and started to sing. 'Jesus lover of my soul, Jesus don't you ever let me go.' When it was finished no one spoke, nothing moved. There was a stillness, and then Angelina and Suzanne got up, taking second coffees around.

Adam got up and walked out of the encampment. Standing still in the dark, he looked up at the stars. The short bible meeting had moved him. Putting his hands together, 'oh my god, look after my family so far away, forgive me for that, just thinking of myself. I want to do the right thing, I also want to succeed. Amen'

'And what of Ronny the Gypsy girl back at Cambridge?' he whispered, feeling the cross around his neck. 'And this Italian well-bred beauty here, he'd been thinking about writing.

As he walked Adam was softly speaking to himself. Ronny's brothers are knife men. You can't make a fool of gypsy young women, especially Caldaresh. 'But I have not wrote yet, and the old mafia woman with that big webley service revolver always in her bag, she wouldn't think twice about using it.'

'You'd better make your mind up which one, or none at all, they're both beautiful and both dangerous. Find some dance hall girls for a couple of years until you're ready to get married. Get your hot gypsy blood under control; you're walking on thin ice' he whispered.

'What's that?' asked Tex. 'Oh nothing, just thinking out loud' as he walked back in the camp.

Adam walked over to the two evangelists. 'I am Adam Boswell from Scotland, England. I enjoyed it.' 'Pleased to meet you. I am Harry and this is my friend Ringo.' They each shook hands. 'Our work is to tell you of Jesus. When Jesus the Savior comes into our lives, we will sin less. So what do you do?' 'I am a gambler, horse dealer, a buyer and seller.' 'And maybe a soldier of fortune?' said Harry. 'I haven't thought about that, I don't wear a gun.' 'Yes to wear a gun can give you protection in this wild country. But you may be challenged and have to kill or be killed' he said. 'How do you live?' Harry smiled, 'God provides for his workers.' 'Would you like another bowl of stew?' asked Angelina. Adam smiled, 'it looks that way.' 'Will you stay in Glen Parva long?' 'As long as god wants us to be there.'

Adam turned, 'wherever I go religion seems to follow me everywhere. Is god trying to tell me something?' he said under his breath.

The fire needed another build up to last through the night for the men to sleep around, leaving the two stage coaches for the women.

Adam followed Tex to one of the stage coaches, going in the boot. They then went around, handing a blanket to everyone.

'I am feeling very tired. The problem is if I go to sleep now, I will probably wake at four or five o clock.' 'You look very tired Mrs Sinata. It's been a long hard day, I am tired, and I am young enough to be your son.'

'23 - 24 - you're close, I am 26.' 'Are you coming over to the stage coach Angelina?' 'No mother, nine o clock is far too early, I'll stay up round the fire and have a talk with the other women.'

'Adam will walk me back over' she turned as she said it. 'Of course Angelina' answered Adam, as he held his arm out to Mrs Sinata. She slowly pulled herself up off the stool leaning on Adams arm. 'Thank you, you have the ways of a gentleman.' Adam never answered.

As they walked towards the stage coach, he opened the door for her. 'Can you leave us for three or four minutes?' 'Of course Mrs Sinata.' Adam walked off, then stopping about 30ft away, waiting to walk Angelina back to the fire.

'Angelina, being your mother I am a little embarrassed to speak to you like this. I know and can see you have eyes for the gypsy gentleman Adam. Please don't deny it. I want better for you one day. If you must flirt, I know he is handsome in a rough sort of way. Don't let yourself down. When a young woman loses her name it can be forgotten but it's never dead.' 'I understand mother.' 'Goodnight and God bless' she leaned to kiss her mother on the cheek.

John B, the Wagon Master stood by the fire talking to the night guards 'you two men first watch to 2 O'clock, then you two till 7 O'clock. Any trouble just fire two quick shots in the air.'

Angelina went and sat with the women. Adam looked around, it was a nice atmosphere, some just laying back smoking, drinking coffee, others talking. John B sat thinking of his wife Seler. He was getting fed up away from home so much. Someone was strumming a guitar. He thought how his mother Delly would sing to it. He suddenly felt a little lonely. John B walked over the second time placing another two big logs on the fire, then throwing a heavy branch on top. Over an hour had passed when Suzanne and her boy William got up, then walking over to one of the stage coaches. Angelina was sat talking and laughing with the two dance hall girls.

Adam stood up folding his blanket, then throwing it over his arm. He could just see Angelina talking and laughing to the left side of the fire. She slowly looked up, knowing he was looking at her. The two dance hall girls had been talking about him earlier on.

As he approached her he smiled, she smiled back. He stopped about 50ft passed her, then turning around. 'Angelina' 'Yes what is it?' answered Angelina. She looked away feeling a little cheap and embarrassed, she caught him up putting her arm through his. He was so different from the courters she knows he is rough, but has manners, something of a gentleman. They continued to walk for another 40-50 yards. He lay the blanket on the ground. As they sat down, he pulled the hunting knife out of his belt and stuck it in the ground. 'What's next Adam?' 'Your pistol, this is an open wild country and you need something.' As they lay on the blanket time seemed to stand still like the moon above. He reached out, it's so close, so big, I feel that I could touch it.' 'Like we're here on earth, I wonder if there are people on the moon.' 'We will never know' answered Adam, as he pulled her to himself again. They had been kissing and caressing for the last 20 minutes. He was so passionate with her. She was finding it difficult to keep control. They had done everything except sex. 'I love you so much Adam. I have been out with three other young men and always kept control. You just hypnotize me my gypsy gentleman. I want to be yours.'

They made wild passionate love again and then again, time seemed to stand still like the moon above them. Leaning on his arm panting just a little he reached over, staring at her, he touched her forehead, it was wet with sweat. He kissed her gently on the corner of her mouth, 'was it good my wild Italian princess?' 'Yes it hurt a little, but a nice hurt', she then looked away embarrassed.

'You won't want me now will you Adam? I will always want you.' 'Yes, I love you' answered Adam as he looked down at her, realizing how quick his answer was. Pulling her to him, he kissed her again, and then stood up. 'It was so overpowering, like nothing I have known, now I feel so close to you.' Adam smiled, looking down at her. It was probably her first time he thought.

'Thanks' said Adam, taking a cigar off Tex. 'No fences, no edges, its vast, who owns it?' asked Adam.

'It's open range, they just brand the cattle and let them free run its poor land as you can see. No one wants to fight to the death and grab it. There's plenty of it' answered Tex.

'You like a long walk before you turn in,' Adam just smiled and nodded. Getting up he walked over to the nearest stage coach, taking a short spade out of the boot. About 8ft back from the edge of the fire; he quickly scraped out a deep trench, then piling the earth up some 9" on the side nearest the fire.

Tex looked at the short deep trench, then at Adam. 'That's what the Indians do at night.'

'It's better than burning' answered Adam. 'What you smiling for? Asked Tex. 'Oh just thinking back, about burning and a bucket of piss.' 'Do you remember about me telling you? Jack ran off with the Lady Elizabeth, and we all left for Blackpool.'

'Yes, I do' answered Tex.

The gypsy family had been gone from Essingbold two days, making their way to Blackpool. It would be a long and hard journey, nearly 150 miles across Yorkshire, and the Lancashire tops. It would take a long hard four days; parts of it would be very hard on the horses. They were three miles out of Halifax.

'Four o clock, I've had enough for today, so has the horses' said Isaac to his wife Nelly. 'There's that lay by up ahead, we've stopped there twice before.' 'Yes, we could do with getting a fire going and a hot meal' said Isaac, pulling the two horses over onto the opposite side of the road, to pull into the lay by. The four wagons were pulled in a row, keeping to one side, so as not to block the lay by off. 'It's a few years since we was here' said Nelson, holding his hands out over the fire. 'Must be six or seven years' said old Byron. The women was skinning and gutting four rabbits, the boys had managed to kill, knocked them over quick and quietly during the day with the catapults. They would need to cook something to go with the four young rabbits. They wouldn't fill eight people.

Adam and Layton was using a weight and line with a rope attached to the short piece of string, thin line that went through the lead bale. They stopped underneath of the big old oak tree, with some of its branches rotten.

Layton threw the small lead bale as hard as he could. It went straight out, and over a branch, and then stopped. As Adam held the rope tight; the ball came to a sudden stop in mid air, then spinning round and round the rotten branch. Both boys then pulled as hard as they could. There was a loud crack as the branch broke, falling to the ground.

'Well done boys' said their father, as they dragged it over to the fire. 'I suppose you will be selling Jack's open lot when we get to Blackpool?' said Adam. 'A small nicely made wagon. I was thinking of keeping it for you two boys to have your own wagon. Like your mother said, you are in your teens now and need some privacy.' The boys turned to look at each other at the same time. 'Well' said their grandfather Isaac. 'Thanks dad.' 'Yes that's really nice of you dad' said Adam. 'I do wish you'd stop talking like a gorger gentleman with your really's.' 'Sorry dad' said Adam. 'I'll send young Jack £30 for it when we know where he's going to' said Nelson.

'Where do you think they'll be dad?' asked Layton. 'It won't be Blackpool. Sir John knows we'll be there. I wouldn't be surprised to see Sir John at Blackpool' said Isaac. 'They'll be at Perth with the Shaw's or Hereford with his sister Jane & George' answered Nelson.

'Were going to miss the comforts we had at Sir Johns' said Nelly. 'All good things come to an end' answered Isaac. 'It's nice to be out on the road again and free.'

Just then, a youth came on the lay by, then walking towards the fire. 'Gorger chowr galling a kiey, (non gypsy youth coming over here)' said Adam.

'Excuse me sir, can I have a warm by your fire?' 'Of course you can, and what is your name?' asked Nelson. 'I am William Forsth. I was fourteen years old today and I have been released, I now have my freedom to go and do what I want.' 'Have you been in jail boy?' asked Isaac.

'No sir, I have been brought up in a Doctor Barnados Home for Orphans on the other side of Halifax.' He stopped, and slowly looked around. 'You are gypsies aren't you?' 'Of course we are. Does that bother you?' He never answered. 'Well I was going to offer you a hot drink and something to eat, but if you're too posh for us, you best be on your way' said Isaac. 'I am sorry, it's just that..' he stopped. 'Go on boy, finish it' said Isaac.

'Well I have heard that you steel babies and kidnap boys like me.' 'We have to work very hard horking and hunting to bring up our own children, without looking after someone else's.'

Layton and Adam would be using Jack's open lot (wagon) that he had left. 'I don't want a gorger cuwer suteing adrey mandys woodross' ('don't want strange people sleeping in my bed') said Adam. 'So where are you going?' asked Layton. 'I am going to Blackburn. I have an aunty there.' 'Did she visit you much in the home?' 'Twice.' 'In how long?' asked Layton. 'In thirteen years' answered William, looking away.

'I wouldn't build my hopes too high young William. You're welcome to travel with us, safer than on your own. We go through Blackburn, were going to Blackpool.' 'Thank you sir.' 'I'll help any way I can.' Nelly had made several cakes. 'That was delicious, what cake or scone is it?' he asked. 'It's gypsy cake in the pan' said Nelly, as she buttered the big slices, giving him a second one. Old Byron had his button keyed molden out, and Nelson, his violin. Delly was leading the singing, all the others sung along. William started singing as well. He looked very happy. The apple sweet cider tasted good.

The three hours seemed to pass quickly. Isaac walked over to William with a small spade. 'Make a deep groove in between you and the fire, don't get too close, here's a small sheet to put on the ground, and a thick blanket to wrap up in.' Layton and Adam had put plenty of wood on the fire. Everyone said goodnight.

Half way through the night, William started to shout 'I am on fire. I am burning - help!' Nelly was the first up. She reached for the night bucket. She quickly took the lid off as she was walking over, then emptied the half bucket over William. 'Oh thank you Mrs Boswell, I had my back to the fire, I was burning.' He then stopped and started to smell the blanket and his coat. 'What was it? Pray tell me?' 'It was the night bucket' said Nelly. 'The piss bucket' said Isaac. 'Oh you should have let me burn' he said. They all laughed as they walked away.

'Did he get to his aunty at Blackburn?' asked Tex. 'Yes, she was pleased to see him, but did not want him. He travelled on to Blackpool with us, got a job there, palled with the gypsy boys. We had two summers there, then left for Scotland. We heard he married a gypsy girl. I suppose a story would go round Halifax where he came from that the gypsy's had kidnapped him.

'If I ask you something very personal, will you take offence?' 'What do you want to know?' replied Adam. 'I err---' Tex was having difficulty. 'Say whatever is bothering you' said Adam. 'I heard your people sometimes take young children, steals them, to work for them or sells them.'

'That is 100% untrue, and completely misinterpreted.' 'You speak so posh, miss-in-what was that?' asked Tex. 'A lie and exaggerated. Sometimes there would be a young girl who had got herself in trouble, and her family did not want the shame of it. She would be told to get rid of the child. They would offer it to a passing gypsy family, and it would be gone.'

'Sometimes there would be six or seven children in a very poor home, and another would be born by accident. My grandfather Isaac had five sisters, one of them was given to his mother Lowizer when she was out hawking big posh houses. He never would tell us which one. As far as we were concerned, they were all our aunts. We loved them all.'

'Somehow we all get fed. We are survivors. We might have to rough it a bit now and then, but we don't go hungry. We will beg, deal and poach. We don't go out of business because we are the business. When the women hork, sell flowers from the basket, and the flowers, they are hard to get or too dear, we don't go into people's private gardens and steal that would be wrong. But we do go to the big government buildings and parks where there are too many. People want flowers and our women want shopping. It's sometimes not always the best way. But it's very rare a gypsy family goes hungry for more than a day.

'If in a works getting half a horses wagon load of scrap, it is best to go in at nearly dinner time, with a written receipt from the office for pounds worth of scrap iron, five shillings in the yard foreman's hand, he will walk away for his dinner and we will come out with a full £5 worth load, there's so much there, it's not missed. This is hard dirty work and possibly trouble. We only do scrap from factories when everything else is bad. It's live and let live, but not with most of the big people, live and others starve. We are survivors.'

'We would never see a little boy or girl brought up in a child's workhouse, if we could help them. They are abused, beat, and go hungry. Sometimes sold, and the passing gypsy gets the blame. If anyone of our families can't take a child themselves, they will get it to another gypsy family. We are god faring and god believing people.'
'You explained that simple and believing. I respect you Adam.'

The Next Day

They pulled up to give the horses a drink and a rest. Everyone was glad to stretch their legs, and have a long drink. Tex and Adam was having a smoke, when Susan walked over. 'Mister Tex?' 'Yes, what is it?' he answered. She looked away, a little embarrassed, as she spoke, then pointing over to some rocks and high bushes about 30 yards. 'We ladies need to go over there for ten minutes.' 'That's alright ma'am, I understand. I'll tell the men to stay here until you come back.' The two dance hall girls Susan, Angelina and her mother also walked over.

'What do you think Tex? When will we reach Fort Montrose?' 'If we keep it nice and easy like on the horses, give them another good rest later on.' 'They're pulling weight and its hot, they'll be spent out' answered Adam. 'You're right, but that will be no problem, there will be six fresh horses for us tomorrow' answered Tex. All of a sudden some of the ladies were screaming, holding their long dresses up, and running back to the stage coaches. A cougar, a young mountain lion must have been in the rocks and bushes. With all the screaming, it was as frightened as the five ladies were, it went running off in another direction. Tex, John B, and Adam just stood there laughing. Malcolm run out, pulling his 44 colt revolver out of the shoulder holster, holding it with both hands, he emptied it, all six shots at the young lion that was running hard in the opposite direction from the ladies. The animal had been hit; it fell rolling over, and then got up, dragging its back half. 'Good shot with a hand gun, must have been 80-90 yards' said one of the wagon drivers. 'I just aimed a foot above it and a foot in front' said Malcolm.

The four men walked out to the wounded animal. It stopped dragging its back end, and laid there. It had been hit twice, in the back and thigh, then looking up at them, its mouth half opened in a snarl, showing its teeth. 'A dam shame, it's only about fifteen months old, what did you shoot it for?' asked Tex. 'It would have grown into a dangerous vicious animal.' 'It was a good shot at that distance.' 'I hit it twice, look' said Malcolm.

Tex slowly cocked the hammer back of his Winchester rifle, pointing the barrel at the big cat's ear, its head just dropped. 'A lovely young animal, it didn't mean any harm, just running away' said Adam, turning, then walked away. Tex could see his friend was annoyed.

Two hours later the left side middle horse just dropped bringing the coach to a sudden stop.

Tex pulled on the reins, then pulling on the handbrake. Adam jumped down following him over to the other stage coach. The horse was laid on its side froffing at the mouth whinering. 'It's wore out, let it loose or it'll die, it's had a slight heart attack' said Adam, he had a bucket of water. He was bathing and splashing water all over its head. They got it up. He held the bucket while it had a drink. Tex undone the harness, then tied it at the back of the stage coach. 'Will it die?' asked Suzanne. 'I don't think so, it's the oldest out of them all. It can't take the heat and the distance' answered Tex. 'It's finished for hard work, its days of pulling stagecoaches is over' said Adam.

CHAPTER SEVENTEEN – GUN FIGHT AT FORT MONTROSE

'There's the fort!' shouted John B. Adam reached down under the seat, coming out with the telescope. He had a good view as the Fort was on high ground. Tex looked at his watch, twenty past five. 'It's been a long day', he dropped it back in his waistcoat pocket. Adam pointed to the horses, they had a broad white sweat line around each side of the harness straps. 'They're spent out.' 'Good job there's fresh horses at the Fort for us tomorrow.' Adam just nodded in reply.

Tex held a horse's bridle with each hand, as he walked between them, following Adam and the man over to the livery stables. 'Give them a wipe over, feed them, then bed them down for the night, they need it' said Tex to the stableman.

'We'll be okay for tomorrow with fresh teams' said John-B. 'Another two days, and we'll be in Glen Parva. The stableman turned, looking at him. 'I don't think so.' 'These horses will need at least a full days rest, maybe two.' 'You've got the horses for the changeover haven't you?' 'Forget the two half shires. They will need four, and we will need six for each stagecoach, that's sixteen horses' said John B the Wagon Master. 'No way, we've got only eight.' 'You've got too many, a wagon, and two stage coaches.' 'We can't use them same horses tomorrow, we will need to give them at least a full days rest, maybe two' said Adam, looking at Tex.

'You're right, they should be having two days' rest.' 'You need more horses' said John B. 'There is supposed to be a couple of boat loads coming over from Ireland next month' said the stableman. 'Well however much we talk about it, it isn't going to alter things. We'll discuss it and see what's what in the morning.' 'I am hungry, I need a clean shirt and need a wash' said Tex, slowly walking away.

Adam glanced around the cantina. The bar was in an L shape, situated in the far corner. There was only seven tables for cards and drinking. Two steps went up with a handrail, to one side was the dining room area being on a 2ft higher level, with a small banister rail across the front. This was the café area. There was three tables and one long table across the back wall.

Everyone had a good night's sleep.

The travelling party just about filled the café area for breakfast. 'I could eat a horse' said Adam, pulling a chair out. 'You might just get a horse steak tonight' said Tex. Adam glanced around.

The wood planked walls were plastered over, not painted. The roof area had been painted white. It was now a yellowy cream with the cigarette smoke. The floor was just wood planks, no rugs, and needed sweeping. The place smelled heavy of cigarettes.

'Disgusting place, it's cleaner eating out on the trail.' 'I agree with you Mrs Sinata' said Adam. Two young Spanish girls went back and forth from the cantina, placing the breakfasts on the tables. Adam looked down at the table, no cloth and there was a few bits of food left between the plank table top. 'Mokerdy chklow tane' he said to himself. 'What was that?' asked Tex. ('Dirty, filthy place') 'I've seen this place cleaner, it's getting worse' answered Tex. Adam looked down at his plate, 'excuse me Miss, have you got a minute?'

'Doesn't he speak nice?' 'Like an English gentleman' said Susan.

'Yes Senor.' 'This belly pork looks like it's going to walk off the plate, its nearly raw, can you put it back in the pan, I asked for it well done, and the eggs are rock hard?'

The cook, a fat greasy woman came swaggering over. 'My food does not suit you senor?' she said quite loud expecting to have her way. Adam slowly looked her up and down as he started to speak. 'The meat is nearly raw. I asked for it well done, and the eggs are rock hard.'

'You'll have to wait.' 'Excuse me, before you go. I haven't finished' 'Yes what is it now?' 'You should get a pinny over those dirty clothes. Pin that hair up and clean your nails.' 'Where do you think you are?' she asked. 'I know where I am, in this dirty dump.' 'I am the one that's eating and paying for it. I'll report this place, I will send a letter to Wells Fargo Huston about this place, it's filthy.' A little thin man came quickly over. 'Sorry Senor, they will cook you a new breakfast straight away.' Tex looked at him with a smile, 'no shouting, fighting, just the right words' he said.

'It does not suit the English Gentleman' said Malcolm with a chuckle. 'He's after you today' said Tex. Adam looked up from buttering the thick piece of bread. 'He'll wish he was somewhere else' said Adam. Bill Hib the Barber's eyebrows lifted up.

Adam looked over as he placed the knife and fork down half way through the meal. 'Angelina?' 'Yes Senor Adam?' 'John B the Wagon Master tells me we are staying here today and tonight, leaving tomorrow. I'd like to give you your gun and teach you a little how to use it. You'll need to practice three times a week for a month to be good with it.' 'That will be fun. Yes I will watch, and how much do I owe you?' asked Mrs Sinata. 'It's a present from me to Angelina.' 'Please let me pay you.' 'It's a gift, a sign of our friendship. Let's say no more about it.' The old lady looked at him, 'he seems to have an heir of importance' she thought.

They walked out the back door, down the steps. There was a rubbish dump at the end of the pathway. Most of the party followed. 'Do you call this a prairie?' asked Adam staring at the trail going as far as the eye could see, disappearing out of sight. There's nothing, not even fence edges, just a few trees. 'That's right, open prairie.'

'We call it free range' said Tex. 'So does anybody own it?' 'Yes, everybody that wants to use it, and many do. See them small herd's way out to the left? They're branded, probably owned by 3 or 4 different spreads, just left to free graze and breed' said Tex.

Adam looked around . 'A burning dump.' 'You got it;' answered Tex. There was three posts in the ground with two planks, one at the top and one halfway. There was many bullet holes in the posts and planks, and this will be the practice shot' said Adam.

Angelina walked over and stood by him. Taking the small revolver out of his belt, he showed it to her. 'It's a good accurate pistol. This is a 32 caliber revolver, and as you can see mine is a 38, bigger and heavier. The first thing you need to know is to use the safety down, and it's on push up and it's off, try it.'

'That's it.' He then showed her how to load it, and gave her the box of ammo to put in her bag. 'You first learn to slowly take aim, lining up the front sight in the back one. That's it.' She was aiming at an old bucket, only 30ft away. 'No Angelina, you are jerking the trigger and closing your eyes as you fire it. Now just slowly squeeze.'

She hit the plank, just underneath. 'It's getting heavy' said Angelina. 'Now I want you to use both hands.' He stood at the back of her, his arms around her, holding her wrists, now were coming up, up, take aim, fire now. The bullet went straight through the bucket, now lower the gun, have a rest. John B had replaced the bucket. Two fast shots, she hit it again with the last one. 'You're still jerking it, squeeze it slowly. Yes it was a good shot.' He smiled, she liked the encouragement. They all clapped her. Adam walked slowly over to Mrs Sinata, 'are you going to get some practice in?' he asked, glancing a her bag on the ground. 'Mr Boswell, I've been able to use this gun for a lot of year's thank you.'

'Oh thank you Adam', she looked straight at him, and never turned away, there was no hesitation, no embarrassment. Her eyes sparkled full of life. He held her gaze. 'You're beautiful' he said. She had hypnotized him and she knew it. If we was on our own, I'd kiss and hold you so tight.' She could feel it and smiled, looking away, then back. 'Your mothers watching' 'I don't care' she answered. He stepped to one side. 'When you're not aiming, keep the safety on. Show me. Very good.'

Her mother could see Angelina was not flirting anymore, she had fallen in love. She was a very astute lady. 'Mr Boswell, Adam, I've heard of your talent with a hand gun, show me something.' 'Have you got a silver dollar?' She looked in her bag. 'No I haven't. I do have fifty cents piece.' 'Well I've never tried one before.' 'There's always a first time' she answered, holding out the half dollar, about the size of a sovereign. Angelina fired twice, and hit the bucket again. 'Next time another day we will move it 30ft further back, that will be your distance, 60ft' said Adam.

'Well Well - if it's not the tin can crack shot, and wearing a gun too' said Malcolm, his gun holster was now on his belt. 'Watch out boys, he's a deadly pistol hero.' 'I've taken a lot of insults from you Gypo. You've got trouble coming from me today.' 'Big trouble, is that so?' said Adam.

His cunning mind was working fast. He took two three slow steps back. He was right on the edge of the scattered rubbish. 'Let's see you do your dancing here' he thought. 'I am here and waiting for you low life' said Adam undoing his gun belt. I'll give you a fight.'

'No, no, keep it on Gypo, I warned you when you wore a gun you'd have me to reckon with, have you got the guts for a gun fight? Well, have you?' Adam never answered. 'You're yellow aren't you Gypo?' 'Didn't think he was yella' said John B. 'I don't think so.' 'I've never seen anyone shoot like him' said Bill. 'Is he fast?' answered John B.

'You've done this a hundreds of times, but this time it's for real' whispered Adam. He felt a little chill run down his spine, taking several side steps away from Angelina and her mother, at that everyone moved well back. Malcolm had stayed where he was at the bottom of the three steps, the morning sun was behind him, just starting to rise over the Fort wall. Adam pulled his Stetson a little lower to shade his eyes. Just then 2 men came slowly down the steps. One was holding a 12bore double barrel shot gun who stood next to Malcolm. The other had a navy 38 colt with carved silver handles in a low black holster.

'We're the Smitt brothers, we're distant cousins of Malcolm you could say. I am Wade, some call me Shyan-Smitt. My brothers Shotgun-Smitt.'

'I've heard of you paid gun slingers, you own the tavern saloon here.' 'My God just where's this going?' said Tex. 'I'll tell you where it's going, every time I tried to have a go at this gypsy tramp, you'd tell me what I could or couldn't do because you had that law badge. You must be in love with him or something. He's going down, look at the state my face is in. He's going down, and anybody gets in the way goes down with him, I aint standing alone no more, I've got back up.'

'If Malcolm doesn't get the dude, the other 2 will' said John B. 'That's not a challenge, that's murder.' Said Henry Hibb.

'On your way law dog' said Shotgun. 'Can't do that, he's my friend, and I am the law here.' said Tex, tapping his badge. 'You're just a contract law man, no Sheriff, and there's no law here. The only law in Montrose is the gun' said the one called Shyan with the silver handled colt, who was now standing some 6 or 7 feet to the right of Malcolm.

Shot gun cocked both hammers back, pointing it at Tex. 'Take the colt out of the holster with your wrong hand very slow and place it on the ground...... that's it. Get clever and I'll cut you in two. Now walk slowly away by your friends.........that's a good boy.'

Angelina was very frightened. 'I must do something, somebody has to its 3 to 1.' Her hand was in her bag. 'Get your hand out, now trust me' said her mother giving Adam a quick stare, then glancing at her bag. 'Please wait, I can't bare to see the killings, we're going to the Cantina' she shouted. 'Come Angelina' not waiting for a reply she started to rush forward up the pathway. 'Never let it be said I was not a gentleman' said Malcolm with a smile. 'Take your time ladies, take your time.'

Adams sharp mind had taken in Mrs Sinata's quick hint. He was ready, but he wasn't sure what for. As Mrs Sinata drew level with the man holding the shotgun her hand came quickly out of the bag. She pointed the cocked Webley 38 at the man's head and squeezed the trigger. He was only 6ft away when the Webley went off like a cannon. The bullet hit him just above the ear going straight through.

Malcolm's face was smothered with blood and white mush. 'I am blind' he said, trying to clear his eyes. The bullet continued, just missing the gun slingers nose by a few inches, putting him off balance. The man with the shotgun crumpled, both barrels went off. The 2 dance hall girls were screaming.

As Tex took 3 quick strides throwing himself down, his 44 colt was in his hand, the hammer cocked back. Adams gun went off more like a bull whip crack, then a bang. Tex's colt 44, bullet slammed in to the gun slinger, centre of his chest. Just 2 seconds after, Adams 38. The 2 bullets was only 3 inches apart. He seemed to walk slowly backwards 3-4 steps, then went down.

Malcolm's hands came slowly down from cleaning his eyes, looking around, his left hand still holding his bandana. Shyan lay on his back, colt in his hand, his chest was one big red patch. Shotgun lay in front to the left, the right side of his head was quite messy, the other side just had a hole above his left ear.

'So Gypo, where would you be without the old Mafia witch and the law dog?' 'I'd be dead like these friends of yours, those 2 pieces of rubbish. You see people know what you are when they're in your company day and night for nearly a week.'

'I received respect, and was accepted. You look down on everybody, so arrogant. I'll let it go. Step away now Malcolm, while you can, or I'll kill you.' 'You're good with tin cans, but you're yella Gypo, you're not bluffing me. You haven't got the guts for it; you haven't got the nerve' Malcolm made several steps forward, then turned sideways. Now only half the target.

'It's a long shot for the dude, must be 100ft.' 'That won't bother him' said Billy Hibb the Barber. 'Is he fast?' asked John.

You could still smell the gun smoke in the air. Everything was so silent. Adam had done this hundreds of times, but this time its for real, he thought, he could feel the warmth from the morning sun, or was it the body heat from the 1750 people in the big tent? He had a slight cruel smile as his eyes looked straight ahead. 'I am your Gypsy boy and gun play is my game. You say when.' 'Yeah, let's do it' said Malcolm.

The bullet took the first 2 knuckles off Malcolm's right hand, his colt had just cleared the holster. He let out a low deep little scream as he dropped the gun. His left hand quickly wrapped the bandana around his damaged hand several times. 'You scum, you've lamed me for life.'

'I won't shoot an unarmed man' said Adam, holstering his gun, he turned walking away. It was Angelina that broke the silence. 'Adam, he's got another gun' she shouted.

He spun; dropping to one knee, the 44 Derringer bullet hit the heel of his boot, then came that bull whip sound. The bullet hit Malcolm just under the right eyebrow, going out through the top of his head. He never felt a thing, just saw a white flash.

They all stood around him silent. He laid on his side, the blood making a dark patch near his head. 'You was lucky, the distance for the derringer, and using his left hand, saved your life.' said Tex.

'He just didn't know when to stop did he?' said Adam. Tex could see it had bothered his friend. 'Man your fast, that was some shot, I am not sure if I blinked or not' said John B. 'Will you teach me to draw and shoot' asked William. Angelina ran over to him, then holding his two hands. 'Thanks Tex for what you done.' Said Adam

'Anytime, but you'd be dead if it wasn't for her.' 'Will you take a little advice from a friend?"

'So' said Adam. 'Stop turning your back and walking away. You did that in the saloon in Aberline. It's not a dual in London or Paris. This is a new wild frontier, if you turn your back they'll kill you. Very rare someone gets shot in the hand unless by accident, it is usually to the death.'

Mrs Sinata looked straight at him. 'He gives you good advice.' As he started to walk away, he turned. 'And I thank you Mrs Sinata.' 'We both owe you.' said Tex. 'I am Costa Nosta, a Dons wife; it seemed the thing to do. I might call on you one day to repay it.' said Mrs Sinata. Adam just nodded, not really sure. Angelina looked away.

'You live by the sword, you will die by the sword' said Harry.

'Maybe I should have let him kill me.'

'Maybe you should not have been carrying a gun' said Ringo. 'Maybe everyone should mind their own business, maybe you two can pray and get him into heaven' answered Adam. 'We'll pray for him, but it's too late for that now.' 'So what kind of vicars or preachers are you, not to pray them into heaven?'

'Because it's too late, if he is not saved, not heard Jesus' call and answered it, he will be in hell however good he thought he was. By the look of him, I'd say his chances are pretty slim' said Ringo. 'If he did hear Jesus' call and answered it, then he was saved, and he'll be in heaven right now.' said Harry.

'I've just killed 2 men, and I haven't got the time or patience for this nonsense. You talk in riddles.' Adam turned and started to walk away. 'Mr Boswell' said Harry. 'Yes, what is it?' 'When we get to Glen Parva, we will be having meetings for a few weeks before we move on again. Why don't you come along to one? Maybe you will get an answer to some of your questions.' Adam hesitated for a minute, 'I don't want to insult your religion. I was brought up to believe the bible, and only the bible, and that's enough for me.' 'Good day'. 'See you there' said Harry. 'Maybe.' said Adam, he nodded and walked on.

He was looking at the Fort as he walked around it with Tex. There was only two of the four high towers left standing with a long high wall in between; with a row of shops in front of the long wall. 'It's a very good idea' said Adam, as he followed Tex into the general store. There was a small saloon next to it called The Tavern, the cantina was over on its own, 'how much to bury them each in a box, a wood cross?' '55 dollars each Senor.' 'I'll bet it's just gone up' said Tex, counting the money out of Malcolm's wallet, placing a piece of paper by the money. 'What does it say Senor?' 'It's says their names.' 'But no age Senor.'

'I didn't know their age' answered Tex. Adam could see Angelina slowly walking looking up at the high tower. 'I'll see you later Tex', turning, he walked away. 'Sure thing' answered Tex.

'Nice to see you Adam.' 'I see you're still wearing your gun.' 'I guess so' he answered, with a slight smile. 'That's American, I guess so' said Angelina. 'Yes it is, you tend to pick it up quickly.' 'Don't lose your accent, and how you speak, it gives you so much character' she said.

'I'd be dead now if you hadn't have shouted.' She never answered as she put her arm through his, they walked looking around the tower, 'it's two houses now'. 'I wonder will this place become a town one day. Adam never answered, as they walked round the side, he slowly pushed her back against the wall, lifted her chin up, slowly kissing her, then gently bit her bottom lip. Her arms reached up around his neck. He could feel her thighs tremble against him a little; his left hand was slowly playing with her hair as they kissed again. Then she suddenly pushed him away. 'No Adam.' She could see the sweat on his forehead, then taking his Stetson off, throwing it on a packing crate, see ruffled his curly hair. His arms went around her waist, pulling her to him, his knee was gently between her legs, her arms was up around his neck again as they kissed, they embraced for several minutes.

She was a challenge, so much different than a paid woman who is there to be used, he thought as he lifted his head from kissing her neck. Slowly she pulled his hand away. I must go Adam, please, I must.' She looked up, then gave him a quick kiss. 'I think I am in love with you.' She walked away.

The second day after leaving Fort Montrose

It seemed like it was never going to end, maybe because it was the last day of the journey. Everyone was so tired; the horses could not have lasted another day.

It had just gone 5 o clock when they came to a stop at the top of a rise, all jumped out following Tex. 'Glen Parva' he said. His outstretched hand pointing down.

Adam walked back to the stage coach, reaching under the driver's seat for the ships telescope, looking down to the left. It was bigger than Aberline, more interesting, good planning could be seen.

The usual long wide main street but with two streets off either side instead of one, and at the top, it went in a circle of just shops, and a second salon. There was a grass circular centre, baskets of flowers hanging here and there at the fronts of the shops and bank, like Cornwall, Adam thought. On the opposite side of the grassed centre was

The Royal Hotel, it seemed to go in a half-circular shape. It was the largest building in town.

Moving the telescope, he could see a wide river at the back of the valley with a bigger and lower valley on the other side of the river that ran between the two valleys, disappearing out of sight.

The grass was deep Brunswick green, there was various types of trees with small flowers near them. 'What do you think?' asked Tex.

'Beautiful, a rose in a garden of weeds' said Adam. Angelina walked over and stood at his side. He handed the telescope to her; she then passed it to her mother. 'It's beautiful, like a painting' said Mrs Sinata.

Adam turned to look at her, 'Perthshire and Fife in Scotland,' he said. 'I haven't been there.' 'Pity' answered Adam. 'It has gone cooler' she said looking at Tex.

'Yes there is a slight breeze from the Gulf of Mexico, less than 40 miles over the other side of that second valley is the sea, the Gulf, 200 miles that way is Coahuila Mexico, and 250 miles to the right is New Mexico. Nearly as big as Texas. It's so vast, it will take centuries to fill this country' she answered.

'So this is nearly the bottom of Texas?' asked Adam. 'About 3/4 ways down.' 'That's Glen Parva's 2 valleys, a Shangri La' said Mrs Sinata. 'The rail road will get here within 5 years, with it will come good and bad and opportunities for those who have money' said Adam. 'Do you tell fortunes as well?' 'I have never tried Mrs Sinata.'

'And what or where is Shangri La?' asked Tex.

'It's a beautiful, magical hidden place.' Mrs Sinata glanced at Adam surprised that a Gypsy would know such a classic story. 'And the river?' he asked. 'The river, it's called The Tay Grande. The Tay runs through Perth in Scotland' said Adam. 'The valleys are nearly 65 miles long.' 'It is nice, I hope it has a lot for me. I've travelled over 2000 miles to make a start here' said Adam.

'Well we have travelled nearly 10,000 miles!' said Angelina. Her mother gave her a quick stare as if to say no more. Adam just smiled. 'The two valleys run side by side with the river between. Glen Parva valley is 5 miles wide and 65 miles long with many farms and ranches along its banks, also some small holdings in the backlands.'

'The fish valley 8 miles wide, 65 miles long, with just one ranch' said Tex.

'Just one ranch you say?' 'That's right mam! They say it's over 150,000 acres.' 'I have never heard of a private place so big' said Mrs Sinata. 'Anything is possible in America' said Adam. Tex glanced at him smiling. 'The Parva's, I met them in New York. Very nice people, they named this place. He is Scotch/Irish, his wife half Mex, very beautiful. They have a daughter and a young son' said Adam.

'You certainly get around. John Parva Junior. One day he will be the richest man in all of Texas. They have a prosperous silver mine as well' said Tex. 'They are both very eligible, and how old is this young man?' asked Mrs Sinata. 'He is 21 in two months' time, she is 26.' Angelina gave Adam a quick glance. 'There is going to be a big party, you will get to know them, everyone will be invited' said Tex. 'Yes of course' said Mrs Sinata looking at her daughter, Angelina ignored her. Adam had taken it all in; his sharp gypsy mind was more than a match for the old mafia woman.

Everyone was pleased to stretch their legs, the men having a smoke. As Mrs Sinata got back to the Stage coach she turned to see Angelina putting her arm through Adams. 'Do you love me Adam?' 'Of course I love you Angelina.' 'You make a fool of me in front of everyone, I would shoot you Adam.' He lit a cigar, he needed a smoke.

'We must get to know the Parva's. Adam is a nice young man, but I want a lot better than a handsome gypsy dealer for my only daughter' thought Mrs Sinata. Angelina knew her mother well and how the Mafia would try matchmaking for their children. Adam was the man she wanted.

'I've noticed you like the woman.' said Tex.

'Can you think of anything better?' questioned Adam. They both laughed.

'All I want is just a few cold beers and a rest up for a couple of days, getting old for this now' said Tex as they climbed back on the stage coach. 'Come to my place for the night. I've always got a big flask of beer in a churn of cold water and my wife will cook us a nice steak. I will show you around Glen Parva tomorrow. I suppose you'll be staying at The Royal Hotel, now you are working the casino there?'

'Not really Tex. I like my own space and thanks, that sounds good to me.' 'Are you really going to run that Casino for the old Lady?' She is Mafia, they're very dangerous people, and anything goes! 'Yes I know.' 'You promised to tell me about the women fortune telling, and that scam your father called the bag?'

'The Persian Rugs. Yes we were at Blackpool for two years. We then went up to Perth and that is where we joined up with the Wild West circus.' 'You can tell us all about it after supper.' 'Cheryl will enjoy it.' 'Cheryl is she French?' 'No she's English.' 'It's good to know some of my own kind are here.' 'Move 'em out' shouted Tex twice as he flicked the reins.

Adam looked at the downhill 2 miles into Glen Parva, it reminded him of the Bridge of Earn, Road to Perth and the Inches Common when they had come up from Blackpool. But there was a big red white and blue Wild West circus tent where they usually camped.

'You're quiet Adam.' 'Oh, just thinking about when we joined up with the Wild West circus.' 'And?' said Tex. 'Our way of life changed, it took us forward 30 years in just 6, and I found there was a big world out there.'

The two stage coaches and the big wagon were going slowly down the slope into the valley. The drivers were pressing on the foot brake, holding the reigns tightly then they were on the flat. They had gathered a little speed, but no one was in a hurry. In the distance they could see a big sign, which read: -

'YOU'RE HERE - WELCOME
TO
GLEN-PARVA'

AND THE STORY CONTINUES…………..

*Nelson Jack Boswell & Wife Delly
Honeymoon Photo*

Author's Great Grandfather (Manx Tommy Boswell) & his wife
of The Isle of Man (father's side)
Pictured around 1890

Author's Great Grandparents (Mother's side)
Isle of Man
Pictured late 1930's
Herrs Robinson - Blackpool
Minna Boswell - Lincolnshire

Author's Grandparents and cousins - The Finney's
Doncaster Races
Pictured late 1920's
Granddad Tom Boswell (2nd left)
Granny Blanch Robinson (3rd left)
Mother Clarice aged 15 (5th left)

Going to Doncaster Races
Pictured late 1920's
Granddad Tom Boswell
Granny Blanch Robinson
Mother Clarice aged 15

Doncaster Races
Pictured late 1920's
Granddad Tom Boswell
&
My Mother Clarice (left)

Author with parents - Nelson & Clarice Boswell
Brother Tommy pictured with Dad
Nelson-Jack with Mother.
Car - Studio-Baker 1936
Photographed in Bristol 1937

Flash Isaac (Scottish) & Nelly Boswell (I.O.M)
Bristol 1937
(The Author's grandparents)
Trailer - New North Star (1937)
Custom Built (Only 3 built).

My Mother - Clarice and Brother Tommy at
The Duckering Shop, Isle of Man
1934

Granddad Tom Boswell & Granny Blanch Robinson
and Brother Tommy (Rhyl, North Wales) 1952
Pictured with USA V8 Ford Car and
New Queen of the North Avendale Caravan.

Weston Super Mare (Bristol) 1953
Authors Parent's - Nelson Boswell (Scottish)
& Clarice Boswell (Chester) and Daughter Clarice
Pictured with New Somerset Royal Trailer 1953
Custom Built - only 8 built.

Authors Wife - Delly Finney
Pictured in the South of America 1960

Delly's father: (American) - George (Joe) Finney,
Mother - Adelaide Smith
Grandmother - Jane Boswell

Finney's & Boswell's in USA Pictured in 1958

Wife Delly's family: Mother, Father, Delly, her sister Meara and cousins

Photographed in 1960

Wife Delly's Granddad - Nat Smith & Granny - Pouse Holdum

Photographed in 1961

My Mother - Clarice Boswell and my eldest son Jack
in Cardiff, South Wales.

Photographed in 1961 in Bristol (The good Old Days)

Jack with Jag